Before Win...

Nancy K. Wallace loves chocolate, Christmas, and fairytales! She collects books of folklore and she houses them in dozens of bookcases (filed alphabetically according to country). She lives with five lovely cats in a 140-year-old farmhouse named *Chevonwyck*. Nancy is the author of 19 children's books plus The Wolves of Llisé series for new adults. Fortunately, her two daughters are excellent at proofreading! She is a Youth Services Librarian and has reviewed YA literature for VOYA magazine for 20 years.

Find Nancy online on Twitter @FairySockmother and her blog http://fairysockmother.com/

For more information on The Wolves of Llisé series, check out www.AmongWolves.net

A7 042 873 5

Also by Nancy K. Wallace

Among Wolves
Grim Tidings

Before Winter

NANCY K. WALLACE

Book Three of The Wolves of Llisé

HARPER
Voyager

Harper*Voyager*
An imprint of HarperCollins*Publishers* Ltd
1 London Bridge Street
London SE1 9GF

www.harpercollins.co.uk

This paperback edition 2018

First published in Great Britain in ebook format by
HarperCollins*Publishers* 2017

Copyright © Nancy K. Wallace 2017

Nancy K. Wallace asserts the moral right to
be identified as the author of this work

A catalogue record for this book
is available from the British Library

ISBN: 978-0-00-818154-3

This novel is entirely a work of fiction.
The names, characters and incidents portrayed in it are
the work of the author's imagination. Any resemblance to
actual persons, living or dead, events or localities is
entirely coincidental.

Typeset by Palimpsest Book Production Ltd, Falkirk, Stirlingshire

Printed and bound by CPI Group (UK) Ltd, Croydon, CR0 4YY

All rights reserved. No part of this publication may be
reproduced, stored in a retrieval system, or transmitted,
in any form or by any means, electronic, mechanical,
photocopying, recording or otherwise, without the prior
permission of the publishers.

MIX
Paper from
responsible sources
FSC
www.fsc.org   FSC C007454

I dedicate *Before Winter* and
The Wolves of Llisé in my husband's memory.
Dennie, you will forever be my comfort,
my rock, and my only love.

Prologue

Jeanette bent over Devin, her brown curls lightly brushing his cheek. When his eyes fluttered open and focused on her face, she smiled.

"Am I dead?" he asked.

She kissed his cheek. "No, my love," she assured him. "You aren't dead but you need help."

He cupped her cheek with his hand, ran his thumb across her lower lip. "My God, I love you," he murmured. "Where have you been? I've been so worried."

"Not far away," she answered. "But I have to go now, Devin, I'm sorry."

He found her hand and held it. "Don't go," he protested.

"I can't help you, Devin," she explained. "But Marcus is coming back."

"Marcus tried to kill me," he said.

She shook her head, her eyes big in her slender face, and rose from her knees. Her dress swirled around her bare feet. "I have to go."

"Don't go!" he begged.

She kissed her finger and stooped to touch his mouth. "I must," she said. "Be still."

"When will I see you again, Jeanette?" he asked, raising his head. The pain sent him back down into darkness, her name still on his lips.

CHAPTER 1

If I Should Die

Devin's head pounded in time with his heart as it slowly pumped his life's blood onto the forest floor. He lay in deep, velvety darkness as rain spattered the leaves of the trees above him and slid in rivulets down his cheeks like tears. Gone was the fragrance of pine, the wind fresh off the ocean. The air stank of burned paper and cloth. The Chronicles were gone … he had tried and failed to save them and now they were lost forever. The entire history of the provinces had been destroyed by ignorance and flame. Ultimately, his trip to the provinces to preserve the Chronicles had led to their destruction and he would forever bear the guilt of it.

He opened his eyes to a dizzying view of tree trunks and rocks spinning in front of him. He swallowed convulsively and tried to shift to his back to see for himself if perhaps some small part of the repository remained. Nausea rolled over him in waves and he stopped moving and lay very still, half on his side, the way he'd wakened. Minutes passed as the sickness that threatened to overwhelm him finally stilled.

He lay stiffly, his teeth clenched, one hand digging into the earth.

Finally, he touched his temple gingerly and found the whole side of his face was caked with a sticky mass of blood, pine needles, and dirt. His hand involuntarily rummaged in his pocket searching for a handkerchief and found it completely empty. Even Marcus' rosary was gone.

Last night seemed decades ago, when he and Marcus had sat and talked on the banks of the stream, weathering a storm together. What had Marcus told him? "Trust me." And Devin had. He had trusted Marcus with his life and Marcus had shot him. So, where was his bodyguard now? In some tavern toasting René Forneaux's bid for chancellorship? Did he regret having shot the current chancellor's son when he had been sworn to protect him? Or did he accept his new position with the same intensity that he accepted his role as Devin's bodyguard? What kind of man was Marcus Berringer, anyway, to change loyalties like the wind?

Devin let out a deep breath. He was on his own now. He'd need to find his way back to La Paix … to Chastel, Armand, and Gaspard. Together they would plan a way to thwart this new regime and Marcus would be forever marked as an enemy, not an ally.

Devin tried again to move … to catch some small sight of the repository that had housed the Chronicles. Perhaps there was something left … even a few pages that could be salvaged and reassembled. But the forest lay shrouded in mist and smoke and drizzling rain; here and there an evergreen branch appeared momentarily before the mist swallowed it again. Everything seemed muffled and unreal. Even the birds were silent.

A frightening notion wiggled into Devin's thoughts like a worm. Perhaps, he would die here after all, only a few feet away from the greatest discovery in Llisé's history. At least, he had seen this arcane library and touched it with his own hands – the collected histories of every province in the empire. For a populace that was forbidden to learn to read and write, they had not only recorded their oral history on paper; they had organized it and filed it alphabetically. If René Forneaux assumed he was fighting ignorant provincials he was going to be in for shock.

Devin hoped he would be there to see it but from the amount of blood that continued to soak the neck and shoulder of his jacket, he was beginning to doubt whether he would. His head ached unbearably and he curled up on his side like a child and waited for morning. Sleep came fitfully, dragging him down into nightmare and releasing him, cold and shivering, into the darkened forest once again.

CHAPTER 2

Vestiges of Betrayal

"Dear God!" said a familiar voice. "Devin?" Hands eased him onto his back. He groaned as the world spun and lingering raindrops fragmented like a hundred prisms of light as the sun's rays pierced the trees.

Marcus was bending over him, slapping him lightly on the cheek. "Can you hear me?" he asked insistently.

Devin nodded, the motion setting off pain that threatened to make the top of his head explode.

Marcus exhaled loudly and sat back on his heels. "Thank God you're alive!" he murmured.

Devin forced words between cracked lips. "No thanks to you."

"I saved your life," Marcus explained calmly. "They'd have killed us both if I'd tried to resist. I asked you to trust me. Shooting you was the only way I could save you."

"Have you come to finish me off then?" Devin hissed through gritted teeth.

"I saved your life," Marcus repeated sharply.

"And your own skin," Devin murmured.

Marcus' face flushed an angry red. "Had I meant to kill you, Devin, do you think I'd have missed at ten feet? I had to get those soldiers away from you until I could come back alone. They had to believe you were dead, so I grazed your head with the bullet. There was lots of blood but I spared your life." He slid a hand behind Devin's back. "Now let me help you, damn it! I need you to sit up."

Devin felt completely limp, like all his bones had turned to water. He let Marcus pull him into a sitting position against a tree but he folded up in agony, cradling his head in his hands.

His former bodyguard produced water and bandages. Dabbing lightly at Devin's temple and the back of his head with a wet rag, he frowned, his craggy face wrinkled and drawn. He wrapped a bandage around Devin's head and buried the bloody rags under a bush. "We have to get out of here," he said. "Can you walk?"

"How far?" Devin asked.

Marcus put his hands under Devin's arms and lifted him to his feet. "Back to La Paix," he replied, pulling Devin's arm over his shoulder.

Devin exhaled, "God!"

"I'll carry you if I have to," Marcus said.

"Don't," Devin protested. He put one unsteady foot forward, his vision still blurry and uncertain. "I can't see, Marcus."

"At all?" Marcus asked in alarm.

Devin waved a hand. "Everything is blurry ... fragmented."

"That's to be expected with a concussion," Marcus assured him. "You smacked the back of your head on a rock when you fell. It should go away in a few days."

Devin looked for the shepherd's hut that had housed the entrance to the repository. He blinked, willing his eyes to focus on what remained. The bank of earth behind it had collapsed; ironically leaving the rickety doorway standing, like a portal to nowhere. Only a mound of dirt was visible and the lingering smell of burning paper. "Do you think there's anything left?" he asked.

"If there is, we can't save it now. I need to get you somewhere safe," Marcus replied. "Come on."

Devin's hand fumbled toward the lining of his coat.

"You still have Tirolien's Chronicle," Marcus assured him. "They never even looked for anything hidden in your coat."

"Thank God," Devin whispered. "Where are Emile and his men?"

"Dead," Marcus said shortly. He urged him forward. "We have to go. There won't be any second chances for either of us now. If we're caught, we'll be shot on sight."

Devin moved with him, staggering through the trees to the top of the hill. They followed the edge of the forest, staying deep within its shade as they made their way painfully back toward the road. At the edge of a field of golden flowers bent low by the rain, Devin tripped over a fallen log and fell.

Marcus went down on one knee beside him.

"Give me a minute," Devin begged.

"A minute," Marcus reiterated. "We don't dare stop for any longer."

Devin closed his eyes, laying his head back against the cool earth. His breath, coming in gasps from the exertion, sounded harsh and jarring under the quiet of the trees.

"Come on," Marcus said too soon, hoisting him upright.

Devin put a hand to his head as the trees ahead of them blurred and spun. He leaned on Marcus and walked, silently counting his steps one after another. They stopped for water at a clear brook that wound its way through the fields above them on its way to the ocean below. Devin washed his hands and face in the cool water, lingering to splash it across the back of his neck before they went on. Above, the gray clouds hung dark and low.

It seemed like hours before they reached the road. The primitive track made walking easier but increased the chance of detection. Marcus stopped frequently, always listening for sounds of pursuit or horses' hooves. They went on for at least another hour, Devin staggering more with every step. Without any warning, his legs just crumpled. He slid out of Marcus' arms and went down, stones tearing through the knees of his trousers. "I can't do this anymore," he panted.

"Just a few more feet," Marcus coaxed. "The cave where we spent the night is right around that curve. If you can make it that far, you can rest for the night."

He struggled up with Marcus' help, half expecting that the promise of rest was only to entice him to keep going, but just around the next curve, Marcus led him down an embankment. Below them was the stream that had swollen to twice its size during the thunderstorm last night. Even with blurry eyes, Devin could see it was still muddy and swirling after all the rain. He sank down gratefully under the layer of overhanging rock and stretched out on the ground. "Thank God," he murmured, closing his eyes.

Devin woke in the night to the soothing sound of water rushing over stone. He shifted cautiously, attempting to keep nausea and dizziness at bay, and felt a hand on his shoulder.

"How do you feel?" Marcus whispered out of the dark.

"I'm still alive," Devin answered back.

How strange that they found themselves together in the same place where they had stopped two nights ago. Devin rearranged himself cautiously on the rocky ledge. "Tell me what happened to Emile?" he asked.

Marcus took a deep breath. "He sent two men home on a ship – one of them took my rosary that they stole out of your pocket. They hoped it would serve as proof of your death to your father."

"He'll know it's not mine," Devin interrupted.

"Exactly," Marcus said. "I hope that we've sent him a message that you are still alive."

"Do you think he has been deposed?" Devin asked.

Marcus shook his head slowly. "I can't be certain, Devin. A lot may have happened in the two weeks it took those men to get here. If he is still in power then Forneaux is only biding his time. Your father may have sent those men to find you and bring you home and instead Forneaux paid them to kill you."

Devin put a hand to his head. "There are too many different conspiracies. How do we sort them all out?"

"We don't have to," Marcus said. "We continue with our plan. If we can reach La Paix before the others leave, we can join them when they go to Coreé."

"I'll be recognized," Devin said.

"Not necessarily," Marcus replied. "You have a good start at a full beard: you've lost at least two stone in weight and in those clothes I doubt your father would recognize you."

"And who will kill Forneaux?" Devin asked, thinking of

8

Angelique's insistence that she wanted to murder the man herself.

"I believe we will have several contenders standing in line," Marcus muttered. "Don't worry about that now. Are you hungry at all?"

Devin shook his head and regretted it.

Marcus handed him a flask. "Drink some water and try to sleep then."

Devin could just make out his bodyguard's profile as Marcus kept watch, his pistol in his lap. When they'd camped here before, he'd trusted Marcus, even confided in him. Last night, he'd been shot by his own bodyguard and almost killed, but Marcus didn't appear to have changed. He had assumed his previous position as though he expected Devin to accept him also. And yet Devin would always see the muzzle of Marcus' pistol aimed at his head and feel the sharp burn of that bullet, the instant before he passed out.

CHAPTER 3

Lavender

Devin dreamed of troops marching in Independence Square, his father standing on the steps of the Chancellor's residence to view them, surrounded by his bodyguards. Devin stood beside him, as did his brothers and his mother. The pound of their horses' hooves hurt Devin's head as they shook the ground. They never missed a step, one hoof after the other, as though the horses had been trained to march in perfect time, but the soldiers' rifles were aimed at the Chancellor and his family.

A hand descended over Devin's mouth, waking him abruptly and yanking him backwards. He struggled, fighting imprisonment and nausea, as rough cloth was pulled over his head and body.

"Be still," Marcus hissed in his ear.

Devin realized the pounding hooves were not a dream but horses passing on the road above them, at least one squad of soldiers, maybe more. Faint light passed through the coarse fabric of the blanket Marcus had hidden them under. The fabric was a sullen gray like the stone that hid them. It would have concealed them from a casual glance but the men passing above them never halted. The hooves and jingling bridles faded off into the distance, leaving Devin chilled and shaking.

Marcus waited a long time before he spoke. He finally pulled the blanket down and dropped it in a heap beside him. "Those may have been your father's men, but I have no way of knowing. They could as easily be some secret squad of Forneaux's sent out to track me down."

"Why would my father deploy a small army to retrieve me?" Devin asked.

Marcus raised his eyebrows. "Because with the political situation so volatile, I'm sure he wants you safely home."

"Is Coreé safe?" Devin asked. "It doesn't seem very secure for my father right now."

Marcus shrugged. "Perhaps Emile told us what he wanted us to hear. The government may be more stable than you think. Your father has a host of supporters. There is very little that Forneaux could present that would discredit him."

"And yet Forneaux feels he has an angle. He'd hoped to add Gaspard's and my deaths to the list of offenses against the provincials but we've managed to avoid falling into his traps."

"Pray it continues," Marcus said.

"Where is Emile's body?" Devin asked after a minute.

"At the bottom of the harbor along with his men. I didn't have time to hide them anywhere else. I needed to get back to make sure you were all right."

Devin raised his eyebrows. "So you weren't sure, after all."

"Sure of what?" Marcus asked brusquely, but the color had begun to rise in his face.

"Sure that I was still alive," Devin answered.

"I never miss," Marcus replied. "I'm an expert marksman."

Devin didn't doubt it. "Then what was the hurry?" he asked.

"I didn't want you to bleed to death," Marcus answered gruffly. He busied himself with rearranging his pack.

"How did you kill them?" Devin asked after a minute.

"Emile and his crew?" Marcus cocked his head, his voice formal but taunting. "That's not something I'd have expected you to ask, Monsieur Roché." He looked away, sharpening his knife against a stone. "I drugged their beer in the Wind and Water Tavern and when they staggered out along the dock, I cut their throats one by one and let them drop into the water. I weighted them down with chains so they wouldn't float to the surface."

Devin turned his head away. He'd wanted to know, but now that he did, the details only emphasized how brutal Marcus could be when he had to. But then when he thought of the smoldering Chronicles, his fists clenched and he thought that perhaps he could have pushed them into the harbor himself.

Marcus changed the subject. "We'll stay here for today. They've already passed by this area so I think we are safe for the time being. You need a day to rest anyway. How is your head?"

"Better than yesterday," Devin answered, although any movement still made his head throb.

"Stay quiet for today," Marcus suggested, pulling cheese and sausage from his pack. "You didn't happen to bring another one of those little crosses that would grant us access to the tunnels, did you?"

Devin fumbled with his jacket, trying to keep his head

still. "Actually, I did!" he said, withdrawing a cross that was still attached to the lining. "I sewed it into the seam because I thought there was some chance we might be separated."

Marcus beamed. "Excellent! Leave it right where it is. You don't want to risk losing it. Now all we have to do is find a church."

"I don't believe there is even a town close by," Devin answered. "At least I didn't see any on our way through here the last time."

Marcus stretched his legs out in front of him. "I believe you're right. The closest church is in Calais and we're not going back there."

"So, we'll walk until we find another," Devin said. "By tomorrow I'll feel more like myself." He closed his eyes against the swirling patterns the leaves made and hoped that tomorrow would be better.

"I thought I might try to catch a fish for dinner," Marcus offered. "Will you be all right alone if I leave for a few minutes? I'll stay within hearing distance."

Devin opened one eye. "Go ahead. There is nothing much happening here."

Marcus threw him the pouch with the bread and sausage. "If you are hungry before I come back, you can eat this then. I think you'd prefer it to raw fish. I'll find a fish for myself and be back shortly." He laid a pistol on the rock beside Devin. "Keep that close at hand while I'm gone."

Devin's head still throbbed but he hadn't admitted that to Marcus. There was no way out of the present situation except to walk back to La Paix and he would do it, whether his head hurt or not. The journey would take longer this time, a week or more, with them having to avoid the roads

13

and any small towns or villages. He leaned back against the rock and closed his eyes; the rushing water of the stream below him formed a soothing backdrop. The forest spoke a dozen peaceful languages around him: birdsong, wind through leaves and needled branches, the scurry of small creatures searching for food.

A cascade of stones and dirt sat him upright, the gun in his hand. Before him was an elderly woman. Her head would have barely come to Devin's chest and he wasn't tall. She was like a wizened child; ragged grayish-brown clothing clung to her slight frame, making her blend effortlessly into the rocks and earth behind her. She squatted down, blinking uncertainly at Devin.

"Who are you?" she asked in a trembling voice.

"I might ask the same," Devin replied. "Who are you?"

She cocked her head as though trying to remember. "I am Lavender. Are you the one those soldiers are looking for?"

Devin feigned nonchalance. "Are they looking for someone?"

"They are," she said with a fearful look at the road above. Her brow furrowed. "They are always looking for someone and then people die."

"They won't hurt you here," Devin replied.

She frowned, giving her brown wrinkled face the look of an oversized walnut. "They don't want me. There is no one else in the forest except that man fishing. And you're on edge," she prodded. "It makes me think they're hunting for you."

"I honestly don't know who they are hunting for," Devin replied. "And what business is it of yours anyway?"

"It's my business to know what happens in these woods," she said defiantly.

14

"Well, this particular matter doesn't concern you." Devin waved the gun in her direction. "You need to be on your way."

She laughed again, a deep humorless sound that put Devin's nerves on edge. "You can't tell me what to do!"

"I can," Marcus' voice said suddenly. He had come up silently behind Devin, his gun in his hand.

Lavender was unconcerned. "You won't shoot me," she said. "The sound of a gun will bring those soldiers back here."

"True," Marcus answered, his voice deadly. "But I can slit your throat and no one will hear a sound."

Lavender's body crumpled, like a bunch of rags thrown on the floor, her gnarled hands went to her scrawny throat. "Why would you kill me? I've not done you any harm. I've done nothing but speak to the gentleman."

"He told you to be on your way," Marcus replied. "You need to leave."

"I will," she said. "I thought we could help each other."

"In what way?" Marcus asked, his voice sarcastic.

"I can show you a way into the tunnels," she whispered.

Devin and Marcus exchanged a look. The tunnel system, which used the natural cave formations of Northern Llisé, would provide them with a safe, protected route to reach Madame Aucoin's house in Amiens. "And what do you want in return?" Devin asked. He realized his mistake too late when her toothless grin revealed her brown gums.

"So you do need to reach the tunnels?" she cackled.

"Devin, shut up!" Marcus growled. "You're only making matters worse."

"I can take you there safely," said Lavender. "For a price."

"And what would that be?" Marcus asked.

"What does the boy have hidden in his coat?" Lavender asked.

"You'll find nothing in my coat but a ripped lining," Devin replied, involuntarily clutching Tirolien's Chronicle to his side.

"Let me see," Lavender asked, reaching out with sticklike fingers.

Marcus slapped her hand away with the barrel of his gun. "Keep your hands to yourself," he said.

She snatched her hand away, holding it against her scrawny chest. "If you hurt me I will tell the soldiers where you are."

"Then I may as will kill you," Marcus replied calmly. "I doubt anyone will miss you."

"Lavender is a story," she protested feebly. "You can kill the bards but you can't kill stories."

Devin leaned forward warily. "What do you mean?"

She wrapped her arms around her as though she were cold, her ragged clothes looking more like a burial shroud. "Stories live on if you keep telling them."

"There need to be bards to tell them," Devin corrected her gently. "The bards tell the stories so that they won't be forgotten."

"You can tell the stories," she insisted. "You can tell Lavender's story."

Devin rubbed at the bandage on his forehead. He wanted to lie down and still the thumping ache in his head.

"Come back tomorrow," Marcus said. "You can tell your story then."

"Lavender's story is part of the Chronicle," she said.

Devin exhaled. "Dear God, Marcus! She can't be the Lavender that Armand taught me about?"

"I agree," Marcus muttered, shifting his gun from one hand to another. "That was centuries ago, wasn't it?"

"I don't know," Devin whispered. "Lavender, is your story about your white pony?"

She nodded vigorously. "Yes, yes," she said, "my beautiful white pony that ran away."

"Where is your father's house?" Devin asked. "Surely there must be someone left who wonders what happened to you."

She shook her head, looking forlorn and afraid. "I can't find it."

"You lived in Arcadia," Devin explained gently. "This is Tirolien. Your story is in Arcadia's Chronicle. I believe that you lived there."

She threw her hands out in supplication. "I don't know where that is."

"We are going that way," Devin said.

"Devin!" Marcus warned. "We can't take anyone with us."

"But she's lost," Devin said. "Surely we can show a little mercy?"

Marcus shook his head unyieldingly. "Not now. Not here."

Devin looked helplessly at Lavender. "How do you live? Where do you sleep?"

"I sleep under the trees. The roots are my pillows. In winter when it is cold, I live in this cave."

"This cave?" Devin asked, nodding behind him.

She nodded, curling her feet around her, pulling the scraps of her clothing down to cover her toes. "I eat berries and nuts."

"This is her cave, Marcus," Devin protested. "We can't stay here."

"I don't mind," Lavender offered. "We can all stay here together."

"We mind," Marcus replied. "If this is your cave, we'll move on."

"Please don't," she whispered. "I have no one to talk to but myself. Once I ate at a fine table, with wine and tarts; there was music and laughter and dancing. Now, I am lost and I don't know where home is."

Devin closed his eyes, thinking wretchedly of Angelique and all she had lost.

"Lavender, how old are you?" he asked.

She shook her head. "I have forgotten." She picked at the fabric of her clothing for a moment. "Did you know my pony is missing?"

"I had heard that," Devin said. "I don't believe you will find him here though. You need to go back to Arcadia."

"Is it a long way?" she asked.

Devin looked at her bare feet worn hard and leathery from walking. "I think you could make it," he said, pointing above them. "You should follow the road."

She made a sharp keening sound, making herself as small as possible. "Men travel the road. They are cruel, cruel men. They burned my father's chateau."

Devin sat forward, making his head throb more. "Your father's chateau burned?"

"It's gone," she said in faint voice. "All my people are gone. There is no one left but me and I have nowhere to go."

Devin put a hand to his head. "Marcus, surely there is something …"

"No," Marcus repeated. "We can't get involved. There is too much at stake, Devin. We need to move on, Madame, and leave you to your cave."

She nodded, sitting in a forlorn heap.

"Do you have any money?" Devin asked.

She shook her head and spread thin fingers. "I have nothing but my friends," she said, gesturing behind them into the small cave.

Marcus whirled, pointing his gun behind them but there was nothing there but the rocky cave floor.

"What friends?" Devin asked.

She crawled behind Devin into the shadows. "These friends," she murmured, collecting small rounded wooden balls from the floor of the cave. She placed one of the balls gently in Devin's hand. "This is Simon."

Devin turned the ball in his hand, revealing features cut deeply into the wood with a knife or stone. The wooden ball was a head with recognizable features: plump cheeks, a bulbous nose, and a mouth wide open in laughter. "Who is Simon?" he asked.

"My father's baker," Lavender said. "He made all the tarts, cakes, and sweets. He always saved me something special in his apron pocket."

Devin reached carefully for another ball. "And this one?"

"My father," Lavender said, her fingers reluctant to release it into Devin's hand. She turned it so the features were apparent but did not pass it to him. The face was strong, the nose long and thin, the smile betrayed a gentleness that Devin recognized in Lavender's own face.

Lavender collected it, cradling it in her lap like a child. "I would like to see him again," she whispered.

Devin looked at her gnarled hands, the skin that hung from her wiry frame and thought that she must have outlived her father by at least fifty years. "I would like to see my father again, too," he answered gently.

She looked up. "Do you know where your father is?"

"I know where I left him," Devin replied. "I hope he is still there but nothing is constant. Time changes everything."

"I went back one time," Lavender said. "There were horrible men there. They had killed my father's guards and burned the chateau."

Marcus returned his gun to his jacket. "When was this?"

Lavender shrugged. "Many winters ago. I saw the men on horseback and the torches and I ran. I didn't even try to help them," Lavender murmured, her voice barely audible. "I carved their faces here, so I wouldn't forget them." She swung her arm out, encompassing the wooden heads. "I have them all except for the stable boy who didn't latch my pony's stall." She chose one head from the collection and held it up. "This is the Captain of the Guard. His name is Amando. He would have fought to the death to protect them!"

Devin glanced at Marcus. "Had you heard about the destruction of this chateau?"

He shook his head. "No, nothing. Although much of what transpires in these far northern provinces goes no further. I doubt your father knows either."

Lavender let out a huge sigh and leaned back against the rock as though the conversation had exhausted her.

"Lavender," Devin asked. "Did you have any brothers or sisters?"

Her little head bobbed up and down as she scrambled forward on her knees. "They are here, too." She lined four wooden balls up on the rocky shelf above them. "Sébastian, Abelard, Michel, and Charles."

Devin felt a shiver run down his back at the detail she had worked into the faces. It was almost as though she had collected a host of men's heads that had been decapitated. He took a deep breath, trying not to show his revulsion. "Is it possible that they might have escaped?"

Lavender began to cry. "I don't know. I ran away. I didn't stay to help them fight. I simply saved myself."

"God!" Marcus commented angrily, his face unreadable in the shadow of the rocks. "This world seems filled with women who have been abused and yet feel responsible for their families' deaths." He remained silent for a moment and then put a hand out to grasp one of her scrawny shoulders. "Lavender, we'll take you back. Surely there is someone who can help you in your own province."

CHAPTER 4

Dreams

"You told me you knew a way into the tunnels," Devin said, extending Lavender a piece of bread.

She nodded as she tore at the crust in her hand. "It is down the mossy steps. A whole town used to be there. It's deserted now. No one has lived there in years."

Devin wished there had been time to read Tirolien's Chronicle. Surely, an entire deserted town would have found its way into the Chronicles at some point. He recalled the map they had found in the Bishop's Book, which outlined the resettlement of people from towns in danger of being wiped out by the government. His nearly perfect recall brought the map to mind with all its details but he remembered no designation for a deserted town in the mountains above Calais.

"What was the town called?" he asked.

"We don't know," Lavender replied, fondling one of the wooden heads of her brothers. "It was very, very old."

"It sounds too good to bypass," Devin replied.

"We're not on an archaeological expedition," Marcus

warned him. "We'll investigate only if it will get us back to Arcadia sooner."

Devin shifted so the back of his head was against the rock face behind him. The coolness of the stone soothed the dull ache that persisted. "Where do the tunnels go, Lavender?"

She shook her head. "We don't know. We don't like the dark." She seemed to grow smaller when something frightened her; she scuttled backwards, nervously cradling the carved heads of all her brothers in her lap.

Devin tried to imagine what her life had been like, to have lived once as a child, in a household of wealth and affluence, and then spend the remaining decades as a wild thing that lived off the land and hid wherever she could find shelter. The parallels to Angelique's life were uncanny but while he found Angelique both endearing and repelling at different times, Lavender merely seemed pathetic. How terrifying it must seem to be elderly with no prospect of anyone to care for you. If she died in these woods or even in the shelter of the cave, she would leave little alteration in the landscape: just a small bundle of bones in a few shreds of cloth.

Marcus arrived triumphantly. Surprisingly, in the short time he had been gone, he had caught two fish. He gutted them on a flat stone and fileted the meat, dividing it into three portions.

"Lavender claims to know a way into the tunnels," Devin said quietly, as Marcus worked.

Marcus looked up, his knife poised in midair. "Can you show us the way?" he asked.

Lavender bit into a piece of fish, mashing its white flesh between her brownish gums. Devin found himself alternately disgusted and then sympathetic to her. "We'll go down the mossy steps," she repeated, gesturing somewhere over her shoulder.

"How far away are the mossy steps?" Marcus asked.

"We can reach them by tomorrow night," she answered, reaching for another piece of fish.

Marcus glanced at Devin. "Is it hard walking?"

Lavender flicked a fly from her bare toe. "We will need to walk carefully. The woods can be cruel."

The woods had obviously been cruel to Lavender, Devin thought. Life had been cruel to her just as it had been cruel to Angelique. One of them had a chance at redemption; whether it was too late for Lavender remained to be seen. He ran a hand over his eyes, hoping his blurred vision corrected itself soon. It left him feeling unsteady and nauseated. He slipped down and rested his head on his hand, letting Marcus' questions and Lavender's staccato answers be drowned out by the wind in the trees and the rush of the stream below them.

Chaotic dreams had the wooden heads speaking to him, one after another, hinting at terror and brutality that existed long before René Forneaux. Their jabber became constant. Each of them interrupted the other, their voices becoming louder and louder until Devin couldn't separate them. Without Lavender to identify them, they might as well have been an angry mob intent on violence.

Devin tossed and turned, chased by terrifying shadows of the past and a clear image of his enemy in the present. The wooden head of the Captain of the Guard suddenly opened its mouth crying "Danger! Danger!" until it dislodged itself from the others on the rock ledge and rolled off down the ravine, its mouth screaming its alarm until it landed

24

with a plop in the stream below. It bobbed along as the stream carried it and its garbled warning off toward Calais and the sea where it would be lost forever. The other heads watched in horror as it bobbed away on the current.

Devin wakened with a start. Lavender lay curled like a pile of rags, her father's head in her hands. Marcus stared out at the woods below them, starlight tracing glistening ribbons in the water. "Don't you ever sleep?" Devin hissed.

Marcus glanced at him. "I sleep better than you, apparently. What was all the excitement about?"

Devin shook his head. "Strange dreams. I wonder whether I'll ever be rid of them."

"Forneaux?" Marcus asked.

"And his ilk," Devin said quietly. "If Lavender's home was burned and this town she's taking us to was destroyed, obviously, there have been evil men at work in these mountains who lived long before René Forneaux."

Marcus stretched out his right leg, the barrel of his pistol glinting for a moment before he came to rest. "There have always been evil men, Devin."

"There's something else, though," Devin said. "Don't you feel it? Lavender must have lost her home fifty years ago, at least. Forneaux couldn't have had anything to do with that."

"I'm not certain you can believe anything she says," Marcus replied. "She thinks she is the Lavender from the Chronicles and that she had a white pony."

"Perhaps she did have a white pony," Devin countered. "She may also have been named for the legendary Lavender and now she confuses the two in her head."

"Those damn heads give me the creeps!" Marcus said

with a shudder. "And she'd better not expect me to carry them for her. There must at least forty of them!"

Devin suppressed a laugh. "If my dreams have any element of truth, there are now thirty-nine. The Captain of the Guard is no longer with us."

"What?" Marcus asked, giving him a strange look. "Go back to sleep. You're as crazy as she is."

"I'll explain in the morning," Devin assured him.

CHAPTER 5

The Wilderness of Llisé

Devin wakened to the sound of sobbing. He rubbed blurry eyes with one hand to see Lavender scouring the ledge above them, her muddy hands feverishly patting the rock. Some of the wooden heads cradled in the remnants of her skirt had fallen to lie in the dirt at her feet. Devin prevented two of them from falling with the toe of his boot as they rolled precariously close to the edge of the ravine.

"He's gone! He's gone!" Lavender sobbed. "We can't go on without him to protect us!"

"The Captain of the Guard?" Devin asked resignedly.

Lavender turned to fix him with a suspicious eye. "How did you know?"

Devin sat up. "I didn't actually know for sure. But I dreamed about him last night. He kept shouting, 'Danger! Danger!' and then he rolled off the ledge and down the ravine. I watched him float down the stream toward Calais."

Lavender rose to her diminutive size, her hands on her hips. "You didn't even try to stop him? To save him?"

27

"I was asleep!" Devin protested. "I saw this in a dream. Have you asked Marcus if he heard anything?"

Marcus shook his head. "I certainly didn't hear him roll down into the stream, Lavender." He gestured at the wooden heads scattered around her feet. "Are you certain he isn't there?"

She flopped onto the dirt, sorting balls into groups around her, murmuring each name lovingly to herself. Devin watched her, wondering how much of reality she had any true hold on. She looked so pathetic, tears drying in dirty streaks down her cheeks, her fingers shaking as she tallied up the only remnants of her family and friends that she had left.

"What have we done to our people," Devin whispered to Marcus, "that they have been left so fragile and pitiful? Angelique's story shocked me when I realized how much she had to bear and then there was Elsbeth, Dariel Moreau's wife. She went to the market and came home to find her husband tortured and murdered on the floor of Tirolien's Bardic Hall. Who knows what unhinged Lavender's mind or how many more there are like her? How many children have watched their parents die and have been left orphaned to ..."

"Just stop!" Marcus demanded. "Why are you so maudlin this morning? It won't help anything to dwell on this. You'll end up spouting gibberish yourself, if you haven't already."

"He's not here," Lavender wailed suddenly. She glared at Devin. "I can't believe you wouldn't help him! He would still be here if you had caught him when he fell."

Devin sighed in exasperation. "Well obviously, I didn't. I wasn't even awake, Lavender. I thought I dreamt the entire thing."

"He took the time to warn you!" she pointed out with an accusing finger. "And it cost him his life."

Devin resisted the urge to point out that a wooden ball was not alive. "He may have warned me," he said quietly. "But he didn't tell me what he was warning me about."

"We can't stay here," Lavender stated, gathering the wooden heads in her tattered skirt. "We need to move on, now. Surely you can understand that!"

"Perhaps he was warning us about the deserted town down the mossy steps," Devin said. "There is more than one place here where we may encounter danger."

"Well, I'm leaving," Lavender said with a huff. "I don't need to be told twice that my life is in danger. If the Captain of the Guard gave his life to save me, I would be foolish to disregard his advice and so would you!"

Marcus dropped his head in his hands. "God! This is insane!"

"Call it what you will," Lavender replied sulkily. "But remember that I warned you."

Marcus clapped a hand on Devin's shoulder. "Let's go! There's no use arguing with her and call me a bleeding-heart moron, but I won't let her go on alone."

Devin smiled and stood up, one hand on the rocks behind him, hoping to hide his persistent dizziness from Marcus. His bodyguard didn't need another thing to worry about.

They slithered down the slope to the stream bed. Marcus persuaded Lavender to let him carry the wooden heads in the food sack after two escaped her skirt on the way down the incline. The smell of earth and pine reminded Devin sharply of his bodyguard's gun pointing at him in another part of Tirolien but he pushed the memory away and concentrated instead on Marcus' broad back ahead of him.

Lavender led them deeper into the woods, where the ferns grew so large they towered over her. They followed the stream as it meandered to the northeast. The air was chilly this morning and wood smoke wafted through the trees.

Marcus put a hand out in front of Devin. "That smoke is from a cooking fire. Those soldiers may have stopped for the night. Walk quietly and be ready to hide should we come across them."

"The smoke is from Martigues," Lavender volunteered. "It is off the road, a mile or so to the north. There are only a handful of houses there. Hunters and trappers, mostly. They sell their meat and furs in Calais until the winter snows make the roads impassable. They are rough men. I stay away from Martigues."

Devin glanced at Marcus and saw a shadow of worry cross his face before they started off again. The smell of wood smoke faded as they moved farther away from the road. Devin didn't believe he had ever traveled so far into the wilderness before. The pines here were as tall as cathedral spires and even in August there were telltale glimpses of autumn color among the maples and aspens. In a heartbeat autumn would be over and winter would be upon them. They had to reach Coreé before roads were impassable and the icy storms on the Dantzig had effectively halted travel for the season. He hoped that Lavender's promise of a way into the tunnels was a legitimate one and not a figment of her irrational mind.

By late afternoon, they reached the deepest part of the ravine. On either side crumbled stone foundations rose up, still attached to the cliff walls. In the center, the stream threaded its way through part of a broken wall in a series of small waterfalls. The streambed below lay scattered with huge stones, as though giants had tossed them in some mythical battle.

Marcus turned to look behind them. "That valley behind us must have been carved out by the lake and these stones are what remain of a dam. There must have been a very powerful storm that overfilled it and then burst through and flooded the land below."

"The dam was burst intentionally," Lavender said. "My father told me. He said the people of the town refused to pay their taxes and the government sent soldiers who sabotaged the dam. They drowned every man, woman and child in the village."

"My God," Devin muttered. "When was this?"

Lavender shrugged. "I don't know. The area has been deserted for many, many years. No one else wanted to rebuild in such a vulnerable spot. Legend says that this was the oldest town in Llisé."

"Really?" Devin asked, yearning to pull Tirolien's Chronicle from his jacket and read it but he dared not risk letting Lavender know that he had it.

"It's said to be haunted," Lavender continued darkly. "But I'm not afraid of a few ghosts." She turned to look at Devin, her eyes glinting. "Are you?"

Devin thought she looked like a wraith herself as she wound through the heavy undergrowth, always keeping the stream to her right. He lost his footing more than once on the rocky edges of the streambed, his vision still taunting him with blurred images of where he needed to put his foot next. One misstep filled his left boot with icy water and he had to stop, hopping on one foot to empty it.

They were so deep in the ravine that the sun had already effectively set for them when they reached the site of the ruined village. Their footing, which had been unsure before, now became precarious. The deep shadows did lend a ghostly quality to the scene before them and mist rose from the water as a chill drifted down the ravine behind them. Tumbled stone lay everywhere; a few buildings were marked by what remained of their foundations. Although, on the left side of the stream what must have been a church nestled into the hillside. Its nave had been ripped apart by the flood waters but its ragged steeple remained. There was something incredibly forlorn about it and Devin found his eyes drawn to it again and again. Moss and ivy softened the harsh lines of the ruins but there was a tremendous sensation of loss that permeated the scene.

"That's it," Marcus said as he called a halt to further exploration for the night. "We'll have no broken ankles or legs to complicate matters." He slung the sack of wooden heads down with a smack which made Lavender jump and murmur something uncomplimentary under her breath. "There's an L-shaped wall over there which will offer some protection for the night."

Devin was grateful to stop. His headache had returned by mid-afternoon and he was tired of straining his eyes to see what lay ahead of them. He slid down the wall that Marcus indicated and rested his shoulders against the stone.

"If you would gather some sticks, Lavender," Marcus said, "I think we could chance having a fire."

Lavender gave Marcus' sack a loving pat and hobbled off to collect wood. Devin glanced at Marcus. "She promised us a way into the tunnels. It seems the church is the only possibility."

"I agree," Marcus responded, watching her slow progress at gathering kindling.

"But where are the 'mossy steps'?" Devin asked.

Marcus pointed up the hill. "Maybe they come down toward the church from the other side, which is odd because she claimed the entrance was 'down the mossy steps.'"

"She must have discovered them from above then," Devin speculated.

"Perhaps," Marcus said.

"You don't trust her?"

Marcus pursed his lips. "I don't trust anyone but the Chancellor and you, Devin."

"Which Chancellor?" Devin asked.

Marcus stopped, a wounded expression on his face. "Do you really need to ask?"

"Yes," Devin replied. "I do. Because I am determined to do everything I can to keep my father in power. I just want to make certain that you feel the same way, too."

"You have my word," Marcus replied, holding out his hand.

Devin avoided his eyes because there was still a part of him that didn't trust Marcus. He wondered if the mistrust would ever be gone, but they seemed to be bound whether he wanted it so or not. He didn't shake Marcus' hand and Marcus was quick to withdraw it when it wasn't accepted.

CHAPTER 6

Spirits

The snap and crackle of flame created a small haven of warmth and safety as the rosy glow of the fire dappled the stone walls that sheltered them. For the first time Devin realized just how silent this valley was. Except for the constant flow of water over stone, there were no calls from night birds or the scramble of small animals searching for food. But most disturbing, there were no wolves here, at all.

An autumnal chill settled into the ravine long before dark and Devin was grateful for the blankets that Marcus had brought with him. Unfortunately, there were only two and Devin found himself sharing one with Lavender who cooed and patted it as though she had never seen a blanket before in her life. Her skin was covered with months of filth, her clothes so dirty that their original color had vanished forever and yet sitting in such close proximity to her, Devin was aware only of a pleasantly earthy, woodsy smell. It was as though Lavender herself had become part of her environment.

After they had roasted and eaten the two small rabbits Marcus had caught for dinner, she excused herself from the group and wandered off into the ruins of the town. Devin watched her until she blended into the earth and shadow around them. When she returned half an hour later she brought a square chunk of wood that had been cut from a larger piece. She laid the piece down, slid her legs and knees under the blanket with Devin and propped herself against the wall. From a little bag of fabric around her waist she withdrew a stone with a sharp edge and began removing the bark, humming a little song as she worked. The sweet, sticky smell of pine filled the campsite.

"Are you carving the Captain of the Guard?" Devin asked, referring to the head that had been lost.

Lavender looked up at him in surprise, her dark eyes fathomless in the dim light. "Amando died to save us," she reminded him primly. "He has gone on to the ocean. I think he would have liked to be buried at sea. I just would have liked to see him off."

Marcus laid another log on the fire, sending a shower of sparks into the air, his eyes on the two of them. "Then what are you carving?" he asked.

She didn't look up, the stone still at work in her hand. Her voice was hushed. "I'm carving you, Marcus, so I won't forget you."

A slow smile spread across Marcus' face as he sat back. "Thank you, Lavender."

Lavender's cheeks looked flushed in the firelight. "You said you would take me home. No one has ever promised to do that before."

Devin felt a lump in his throat. He wondered what Lavender's home was like now. Had it been destroyed or was it held by some rival family? Would there be anyone left there who remembered the little girl who had run off to hunt for her pony? She was wiry and flexible as a child but her skin was as wrinkled as a great-grandmother's. Surely she had outlived all her family.

Devin volunteered to keep watch while Marcus slept. He gave Lavender the blanket, fearing the extra warmth might make him sleepy, and slid away from the wall. Putting the fire at his back, he looked out at the landscape clothed in night. The ruined buildings seemed to have weight and form even in the darkness and he thought he could chart their positions correctly although there was no moon. Lavender had hinted that this place was haunted and he could almost feel the panic of the villagers, as a wall of water and stone tore through their homes. There would have been no warning; those who sought shelter in buildings would have drowned as surely as those who had run. He imagined fathers carrying children on their shoulders being catapulted into the waves of water as their feet were swept out from under them, mothers with babes at their breasts drowning with their infants still clasped in their arms.

His eyes went involuntarily to the hill where the steeple still stood. It was possible that a man standing at that level might have survived, that the priest might have found safety in the height of that steeple even as the nave was ripped away below him and scattered by the flood waters. Obviously, someone had lived to tell the story. Lavender knew the tale as one that had been repeated even in her father's hall, another province away. Was there a cemetery above the ruins of the town or had it too been swept away by the raging waters of the burst dam, leaving the remains of the ancient dead to mingle with the recently drowned? If a cemetery did still exist, did it contain the ancestors of the villagers or the victims of the flood? Tomorrow he would climb the slope and if he found a mass grave or a number of graves from the same day, he would try to find evidence of who might have buried the people who died in an instant during that disaster.

The fire had died down to just a bed of glowing coals, when Marcus woke to relieve him of guard duty. Devin felt strangely awake as though the village around him had so much left to tell him. He wondered if he would have felt the same way had Marcus stayed wakeful all evening to discuss it. Now, with Marcus beside him, he found he didn't want to talk about it. It was difficult to explain the strange attraction this valley had suddenly acquired for him. He accepted Marcus' blanket without comment and went to lie down beside Lavender, afraid of breaking the spell by speaking.

Devin barely closed his eyes as the village seemed to spring to life around him. There was the millhouse, the smithy, the bakery, and several dozen houses clustered along the stream. Women laughed and talked as they washed clothes in the flowing water and spread them on the rocks to dry. Men gathered at the smithy, where a stone marker proudly displayed the town's name, discussing planting crops, last frosts, and spring rain. The air was warm and a few flowers poked out between the roots of some ancient oaks on the hillside. Three boys took turns swinging from a rope over the stream, ignoring their mothers' admonitions to not fall in – the water was too cold. A baby sat by her mother's side playing with her own bare toes, while a gray cat rubbed against her tiny back.

And high above them, he saw the priest running toward

the steeple of the stone church. The clanging of the bell brought silence to the people below, then parents grabbed their children and began to flee up the slope. Rushing water and crashing stone drowned out the sound of the church bell clanging out its alarm. Water roared into the valley, sweeping everything and everyone from its path. And above the chaos of screams and death, the priest fell to his knees, the bell rope still in his hand. The insidious water filled the valley, tearing away the nave of the church and leaving no one alive in its wake but him.

Devin scrambled from his blanket. Stumbling partway down the stream, he ignored Marcus' admonitions from behind him, till he found the spot he was looking for. Excavating centuries of leaves and dirt, he dug at the earth with his hands like a dog. At last, he uncovered an engraved stone near where the smithy used to stand. Carrying it back to the feeble light of the fire, he brushed at the clinging earth to uncover the letters on it with dirt-encrusted hands.

"This was the village of Albion," Devin said reverently, sitting back on his heels. "May its villagers rest in peace." He looked up to see tears streaming down Lavender's face and realized his own eyes were wet, too.

CHAPTER 7

Albion

Marcus directed him back to the fire as he stood shivering, the stone clutched in his hands. "How did you know where to find it?" he asked, throwing more wood on the fire and placing his own blanket over Devin's shoulders.

Devin sat, looking at him stupidly, as though he had found Marcus and Lavender existing in the wrong century. "I dreamed it ... just now ... right after I fell asleep."

"You've been asleep for hours," Marcus said, sitting back on his heels.

Devin saw it was true: the first rosy light of dawn lit the eastern horizon, touching the fog rising from the streambed. Lavender sat, clenching her blanket to her chest. "I didn't mean to startle either of you," he said. "I dreamed about Albion and the villagers. It was as though I was there among them. When I woke, I felt that finding the stone was the only way to substantiate what I'd seen."

Marcus eased the stone from his hands and cleaned it off with a handful of leaves. The letters had been cut by an expert stone mason, not even water and centuries of burial

39

in mud had diminished the precise word chiseled into the rock. Marcus sat back against a tree trunk. "I haven't ever heard of Albion, have you?"

Devin shook his head. "I don't remember the name from the Archives. I don't even have a clue as to how long ago these people perished or why. If my dream actually holds some truth, then the priest was the only one who survived. He ran to ring the church bell to warn them but it was already too late. People were washed away in seconds."

Lavender sat listening, her eyes as large and round as a child's. "Do you know the name of the man who ordered this?" she asked softly.

"I don't," Devin said. "I'm sorry. It was as though for a moment I glimpsed the everyday life of this village and then in an instant it was gone, washed downstream in a swirling chaotic flood of adults, children, homes, and animals. Dear God, rest their souls. What a way to die!" He rubbed a hand over his eyes, realizing that in his dream everything had seemed crystal clear; now that he was awake his eyes were blurry again. "I want to explore what's left of the church. Can we go now?"

Marcus' movements were slow and studied as he heated water in a small pan. "Let's eat first. We never know when we may have to hide suddenly. The fire is an advantage we aren't often blessed with and we should use it."

Devin stood up restlessly, glancing at Lavender who was whispering to the head of one of her brothers. God, he thought, they were all going mad! Marcus was the only sane one among them. He walked along the streambed to escape Lavender's insane mutterings, pacing off the buildings he remembered from his dream. There had been a small bridge across from the baker's, spanning the flow of the stream

40

below the dam. There was no sign of it now, though he searched for stone pilings on both sides of the water, soaking his boots in the process.

A few foundations remained, many of them filled with water from recent rainfall. These small stone squares that had supported homes and shops were most apt to contain small artifacts that chronicled the inhabitants' lives. He sifted through dirt with his hands at the millhouse, where the millstone still stood, tilted on its side, resting on a random stone that had been flung from the center of the dam. He found a knife, its blade nearly rusted away, and the remains of the rotted rim of a wooden bowl. There was nothing personal here, nothing that spoke of the hopes and fears of the people who had lived out their lives under the shadow of the dam. They had, apparently, never feared death by drowning. How long had the dam stood before it was sabotaged?

"Devin!" Marcus called.

Devin looked back and saw that Lavender was already consuming something out of a cup. No doubt they would have to share. There seemed no need to rush when she was already occupied with breakfast. He made his way back slowly, mentally placing each building where it had stood in his dream. He joined Marcus just as Lavender finished.

"Will there be more?" she asked, patting the heads she had gathered in her skirt. "We are still hungry."

"There is only enough for each of us to have a cup," Marcus replied.

"What is it?" Devin asked, looking suspiciously at the pan.

"Stew," Marcus answered, "from one very small fish."

"She can have mine," Devin offered.

Marcus quelled Lavender's eager smile with one word.

"No! We have a long way to go and we all need to eat if we are going to make it home."

"Home?" Devin asked. It was a strange choice of words for Marcus. Devin would be happy to reach La Paix but Marcus obviously had greater expectations.

Marcus scooped up a cup of the foamy stew and handed it to him. "Winter will be upon us before you know it, Devin; autumn is short in the mountains. We can't go by ship back to Coreé. We have to cross the mountains into Vienne and it has to be done soon. We must reach Coreé before winter."

"Or it will be too late?" Devin added. The words were implicit. Not only did winter's snow and ice hang over them ominously, but his father's life depended on them arriving in Coreé quickly. René Forneaux's power was growing among Council members. Already, he was recruiting men from Vincent Roché's personal guard and it was evident that he was planning a takeover soon.

Marcus didn't answer. His eyes were lined, his face pinched with worry. His allegiance lay first with Chancellor Roché, with his son second. Devin could only imagine the conflicted emotions he must be feeling right now.

Devin finished the tasteless stew and handed the cup to Marcus who rinsed it in the stream before filling it with the dregs from the pot for his own meal. "I'm going up to look at the ruins of the church," Devin said, standing.

"Sit," Marcus said quietly. "Let me finish my breakfast. We'll all go together."

"We're wasting time," Devin protested.

"Sit," Marcus repeated. "There is nothing there that hasn't been waiting for centuries. Ten minutes more will make no difference."

Devin flopped down beside the fire, watching Lavender endlessly sort her collection of heads. He swore if they reached La Paix, he would have one of the seamstresses design an apron with a pocket for each one. Maybe if Lavender knew each head was safe and securely tucked away in its own little compartment she would cease counting and playing with them. He knew he shouldn't let her behavior bother him but it did. This valley seemed laden with the hundred ghosts of its past residents; he didn't need Lavender's creepy heads reminding him of all the ghosts that seemed to travel in her wake, too.

Marcus took his time eating, washed his cup and the small pot he'd used to cook their stew in, and finally began to pack their things.

"We're not coming back?" Devin asked, his mind still on his exploration of the ruined church.

"I see no reason to," Marcus replied. "Should the tunnels beneath the church look promising, we won't have any reason to return. If not, we'll continue up and over the hill. This valley has turned south and we need to go east to La Paix."

Devin squatted down and drew a quick diagram on the wet earth near the stream. "The tunnels under the church don't connect to the ones on the map," he said after a moment. "I should have realized that before."

Marcus looked at him sharply. "How do you know that?"

Devin gestured at his drawing. "I memorized the map."

Marcus took a step closer. "The one in the Bishop's Book?"

Devin nodded.

"How long did that take you?" Marcus asked.

"Not long," Devin replied. "I only have to see a page for a moment or so and I remember all of it."

Marcus raised his eyebrows. "No wonder school was so easy for you. It seems you have an unfair advantage."

"Unfair, perhaps," Devin replied, "but quite useful in this instance, don't you think?"

"Perhaps," Marcus agreed. "But then there is no reason for us to pursue these tunnels below the church."

Devin jumped to his feet, his hands shaking. "Please, allow me to take just a few minutes."

Marcus' gaze was wary. "You seem to be unusually agitated about this."

Devin attempted to still his hands. "I know and I can't explain it. It feels strangely important. It's almost as though I lived through this massacre last night." He glanced across the valley, tendrils of mist rising from the water and weaving through the tree branches above. "Can't you feel it? It's as though this valley is haunted by all the souls of those who lost their lives."

Marcus was slow in answering. "I'll admit I feel something but it makes me want to leave as soon as possible. Whatever happened here has nothing to do with us."

"But don't you see, it might?" Devin said. "I feel as though all of this is connected in some huge web of treachery that we have only just begun to untangle. We cannot fight it unless we have all the information we need."

"And you expect to find it here?" Marcus pressed him.

"Perhaps," Devin said desperately. "Perhaps not, but I need to look."

Marcus exhaled. "Go on then."

Devin scrambled up the incline toward the ruins of the stone church, finding handholds in the twisted roots of the ancient oaks. Behind him, he heard voices, muted and strange and then all of a sudden around him he heard the cries of

44

people being yanked from their precarious holds by water blasting through their peaceful little valley. He dropped to his knees, his hands over his ears, trying to shut out the sound of women and children screaming for help and the anguished cries of men, unable to aid their families, as they were swept away themselves.

Marcus latched onto Devin's shoulders and shook him. Devin focused on Marcus' face and the undisturbed forest around them. The voices were gone, hushed as absolutely as though they had ... died.

"Devin!" Marcus blustered. "You're scaring me! What on earth is the matter?"

Devin wiped his dirty hands on his trousers. He bit his lip, his breaths coming in uneasy wheezes. "You didn't hear it?"

"Hear what?" Marcus asked. "All I heard was you taking off up this hill as though the devil himself were after you."

Devin shook his head. "I heard their voices again," he said, looking at the earth in front of him. "I heard them dying, Marcus. It was as though if I didn't climb the hill in time, I'd drown, too."

Marcus, who didn't quail at facing a dozen armed men, crumpled. He turned Devin's head toward him, one hand reaching to lift the bandage over his temple. "Did I do this?" he asked, examining the injury. "Is this some side effect from the gunshot wound?"

"I don't think so," Devin replied. "It's something about this place. It's as though I'm having a waking dream. It's not your fault, Marcus. None of this is."

"We need to get out of here, Devin," Marcus said, pulling him upright. "Something's not right and I'm not going to risk your life by staying here a minute longer than necessary."

"But it is necessary," Devin told him. "There is something here that we need to know, something important. Those voices simply drove me upward. The answer is in that church or below it and we need to find it before we leave." He pulled away, leaving Marcus and Lavender to climb the slope after him through the mist and shafts of sunlight.

CHAPTER 8

The Key

Devin halted at a chasm that yawned open where the nave of the church had been. Near the altar, which hung suspended above the abyss, a spiral of mossy stone steps wound downward, disappearing into the darkness below.

Lavender came to stand beside him, humming some tuneless lullaby as she rocked one of her brothers' heads in her arms. "The mossy steps," she pointed out proudly, as though she had created them herself.

"What's down there?" Marcus asked her.

She jerked one shoulder nervously and avoided his eyes. "The tunnels," she said. "But I don't go there."

Marcus huffed in exasperation. "Then how do you know what is there?"

She rubbed one of her brothers' heads against her cheek, like a child with a comforting toy. "I went there once with my brother when the church was still here. There was a room in the cellar but the door that led into it was locked."

Devin glanced at Marcus. The key in his jacket was a token of passage, not made to open a lock. "Perhaps we can open it. If the door is wooden, it's bound to be rotted by now. We could force it."

"You need the key," Lavender said.

"Do you have it?" Devin asked.

Lavender shook her head. "You have a key. I know you do," she insisted.

"I don't have the key to this door," Devin replied irritably.

"You need the key to reach the tunnels," Lavender insisted. "He told me that you need it!"

Marcus grabbed her shoulder and spun her around. "Who told you that?"

Lavender shook in his grip, her face as white as a sheet. "Sébastian," she whispered. "Sébastian told me."

"Who is Sébastian?" Marcus shouted.

Devin stepped between them, breaking Marcus' hold with his shoulder. "Her brother," he said. "She says her brother Sébastian told her."

Marcus put a hand to his head. "Holy Mary Mother of God!" he muttered. "I swear I'm the one who's having nightmares. I just pray I'll wake up soon. What possessed me to allow you to come with us, Lavender? This has been nothing but an ill-fated, insane undertaking from the start!"

"Can I go down?" Devin asked.

"We have no light and apparently we have no key to open the door at the bottom." Marcus threw up his hands in disgust. "I can't even see the bottom of the steps, Devin, let alone inside these tunnels she's babbling about. Leave this, would you? We need to be on our way!"

Lavender sank down on a rock, a stray tear rolled down one cheek before she swiped at it with her ragged sleeve. She began rocking back and forth and humming, her arms

48

clasped tightly around her. Devin felt she had never seemed so pathetic.

"Surely, we can make a torch from pitch," Devin suggested. "This pine will burn."

"Of course it will," Marcus answered roughly. He glanced at the sun climbing the eastern sky. "I will give you until noon, Devin, and then we leave whether or not we have found whatever you think is waiting to be discovered here." Devin started to object but Marcus interrupted him. "That's the deal. Take it or leave it!"

"I'll take it," Devin said. He cut a sturdy branch from a spruce tree and dipped the tip in the excess sap that seeped out of the trunk. He held out a hand to Marcus who reluctantly put his flint in it.

"That's the only flint I have," Marcus warned him. "Don't lose it!"

"I won't," Devin assured him. He glanced back at Lavender, wanting to say or do something to counteract Marcus' harsh words. He held out his hand. "Will you come with us, Lavender?"

She shook her head, her eyes brimming with tears. "I don't want to," she whispered.

Devin touched her shoulder gently, afraid of upsetting her more. "Call down if you need us."

She glanced up, her face softening for a moment. "Thank you," she said quietly.

Devin turned toward the ruined church, feeling Lavender's desolation and Marcus's irritation following him like a malevolent cloud. The steps were remarkably easy to descend although Lavender stayed behind, sitting dejectedly on her rock. Whether she was hurt or angry at Marcus or simply afraid of the tunnels, she seemed anxious to keep her distance from both of them. The moss provided a cushiony if slightly slippery layer to the stone as they made their way down. The smell of dampness, earth, and rot was overpowering. Ferns had rooted here, too, pushing up feathery foliage from fallen tree trunks long since decayed, surrounded by clusters of red mushrooms with yellow spots.

Devin thought of supper. "Those are beautiful. Are they ...?"

"No!" Marcus snapped. "They're not. They're *Amanita muscaria* and they are poisonous!"

Devin raised his eyebrows. "That's good to know."

The steps ended, lost in the deep shadow from the walls above. In places part of a floor remained, cut from massive squares of stone and fitted together almost seamlessly. In the corner, there was a door, arched at the top as the original church door might well have been, too. There was no ornate locking mechanism, just a simple keyhole. Marcus gave it a hefty yank but it didn't budge. Devin slipped out the tip of his knife and fitted it into the lock, feeling it jam after half the length of the blade had entered.

"It's locked from the inside," he said. "I can feel the key."

Marcus looked askance. "I had no idea you'd trained as a locksmith."

Devin laughed. "Oh, never a locksmith, Marcus, but I didn't get through the *université* without learning how to pick a lock."

Marcus went down on a knee and ran his finger under the door. He turned to see if Lavender was watching. "Can you give me a piece of parchment from your jacket?"

"The only parchment I have is Tirolien's Chronicle," Devin hissed.

"Don't you think I know that?" Marcus whispered. "If

I slide it under the door do you think you can loosen the key enough that it will fall onto the parchment? We can slide it out under the door."

It was easier said than done. Devin tried manipulating the knife but the blade wasn't long enough. The blades on two of Marcus' knives were too thick to enter the keyhole but the third one, that he withdrew from his boot, looked long, slender, and deadly.

"What's that one for?" Devin asked.

"If you have you to ask, you're not as smart as I thought you were," Marcus remarked lightly. He stood up stiffly. "Here, you get down on your knees with the damn parchment! You're less than half my age."

Marcus fit the narrow knife into the keyhole, jiggled it several times and gave it a practiced twist. The key dropped but when Devin started to withdraw the paper, he could hear it bump the door.

"Don't! Don't! Don't!" Marcus cautioned, extending a hand. "Let's see if we can dig out under the paper a bit and give it more room. It's probably a thick key."

They cautiously brushed dirt away from the threshold as the sun rose higher in the sky. Not once did Marcus comment on the time of day or urge their departure. He lay with his eye on ground level, carefully shifting the parchment back and forth. Finally, he maneuvered the parchment forward, bringing a heavy iron key with it.

"Got it!" crowed Marcus, swooping to grasp the key from the parchment. Holding it aloft, he squinted over his shoulder at Devin. "Would you like to do this or shall I?"

Devin bent to retrieve the parchment, brushing it off before returning it to his jacket. He took a step back and motioned to Marcus. "You can open it."

CHAPTER 9

Whispers from the Past

As Marcus turned it, the key rasped in the lock, metal scraping metal. Devin heard something rattle and shift, sending a chill up his spine, and the door cracked open. A dry draft of air billowed outward as though it had been trapped there for centuries, and both of them seemed frozen in time for an instant: Marcus, so strong and confident, gripping the key in one hand and the knob in the other, and Devin, tense with a strange suspicion of what they would find inside. He stooped quickly as the door fell open, cradling the skeleton in his arms, lest it crumble on the stone floor.

"God!" Marcus whispered. "The priest! Did you know he was in here?"

"I had a feeling," Devin answered, afraid to move for fear part of this man of God might shatter in his arms.

"You might have warned me," Marcus grumbled, bending over. "Let me help you."

Only scraps of his clerical robes held the bones in place. The priest's skull seemed to drop naturally into the crook of Devin's shoulder. Devin doubted if he lived to be a hundred that he would ever forget the feeling.

Marcus seemed to be at a loss. "Where shall we put him?"

Devin nodded toward the open door. "Back inside? He died there. It seems we have disturbed his tomb. Perhaps we should restore things to the way they were."

"He must have died leaning on the door," Marcus observed. "Let's prop him against the wall instead."

He slid a hand carefully under the skeleton's lower half while Devin supported the top, feeling bones loosen and shift as fabric and leathery strips of skin fell away. They moved him into the dark interior of the tunnel, arranging the remains as reverently as possible against the far wall.

Devin stood up, tried to restrain a violent shudder and failed.

Marcus retrieved the spruce branch. "My flint?" he asked, holding out his hand.

Devin tried to pull it out of his pocket but was unsuccessful; his hands were shaking so badly. Marcus reclaimed it himself and struck a spark to their spruce branch, the torch throwing its flickering light into the darkness.

The "tunnel" consisted of one austere room: a shelf held empty bottles of communion wine. The floor held only the tatters of a decayed blanket, a Bible and a small leather-bound book. Devin bent to pick the book up, disturbing a quill that rolled off across the floor. An empty ink well rocked back and forth on its side.

Devin opened the cover, his eyes squinting to keep the words from blurring: *Father Sébastian Chastain, 12 Avril 1406.* "God," he breathed. "Can you believe this? It's a journal, Marcus!"

"And this is nothing more than a safe house, Devin," Marcus replied, gesturing with the torch. "You were right. It doesn't connect to the other tunnels but it must have served as a secure place to hide someone who might have been running for his life."

Devin barely listened; he turned the pages reverently, tracing the writing that grew more spidery and shaky toward the end. Not only did the writing itself change but so did the ink. Devin swallowed, hardly wanting to put his observations into words. He'd seen two other manuscripts like this once before in the Archives. He cleared his throat but it didn't stop his voice from shaking. "He finished this by writing with his own blood, Marcus. Imagine having something so important to say that you ..." He couldn't finish.

"I think we need to leave," Marcus said firmly. "Take the journal with you. Hide it in the lining of your jacket with Tirolien's Chronicle. If Father Sébastian died recording all of this, then it needs to be preserved and remembered."

"He voluntarily starved to death to preserve this account of what happened, Marcus," Devin whispered. "He died for Albion and its people and we would never have known if Lavender hadn't led us here."

"We need to leave now!" Marcus instructed as Devin still stood mesmerized, fingering the journal in his hands.

Devin slipped it through the ripped seam in the lining under his left arm, feeling its weight drop toward the hem below. What did he carry with him from this place and what providence led them to find it?

Marcus shoved Devin outside, taking one final moment to place the Bible gently in Father Sébastian's lap before closing the door. He gave the key a turn in the lock and slipped it into his pocket. "When we reach La Paix," he said, "I will drop this key from the top of the waterfall. Father Sébastian deserves to rest in peace now that he has passed on his legacy."

"Sébastian." Devin repeated the name suddenly. "That's what Lavender told us. She said Sébastian had told her we needed the key. Maybe it wasn't her brother she was talking about."

Devin turned away from Marcus, anxious to test his theory. He took off up the winding steps, each step firm and secure, as he dodged fallen branches, trees, and rocks.

"Devin, stop!" Marcus called behind him. "You'll break your neck!"

But Devin climbed higher and higher into the sudden brilliant gold of that late-August afternoon, the reassuring weight of Father Sébastian's journal in his pocket.

He stopped at the top, blinking in the strong shafts of sunlight that enshrouded the church. Lavender was gone. He knew she would be. He circled the empty crater where the church once stood but there was no sign of her dirty gown or brown, wrinkled face. In the valley below nothing moved but the water of the stream flowing endlessly to the south. A gentle wind tossed the branches above his head and he realized that up here the air was much warmer. He was glad Marcus had packed their things this morning, because he didn't want to go back down to spend another night among the valley's shifting mist and ghostly whispers.

Marcus reached the top of the steps. "Damn it, Devin!" he gasped, bending over to catch his breath. "What's the hurry?"

"Lavender's gone," Devin said, reaching to retrieve the freshly carved head she had left for Marcus on the rock where she had been sitting. He held it out to him.

Marcus made no move to take it. "What are you trying to say?" he asked.

Devin shook his head and gently placed the wooden image of Marcus into his bodyguard's hand. "I'm not trying to say anything, Marcus. I'll let you draw your own conclusions."

CHAPTER 10

Mysteries and Discoveries

Marcus insisted that they look for Lavender, and they did, but if she still existed, she had blended back into the landscape like a native flower or shrub. Nothing remained but the little carved head of Marcus and their memories of her.

"I made her cry," Marcus said gruffly, stuffing the carved head in his pocket.

Devin sighed. "Perhaps it wasn't you as much as the situation. It's been hard on everyone."

"Do you think she was ..." Marcus hesitated.

"A ghost?" Devin asked. "Perhaps. But we touched her, smelled her, she ate our food."

"The food sack," Marcus said suddenly and set it down to rummage through it.

Devin knew what Marcus would find before he announced it. "The heads are all gone. Every last one of them."

"Except the one she carved for you," Devin pointed out.

Marcus withdrew it from his pocket, held it humbly in his hands for a few moments. "Did I ever thank her?"

"I'm sure you did," Devin replied.

Marcus slipped the token back in his pocket.

Devin's eyes still searched the rocks and bushes around them, hoping that he might catch sight of a scrap of tattered brown fabric or a tiny footprint to convince them that Lavender had traveled with them and touched their lives for several days.

Marcus grabbed his sleeve. "Come on, then," he said finally. "Night falls earlier now. We need to go."

They left the ruins of Albion's church behind. Above the deep ravine, the terrain flattened out. Statuesque spruce trees circled a small clearing knee deep in long grass and scattered wildflowers. Here hawks soared, and rabbits and deer grazed in the late-afternoon shadows. It was like another world compared to the valley behind them. Light, fragrant, and warm.

Devin tripped on a raised stone. He dropped his pack, hoping it might be a headstone, and knelt to pull the weeds away.

"The Town of Albion, Destroyed by Flood, 12 Avril 1406," he read as Marcus bent to look. "It's the same day Father Sébastian's journal begins."

Devin walked in a wide circle from the stone, swinging his foot to crush the tall grass. "I'd hoped there might be some gravestones," he said in disappointment.

"The bodies would have washed downstream and Father Sébastian couldn't have dragged bodies up that slope anyway, Devin!" Marcus said. "Not only that, whoever destroyed the dam, would have searched for survivors. Had even a few of the bodies been buried, it would have been obvious that someone survived. Anyone who knew the truth about what happened would have been killed."

"And yet, Lavender knew the story."

58

"The person who created the story may have made an assumption as to who destroyed the dam."

"But the Chronicles are very precise," Devin objected. "The story of Albion's destruction would never have been included in Tirolien's Chronicle if there was some doubt about its veracity."

"Lavender never said the story came from the Chronicles, Devin," Marcus pointed out. "She said that her father told her about it."

Devin inclined his head. "That's true." His eyes drifted over the clearing, watching as the tall grass bent like waves in the wind. "But if this really was one of the first settlements in Llisé, it existed for hundreds of years before its destruction. There would have had to be a cemetery for the church. All of those graves would predate the flood."

"I'm sure you're right but we don't have time to look for a cemetery, Devin. We need to get back to La Paix as quickly and safely as possible. I'm sorry."

Devin exhaled. "I understand."

Marcus skirted the clearing, startling the deer, their white tails flashing as they dashed into the forest beyond. "Perhaps the journal will answer some of your questions."

"I hope," Devin said. It was as though the book was physically hot, burning a hole in his jacket lining. He wanted desperately to take it out and read it, to sit down right in this field and discover the secrets it contained. Had it been possible, he would have read it as he walked.

"Perhaps Father Sébastian wrote a list of the dead in his journal," Marcus suggested.

Devin nodded. "I saw a list of names when I was flipping through the pages." If Father Sébastian left a journal chronicling the fate of his parishioners, Devin felt certain it was meticulous. How strange that it had lain there waiting several hundred years to be found and read!

"We'll look at it tonight," Marcus promised. "We need to find a protected place to sleep. Despite what we left behind us, that valley sheltered us well and kept us safe."

They continued around the clearing, but much to Devin's disappointment they discovered no gravestones along the way. He wanted to stay and search, to learn all the secrets this valley had to offer but he knew it was impossible now. In the few minutes he had spent with the villagers in his dreams, he had felt a connection to them in a raw, emotional sense. He'd shared their laughter and their terror and they were bound to him in a way he couldn't explain to Marcus or anyone else, except maybe Jeanette.

Perhaps in the future he and Jeanette could return together just as he hoped they could go back to the ruined Archives and discover whether anything remained there. The more he saw of the provinces, the more he loved them. Each one held riches that the residents of Coreé never could dream of in their insular little worlds. Perhaps there was a way of combining his love of the Archives with his desire to add the wealth of history the provinces also offered.

Their route dipped into one valley after another and by twilight their legs were tired from climbing. "I see now why the road was built where it was," Devin observed, as he dropped down onto a grassy knoll where oak trees' massive trunks formed a kind of fortress.

"It's too dark to walk any further," Marcus said. "This will do as well as any other for a place to spend the night."

Devin let his pack slide from his shoulders, his hand immediately working the journal up through the tear in the lining and slipping it out. He stretched out for a moment, the journal open in his hands. "It's too dark to read," he said in disappointment. "I don't suppose you'll allow us a fire?"

"No," Marcus said. "I've no idea how far we've come and what villages might be nearby. It's best to be safe. And put that book away if you can't read it. We're not at an inn. You have no idea when we might have to leave suddenly."

Reluctantly, Devin slid the journal back in its hiding place. It was only after they had decided to stay for the night that the ground seemed overrun with exposed roots. Under the trees, there was little grass and the ground was hard as rock. Marcus produced a bit of moldy bread for dinner; it was too late to hunt. They drank their fill of the water from the skins Marcus had replenished earlier and resigned themselves to empty bellies until morning brought another chance for a meal.

Devin's mind was busy with the details of the safe room they had found. "Father Sébastian locked the door from the inside," Devin observed. "He must have been afraid for his own life."

"I'm sure he wanted it to appear to whoever blew up the dam that everyone in Albion was killed," Marcus said. "If Father Sébastian was seen, he would have been hunted down."

"And yet Lavender claimed he told her that we needed the key to unlock the door," Devin reminded him.

Marcus unrolled his blanket. He raised his eyebrows at Devin. "I don't believe Father Sébastian appeared in person."

"She did have a brother named Sébastian. You don't think they could be one and the same?"

"Only if she were a ghost, Devin, and I'm not ready to

accept that explanation yet," Marcus replied. "I think she was a very sad old lady who somehow lost her family and her way. I'm not sure anything she told us was accurate."

"But those carved heads were so meticulous. May I see yours?" Devin held out a hand.

Marcus handed it over with reluctance, placing it on Devin's palm.

Devin traced the carving with his fingers; the frowning forehead and spray of wrinkles around Marcus' eyes were typical. Only the mouth was unusual. "She made you smiling!" he said in surprise.

"Well, I do smile occasionally," Marcus blustered. "Give that back!"

Devin chuckled and handed it over. "If Lavender was a spirit, she could actually have been the little girl who lost her pony in Arcadia's Chronicle."

"Then why didn't she appear to us as a little girl?" Marcus asked.

Devin shrugged. "Because she may have lived a long time, searching these mountains for the pony she loved. We have no idea how old she was when she died."

"I'm not sure we will ever discover exactly who or what Lavender was. There is really no sense speculating about it when there is no way to prove whether one theory or another is correct!"

"That's true," Devin agreed. "But I would rather think she was a spirit than a very old woman wandering alone out here in the night. I do wonder about her brother named Sébastian."

"Do you know the last name of the Lavender who appeared in Arcadia's Chronicle?" Marcus asked.

Devin shook his head. "I don't believe Armand ever told

me. So many of those stories aren't dated either; we can only assume they took place at a certain time from hints in the story. Even if the Chronicle doesn't specify her last name, Armand might still know."

"You'll have to wait to ask him then," Marcus said, stifling a yawn.

Devin pulled his knees up and crossed his arms on them. "Do you want me to take the first watch?"

"If you like," Marcus answered. "How do you feel? No more voices in your head?"

"None," Devin answered. "I believe those voices were only meant to lead us to Father Sébastian and this journal. I don't think I will hear them again."

"Still," Marcus said, wrapping his blanket around his shoulders and curling into a ball at the foot of an oak. "Wake me if you do."

Devin smiled. "You'll be the first to know." He looked west, toward Calais and the sea and saw the full orange globe of the moon rising. The wind increased, rattling the branches in the grove of oaks and the air smelled of rain. Overhead, an owl asked questions of the night as small animals scurried through the grass. In the distance, a wolf howled and was answered by another.

It was a relief to hear normal night noises and not the unearthly quiet of the valley where Albion had stood. If ever a place was haunted – that one was. He thought of Comte Aucoin's chateau and the ghosts that seemed to chasten Angelique. If spirits linger simply to correct a wrong, why had Angelique's family tormented her dreams, turning them into nightmares? Or were nightmares something else altogether?

For the past few days, he'd felt as though his dreams had become muddled with his daily life and it was hard to separate one from the other. He'd always had a problem with "waking dreams." It had started when he was a child and seemed to happen when he was just at the point of waking up. Something or someone in his room would appear to be something else – usually something frightening. The malady had followed him into his adult years and had proved a great source of amusement to his roommate and best friend, Gaspard, when he was at the *université*. After Dr. Verstegan, a friend of one of his older brothers, had prescribed valerian before he went to bed, the dreams had stopped, only to return on this trip. Lavender had brought back the uncertainty of what was real and what was not. Thankfully, Marcus had seen her and spoken with her, too, or he might have doubted his own sanity.

A few hours after midnight, it began to rain, a damp misty drizzle at first and then a downpour, bringing Marcus upright, his blanket over his head. "What in God's name!" he grumbled.

Devin turned to look at him. "Sorry, I can keep watch but I can't control the weather."

Marcus gave a shiver, pulling his sodden blanket around him. "It's late. Why didn't you waken me?"

"I could feel the rain coming," Devin answered. "I thought I'd give you a chance to sleep while it was dry."

"Not so great for you!" Marcus observed. "Where's your blanket?"

"I'm sitting on it," Devin replied. "I thought I'd keep it as dry as I could. I'm worried about the journal."

"Why don't you sleep against one of the trunks?" Marcus suggested. "Put the side of your jacket with the Chronicle and the journal against the tree. You can have my blanket, too, if you like."

"No, thank you," Devin said, sliding over to hug the nearest oak tree. "It's already soaked."

He moved to snuggle against the tree trunk and found the bark ridged and unyielding. He doubled his blanket over his shoulders and closed his eyes but the drip from overhead branches made sleep impossible. After several unsuccessful attempts, he watched a gray dawn touch the eastern horizon with Marcus.

"Can we move on?" he asked.

"If you're ready," Marcus answered. "This doesn't appear to be letting up. We may as well be on our way."

The rain continued all day, leaving their clothes and boots soaked. Finally, by late afternoon the storm clouds scudded off, leaving the sky brilliantly blue and cloudless.

"It's going to be cold tonight," Marcus predicted. "We need to find shelter – somewhere we can dry our clothes and get warm."

"Do you have any money?" Devin asked.

"I picked the pockets of the men I dropped in the bay," Marcus admitted. "What are you thinking?"

"Finding an inn, perhaps?" Devin suggested. "If I tie this bandage around my eyes and find a stout stick, I could pretend that I am blind and you are my father. We'd hardly fit the description of the men the soldiers are seeking."

Marcus shook his head. "That's risky, Devin. I think we need to stay out of any populated areas."

"A cave then?" Devin asked hopefully, thinking of the misery of sleeping outside on a cold night in wet clothes.

"We'll see," Marcus said without agreeing.

They crossed fields, slithered down into ravines, and clambered over stone walls, all to avoid the main road. As the light began to dim, Marcus spotted what looked like a low shelter for livestock at the corner of a pasture.

"That looks promising," Marcus remarked cheerfully. "Stay here in the hedgerow while I check it out."

He was only gone for a few minutes, skirting the field and soundlessly approaching the shelter from the back. For a man on the far side of forty, he moved like a cat, swiftly and silently covering the distance. Devin lost sight of him when he disappeared inside. A moment later he motioned Devin ahead.

"Luck is on our side," Marcus said with a grin. "This is a shepherd's hut. There's dry straw to sleep on and even a lantern filled with oil!"

"Too bad there is no roast mutton hidden away," Devin said as his stomach rumbled.

"That I don't have," Marcus replied. "But there is time enough for me to hunt and you can read your precious journal tonight as long as you keep the lantern shuttered."

Devin dropped his pack and felt for the pages of the Chronicle in his jacket. They were warm and dry and so was the journal. "We're lucky indeed," Devin agreed.

Marcus left his pack on the straw. "I'll be back in a few minutes with something to eat."

Removing the journal, Devin took off his jacket and hung it to dry on one of the branches which had escaped the interwoven tangle of limbs which made up the walls of the hut. Though the structure was open on one side, the three remaining walls broke the wind. He propped his back against the corner and opened the journal.

The first page recording the date was written in larger handwriting than the contents of the journal. Devin squinted at the first entry in frustration as the letters and words blurred together. He rubbed his eyes but no matter how he struggled, the words were as indecipherable as though they were written in a foreign language. What if this problem with his eyesight was permanent? He could never return to his work at the Archives. Of what use was an archivist who couldn't read or copy manuscripts? He put the journal back in his jacket. He'd had little or no sleep last night, he rationalized. Perhaps that was part of the problem, and admittedly the light inside the hut wasn't good either. He put his head back against the wall and closed his eyes. A short nap might improve things.

Marcus entered, wakening him. He laid two skinned rabbits down on the hay. "I thought you'd be devouring that journal!" he said in surprise.

Devin passed a hand over his eyes. "I guess my lack of sleep got the better of me. Perhaps we can read it together after dinner."

"Read it to me while I cut these rabbits up," Marcus directed. "I think we might be able to roast them a bit over that lantern."

Devin slid forward. "I can't, Marcus."

"You can't what?" he asked, busy with his rabbits. "I know you don't like raw meat. I just said I'm going to try to cook it for you."

"It's not that," Devin answered.

"Then what's the matter?" Marcus asked, sparing him an annoyed look.

"I can't read," Devin blurted out. "My eyes are blurry all the time. I can't see straight."

Marcus dropped his knife and turned around. "When you first mentioned this, I assumed it was temporary. You read the date in that journal to me yesterday."

Devin turned the book so he could see it. "The date and Father Sébastian's name are written much larger. I was able to make that much out. But in the journal entries ..." He turned a page and held the book up for Marcus, "the writing is much smaller. See for yourself."

"God, Devin, I had no idea! You should have told me," Marcus replied. "It's only been five days, maybe it will go away."

"Maybe," Devin conceded.

"Have the headaches stopped?"

"Yes, and the dizziness, too. It's only the blurriness in my eyes that's remained."

"What can I do?" Marcus asked.

"Read the journal to me tonight," Devin said. "We need to know what's in it. If something should happen – if the book were captured – no one would know the truth about what happened at Albion."

"Anything," Marcus promised. "I don't know what to say, Devin. You know I shot you to save your life."

Devin nodded. Marcus' concern seemed palpable. He had no desire to reassure him; he didn't have the heart. Losing his eyesight would bring all his dreams crashing down and he wasn't ready to deal with that now.

The lantern proved efficient at cooking bits of rabbit on wet sticks. The edges were crisp and the center tender and juicy. Devin couldn't remember having enjoyed a meal more. They were both famished after last night's lack of dinner and this was certainly an improvement over moldy bread!

Marcus disposed of the remains of the rabbits and returned with two full waterskins. He sat down next to Devin against the wall and pulled the lantern to his side. "Let's have that journal," he said.

Devin handed it to him, watching as he opened it to the first entry. *"I, Father Sébastian Chastain, priest to the people of Albion and Rodez ..."*

"Rodez?" Devin interrupted. "That's another very small village. It's not far from the Arcadia border."

"I'm not familiar with it but if their priest disappeared, there might be more information at one of the churches close by." Marcus glanced at Devin. "You know we can't take the time to look for any more information now?"

"I know that," said Devin, trying to keep the irritation from his voice. "It simply adds more validity to the journal, especially if there are secondary sources describing the destruction of Albion. Go on."

"... must record the events that led to the destruction of Albion and all its citizens. On 12 Avril 1406, Gascon Forneaux ..."

"Forneaux?" Devin yelped. "Is it possible that this could be René Forneaux's ancestor?"

"We'll never know if you keep interrupting me!" Marcus snapped. He took a deep breath and began again. *"Gascon Forneaux and some of his men destroyed the dam holding back the waters of Gave d'Oloron, subsequently flooding the town of Albion and drowning all of its inhabitants. I saw the waters coming over a great distance from the hill above the church and rang the bell to alert my parishioners but my efforts came too late. Every man, woman, and child was swept away by the onslaught and I will forever bear the guilt of their deaths. Had I only reached the church bell sooner, I might have saved some of their lives."*

Devin exhaled. "What a burden to bear! He blamed himself and yet he couldn't have done more than he did."

"I am leaving this journal in the hope that my sister

Lavender or one of my brothers may find it and give it to my father. They are the only ones that I have shown this safe room to. News of my death will bring them here to search for answers." Marcus dropped the journal on his knee. "Now that is just scary! So, Lavender actually was Sébastian's sister?"

"His little sister," Devin reminded him. "The Lavender that the story made famous was a child when she ran after her pony. What would have brought her to Tirolien, do you think? Even had he shown her that room as a child, she wouldn't have been able to travel all this way by herself."

"But maybe as an adult she did," Marcus said. "Maybe she was drawn here because of her brother's death."

"She said she had heard the story from her father," Devin added. "So her brother must have died before she ran away. Could her brother have written to his father expressing his concerns about Gascon Forneaux and the villagers' refusal to pay their taxes? Do you suppose he expected retribution?"

Marcus shook his head. "This is all too complicated for me. I feel as though I've fallen into a fairytale."

"Keep reading," Devin urged.

"*It is incomprehensible that the rivalry between two brothers could have cost so many innocent people their lives,*" Marcus continued.

"Two brothers?" Devin repeated. "Does he give the other brother's name? I think there was a Forneaux who was elected as Chancellor several hundred years ago." He heard the faint sound of voices. "What is that?" he asked, holding up a hand for silence.

"It sounds like people talking," Marcus said.

Devin stood up. Through the trees he saw the intermittent light of lanterns swinging. "Someone's coming."

Marcus was on his feet, too, snuffing the lantern but taking it with them. "Devin, pick up your pack! We need to get out of here!" he hissed.

They stumbled through the dark, tripping over rocks and tree roots, hoping desperately that their hasty escape wouldn't be heard by the group moving into the pasture behind them. They made their way to the far side of the field and scrambled below the brow of the hill, pausing long enough to glance back. A group of twelve people with several lanterns between them gathered at the shepherd's hut Marcus and Devin had just left.

"Who are they?" Marcus whispered.

"Druides?" Devin guessed.

Marcus turned to look at him. "Seriously?"

"I don't know," Devin whispered. "I don't have any better idea than you do!"

The group sat down on the ground, putting the lanterns in a circle in the middle. As they had crossed the field, Devin noticed in the wavering light of their lanterns that none of them were dressed alike. They wore no robes that identified them as a group or a cult and most importantly, they carried no visible weapons.

"Stay here," Marcus directed. "I'm going to do a little reconnaissance. If I'm captured or killed – do your best to get back to La Paix without any further mishaps. I fear leaving you on your own more than anything." He crossed himself elaborately and winked at Devin. "Don't do anything rash," he whispered as he crept forward, soundlessly crossing toward the back of the shepherd's hut.

Devin waited in silence, his hands sweaty, and his heart thumping until Marcus finally arrived behind the hut. At last, Marcus crouched, still and immovable as the trees that bordered the field. The moments stretched into more than an hour and Devin began to feel the air chill as the wind dropped. He slid his wet coat on and buttoned it. Slipping his pack over his shoulder, he prepared to run should Marcus indicate that it was necessary, but Marcus was as still as stone. What was he doing, anyway? Was he afraid to draw attention to himself by leaving or was he gathering information? It was all Devin could do to keep from scrambling over the hilltop to join him.

And yet the minutes dragged on. The waning moon shone overhead now, having lost only a bit of its fullness. Its light outlined the roof and the slope of Marcus' shoulders and made the way back toward where Devin hid seem a little less treacherous. Devin flexed his legs and hands to avoid stiffness, but Marcus showed no sign of moving. After several hours, the group that had gathered in the hut finally stood up, retrieved their lanterns, and went back the way they had come, disturbing nothing at all with their passing. Most fortunate of all, they seemed to have no knowledge at all of Marcus' presence.

CHAPTER 11

Stolen Secrets

Marcus slithered unceremoniously down the slope and landed next to Devin. "Those people were from Rodez. They had actually gathered to learn Tirolien's Chronicle. One man was a friend of Absolon Colbert, Dariel Moreau's apprentice. He'd heard Absolon tell the tales from the Chronicle over and over and learned many of them himself. He's passing them on to the others."

"So they had already heard of Dariel and Absolon's murders?" Devin asked.

"News of a murdered Master Bard and his apprentice travels fast," Marcus said. "Dariel's murder was more lurid than most. There was no attempt to cover it up as an accident or natural causes. When Absolon was murdered as well, there was no evidence to prove that the murders might have been prompted by robbery. The people of Tirolien are furious!"

"As well they should be," Devin agreed. He gave a violent shiver. "Aren't you cold? I'm about to freeze to death. Is it safe for us to retake our hut?"

"Yes, they've all gone home," Marcus said, scrambling back up the hill. "I'm chilled, too, but I thought you'd be relieved that at least Tirolien's stories are being retold."

Devin followed him up, his wet boots rubbing his feet in a dozen nasty places. "I was just afraid you were going to get caught, lurking behind them like a thief," he said. "I had hoped that some of the bards who knew the stories would retell them and teach them to others; even though that isn't the way that tradition dictates that the Chronicles be taught. I hope it happens all over Llisé and the stories of their murdered Master Bards spread across this empire like a plague!"

The moon slipped slowly toward the western horizon, leaving the stars to shine bright and glassy in the dark sky. The grass crunched beneath their feet as though a crust of frost had covered it in the still, cold air after midnight. It seemed that fall had already laid its icy fingers on the northern part of Llisé and their mission seemed more urgent than before.

The hut felt warm and still held the smell of lamp oil, wool, and sweaty bodies. Devin dropped down on the hay, shrugging out of his wet jacket and rehanging it on a stray branch.

Marcus began shifting the hay around by the wall, piling it up and spreading it out again, his back to Devin.

"It's unfortunate when you are warmer without your jacket on than with it," Devin observed, scooping out a small nest for himself in the hay.

"Don't!" Marcus said suddenly.

"Don't what?" Devin asked.

There was a sudden deafening silence. Devin looked up but Marcus' face was hidden in shadow. His voice when it came sounded ragged. "Don't move the hay around. I left the journal here when we ran. I think it's gone, Devin."

Devin fumbled for the lantern, jamming it into Marcus' hands. "Light the lantern so we can see!"

Marcus struck a spark and the lantern illuminated the small space. Though they searched for at least an hour, moving every wisp of hay at least twice, there was no sign of the journal in the hut.

Devin fought an irrational urge to yell at Marcus. "You could hear what these people who met here were saying, couldn't you?" he snapped.

Marcus nodded. "Most of it. I wasn't close enough to hear everything."

"Did they mention the journal?" Devin demanded. "Did anyone say anything about it?"

Marcus shook his head. "No."

Devin paced the small space, his breath misting in the cold air. "Do you think that whoever took it, kept it a secret? Just pocketed it until he could look at it later?"

Marcus threw out his hands. "I don't know. I'm not even sure where I dropped it. When we heard the voices and saw the lanterns, my only thought was to get you away safely. I realize what I've done, Devin, I'm not minimizing it. It was what I warned you about doing and why I told you to put the journal back in your jacket lining when you weren't using it."

"You didn't …?"

Marcus patted his pockets. "No, I've already checked."

Devin sank down on his knees.

"I know how much it meant to you," Marcus said.

Devin steepled his hands against his mouth. "I felt as though we were on the verge of understanding the beginning of this Shadow Government. Father Sébastian mentioned the Forneaux family and the fact that there were two brothers and some apparent feud between them. It sounded as though the people of Albion might have become innocent victims of that feud. We have to find the journal, Marcus. It would strengthen our case if I had some written evidence to present to Council."

"We can't take the time to look for it, Devin," Marcus said. "I'm sorry. If we are to get back to Coreé before winter, we have to reach La Paix as soon as possible."

"And yet, Rodez is on the way," Devin pointed out. "It's only a few miles north of the route we took when we went to Calais to search for the Provincial Archives. We didn't pass it then because we stayed on the main road."

"We don't have time, Devin," Marcus repeated.

"We'll have to stop for food," Devin rationalized.

"How would you determine which person took it?" Marcus asked. "There were ten men and two women here tonight."

"Who seems most likely?" Devin asked.

"No one!" Marcus snapped. "No one seemed like the type to take it without telling the others. They were here to remember and repeat their history. They were meeting in secret … afraid for their lives. Something like that journal would only have added to their goal. They would have been happy to discover any information against the government."

"But none of them could read!!" Devin exclaimed suddenly. "They would have taken it to someone who could, probably the closest priest! I wonder if there is still a church in Rodez?"

"Was there a church there on the map?"

Devin nodded. "Yes, but that map was old. There was

no indication when it was drawn up or by whom. It's worth taking a chance though, isn't it, Marcus? It would only mean a few hours out of our time and it might provide valuable information."

Marcus sighed. "Get some sleep. It'll be dawn before you know it."

"Marcus, we can't allow this journal to disappear," Devin begged.

Marcus held up a hand. "Don't push me. If you do, the answer will be 'no.' Let me think about it. In the meantime, shut up and get some rest."

Initially sleep seemed impossible, but Devin did finally nod off. His dreams were filled with soldiers, floods, and last of all, just before he wakened, Lavender appeared. She held the journal in her hands. "We gave this to you," she said. "If you lose it, there isn't another one. We're depending on you." He woke with a startled exclamation and the determination to find the journal whether Marcus agreed or not.

"What's the matter?" Marcus asked.

"I'm going to go to Rodez," Devin said, "with or without you. I can't let you dictate whether this journal is significant or not, Marcus. I need it to present to Council and I intend to find it before we go back."

Marcus raised his eyebrows and bowed his head, with a grand sweep of his arm. "Then I guess I'll have to go with you, Monsieur Roché," he acquiesced, his jaw clenched.

Rodez was only two miles from the main road, which Devin and Marcus were closer to than they realized. The rural community consisted of a scattering of houses, a small bakery, a store, and a stone church, much like the one at Albion. They heard the bell in the tower as they topped the small rise leading into town.

"Is it Sunday?" Devin asked.

"I have no idea," Marcus responded. "If it is, I don't think it's wise to join the congregation. It makes it much more obvious that we are strangers and a lot more people would be able to attest to our whereabouts."

Devin went off the road into a tangled shrubby area with a good view of the front of the church and sat down. "Then we'll wait."

They didn't have to wait long. Mass must have begun before they arrived and the parishioners trooped down the steps in a little over an hour, saying their farewells to the large priest who greeted them at the door.

"Do you recognize anyone?" Devin whispered.

"That man," Marcus pointed out, "is Absolon's friend. He seemed to be the leader of the group. If I had to guess, I might think he had taken the journal."

Devin watched as the tall, lanky young man bent to speak privately with the priest. "He could be making arrangements to meet him later or confiding that his wife is expecting another baby. It's impossible to know."

Marcus grabbed his arm. "That woman was there, too. I remember the unusual white streak in her hair."

The woman shook the priest's hand and descended the steps, holding a small boy by the hand. Several people followed in quick succession; none was anyone that Marcus recognized until a very large man gripped the priest in a bear hug.

"He was there," Marcus added. "It makes you wonder if he might be the priest's brother. They are surely built the same."

Devin sighed. "Anyone else?" It was well past noon and his stomach was rumbling. How nice it would be to go to the baker's and buy some fresh bread. But in a village this size, strangers would be noticed right away, and possibly reported to the nearest authorities. The people of Northern Llisé were afraid for their lives. Their bards had been brutally murdered and their heritage was in jeopardy. Any stranger had become a potential enemy.

Marcus shook his head. "There is no one else that I recognize. It was dark and I was peering through the branches on the wall of the hut. I think I was lucky to have remembered three of them. Wait a few minutes and we'll go in and speak to the priest."

"I pray he doesn't have another service to perform at a nearby church, the way Father Sébastian did," Devin commented.

"It's entirely possible. I doubt that a village this size could support a priest," Marcus said.

The area around the church had cleared and Devin and Marcus stood up. Devin pulled the bandage from his head, scrunched it, and placed it in his pocket. He combed his hair down over his wound with his fingers as they moved out from their hiding place.

The priest was just swinging the one door closed as they reached the church. "Good afternoon," he said, shading his hand against the sun. "Do I know you?"

"No, Father," Devin said. "May we speak to you?"

"Of course," he said. "I'm Father Mark. Would you like to come inside?"

"Please," Devin said, as Marcus surveyed the empty street for observers. The priest held the door for them and they entered the darkened nave; sparse sunlight pierced the only two windows.

"How can I help?" Father Mark asked. "Are you in need of food or lodging?"

Devin's stomach took that inappropriate moment to growl loudly.

The priest threw his head back and laughed. "I see what the trouble is. I have some food in the back. Let me get it."

Devin restrained him, his hand light but insistent on his arm. "We don't need food, Father, but information. I hope you can help us."

Father Mark sobered. "I believe your stomach would differ with your words, young man, but tell me what you are looking for."

"Last night a journal was taken from the place where we camped. The contents are valuable. We believe the person who took it lives in Rodez and might have brought it to you. It is vitally important that we have it back," Devin said.

Father Mark nodded slowly. "If I were in possession of such a thing, would the person who took it be subject to charges of theft?"

"No," Devin replied. "We simply need it back."

"I've looked at the journal. The book seems to have value to the parish of Rodez also," Father Mark declared. "It fills blanks in the history of our church and the men who have served it."

"It does," Devin replied. "But it also provides background for some of the current political turmoil. There is not only unrest here, in the provinces, over taxes and education, but a man is vying for Chancellor Roché's position in Coreé, as well. I ask you to trust me in this. If you allow us to take the journal with us now, I will see that a copy of it is returned to you."

There was a sudden flurry of activity outside, the sound

of horses' hooves and men shouting. "Soldiers," Marcus hissed. "Is there somewhere we can hide?"

Devin rummaged in his jacket, coming up with the tiny key they had taken from the Bishop's Book, which supposedly granted them access to the underground tunnels. He held it flat on his palm and extended it to Father Mark.

Father Mark hesitated only a moment then motioned with his hand. "Come with me."

They ran the length of the nave and crouched behind the altar. Father Mark, who was a bear of man, hoisted a stone from the floor himself, handed them an unlighted candle and sent them down a ladder just as the doors to the sanctuary were thrown back against the walls of the church. The stone locked down smoothly in place, leaving Marcus and Devin in total darkness.

Devin felt carefully for each step until he reached the bottom rung. He held out a hand to guide Marcus down, then with arms extended, he felt his way toward the foundation wall of the back of the church. The wall ran straight until it reached the corner and there he and Marcus sat down in complete darkness and waited.

CHAPTER 12

Sanctuary

Devin and Marcus could hear nothing except for the sound of boots on the stone floor above them. Never in the history of Llisé had any group dared to question or harass the church or its priests and yet Devin feared they had left Father Mark in an untenable position. If someone had seen them enter the church then the priest would be expected to reveal their location. He hadn't known Devin and Marcus. He had no reason to trust them, apart from the key they had given him, which guaranteed any bearer asylum in any church in Llisé. But if their presence here jeopardized the safety of Father Mark's town and parishioners, he was well within his rights both ethically and morally to reveal their hiding place. And yet, he didn't.

They spent at least an hour in silence, afraid to speak or move and risk being heard in the sanctuary above. At one point, at least some of the soldiers left the church. Finally, Marcus dared light the candle, illuminating their small corner which was far away from the ladder and the stone hatch that granted entrance to their hiding place. Devin scanned their self-made prison. The room was no bigger than the safe room at Albion.

It was then that he saw the journal, lying on an old table against the wall. He jumped to his feet but Marcus tugged on his jacket, putting a finger to his lips. Devin pointed at the journal and Marcus motioned for him to sit down. Marcus removed his boots and padded across the stone floor as silently as a mouse and returned with the journal in his hands. He bowed when he handed it to Devin.

Devin smothered a grin. Marcus was apparently still angry about his insistence on finding the journal. And perhaps, Marcus was right. Devin turned the pages, frustrated by the lack of light and his own faulty vision. At least they had it back, although he felt some regret for just taking it without Father Mark's permission.

He feared they had exposed Father Mark to terrible danger. If the priest had been hauled away for questioning, the church was probably under guard, and there was no hope of Devin or Marcus escaping by the only door, even if they could raise the stone themselves to get out. The worst that could happen was that their hiding place would be discovered and the entire system for protecting the provincial people from the tyrannical rule of its government would be exposed. It seemed that, as usual, Devin had made a situation worse by insisting on his own way. Had they simply continued on to La Paix, they wouldn't be in this predicament.

Devin closed his eyes, recalling in detail the map they'd found in the Bishop's Book. It had designated all of the churches and the tunnels and caves that connected them. The church at Rodez had been included, which meant somewhere in this room there was a hidden passage which joined the underground warren that crisscrossed the northern part of Llisé like a maze. He took a small knife from his pocket, gestured to Marcus to gain his attention and drew a map on the earthen floor. There was salvation here if they could only find it.

Marcus went to examine the wall, running his hands across the stones until behind a shelf he discovered a wooden door, ingeniously covered with slabs of stone. Quietly, he put the wine bottles on the table and removed the shelf, laying it against the wall like an extra piece of lumber. He opened the door carefully, revealing a dark passageway, and beckoned to Devin.

They had only one candle and the lantern they had taken with them this morning but as Devin pulled his own boots off, Marcus returned with another lantern from inside the passage. There was no question that they should leave as quickly as possible and yet Devin felt an obligation to the priest who had endangered his own life by saving them. The soldiers must have been looking for Marcus but they hadn't found him. Hopefully, they would leave Rodez and its priest and people and go on their way.

Marcus must have sensed his hesitation and shook his head and silently pointed toward the passageway. With a pang of guilt, Devin slid the journal back in his jacket and preceded his bodyguard out of the safe room and into the dark corridor. Marcus closed the door and dropped a bar that sealed it from the inside.

"Leave your boots off," Marcus whispered, "until we've cleared the area around the church."

They followed the first tunnel for only about thirty feet before it ended in a steep set of steps carved into the rock. The winding staircase twisted its way downward, ending thirty feet below the level of the church's cellar. Directly in front of them a passageway continued several hundred feet until it ended in a T with a left and right branch. "Which way should we go?" Marcus asked.

Devin closed his eyes, visualizing the map, its endless twists and turns that led from one village to another, from one small church to the next one. The Catholic Church had used Llisé natural geology to construct a route across four provinces and never in several hundred years had that route been compromised. He hoped desperately that he wouldn't be the one to bring that mission to an end.

"Which way, Devin?" Marcus asked again.

"The right branch will lead us back toward La Paix," Devin replied without hesitation. The dark expanse before him reminded him vividly of the cave-in when they traveled through the tunnel from Comte Aucoin's chateau to La Paix. "Does this look stable?" he asked. "I don't want to die down here."

Marcus turned to look at him, apparently aware of what Devin was thinking. "Comte Aucoin's tunnel was dug by hand and shored up with wooden timbers, except for the short passage into the cellar of the church; most of this follows natural formations. These caves have existed for thousands of years." He grinned suddenly. "Besides, I'm not planning to die for a very long time and certainly not here. When I die, I plan to end up on the wrong end of a jealous husband's sword with at least ten lovers to mourn me."

Devin laughed. As far as he knew, Marcus had never even mentioned a lover, only his devotion to the Chancellor and his rigid responsibility to his job as his bodyguard.

Marcus grinned again. "You think I am joking, no?"

"Maybe," Devin replied.

"You think a man in my position has no time for lovers?"

Devin held up a hand. "What you do on your personal time is private, Marcus. I'd rather not know."

They walked quietly for a few minutes. "So how do you imagine your own death?" Marcus asked.

"I've never thought of it," Devin replied.

"That is the curse of youth," Marcus said. "I would have thought your multiple brushes with death on this trip would have changed your thinking." He raised the lantern as the tunnel sloped steeply downward. "Let me rephrase the question: How do you see yourself living out the rest of your days?"

Devin shrugged. "I have always wanted to be an archivist. It has only been on this trip that I have felt that perhaps, that would not be enough to satisfy me. I've enjoyed traveling. There is so much of Llisé that I have still never seen. I wish that all the residents of Coreé could experience each and every province. Perhaps we could bring painters to capture the beauty of the landscapes, create a museum that celebrated one province in each room, and archive the Chronicles and the music in Coreé."

Marcus ducked through a low portion of the ceiling. "That would require your father's blessing and Council's as well. It's no small undertaking, Devin."

"So is acquiring ten lovers," Devin quipped with a sly look at Marcus. "I don't know what my father would think of the idea, but if we survive this, I would like to finish collecting the Chronicles, at least. Already so much has been lost." He sobered suddenly, the burning of the Provincial Archives still fresh in his mind.

"And yet, right here, the people of Tirolien are attempting to retrieve the stories that they can remember," Marcus reminded him. "Don't you think that will happen all over Llisé?"

"I would like to think so but there still needs to be some central means of keeping and recording all of them."

Marcus grunted. "That plan has not gone so well, *mon ami.*"

"You're right," Devin agreed. "It has not."

They walked in silence for a few minutes until Marcus cleared his throat. "You still haven't answered my question. How do you see yourself living out your days? Is this museum you dream of enough to keep you warm and content at night?"

Devin smiled. "Is this confidential? I don't want to hear you repeating it all over the capital when we go home."

"Of course, Monsieur Roché," Marcus answered with a slight bow, returning playfully to the formal means of address that he had used when they started this trip four months ago and which he continued to resurrect when he was angry at Devin.

Devin didn't answer immediately. Was he doomed to only touch or kiss Jeanette in his dreams? Finding the map had given him hope that the people of Lac Dupré still existed somewhere in Llisé. But the empire was huge and the priest of Lac Dupré had disappeared along with his people. There was no one to ask, no logical place to search. Somewhere Jeanette might be longing for him just as he longed for her. Was it possible that they might never meet again even if they both survived the growing unrest that the dark powers of the empire were trying to smother?

They journeyed silently in the small circle of light from the lantern for a few minutes. "I didn't realize that was such a difficult question," Marcus commented, turning to walk backwards so that he could speak to Devin face to face.

"I wish ..." Devin said and then shook his head. "I think perhaps I can't put it into words just yet, Marcus. I'll tell you when I'm ready. There is still so much that is uncertain."

Marcus raised a shoulder in a halfhearted shrug. "As you wish," he said as he turned back around. He stopped so fast that Devin ran into him. "I believe we may have taken a wrong turn," he said, pointing.

Ahead the passage opened into a cave. The lantern seemed feeble faced with what looked like a wide expanse of water before them. The light didn't touch the walls but it glittered off a lake that lapped softly at the floor no more than twenty paces from their feet. Marcus picked up a handful of small rocks and threw them one at a time, each in a different direction. None of them struck rock, only water.

CHAPTER 13

Unexpected Delays

"Which way do you suggest we go now?" Marcus asked.

"Let me have the lantern for a moment," Devin said. He handed his own unlighted one to Marcus and walked to the edge of the water, peering as far as he could in one direction and then the other. He'd hoped that there might be some small shore that extended beyond the water's edge but on each side the lake lapped up against a sheer rock wall. "How deep could it be?" he asked.

"As deep as any inland lake," Marcus responded. "And I've heard stories of the creatures that inhabit underground waters. I don't believe we want to swim across it."

"Then we'll have to go back," Devin said. "If we take the left-hand fork it will lead us quite a distance out of our way before we can turn back again."

"I supposed as much," Marcus replied. "I'd rather be delayed in arriving than eaten by some underwater monster."

Devin laughed. "There are no monsters. Underground fish are pale and blind. Maybe they look like monsters to some people."

Marcus took possession of the lantern again as they reversed their course. "And how do you know this?"

"We learned that in first-term zoology at the *université*," Devin replied.

"Would you want to swim in that lake?" Marcus asked.

"No," Devin answered. "But not because I am afraid of monsters! Keep in mind that map was old. Rocks may have shifted, passages may be blocked. It would be a great waste of time if we swam the lake only to find no passageway on the other side. We'll simply have to improvise."

"I'd rather improvise above ground," Marcus replied. "Where I can see what I am getting into."

"This may not be the most expedient way to travel," Devin said. "Should the left branch of the tunnel be blocked, we will have to try to escape at Rodez and take our chances. If the tunnel is still in use as a route for refugees, surely most of it is open to travel." But was it still in use? There had been no sign of recent travelers, except for the lantern filled with oil hanging inside the door from the safe room. Did the church maintain the routes or simply guard their entrances and exits? Had they been given the time to ask Father Mark, would he have warned them against using the tunnels because of the danger of rockfalls and dead ends?

They traveled silently as they reached the left fork, not knowing whether the soldiers above in Rodez might have found their hiding place. This path began smoothly enough, its sides obviously sculpted by human tools, but it rapidly deteriorated into a rough uneven passageway, littered with rocks and debris. Twice they scrambled over boulders that blocked the way.

Afterward the route led steadily upward. They stopped after several hours, their breath rasping in their chests and their calves aching from the climb. A wide cavern nearly as large as the one that held the lake, spread out before them. Devin took the lantern and set off to explore its width but Marcus called him back.

"We've gone far enough," Marcus said. "We'll stop here for the night, if it is actually night in this God-forsaken place." He dropped his pack and slid down against the cave's rough wall, resting his head on his drawn-up knees.

"How much lamp oil is left?" Devin asked.

"Several hours," Marcus said. "The other lantern is nearly full."

"What happens when it burns out?" Devin asked.

"I would hope we might have reached another church or at least the entrance to a safe room where we can find another lantern. I wish I'd thought to fill our waterskins at the lake."

Devin grimaced. "I'm glad you didn't. That water was an odd orange color and it smelled like sulfur."

"You'd be surprised what I've been forced to drink," Marcus said. "Anything that wets your throat is welcome when you're so thirsty that drinking ..." He stopped abruptly. "Can you hear that?"

Devin stood in silence, straining his ears until he heard a faint but steady sound. "Water?" he asked.

Marcus heaved himself up. "Let's find out what's up ahead before we sleep. It's possible that's fresh water and that would be a blessing."

The sound of water grew louder as they continued up along the side of the cavern. A small waterfall cascaded down the cave wall and disappeared below the cavern floor through a ragged hole. The waterfall, rolling down over the rocks, sounded almost musical in this world of stony silence.

Devin leaned forward over the chasm to put his hand in the water but Marcus held him back.

"Make certain this floor is secure," Marcus warned. "If you fall through that, there will be no saving you." He stepped forward cautiously, placing one foot before the other. Finally, he stuck his finger in the flow and licked it. "Fresh as a mountain stream!" he exclaimed with satisfaction. "Let's fill both of these waterskins. I'll do one if you do the other."

"I'll do them both," Devin offered. "Get some sleep and I'll wake you in a couple of hours."

"Just don't drop them," Marcus cautioned. "We can go a long time without food but without water we are dead men."

Devin bowed playfully. "Thank you for your words of encouragement, fearless leader."

Marcus rolled his eyes and trudged off to find a spot along the cavern wall to sit down. He leaned back, crossed his arms over his chest, and was snoring in minutes.

Devin was famished. Neither of them had mentioned food for a long time. When something interesting or unusual about their route distracted him, he could forget about his stomach for a while but then his hunger returned, empty and gnawing. He was almost ready to start fishing for those poor blind fish if they came across another pool of water. But what would they find down here to use for bait?

Devin took a long drink of water from the first waterskin after refilling it. The water was so cold it made his head ache. Supposedly in the northernmost parts of Llisé, snow covered the mountaintops year round. He could believe that this water originated in the meltwaters below some distant peak where humans had never even traveled. Even the professional cartographers at the *Académie* were vague about the northernmost reaches of Llisé as well as what lay beyond the oceans that surrounded it.

He considered their own map with apprehension. Unfortunately, he and Marcus hadn't been able to turn back toward La Paix yet. The route was leading them constantly upward and almost directly north. The next church on the map was at Yvoire, probably twenty miles north of the main road. He debated whether to share that information with Marcus. Their hasty escape from Rodez would lead to a long delay in reaching La Paix. He wasn't even certain they could leave the tunnels at Yvoire. There was no way of telling whether that church was still in existence or if the entrance from the tunnels had been sealed shut.

It was possible even now that Madame Aucoin, her grand-daughter Angelique, and Jules, their bodyguard, might already have left La Paix for Amiens. He could only hope that Armand, Chastel, and Gaspard would wait for his and Marcus' return to depart. The plan they were in the process of carefully sculpting to defeat and kill René Forneaux would be of no use without all of its players and he and Marcus were delayed without explanation. If news of Devin's supposed death reached La Paix, the men might abandon their plan altogether.

Madame Aucoin had given Devin a button with a falcon on it, as a token to gain entrance to her house in Amiens. He was to give it to her Head of Staff, who would, in turn, summon Jules down from the mountains to escort them through the tunnel system back to La Paix. The exact route from Amiens to La Paix had never been disclosed to Devin. The mountain retreat's location was a closely guarded secret and apparently Madame Aucoin intended to keep it as one. Unfortunately, when Armand had injured his knee on their way back from Calais, Devin had passed that button on along with another key to gain access to the underground passages through one of the churches, should they need it. Devin had two keys but only one button, which presented a problem. Without it, he had no way of proving that he was in need of Madame Aucoin's assistance to her very vigilant Head of Staff.

His daydreaming caused the second waterskin to overfill, splashing his boots and soaking the dusty earthen floor. He was wasting lantern oil and they had no idea how much further they needed to travel within this labyrinth. He sealed the waterskin and went back to keep watch while Marcus slept.

CHAPTER 14

Discoveries

Devin sat with the lantern beside him for a few precious minutes and took the journal in his hands. He could only make out a word here and there but even that showed his vision was gradually improving. He perused the pages, looking for sections that might stand out as being important. The Forneaux name appeared several times in the beginning of the book, the end held what he assumed was a list of the drowned residents of Albion. He wanted to know those names, so he could try to match them to the faces he had glimpsed, if that was possible. How could he forget the baby playing, blissfully unaware of impending death, or the elderly man who sat by the bakery playing an ancient harp? It was as though the people of Albion had become part of his soul and he would carry them with him forever just as he would carry Dariel Moreau and his apprentice, Absolon.

The harp made him wonder if perhaps the elderly man had been a visiting Master Bard. Harps were expensive instruments – even old battered ones. Perhaps Armand would know if Tirolien's Master Bard had died in the flood at

Albion several hundred years ago. The Master Bards formed a brotherhood and each protected and encouraged the others. Surely, their deaths were remembered as well as their lives.

Devin reluctantly snuffed the lantern to conserve oil and sat quietly in the darkness. The ghosts of Albion seemed to draw strength from the obscurity and he saw them more clearly in the total absence of light. Over and over he watched the idyllic scene turn into chaos and death until he was weary and drained.

Devin startled as Marcus woke with grunt. He held out a hand in Marcus' general direction. "May I have the flint?" he asked, anxious for light again, even a light as feeble as the single flame of one lantern.

Marcus blinked as the lantern sprung to life and ran his tongue over his lips, scanning his surroundings. "God," he said. "I hoped I'd dreamed this."

Devin put the book down and got up to hand him a waterskin. "You don't like caves?"

Marcus took a long drink and rested the waterskin on his thigh. "I abhor caves. I always have. Don't even try to talk me out of it."

Devin laughed. "I won't. I'm sorry. They are not my favorite either but if they can help us reach Amiens safely, I might change my opinion." Oddly enough, he didn't share Marcus' dislike of these caves. The open passageways and wide caverns had a completely different feel than the tunnel from Comte Aucoin's chateau to La Paix. The only thing that worried him here was the complete and total darkness that would descend if the lanterns burned out. He thought about the dwindling amount of oil that remained and then tried to put it out of his mind.

Marcus stood up and stretched and flexed his shoulders.

"I spent a short time looking at the journal," Devin said. "Would you read me some of the names that are listed in the back?"

"Not now," Marcus replied. "I'm not wasting oil on reading when it could mean not getting out of these God-forsaken caves!"

"But you'll read them to me later, won't you?" Devin asked.

"We'll see," Marcus barked. "Get some sleep. We need to travel quickly if we're to reach La Paix before everyone leaves for Coreé. I pray they haven't given us up for dead."

"Do you think the news that you shot me could have reached them already?" Devin asked.

Marcus shrugged. "Madame Aucoin has her own complex web of informants. If she doesn't know now she will soon. That's why we need to reach La Paix or Amiens as quickly as possible. Now will you stop talking and get some rest!"

Devin gave Marcus the extra lantern and lay down against the cavern wall, his head propped on his pack. Sleep seemed impossible. A dozen gloomy thoughts swirled in his head. Gaspard would lose heart for this entire enterprise if he thought Devin was dead. He couldn't see him continuing without Devin's support. And Angelique was such an unreliable accomplice. The murder of her family and her life alone in her father's chateau for twelve years had left her mentally unbalanced and emotionally crippled. Devin doubted her ability to play the part she had demanded in their plan. The slightest alteration might set her off and then everything would fall apart and they'd all rot in prison for treason, or worse yet, hang.

Their plan seemed held together by fragile hopes and insubstantial expectations. They had all agreed that only by eliminating René Forneaux would the Shadow Government lose momentum. Everyone said that the only way to kill a snake was to cut off its head. So that was what they intended to do. Madame Aucoin expected that she and Angelique would be invited to some of the holiday galas where Forneaux would be in attendance. Angelique claimed that only she might be able to get close enough to stab him. Reluctantly the others had agreed but Devin continued to be uneasy about both the plan itself and Angelique's participation in it.

Devin sat up and collected his pack and the extra lantern. "I can't sleep, Marcus. Can we just continue?"

Marcus inclined his head. "Whatever you like, but don't whine later if you're tired."

"I won't," Devin replied. "The passageway we need to follow if we go to Yvoire continues on the other side of the falls. I walked down to look while you were asleep."

They started off again with cold water for breakfast. Devin's stomach was so empty that he swore it sloshed as he walked. Marcus spared no time for talking and set a faster pace than he had yesterday. Here the passageway remained clear of obstructions and they wasted no time negotiating fallen debris. After only an hour, the lantern began to run out; the flame sputtered and flickered fitfully. Devin passed Marcus the second lantern, fully aware that when they lit it, they had one chamber of oil between them and unremitting darkness.

Several hours later, they passed into another chamber, smaller than the last but with its own water source as well. A small pool bubbled merrily, fed by some underwater source. In the center of the cavern, stones had been gathered into a large fire ring, the ancient ashes still visible in the center. Animal bones were gathered in a pile, bleached and white as though they had been left in the desert sun. "People must have lived here hundreds of years ago," Devin said with reverence.

"Don't even suggest that we take time to explore the remains, Devin," Marcus warned him. "I won't waste time on the dead while I still have a chance of keeping us alive."

"I wasn't suggesting that, Marcus. But that pile of bones means, if they actually lived here then they must have had access to go outside to hunt. There has to be an exit here somewhere."

"We'd need to find it quickly or continue," Marcus said. "I won't waste time or lamp oil searching for an exit."

"That's hardly the point," Devin answered, picking up the empty lantern. "We don't need to search at all. It's your decision which direction we take. Do you want to follow this passage clear to Yvoire or do you want to leave now if we can and take our chances out in the open?"

Marcus hesitated. "How far are we from Yvoire?"

Devin shook his head. "The map was inexact as to distance. It's very difficult to judge. Most of the time, the tunnels shorten the distance between towns but not always. I do know that Yvoire is about twenty miles north of the main road we need to reach before we can travel toward Amiens."

"Twenty miles!" Marcus bellowed. "That's more than another day's travel! I say we leave the tunnels here if we can find a way out. Take the candle and search the right side of the cavern for a passage. I'll take the left. We can't waste a lot of time on this. It would be a godsend if we could find a way out but if we can't, then we'll just have to keep going."

Marcus lit the candle and passed it to Devin. He whisked off toward the left side, leaving Devin with only the feeble candlelight. The chamber held a number of air currents and the flame flickered wildly. The air movement itself seemed to promise access to the outside, which was encouraging. Devin protected the fragile flame with his hand and scanned the walls as he walked.

He had only covered half the distance when he came across something that stopped him dead. The walls were covered with primitive paintings, the muted colors drawn from earth and stone. Devin fell to his knees, running his hands over the ancient images that had lain undiscovered for centuries, protected from the wind, rain, and snow outside. He cursed the feeble light of the candle as it failed to cover the full scope of the paintings' historical significance.

"Marcus!" he yelled. His voice echoed through the rocky expanse as the sound of running footsteps and the light from the bobbing lantern ran toward him.

"What's the matter?" Marcus demanded, gasping for breath.

"There are paintings on this wall," Devin said, pointing. "They continue almost to the end of the chamber."

Marcus growled. "You called me over here just to see pictures on the walls!" he said angrily.

Devin grabbed his arm. "They're not just pictures, Marcus, look! They depict our ancient history! There were people already living here before any settlers came to Llisé. There were native people who hunted in these forests and fished in these streams. They apparently retreated to the caves in fear of the newcomers."

Marcus' jaw tensed. "I don't really care, Devin. I'm trying to save your life. I don't have time for a history lesson."

"You will care, if you hear me out," Devin insisted. "It was the native people who were the ones who lived here in these caves and painted these pictures."

"And finally they got braver and came out and intermarried with the settlers?" Marcus snapped. "What difference does it make?"

"Lend me your lantern," Devin begged, reaching out for it and shoving his own candle into Marcus' hand. He went back to the beginning and pointed out the important parts to Marcus as they moved slowly along the wall, Devin still on his knees, Marcus bending over him. "The native people did eventually intermarry with the settlers but that's not what's significant," Devin continued. "In the beginning, there were apparently two different families or clans. The first picture shows them living peacefully together outside. The second shows them watching some newcomers land in boats. In the third, they retreat to the caves. In the fourth and last painting, in order to be able to hunt safely, the first clan learns to shape shift into wolves and the other clan learns to change into falcons!" Devin stopped, allowing the information to sink in. He was pleased when Marcus' grim expression changed.

"My God," Marcus said. "The clans must have been the Chastels and the Aucoins!"

Devin nodded, his heart pounding in his chest. "I have absolutely no doubt of that! Do you remember that Angelique told us that her father said the Chastels had their very roots in the earth of Llisé? Perhaps the Aucoins did, too. We just haven't seen any proof of it yet."

"So those two families are Llisé's only native people," Marcus repeated.

"But those two clans must have intermarried before the

settlers came," Devin pointed out. "Perhaps the ability to shape shift into both wolves and falcons extends to some people in the line of descent. Do you realize what this means? It's possible that Chastel may be able to change into a wolf and a falcon!"

"Don't you think he would have mentioned it?" Marcus asked. "He trusts you with his wolf persona. Why wouldn't he tell you this, too?"

Devin shrugged, his nerves jangling with this new information. "And why wouldn't the Aucoin children have fled from their attackers if they could fly? There is a great deal we don't know."

Marcus remained silent for a moment. "So we took away the hunting grounds of Llisé's native people and divided up their lands, changing Llisé into an empire with a whole new set of rules and squeezed them out."

"Maybe at first," Devin said. "But oddly enough, both families managed to rise to influence and prestige in this new world that we built.

"Marcus, I came here intent on memorizing the Chronicles and I have found instead that there is so much about this empire of which we are ignorant," he continued. "The 'provincial history' that is maintained in the Archives concerns battles, uprisings, and stories of the plague. I believe that a great deal of those stories attempt to explain the deaths of thousands of provincials at the hands of the Shadow Government. The rest of the Archives revolves around Vienne and its capital, Coreé. We have yet to read the full story behind the Forneaux family in Father Sébastian's journal and today we been confronted with this new revelation that raises questions about who and what we are."

"Apparently, we are thieves first of all," Marcus commented grimly.

"It may not have been as blatant as that," Devin replied. "Those first settlers were explorers. They must have come from islands off the west coast of Llisé. That is what Lisette's Lament implies. Do you remember when I tried to pin Armand down about that when we were discussing that ballad? It was almost as though he knew more than he intended to share."

"Don't ever forget that Armand is a Chastel, even though he claims his mother's last name. The same blood runs in his veins and he is tied to this ancient clan, just as surely as his brother is," Marcus said.

"It's almost too much," Devin commented. "I realize that I was naïve to think I could learn all of Llisé's Chronicles, in the fifteen months of my third year at the *Académie*. Now there is this to sort out, too! I wonder if there are any records of the first settlers who came here? And surely there is something more than one ballad that concerns the erection of that path of monoliths that troop across Llisé like a battalion of stone giants."

"I believe both your father and your brothers warned you that you had bitten off more than you could chew," Marcus pointed out. "Now, we have men trying to kill us, only enough lamp oil for less than another day, and René Forneaux trying to overthrow the government. That is personally almost more than I can deal with in a day."

Devin laughed. "Almost?"

Marcus nodded. "Almost, but not quite. Are you finished here?"

"There are some empty pages at the end of the journal," Devin said, realizing he was pushing Marcus' momentary good humor. "Could I please copy these pictures? I want to show them to Chastel and Madame Aucoin. I'll do it quickly. They just need to be recorded."

Marcus lost his smile. "I have nothing to write with, Devin, and we really haven't the time to spend on this."

"I can use a piece of charred wood from the fire," Devin suggested. "It's important, Marcus. I'll recopy them later on archival paper."

Marcus sighed and nodded, returning the candle to him. "Go ahead but be quick about it."

"I will," Devin replied, sticking his candle in a crevice in the wall. He sprinted across the cavern as Marcus held the lantern up to shed more light. There was more than one piece of charred wood that would do and several rocks that left tinted lines when he scratched them across a page from the journal. The sketches would be crude but then so were the original paintings. He ran back with his drawing supplies and laid them below the paintings on the cavern floor.

"I'll keep looking for a way out," Marcus said. "There is nothing on that side at all; perhaps this one will be better." He turned a moment, watching Devin begin to sketch the paintings. "If you're not finished when I come back, you'll have to stop. This still isn't worth losing our lives over."

Devin nodded. "I understand."

Devin's skill at transcribing manuscripts should have improved his precision at copying the pictures. The size of the cave paintings made them easier for him to see but his eyes betrayed him as he tried to work quickly. He was continually frustrated as he copied them into Father Sébastian's little journal which seemed to grow more valuable by the minute. He finally finished, unsatisfied with the smudgy representations he had added on the small pages.

Dusting his hands off on his trousers, he secured the journal back in the lining of his jacket, retrieved his half-burned candle and went to look for Marcus. It had been a long time since his bodyguard had left and he didn't see the lantern light anywhere in the cavern.

CHAPTER 15

Free Again

"Marcus?" Devin yelled.

There was no response and he called again, his voice echoing down the passage in front of him, as though mocking him with its repetition. He continued forward. Obviously Marcus wasn't in the cavern behind him, but it seemed odd that he would have gone on so far ahead.

"Marcus?" he called a third time, as his candle flame bent nearly horizontal in a sudden gust of air. The passageway seemed lighter here and he looked up to see a ragged square of blue sky high above him. So, that was how the falcons left the cave! They flew up and out of the cavern to hunt and then returned with their kill. But an entrance sixty feet in the air wouldn't have aided a wolf or a man intent on reaching the forest and meadows where he longed to hunt. There had to be another way out.

Hot wax dripped on his hand and he realized just how little of the candle he had left. If Marcus was gone or missing, he had only a few minutes to find him or an exit before he would be left alone in here with no light at all. He walked as quickly as he could without extinguishing the candle flame but the rough stone gave no hint of another passageway other than the one he was traveling in.

Could Marcus have left him? Was that part of the plan – to abandon him here where he had no escape? Marcus had never suggested leaving the lantern for Devin while he sketched and that he himself would take the candle. Marcus knew the candle was good for only about another hour before Devin would have no light, and yet he left him with it rather than divide the lamp oil between the two lanterns.

Devin's heart beat faster. He realized that not only did Marcus have the lanterns, but he had taken both waterskins, as well. Nausea that had nothing to do with his constant hunger knotted his stomach. He was alone, with no water, no food, and very soon no light. The chances of him reaching Yvoire were slim and his chances of reaching La Paix slimmer. Without Marcus, Devin was doomed and he was the first one to admit it. With his heart pounding and hands sweating, he hurried as fast as he could without having the candle blow out prematurely.

But maybe he was wrong in suspecting Marcus. Maybe something had happened to him. Reason began to soothe his anxiety, if not his heart rate. If Marcus truly intended to kill him, he'd already had that chance and hadn't taken it. Instead, he tried his best to fake Devin's death to fool Emile and his men. Devin was only alive because of Marcus and if his bodyguard wasn't answering now, it was because something was wrong.

These caves had deep holes that plunged hundreds of feet down. If Marcus had fallen into one, Devin would have no way of knowing where and no means of rescuing him. Without light, Devin would have no way to identify any other holes himself before it was too late. And yet, he'd passed no rock falls, no chasms, or fallen debris. He obviously hadn't found Marcus lying on the floor unconscious from a fall or head injury. But if he wasn't here along the passageway, where was he?

"Marcus!" he shouted again with a note of desperation in his voice. The caves were so silent, recalling an unwelcome memory of the valley where Albion had been destroyed. At least that valley had sunrises and sunsets, rain that fell from the skies, and stars at night. This silence was the silence of the grave. What would it be like to die of thirst or starve to death, he wondered, thinking uncomfortably of poor Father Sébastian who had voluntarily sentenced himself to exactly that fate?

Devin slowed to negotiate a huge curvature of rock that blocked most of the passageway and stopped in amazement. The rock face was studded with quartz that glittered in the light from the dancing golden rays of the sunset.

Vining plants tumbled down, curtaining the wall of the cave on the outside but allowing the intense rays of the sun to flicker between the leaves. Devin parted the vines carefully with his hand. Marcus stood with his hands clasped behind his back. His eyes were on the glorious purple-and-gold sunset, spreading in opulent glory over the mountains to the west. Devin extinguished his candle and joined him, trying to still both his heart and the shaking of his hands.

He took a deep breath. The air smelled of evergreen needles, damp earth, and late-summer grasses. Yellow and purple wildflowers dotted the slope where the tree line had left a few clearings. In the distance, the mountain peaks were covered in a dozen shades of green with an occasional splash of autumn color. A flock of ravens flew over, sharing their conversation with the entire mountainside. There wasn't a house or building as far as he could see. Devin had never felt so happy to be outside before!

"It's glorious, isn't it?" Marcus said smugly, as though he himself had painted those spectacular colors in the sky. "God, I'm glad to be out of those caves." He took a deep breath and spared a glance at Devin. "For Christ's sake, what's the matter? You look like you've seen a ghost." His gaze fell on the candle stub in Devin's left hand.

"God, did your candle burn out?" he asked in concern.

"No," Devin said. "It came very close to it though. I didn't know where you were."

"I told you I was looking for a way out," Marcus replied. "I thought it would take you a while to sketch those pictures so I was just enjoying the fresh air and the sunset. Are you upset?"

Devin shook his head. "I'm not upset," he said, although he couldn't stop his hands from shaking.

Marcus snorted. "Did you think I'd just leave you in there with no light and no water?"

"Let it go," Devin replied, masking his irritation. "The mystery of your disappearance is solved and I'm relieved. May I have a drink?"

Marcus swung the waterskin over to him. "Devin, if I haven't proven my loyalty by now ..."

"You have," Devin replied firmly. "But I thought you might have fallen down a hole or been buried in a rock fall. I called you half a dozen times."

"I probably couldn't hear you out here," Marcus replied, his eyes returning to the sky. "Once I walked outside, I couldn't persuade myself to leave all this and go back inside."

"I can understand that," Devin said, coughing. "I feel as

though I have a handful of dust in each lung. I wonder if that feeling will ever go away."

"It will," Marcus assured him. "But that dust is murder on your lungs. Miners who work underground die young."

"Isn't there anything that can be done about that?" Devin asked. "Would masks help them?"

"Maybe," Marcus replied. "They tie scarves over their faces but it's a brutal place to spend your days. You and I were just sightseeing in comparison. Leave it, Devin, you can't change the world."

"But my father asked me to be his eyes and ears in the provinces. Surely, this qualifies?" he retorted. Devin sat down and then stretched out full length on the damp grass, his eyes drawn upward by the swift movement of wings.

A lone falcon glided on the wind above them in lazy circles that brought it lower and lower to the ground. Suddenly, something bright and shiny dropped from between its talons and bounced onto the ground at Devin's feet.

Devin stood up and searched for the object in the long grass, his fingers grazing the back of a brass button. He held it up for Marcus to see the falcon emblazoned on the front. "Someone is looking after us," he said, excitement bubbling in his chest. "Do you think that was one of the Aucoins?"

"God only knows," Marcus murmured. "If it was, I hope those waiting for us will be informed that we are both still alive and making our way east."

Devin rolled the button on his palm in amazement, watching the falcon shrink to a tiny speck in the blue sky and then disappear entirely into the distance. "I wonder what day of the week it is," he said after a moment. "And how long we have been gone."

"I have no idea," Marcus answered. "We may have been in those caves for days. To be honest, it felt like weeks to me. I hope we won't have to repeat that again soon."

"Do you have any idea where we are?"

"That's Mount Graig," Marcus said, pointing toward the highest peak in the eastern sky. "I'd say we are halfway back toward Amiens but way too far north. I think you had already determined that."

"Do you want to travel anymore tonight?"

"No, we'll stop. You haven't had any sleep. Tomorrow we'll try to travel as fast as we can. I hope the patrols have moved on. I'm not certain how intent they are on finding me."

"Or me," Devin added.

"I doubt that they are hunting for you. I think they are convinced you are dead," Marcus said.

"But there was no body," Devin reminded him. He felt a pleasant lassitude as the light slowly began to leave the sky.

Marcus looked down at him. "Your body could have been eaten by wolves or buried by fishermen who stumbled upon it on the hill above the sea. Emile's two conspirators returned to Coreé reporting your death at my hands. That is the only truth anyone knows at this juncture and it works to our advantage. I watched those men board the ship myself before Emile and the rest of us went for a celebratory drink." He held out a placating hand to Devin. "I was not celebrating, just so you know, and now I am a wanted man. You are anonymous and if possible I would like to keep it that way. If we could just create a new persona for you – that would be ideal."

"I've already suggested a blind man," Devin said. "I

would play a bard but that would probably get me killed."

"I could cut off one of your legs and make you a cripple," Marcus suggested with a glint in his eye. "But then you'd slow me down."

Devin rolled his eyes, "Anything short of death or dismemberment is all right with me. Use your own judgement."

"Ah," Marcus said laughing. "You say that now but several minutes ago, you were wondering whether I might have left you to fend for yourself in those caves."

A sudden movement to the left sent Marcus whirling. Devin leaped to his feet, reaching for his pistol, but it was only two deer, startled out of the brush by their laughter.

Still laughing, Devin bent over, one hand on his stomach. "Oh, what I'd give for some venison right now. I don't think I've ever been this hungry before."

"Hunger is good for you," Marcus said. "It helps you identify with at least half of Llisé's people who go to bed hungry every night."

"I'm trying to change that," Devin said, the laughter leaving his heart.

Marcus' face sobered. "Devin, you have no power. Your only advantage is the influence you may hold over your father."

"I have the power of the written word," Devin protested. "I can write and speak about the plight of the provincial people. If I posted the stories in the newspaper I could reach hundreds of ..."

"Hundreds of affluent people who really don't care if people are starving in the provinces," Marcus finished for him. "People in Coreé only worry that their wines, cheeses, and fine fabrics are delivered on time. Don't delude yourself into believing that without René Forneaux, life in the provinces will be better. The problems run much deeper than that." He handed Devin his pack and the other waterskins. "Take these back into the cave entrance. As much as I prefer not to, we'll sleep in there tonight. I think it's safer. I'll see if I can find some game. There should be some rabbits about this time in the evening."

Devin stood gaping at him, the pack and waterskins hanging from his hands. "Do you really believe after all we have discovered, I've accomplished nothing by this trip?"

"I believe that your idealism blinds you to so much of what's going on in the real world, Devin. Your trip has brought us to the brink of war, your father's power is in jeopardy, and most days I doubt I will be able to get you home alive. Let's leave it at that for tonight." Marcus turned his back and walked into the darkening twilight.

Devin lit the lantern and carried their gear back into the chamber where he'd found the cave paintings. He threw the packs on the floor, gratified when Marcus' extra shirt spilled out onto the floor. Marcus' words had stung. He and Gaspard hadn't started out on this journey to change the empire! They had come to gather as many of the stories and songs from the Provincial Chronicles as they could.

It was unfair of Marcus to blame him for the unrest that had unfortunately coincided with his trip. If he could reach Coreé in time, the journal that he carried, in addition to Angelique's testimony, would not only bolster support for his father's Chancellorship, but it would expose René Forneaux's Shadow Government, and bring attention to the plight of the provincial people, too! All of those were things that no one would have been in a position to do had he not decided to visit the provinces!

Waiting patiently for Marcus' reappearance was unappealing, so he refilled the waterskins. The water in the last cave had been pure and clean; if this pool provided fresh water as well, they would be supplied to start in the morning. He tasted the water first, as he had seen Marcus do, noticing that it seemed less frigid but no less sweet. He drank again from the waterskin and refilled it, leaving it on the floor with the packs.

Devin took his time walking back toward the exit. At one point along the passageway, it appeared as though a symbol had been carved into the stone and he knelt with the lantern to see what it was. The symbol was a stylized image of a wolf. Its head pointed toward the passageway that eventually led to Yvoire; its tail pointed back toward the cavern he had come from. Marcus hadn't returned so he continued down the passageway into another chamber, smaller than the one before, with a lower ceiling.

Devin could smell and feel the damp chill of the night air from the exit seeping down the passage behind him but a musky odor permeated this chamber. Aware of a presence inside, he halted at the entrance but he heard nothing move in the darkness around him. He took a tentative step forward, holding the lantern above his head but the light didn't touch the back of the cave wall. He swung the lantern to the left and then to the right. A dozen glowing eyes blinked at him from the shadows and a low growl reverberated from the stone walls.

CHAPTER 16

The Way of the Wolf

Devin's retreat of several steps brought another low growl of warning that he recognized as a wolf. The guttural sound rumbled through the chamber as several other wolves took up the call, threatening any interloper who dared breach the security of their den.

He had a pistol in his pocket but it only held two shots, not nearly enough to wipe out a wolf pack, even a small one. He stood still, remembering Chastel's wolves and their complete devotion to the man they called master and doubted he'd have the heart to kill them, anyway. Finding them here as he had, what guarantee was there that these wolves weren't associated somehow with Chastel's pack?

Had he and Marcus decided to continue to Yvoire, they would have encountered these same wolves tonight. Marcus would have tried to fight his way out and not only would they have slaughtered a number of wolves but they probably would have died themselves. It was up to him to find a different solution, one that left both him and the wolves alive.

He bent forward and placed the lantern on the floor, lowering himself to sit beside it. The lantern shone on his face, showed that his hands were empty, and that he was lowering his body in deference and rendering himself harmless before them. Growls continued but none of the wolves moved any closer. The glowing eyes remained sequestered in the back of the cave. Devin didn't speak, he sat silently, not moving, willing his body to emanate calm. It seemed like hours until the growling finally stopped and then, he heard heavy footsteps in the corridor behind him.

"Devin?"

"Don't come any closer," Devin said softly.

He could feel Marcus' presence hovering in the passageway. A second human had tipped the scale against the wolves. A single snarl broke the silence.

"Go back outside," Devin whispered. He heard footsteps retreat and exhaled slowly.

Devin continued to sit still, trying not to breathe too fast, or sweat, or squirm, or anything else that might indicate his fear to the wolves in the cave. Still they remained, quietly gathered in the back, their eyes blinking occasionally. Devin considered extinguishing the lantern but that would only make it harder for him to see; the wolves could see him with no trouble at all.

He waited at least an hour and then quietly stood up. Some of the glowing eyes shifted higher as though several of the wolves had stood up, too. Devin waited, standing quietly until he heard no further signs of agitation. Picking up the lantern, he backed out of the cave and into the passageway. He resisted the urge to run or to turn around constantly to look behind him. He walked slowly and purposefully back to the exit to the outside.

Marcus waited with his pistol in one hand and a knife in the other. "God, Devin what did you get yourself into?"

"A pack of wolves," Devin replied softly, "literally. There is a smaller chamber there that we would have had to travel through if we continued to Yvoire. There are probably at least half a dozen wolves in it, maybe more. Could they have been mothers with young pups?"

"Pups are born in May and June," Marcus answered. "It's late for that. Young wolves are hunting with the pack by now."

"I think we need to drop back to the cave with the pool if you're intent on sleeping inside. I don't think the wolves will follow us but I have no way of knowing that for sure."

"I can't say I'll rest comfortably knowing we have wolves for neighbors," Marcus said, grabbing the packs from the floor where Devin had left them. "There's no way of securing our safety in here."

"Or outside either," Devin said. "Don't those pistols only carry two bullets? There was no way I was going to start shooting."

Marcus nodded. "What did you do?"

"I simply sat down. I thought if they saw me being submissive they would leave me alone."

"You took a very big chance," Marcus said, as they retraced their steps to the larger chamber. "What if they hunt us down and follow us in here?"

"They obviously were aware of our presence earlier and they left us alone. I doubt tonight will be any different. I hope I showed them that we are not a threat."

"You may not be a threat but I am," Marcus argued, gesturing with his pistol. "We haven't gotten this far just to be picked off by a pack of wolves."

"And we won't be," Devin assured him. "I'll take first watch if you like."

"No more of that," Marcus objected. "You're no good to me bleary eyed from looking through that journal."

"If I'm bleary eyed, it's not from reading," Devin responded and then wished he hadn't. Marcus' face turned grim and he didn't continue the conversation.

There was rabbit for supper and Marcus even used the ancient fire pit to cook it. Smoke rose and hovered in ghostly shapes near the ceiling, curling into fantastic curls and tendrils before it disappeared, whisked away by some high air current into the world outside. Devin could barely wait until the meat was cooked. The juices dripping on the hot coals seemed like the sweetest scent he'd ever smelled.

Finally, Marcus handed him a stick with skewered bits of roasted rabbit. "Eat it slowly," he cautioned. "We've eaten next to nothing for days. Don't waste this by making yourself sick."

Devin paced himself, savoring each morsel of rabbit in his mouth and chewing slowly before Marcus handed him another stick full of meat. "Did you get enough, Marcus?" he asked before biting into it.

"I did," Marcus answered. "I caught four rabbits. There is more than enough. I'll smoke the extra meat and keep it for tomorrow. Meals have been scarce on this trip."

A shadow crossed Devin's vision and he had the sudden feeling they were being watched. In the doorway, a big gray wolf stood, its eyes glowing in the dark. "Where are the bones?" he asked Marcus.

"What do you want with the bones?" Marcus asked. He followed Devin's gaze and swore.

"Just give them to me," Devin said. "I don't think we

are about to be attacked. I think the smell of meat attracted him."

Marcus handed him the bones wrapped in some leaves he had gathered outside. "My pistol will be aimed at his head if he even takes a step toward you," he said quietly.

"Understood," Devin said. He took the bones and crossed the chamber slowly. The wolf didn't budge from the doorway but stood expectantly as Devin approached. He stopped about twenty feet away and laid the bones on the cave floor and then backed away.

The wolf hesitated a moment and then walked forward tentatively. He bent his head down but kept his eyes on Devin. Taking two of the bones in his mouth, he exited the chamber. In a few minutes, he was back for more. This time, he ignored Devin and snatched up a mouthful of bones. He returned twice more and carried off the rest.

Devin went back to sit down with Marcus. "I'd say you've made a friend," Marcus admitted. "Though I wouldn't have believed it if I hadn't seen it. How did you know he didn't intend to just take the rabbits from us?"

Devin shrugged. "A feeling, I guess. They let me leave their cave without incident. I felt as though I should return the favor."

Marcus shook his head. "Some days I think you're as crazy as Angelique."

CHAPTER 17

Loss and Remembrance

"I think you'd make a good pirate," Marcus commented over a mouthful of cold rabbit.

"A what?" Devin asked, adjusting his pack. They'd risen early and walked outside to a misty dawn. The evergreens rose above the white wispy tendrils of fog like isolated islands on a huge lake.

"A pirate!" Marcus answered. "We can make a patch for your eye – it will cover your wound – and tie a scarf over your hair. It would make a wonderful disguise."

"Where will you get the scarf and the eye patch?" Devin asked. "You can hardly go shopping when you are a wanted man."

Marcus smiled wickedly. "Ah, that's the beauty of my plan. I can tear off a bit of fabric from my shirt. There will be no shopping needed."

Devin jumped down off a slab of rock as they headed south. "And what is your disguise?"

"I'll be a seaman, too," Marcus said. "Perhaps we can rub a bit of clay on my face and arms to change the color of my skin."

"A seaman?" Devin asked. "Not a pirate?"

"They are one and the same."

"Hardly," Devin scoffed. "One man steals for his living and another man works hard for his. If we are going to be traveling together, we have to look as though we belong together."

Marcus' grin faded. "Then let's both be seamen, or fishermen if you like."

"In the mountains?"

"Well, even a man of the sea goes home to visit his family occasionally," Marcus replied.

"Only if he can afford to," Devin said, ducking under some evergreen branches. "From what you've told me, many of these people send their children off to sea and never see them again."

"That's true enough," Marcus agreed. "But remember how Lavender told us the men brought their furs down from the mountains to sell? What if our captain has a plan to sell those furs halfway around the empire in Sorrento? Our ship would take furs to Sorrento and bring back wine to Calais."

"That's not half bad," Devin remarked. "Did you think that up all by yourself?"

Marcus swatted him with a pine branch. "Yes, I did. I stayed up half the night planning it."

Devin stopped to brush needles out of his hair. "How is this going to help us?"

"It'll allow us to travel through towns between here and Amiens and to stop and have a decent meal and a glass of wine every day or so," Marcus answered.

Devin inclined his head. "I don't know. I'd rather stay out of towns, Marcus. We've made it this far, it seems foolish to draw attention to ourselves."

"Every stranger draws attention to himself in a small village," Marcus replied. "I'm not certain we can return without passing through a village. These places are so small, a handful of houses and a tavern! I'm guiding us to Amiens by the Lord's own four winds. There's no map in my brain like the one in yours."

"I simply remembered the map of the tunnels," Devin replied.

"Do you remember others as well?" Marcus asked. "You must have used the maps in the Archives when you laid out this trip."

"I did," Devin said. "The trouble is, I don't know where we are right now. Once I have some definite points of reference I can guide us to Amiens."

"I pointed out Mount Graig," Marcus said.

"I need two points of reference to find Amiens," Devin replied.

"That makes sense," Marcus agreed. The sun broke through the mist, throwing everything into either highlight or shadow. "Would you look at that? For a while I thought we might not see the sun again."

Devin stopped for a moment to appreciate the sight before them. "It's strange how our perceptions change as we get older. I saw 'May you see the sun again' carved as an epitaph on a tombstone once in Coreé. I thought it was very sad at the time but I didn't really understand it." He shrugged. "I think it's still sad but I can identify with it now."

"As a young man, you spent way too much time in cemeteries," Marcus said. "It used to worry your father."

Devin turned back to look at him. "Did it? I never would have thought he'd notice."

"He noticed a good deal more than you might think,"

Marcus told him. "You were his youngest – the child that neither he nor your mother expected. He worried about your mother while she was carrying you and he worried about you when you were born. Sometimes I believe that parents view a child born later in life as a bonus and somehow destined for greatness."

"Well, I've failed him there," Devin replied.

"No, you haven't. If I've given you that impression, Devin, then I'm sorry. I was wrong to tell you that this trip hasn't made a difference – it has. We've gathered a lot of vital information. The problem is getting it back to your father. I'm worried about the instability in Coreé and the insecurity of his position. Obviously Forneaux plans some kind of coup."

"And my death was to be a part of that," Devin said.

"Only in that it would silence any evidence that you might have dug up on Forneaux. Remember he planned to sacrifice his own son, too. He doesn't want anyone exposing him for what he truly is, especially Gaspard. All joking aside, Devin, that's why I think it's important that we disguise ourselves. You have no idea when we may meet someone and it's very important that we not be recognizable." "So make me an eyepatch," Devin said.

Marcus grinned and laid his pack on a convenient rock. Drawing out his extra shirt, he dislodged several other items which fell to the ground. Devin bent to retrieve them and stuff them back in the pack but an envelope with his name scrawled across it, stopped him.

"What's this?" he asked. The handwriting was his father's.

Marcus made a grab for it but Devin stepped back. "This letter is for me," he said, "and yet you never gave it to me?"

Marcus avoided his eyes. "There was no need," he muttered inadequately.

"No need?" Devin asked. "Did you make that decision? How long have you had it?"

"Emile gave it to me," Marcus admitted.

"The Emile that you stabbed and drowned in the bay?" Devin asked sarcastically. "That Emile?"

Marcus stood awkwardly. "Yes," he said. "He brought it with him from Coreé. Your father gave it to him before he left, never realizing that Emile had been paid off by Forneaux."

"You had a recent letter from my father and you didn't think it was important to give it to me?" Devin turned the envelope over in his hands and saw the seal was broken. "So, Marcus, did you open it and read it, too?"

Marcus' face was ashen. "The seal was already broken but yes, I did read it," he said.

Devin turned away from him, angry at Marcus and yet apprehensive about what the letter might say. The words were blurry even though his father's handwriting had always been large and bold. He threw it back at Marcus. "I can't even read it! Do you suppose you could humor me and read it aloud?"

Marcus avoided his Devin's eyes. Bending down, he retrieved the letter from the ground.

"*My Dearest Devin,*" he began.

"*I pray that this letter finds you well. The empire is full of disturbing rumors about your whereabouts and the status of your health or lack of it. I truly wish I had never allowed you to go on this trip but I cannot change that now.*

"*I am writing with some heartbreaking news. Please know that you bear no responsibility in it, but your mother passed away last week. I would have written sooner but I couldn't bring myself to put her death into words. Forgive me for not sending this missive sooner."*

Devin dropped to his knees, his hands shaking. "When was this written?" he asked, his voice choked.

"Several weeks ago," Marcus answered quietly. "Shall I go on?"

Devin nodded.

"I found her in the garden, sitting in her favorite chair by the roses just before lunch. I thought she was just sleeping but alas, I was wrong. The doctor feels that her heart failed. We have always suspected that she had a weakness there. That's why she kept to the house so much. She has had a cough for months and seemed to get winded when she walked very far. You know how your mother always was; she always passed everything off as a cold. She was, of course, terribly worried about you.

"I cannot say how much I hate to tell you this in a letter. It seems so impersonal, son. I'm sorry that you couldn't be with us in Coreé for the funeral. Please know that she loved you very much. She talked about you daily, worrying that you wouldn't be home to celebrate Christmas with us.

"This brings me to my own selfish request. Please come home, Devin. The Northern Provinces are nowhere to be when the snows pile up over the windows and people sit freezing by their hearths for six months out of the year. This year's holiday will be difficult enough without us missing two of our family members. The empire is a dangerous place for all of us, at the moment. Please make all haste to return to Coreé.

"Come before winter and relieve your poor father's heart that his youngest son is safe, at least.

"Affectionately,
"Your Father."

Marcus handed Devin the letter but he let it fall into his lap. The wind teased the pages apart and lifted them fluttering into the air but Devin made no attempt to rescue them. It was Marcus who caught them, folding them carefully and returning them to the envelope. He slid the pack off Devin's shoulders and slipped the letter inside.

"Devin ..." Marcus said softly.

Devin interrupted him. "How could you keep this from me?"

"I wasn't sure ..." Marcus began again.

Devin turned on him. "You weren't sure whether you'd killed me?" he asked acidly. "You've been certain of that for days!"

"I didn't mean to hurt you," Marcus replied.

"By shooting me or not giving me the letter?" Devin snapped. "Be specific. I'm sure I don't understand the way you think!"

"I didn't mean to hurt you by not giving you the letter." Marcus' voice faltered. "You were so badly hurt and sick when I found you. I couldn't give it to you then. I've thought of it several times but it didn't seem like the right opportunity. When we were lost in the caves, I wasn't certain we would ever get home. There was no reason to make you feel worse than you already did."

"It was never your decision to make," Devin answered through gritted teeth. "It was my letter, from my father to me. It was never intended for you. Why did you open it?"

Marcus exhaled. "I didn't. Emile did. I believe he planned to taunt you with the news when he captured us, but he forgot. After I shot you, he gave the letter to me in Calais

126

with the comment that they were 'taking out the Chancellor's family one person at a time.'"

"What?" Devin asked incredulously. "Do you think they killed my mother?"

Marcus shook his head emphatically. "No! I don't believe that, Devin. I think he was gloating. He thought I'd killed you. I think he felt that both a son's death and a wife's would be enough to demoralize even a strong man. He simply meant that, as far as he was concerned, two members of the Chancellor's family were dead."

Devin wiped a hand across his eyes, erasing the tears that were brimming over. "She didn't want me to go."

"I know," Marcus answered. "I was there." He made a move to touch Devin's shoulder but Devin shrank away from him. "I apologize for not giving you that letter sooner. You had every right to know and you should have known before I did. I was trying ..."

"To protect me," Devin finished. "I know that, Marcus, I truly do. I'm just angry. She hasn't been the first thing on my mind."

"We've been running for our lives," Marcus said. "That's understandable."

Devin exhaled, well aware that tears were streaming down his face. "I just feel that if I had known, I might have acted differently. I might have paid homage to her in some way."

"You still can," Marcus suggested. "Is there something that we can do that would be an apt memorial?"

Devin glanced around them, the flowered slopes, the rugged mountains, and the pure blue sky above them. "In some provinces they raise a cairn of stones as a symbol of remembrance," he suggested.

"Would you like to do that?" Marcus asked.

Devin nodded. "Yes, I think I would."

"There are plenty of different rocks available," Marcus said. "And there's a beautiful view of the valley nestled between the mountains. Do you think she would have liked it here?"

"She would have loved it," Devin said, looking at the wildflowers covering the slopes in front of them. "She loved any kind of flowers and she would have thought these were lovely."

"Would you like to pick out the stones that we use?" Marcus asked.

"We hardly have time for that," Devin said.

"We'll make time," Marcus assured him. "I'll bring some for you to look at. Choose the ones you like the best."

Suddenly, the morning wasn't going as they had planned at all. Devin gathered some stone slabs to form a base as Marcus piled a variety of stones next to it. "Is there any of that sparkling quartz that we saw in the cave? I thought a piece would look nice at the very top."

"I'll see if I can find some," Marcus replied, moving off to search for it.

Devin gathered the rest of the stones, stacking and restacking them so that they meshed together and didn't shift. There was some release in hard physical work and he found himself lifting weight that he would never have been able to move six months earlier. The provinces had changed him, worn off his soft edges, and strengthened both his body and his mind.

He would never be the same; his family would never be the same either. His mother, who ruled her sons and husband with just an occasional indication of displeasure, had left her mark on them forever. Here on this mountain, Devin would leave a memorial to her. No one but he and Marcus would probably ever see it or know of its significance. But it would last through many snowy winters and rainy summers. And even when time shifted the stones and brought them tumbling down, his mother's memory would last forever in Devin's heart and the hearts of any children he might have. He would make certain that she would never be forgotten in his lifetime.

They worked silently but quickly, discarding their shirts as the sun climbed higher in the cloudless blue sky. They capped the mound with a glittering piece of quartz that Marcus found and both knelt as Devin prayed the rosary, counting out a line of pebbles with his fingers, in place of his missing beads.

As the sun reached its zenith, they continued down the mountain. Neither of them talked. Devin's thoughts were all for his childhood and missed opportunities to spend more time with his mother. Marcus seemed equally morose, his shoulders slumped and his stride less vigorous than usual. When they reached a trail at the foot of the mountain, they followed it eastward. They were still miles north of the road to Amiens but at least this track headed in the correct direction.

By evening, they saw smoke from several chimneys in the air ahead of them. Marcus drew Devin to the side of the trail in a small copse of trees. "There seems to be a village ahead. Are you willing to take a chance at discovery for a hot meal?"

Devin shook his head. "I'm in no mood to play a character tonight, Marcus. And I don't really care whether I eat or not."

"We'll camp then," Marcus agreed quickly.

They went off the path and bypassed the settlement ahead. Through the trees they saw there were only four houses and no tavern. Only two men stood talking outside. The rest of the village seemed deserted. A dozen sheep bleated on the slopes below the trail and they kept a sharp watch out for their shepherds. Only an ancient black-and-white dog seemed to be in charge, harrying the sheep that wandered farthest from the pasture. Below them, a huge lake filled the valley, and Devin finally knew where they were.

"That's Lac d'Asti," he said. "Amiens is on the middle of its eastern shore. We should be able to reach it by tomorrow evening."

"Thank God," Marcus said.

They continued down the mountain until it was too dark to travel any further and camped beside a rushing stream, heading down to deposit its sparkling waters into the lake below them. Devin wasn't surprised when Marcus produced a line and hook from his gear. The ground was damp along the streambed and Devin dug up a few worms with a stick for him to use as bait. In half an hour, Marcus had landed four large fish which he filleted on a stone slab by the water.

"I think we could risk a fire," Marcus said. "It's going to be clear and cold tonight; the mist is already rising from the water. A bit of smoke will mix right in."

A small grove of trees provided a secluded campsite, shielding them on three sides from everything but a view of the stream. Devin built a small fire, huddling over it as the fish sizzled and spat on a stone. He felt cold, physically and emotionally. Had he been in Coreé for his mother's funeral, he and his father and brothers would have supported each other. They would have shared stories and drunk a toast to the cunning but beautiful woman who had ruled the most powerful man in Llisé with nothing more than a smile.

Here, while Marcus understood his distress, it was not the same. Devin bore the aching emptiness of grief in silence. One loss after another had seemed to dog their progress. This trip had proven a catalyst for change, for Devin, for the empire, and certainly for the people of Llisé. But how many of them would still remain when this turmoil was over?

Devin ate one small piece of fish to please Marcus. It was well cooked, the skin crisp and the inside tender but he wasn't hungry. Marcus cooked all of it, wrapped the remainder in cool leaves and set it aside for tomorrow. He left the fire burning. It had reduced itself to coals but the warmth and light were welcome. Tomorrow, Devin promised himself, they would find Madame Aucoin's house in Amiens and then they could go back La Paix. If ever he needed its tranquil setting, it was now.

CHAPTER 18

Amiens

Devin didn't sleep. His thoughts turned constantly to his mother's death and worry for his father who carried the weight of the empire on his shoulders and had just lost his only love and confidante. He was actually relieved when Marcus began making preparations to leave long before daybreak when the air was damp and smelled of earth and verdant foliage. They ate cold fish and packed quickly. Today, they had only to reach Lac d'Asti's eastern shore and they would be among friends again.

"I hate to bring this up," Devin said, just before they were ready to leave. "But do you think it would be wise to bathe and at least change our shirts before we leave?"

Marcus raised an eyebrow, obviously intent on lightening Devin's mood. "Are you saying I smell?"

Devin smiled. "I'm saying we both smell – rather badly. If I were Madame Aucoin's *sénéschal* I wouldn't allow us into the house."

"I understand your concern, Devin, but the cleaner we are, the more we are apt to look like ourselves," Marcus pointed out. "When we left La Paix, there was nothing that tied us to Madame Aucoin. It is vital that be maintained. It would be better to appear like two beggars in search of a free meal than the Chancellor's son and his bodyguard."

"All right," Devin agreed. "I just feel disgusting."

"You can stand it one more day," Marcus advised. "It will be safer."

Devin allowed Marcus to disguise his wound by tying a piece of cloth around his head, which also covered his eye. Nothing more was said about who they might pretend to be, but should they be asked, Devin decided to leave the talking to Marcus.

They headed south in the gray light before dawn, moving as quickly as possible toward the main road that led into Amiens. They heard it before they came to it. The lilt of voices mixed with the tramp of feet, and the squelch of wheels through mud. They had planned to walk parallel to the road wherever possible but here there were many other travelers with whom they could mingle and they merged with the growing throng headed for the city. Wagons filled with bleating sheep, wheels of cheese piled high in wheelbarrows leaving a pungent trail behind them, men bearing baskets of fresh vegetables, women carrying intricate lace pieces wrapped in folds of cloth over their arms, all shared the same road, bumping and shoving with a palpable sense of urgency.

"What's the rush?" Devin whispered to Marcus.

"It must be Market Day," Marcus answered. "Whoever arrives first with their goods is apt to sell out most quickly."

A woman with four miserable, cackling chickens crammed into two small crates crashed into Devin, intent on overtaking another woman with three brown chickens squeezed into an even smaller crate. She offered no pardon and Devin didn't expect it. These people were determined to outdo one another both in the quality of their products and their resolve to plunge onward, hoping to be able to set up their wares first and attract the most buyers.

At the crest of a ridge, Lac d'Asti spread out before them, dawn turning the water a rosy gold. The harbor held hundreds of fishing boats, bobbing on the shimmering water. For today, the boats lay moored as the fishermen crowded the market with their fish to sell. It seemed impossible that Amiens could support so many tradespeople but the market, when they reached it, was teeming with buyers as well as sellers.

Cooks from the great houses, trailed by underlings with baskets, chose carefully only the very best produce and meats. They rushed this way and that, obviously preferring some sellers to others. The smell of meat pies, fresh bread, and hot coffee made Devin's mouth water.

Most men and women carried their own baskets, visiting one booth and then another, haggling with the sellers to obtain the best prices. Children ran giggling, dodging between the adults. Some gnawed on the summer's first apples or smacked each other with sticks in mock fencing matches. Most played hide and seek, darting behind the sellers' stalls and hiding among the produce until someone rousted them out or returned them to their anxiously searching parents.

As prevalent as the children were, so were the pickpockets, some of them little more than children themselves. They stole goods as well as money, stuffing their pockets with produce and baked goods from the perimeter of crowded stands. They lagged behind those with the largest purses, sidling in as bargains were struck and artfully lifting bills or coins while the owners were blissfully unaware.

"Did you see that?" Devin asked indignantly, as a man dressed as a beggar slipped up behind a buxom woman buying eggs and deftly removed the change from her pocket.

"I did," Marcus replied. "And you'll do nothing about it. The last thing we need to do is draw attention to ourselves here. Walk slowly away from the market toward the docks. I'm going to buy us something to eat."

Devin turned away, nearly colliding with the pickpocket who was just backing away from his victim.

The man spun around, his chin split by a puckered scar. "Watch where you're going!" the man snarled.

Devin bent closer to him, close enough to smell his greasy hair and rancid breath. "Give her money back," he hissed in his ear. "Or I'll report you to the authorities."

The man opened a toothless mouth in surprise and stopped dead. His red, bleary eyes surveyed Devin and then he began to grin and laugh loudly. "Trying to move in on my territory, are you, boy? Well, I'll be the one reporting you to the authorities. Move on, before I slit your throat or your wrist!" He flicked a narrow blade from his pocket, slashing a long rent in Devin's sleeve, and ran off. His maniacal laughter rang through the crowd and people turned to watch him go, their eyes wandering back to Devin as well.

Marcus grabbed Devin's arm hard. "That was foolish!" he chided. "What happens in this marketplace is no concern of ours. It would be a tragedy to have come this far and lose you in a knife fight with a frenetic pickpocket."

"He bumped into me," Devin protested. "I didn't intend to start a fight."

135

"Just don't give me any more reasons to worry," Marcus replied. "Stop trying to right every wrong in the empire! It simply isn't possible. Go down to the docks!"

Out of the corner of his eye, Devin saw three soldiers bearing the Chancellor's colors standing by a fountain, a bottle of wine on the wall beside them. "Marcus," he said quietly, inclining his head in their direction.

"I'm well aware," Marcus murmured. "Go!"

Devin pieced together his damaged sleeve and walked away silently. Leaving the bustle of the market behind him, he walked down to the tranquil harbor. Moments later, Marcus caught up with him, a loaf of bread and a bottle of wine tucked under his arm. They found a deserted spot to sit on the edge of the dock. Marcus split the loaf of bread lengthwise, and placed a piece of hot grilled fish inside. They sat quietly sharing the fish and bread along with the bottle of cheap wine that Marcus had purchased.

"Did you know those soldiers?" Devin asked.

"Not personally, no, but one of them is a friend of Emile's."

Devin swallowed a bit of fish and bread before asking, "So they are here looking for us?"

"Not necessarily," Marcus said. "Amiens is the only large city this far north. Placed as it is in the middle of these mountains but with access by water to the provinces farther south, it maintains a garrison of soldiers."

"These wore my father's colors," Devin said.

"As I told you before, your father gave me contacts in every area where we intended to travel. The intention was to enable us to get assistance wherever we were. I don't think he ever imagined that Forneaux had so thoroughly infiltrated his Guard. Those men back there might be able to take us home safely or they might slit our throats as soon as we are alone. Since I'm not a mind reader, I choose not to take the chance of asking for help."

Devin stretched his legs out in front of him. "Did you ever hear Armand tell the story of Bastien's Folly?"

Marcus shook his head.

"A prosperous farmer named Bastien owned land that divided another man's property into two separate sections. Over a period of years, Bastien refused every offer his neighbor, Jean, made to buy his small farm, even though each of his offers was quite generous.

"Both men's properties fronted on a river and during a particularly rainy season, the river rose higher and higher until it lapped at the steps of the farmer's house. His neighbor, in much the same circumstances, decided to leave the area by boat until the waters receded. Before leaving he rowed past the farmer's house and called out to him, 'Bastien, come out! The waters are getting too high. Come with me and we will stay in town until the river recedes!'

"Bastien went to his door and shouted, 'No! You will drown me in the river so that my property can be yours!'

"Again Jean pleaded with Bastien. 'I mean no harm. You will drown if you stay here, my friend. Come out and get into the boat.'

"Again Bastien refused and finally his neighbor rowed on and left him to fend for himself. That night a vicious storm rolled in. It rained for three days and three nights and Bastien's house was completely submerged. Bastien drowned in his own home, protecting it from his neighbor whose only intention was to help him. After his death, Bastien's property was sold at auction for only half its worth to the highest bidder, who just happened to be his neighbor, Jean."

"This isn't like that," Marcus responded. "I don't know these men. I can't vouch for their loyalty. If I ask for their help, it could cost you your life!"

"I don't doubt your decision," Devin assured him. "It only reminded me of the story. I'm woefully out of practice telling them. I'm sure Armand will take me to task for not having rehearsed more on our way back."

"Armand wasn't dodging armed killers as he walked. If he has a problem with your lack of practice, send him to me," Marcus answered.

"Armand has his own demons to fight," Devin reminded him. "It is difficult to perform when your heart is broken."

"You seem to have done rather well," Marcus commented and then apologized. "I'm sorry, that was callous. Forgive me."

"There's no need to apologize," Devin murmured. "I thought that telling stories might take my mind off my mother's death and Jeanette's disappearance. But they will always be with me, sometimes when I least expect it, I'm sure. If you meant that as disrespect, I choose not to take it as such. You have no idea what lies heavy on my heart, Marcus, just as I don't with you."

Marcus turned to face him, opened his mouth to say something, and decided against it. He passed the wine bottle back to Devin and went back to trailing a small sapling in the water. Minutes passed with not a word of conversation from either of them. The sound of the water lapping the dock was soothing and Devin leaned back against one of the posts as he felt his eyes closing.

It was late afternoon when he awoke. Marcus sat next to him carving a piece of wood with his knife. "Why didn't you waken me?" Devin asked. "We're almost safe.

There was no reason to risk being discovered here at the docks."

Marcus didn't take his eyes away from his work. "It didn't hurt anything to let you rest. I'd rather not arrive at Madame Aucoin's in broad daylight, anyway. Hopefully, we won't be noticed as dark comes on." He put the rounded piece of wood and the knife in his pack. "If you're ready, we can go."

Devin almost asked him what he was carving but it looked suspiciously like one of the wooden heads that Lavender had made and carried. What could have prompted Marcus to take up the same pastime? Devin was mystified. And yet he'd been right in what he had last told Marcus. Spending an inordinate amount of time with someone didn't guarantee the sharing of intimate personal information. Marcus knew very little about Devin and Devin knew very little about Marcus.

"What were you carving?" Devin finally asked when his curiosity got the better of him.

Marcus remained silent for a long time as they left the dock. When he answered, his voice was soft. "I thought I might do Lavender the favor she did for me. I haven't her skill at carving but I wanted to remember her face."

"Will you show it to me when it's finished?" Devin asked.

Marcus nodded. "I will. If I finish it and it looks like her, at all. It's just for me. I have no aspirations of becoming a sculptor."

"I wonder what she looked like as a young girl," Devin mused.

Marcus inhaled deeply. "I imagine she was beautiful."

They continued back toward the market. All of the vendors had left for home, their goods sold or returning

139

with them. The ground and warped wooden tables were littered with spoiled or damaged produce left to rot. Small children and the elderly, sometimes working in tandem, quickly gathered the remaining food into cloth sacks. Thankfully the pickpockets had departed, too, their day's work done. These remaining people had nothing to steal but leftover food that no one else had wanted. One stray brown chicken pecked for breadcrumbs along the cobblestones, loudly evading any attempts at capture. Devin applauded her success at escaping. Her exuberant search for food brought a smile to his face although he was certain her owner was cursing her independence.

The city seemed to be designed like a spider web. The fountain in the marketplace served as the center. All streets seemed to fan out from there. From this principal area several of the streets widened, leading toward the top of the mountain. Not seeing any signs to direct them, Marcus picked a street at random. As they continued to climb upward, away from the market district, the street was lined with large houses with trim green lawns in front of them. Shrubbery shaped like animals or urns lined cobbled walkways, each more elaborate than the next.

"What street are we looking for?" Marcus asked as they approached a signpost.

"It's Number 31, Rue de Saint Jacques," Devin answered.

Marcus grinned. "Well, there's a piece of luck I hadn't counted on! We are actually on the correct street."

Devin scanned the houses ahead of them as the street continued up the hill. Few had numbers but the ones that did were in the hundreds. "It's much higher up," he said, noting that as the numbers decreased the size of the homes enlarged into mansions.

The street took a turn at the top, forming a circle. Here, the most extravagant mansions fronted toward the lake, a view that took in all of the harbor and the wide waters beyond it. The sun setting over the mountains threw its amber glow on the water, just as the sunrise had this morning. "This is really beautiful," Devin said. "I don't know why I would have expected anything less from Madame Aucoin."

"The old Comte must have left his wife well provided for," Marcus said. "They raised horses and had vast farms but I think a great deal of their wealth must have been inherited."

"Madame Aucoin has surely been good to us," Devin said.

Darkness began to fall quickly, as soon as the sun dropped behind the distant mountains. The clear sky promised another cold night. Despite his afternoon nap, Devin felt exhausted. This had been a very long, hard trip. The Provincial Archives they had gone to save had been burned, Tirolien's Master Bard and his apprentice had been brutally murdered, and Devin's mother had died. It didn't bode well for the future and Devin's dwindling hope that somewhere Jeanette still waited for him. Hope seemed to flicker less brightly in the twilight creeping through Amiens' streets.

They stopped in front of a compact but elegant mansion, its four stories alight with candles that shed their warmth onto the lawn and street in front it. Devin felt in his pocket for the button that had been delivered to them by a beautiful airborne visitor. "This is it, Marcus, Number 31."

Marcus hesitated. "Should we just go up to the front door? Or head around to the servants' entrance in the back?"

"I actually think we will have more chance of being turned away at the servants' entrance," Devin said. "Let's just hope for the best. If we should be turned away here, we are on our own."

Devin went first, untying the piece of Marcus' shirt from his head and shoving it into his pocket. He knocked firmly and stood back, aware of the falcon-shaped topiaries that seemed to survey him suspiciously from the lawn.

CHAPTER 19

Refuge

When the door opened, it threw warm light onto the doorstep and onto the two dirty travelers who waited there. The *sénéschal*, dressed impeccably in a crisp white shirt and black jacket, looked askance at them. "Can I help you?" he asked, his face carefully impassive.

"I hope so," Devin replied. "Madame Aucoin gave me this to identify ourselves." He dropped the button into the *sénéschal*'s hand, wondering wildly if there might be some slight difference between this one he'd found and the button Madame Aucoin had actually given him.

The *sénéschal* folded his fingers over the button and held out a hand to usher them in. "Yes, of course, monsieur. Come this way."

Could it be that easy? Devin wondered. After all the twists and turns of this journey, could a simple button gain them access to one of the most prestigious homes in Amiens? They wiped their feet outside the door, though it did little good, and walked into a gleaming white-tiled entrance hall. Devin was painfully aware of their appearance, their stench, and the beautifully immaculate condition of Madame Aucoin's house.

"Dev?" yelled a familiar voice, and feet pounded as Gaspard came leaping out of a sitting room on the right. His arms went around Devin in a bear hug and he started slapping him on the back. "Good Lord, we thought you were dead! Do you realize how long you've been gone?"

"Obviously, I'm not dead," Devin answered, disentangling himself. "I have no idea how long we've been gone and Marcus didn't try to kill me, no matter what you've been told."

Gaspard paused, mouth open, apparently at a loss for words. "I never believed that he would," he said finally and held out a hand to clasp Marcus'. "It's good to see you as well, *mon ami*."

Angelique, in a peach confection of ruffles and lace, flew through the sitting-room doors and threw herself into Devin's arms. "Oh don't, Angelique!" he warned her. "I'm filthy and I smell like an old goat!"

His warning didn't deter her from kissing him on both cheeks. "I don't care! Do you know how I cried when we thought you were dead?" Her fingers hovered above the groove Marcus' bullet had traced in his scalp. "Your poor head," she fussed. "Which of those soldiers shot you? I'll kill him with my bare hands."

"It's complicated," Devin responded, glancing at Marcus. "Did Chastel and Armand arrive safely?"

"They arrived over a week ago," Gaspard volunteered. "They're still upstairs changing for dinner."

"*Grandmère* is changing, too, although I will run up to tell her you are here. She will be so relieved," Angelique said, bouncing from foot to foot. She looked so childlike and happy that Devin had to smile.

"We would like very much to change also," Marcus said.

"Of course," said the *sénéschal*. "Madame Aucoin has had rooms prepared for you since she arrived here. I can take you up immediately."

"We would be very grateful," Devin said. "Under normal circumstances, I would never have appeared at your door in this state. We've had a difficult trip."

"We can talk once you've had a chance to clean up," Gaspard replied. "You do smell rather like an old goat, Devin, but I'm so very glad to see you that I don't even care!"

"I'm glad to see you, too!" Devin said, noting that for the first time in many years, it was evening and Gaspard appeared to be completely sober. "But I don't quite understand. Why is everyone here? I thought the arrangement was to meet at La Paix?"

"It was," Gaspard agreed, "but when the reports we heard indicated that you had been killed, Devin, we had to readjust our plans."

"To what?" Devin asked.

"I'm sure we can discuss this later," Marcus said, hurrying him along. "It's best we wash and change before Madame Aucoin thinks twice about letting us into her dining room."

Devin turned as the *sénéschal* eased his pack off his shoulders. "There is some valuable information in there. Please don't lose anything."

"I'll put it in your room myself, sir," he promised. "If you'd like, you can follow me up now."

Devin had so many questions but they left Gaspard and Angelique to tell Madame Aucoin of their arrival and followed the *sénéschal*. Devin held out his hand. "I'm Devin Roché, I'm sorry but I don't know your name."

"Georges Mazzei," he replied. "I knew who you were, monsieur, everyone has prayed that somehow you might have survived. Every time there has been a knock at the door, everyone runs to the hall hoping that you are back, safe and sound."

Devin felt tears dim his eyes. "That's very kind of them," he murmured. His response felt inadequate to the appreciation he felt that here people cared about him and would have mourned him had he died.

Marcus dispelled the awkwardness by introducing himself. "I'm Marcus Berringer, Georges."

The main rooms opened off the wide hallway with double doors of multi-paned glass. The broad stairway, with an ornate gold-and-white railing on each side, split the space about three-quarters of the way toward the back of the hall. The steps were covered in luxurious Sorrento carpet in a pattern of soft blues and greens. While the space was much more formal than La Paix, it exuded the same peaceful ambiance, something Devin was certain now emanated from Madame Aucoin's personality as well as the choices she made in the furnishings for her homes.

Devin and Marcus followed Georges up the staircase to a hallway that ran the width of the house. He found himself counting doorways as Georges assigned their rooms. Marcus' was right next to Devin's and apparently Gaspard's was on the other side. Georges opened the door to soft-cream walls and carpet. The bed, buried deep in soft pillows, exhibited a coverlet in the same cream color below a headboard that was quilted in sumptuous brown velvet.

Devin fought the desire to find some excuse to just stay here, safe and protected. How easy it would be to put off planning Forneaux's assassination, facing his mother's death,

146

and traveling hundreds of miles over a mountain range that hovered on the verge of winter. As dirty as he was, he wanted to fall into that cream-colored bed, pull up the coverlet and sleep through this winter when war threatened to change everything he knew and loved.

He realized Georges had opened another door in the bedroom. God, he had his own bathroom! And there was running water! Maybe he had died and this, at last, was heaven! But if it was, where was Jeanette? He pictured the curve of her cheek, her slender neck and small hands, the taste of her lips as she had kissed him in Chastel's chateau the night she disappeared.

Georges took his arm. "Are you all right, Monsieur Roché?" he asked, his heavy brows furrowed.

"I am," Devin replied. "I'm just tired." He gestured around the room. "You have no idea how this house appears after having slept in fields and caves and eaten raw fish and rabbit because we couldn't even have a fire."

Georges gestured to the fireplace. "Would you like a fire, monsieur? It will turn colder later tonight and a fire might be welcome."

Devin shook his head. "I'm fine really. I'd like to cause you as little disruption as possible."

Georges smiled, his kind face wreathed in wrinkles. "Making a guest comfortable isn't a disruption, monsieur. It's my job. I'll see that a fire is lit before you go to bed."

Georges turned on the taps in the bath tub and Devin almost wept. They were the same polished brass as the ones the Chancellor's mansion had at home. Devin reached a hand out and caressed them in disbelief and then turned to Georges. "Do you know how long it's been since I've had running water?"

"I know La Paix does not have running water," Georges said. "So, I'm guessing that you had it last at home in Coreé."

Devin nodded. "It's not that I can't live without it but it is surely a convenience."

"It is indeed, monsieur," Georges agreed. He glanced at Devin's ripped and worn clothing. "I doubt your clothes can be mended. May I have your permission to burn them? Madame Aucoin has supplied you with anything you might need in the armoire in your bedroom."

"Just a moment," Devin said, divesting himself of his jacket. He slid his hand into the lining and removed Father Sébastian's book and Tirolien's Chronicle. "I risked my life and Marcus' for these. Is there somewhere safe that I can put them?"

"Of course, monsieur," Georges said. "Follow me." They returned to the bedroom. Georges removed a small key from the ring at his waist and unlocked a drawer that was fit almost flawlessly into the pattern of carvings on the armoire down near the bottom. "Put them in here."

Devin bent and slid them in, closing the drawer and running his finger around the edge to make certain that it was again indistinguishable from the rest of the carved wood.

Georges slid the key off his ring. "There is but one key, monsieur. You may put it anywhere you like or carry it with you."

Devin bowed, delighted by the clever secret drawer. "Thank you," he said. "Thank you for everything."

Georges bowed too and grinned, apparently happy that he had pleased Devin. "The bath will be almost full. Just leave your clothes on the floor. I will dispose of them later. There is soap in the bathroom and the towels beside the tub are on a heated rack, monsieur. Hot water flows through them continuously."

"This is heaven," Devin told him. "Really, it is."

Georges just smiled. "Should you need anything else, there is a bell pull by the door."

Devin shed his clothes on the spotless bathroom floor, a pile of filthy fabric that he never cared to see again. His boots he set aside. They might be scuffed but they were still serviceable and he might need them again for their trek over the mountains to Coreé.

He ran his fingers through the hot water and turned off the taps. Easing down in the tub, he felt every bump, scratch, and bruise. But the discomfort was momentary. The heat relaxed his sore muscles and eased every ache and pain. He washed his hair for the first time, carefully circumventing his wound. Dried blood turned the wash cloth brown so finally he dunked his head under water, coming up sputtering, and then leaned back just to soak.

Finding this oasis of peace in a country rife with rumors of assassination and war, felt dreamlike. Here he was safe, protected, warm, and comfortable for the first time in weeks. This house in Amiens offered shelter just as well as La Paix and there were times he feared they would never reach either destination. He'd been greeted by friends who truly cared about him and tonight would be a time of celebration. The warmth of water soothed his soul and eased his heartache. He would grant himself a few moments peace before they convened their Council of War.

CHAPTER 20

Dinner Conversation

When the water finally cooled, Devin dragged himself from its depths and wrapped a warm towel around his waist. Even the Chancellor's residence didn't have heated towel racks! Perhaps those niceties had been eliminated because Vincent Roché assumed office as a relatively young man with two sons still at home. Had they imagined he and his brothers would misuse the towel racks by frying eggs or frogs on them?

He swiped at the fogged mirror and shaved. Afterwards he dried his hair with a towel and combed it, so that his wound was less visible. Walking to the armoire wrapped in a towel, he discovered an entire wardrobe exactly his size with boots and shoes to match. Angelique had certainly found a fairy godmother in Madame Aucoin. So, apparently, had he.

He dressed in a formal white shirt, black trousers and jacket, similar to what Gaspard was wearing. Even after a thorough scrubbing, his hands still looked scraped and raw. His fingernails were broken to nubs. But tonight there would only be friends to deal with. He slipped on a pair of polished black boots and opened the door to the hall.

He hesitated on the threshold in surprise. Madame Aucoin stood just outside along with Armand, Chastel, and Jules. Gaspard and Angelique had also joined the gathering. As he stepped out into the hall, they began a slow heartfelt applause. Madame Aucoin moved forward and enfolded him gently in her arms. He bent to lay his head against her shoulder, fighting tears at her genuine affection. How fortunate he was to have this group of people on his side!

He took an awkward step backward. "I don't deserve your applause. I didn't accomplish anything I set out to do," he murmured. "The Provincial Archives were burned by Forneaux's men, Armand. I wasn't able to save anything but the Tirolien Chronicle that I got from Dariel Moreau's wife in Calais."

"You saved yourself, Devin," Armand said quietly. "The empire was spared one casualty in this war. We are just glad to see you alive and well."

"It seems a poor substitute for all that we planned," Devin answered. "How is your knee, Armand?"

"Better every day!" Armand said with a smile. "Madame Aucoin is an amazing physician."

Devin laughed. "I've no doubt of it. She is amazing at everything! There seems to be very little that she can't do." He held out his hand. "Chastel, how are you?"

"I am well," he answered. "My wolves and I are ready to lead you through the mountains to Vienne and then on to Coreé."

"Where are the wolves?" Devin asked. "I didn't see them when I came in."

"Close by," Chastel replied. "Jules has been taking good care of them."

"It actually concerned me that we saw and heard very few wolves in the Valley of Albion," Devin said.

Chastel gave him an enigmatic smile. "We'll discuss that later."

Marcus' door opened down the hall. "There seems to be a great deal of excitement out here," he said. "What have I missed?"

"Nothing except that we are so relieved to have you both back safely," Madame Aucoin replied. She began to shepherd them toward the stairs. "I imagine you are both starving. Georges said you've been dining on raw fish and rabbits! Let's go down to dinner."

Angelique maneuvered her way over to Devin, entwining her fingers with his. "Walk with me?" she asked, her lashes fluttering.

There was no way to refuse so Devin did, watching a look of disappointment cross Gaspard's face. He wove his way through to his best friend and said, "I think the three of us should go down together." They put Angelique between them and descended the staircase as though they were attending a ball.

The dining room was tranquil and candlelit. Gold draperies covered the long windows that would have looked out upon the lake. Devin took a moment to pull the fabric back, revealing the bay below them. The horizon glowed softly with luminous blue after-light. The house was positioned so that it viewed Lac d'Asti from the harbor side, so that both sunset and sunrise would be visible from this position. Devin marveled at the architectural genius behind both La Paix and this city house. Both designers had an unusual flair of blending buildings with their natural surroundings.

A series of exquisite courses followed one after another until Devin had to refuse any more food. After living on so little for so long, he found that he was overfull after the second course. He laid his silverware down on his plate and decided to concentrate on conversation instead. "Armand, do you remember the story you told me about Lavender, the little girl who lost her pony?"

Armand forked another piece of chicken swimming in cream. "Yes, of course."

"Do you happen to know Lavender's last name?

"I believe it was Chastain," Armand answered. "Why?"

Devin glanced at Marcus. "Well, it's rather a strange story. We met an old woman in the woods above Calais, right after I was shot."

Madame Aucoin held up a hand. "Wait, please. I am more interested in you, Devin. The reports we heard were that Marcus had killed you. Obviously, that's not true but what really happened?"

Devin exhaled and glanced at Marcus. "Marcus and I found the Provincial Archives exactly where Armand said they would be. We had every intention of saving it by removing the contents to another location but unfortunately Forneaux's men had arrived before us. Marcus recognized at least one of them from my father's Personal Guard. My father had sent them to find me but apparently René Forneaux had bribed them to carry out his orders instead. They scoffed at my interest in the Archives but they did allow me to take a torch down to look at it. It was impeccably organized, Armand! Every province had multiple fabric bags protecting the pages of the Chronicles inside. They were arranged alphabetically on shelves. Now it has been destroyed and it can never be replaced. I could have spent the rest of my life there just reading all of those documents."

Devin hesitated a moment, focusing on the candles whose cheery glow blurred into multiple spikes of light before his eyes. He couldn't help wondering if he would ever be able to read well again, or was that just wishful thinking? He cleared his throat and continued. "I kept thinking that the people in Coreé assume the provincials are illiterate, and here they had developed this elaborate system for preserving the Chronicles in written form. It was truly amazing! I wish you had been there to see it."

Armand leaned forward, listening to every word. "I wish I had been there, too."

"Had Armand and Chastel come with us, I would never have been able to protect all three of you," Marcus said grimly. "I think I would like to tell the next part of this story myself, if you don't mind, Devin. The rules of this game have changed since we left Coreé. There are some things I haven't even told you and I think it's time I was honest."

"What haven't you told me?" Devin asked, puzzled.

"Do you remember when Chastel allowed you to read his grandfather's journal?"

Devin nodded, wondering where this conversation was going.

"I will spare the rest of you the details, but many years ago Chastel's uncle was suspected of being a werewolf. The villagers of Lac Dupré turned against him and, during a scuffle in the marketplace, his uncle killed a man. The incensed villagers turned against him, clubbing and beating him. Chastel's grandfather shot and killed his own son before an angry mob could beat him to death or hang him. At the time he read it, Devin was appalled by the thought of a man killing his own son."

"As well he should be," Madame Aucoin murmured. "That is a terrible story."

"It is a tragedy," Marcus agreed. "I don't mean to minimize it, but it is vital to see that the father's action was still prompted by love. I tried hard to make Devin understand that Chastel's grandfather was protecting his son in the only way he had available to him at the time."

A cold lump lodged in Devin's stomach and he was aware that Madame Aucoin was looking at him.

Marcus didn't speak directly to Devin but addressed the entire group as a whole. "When Devin's father assigned me to accompany him on this journey, he was afraid that Devin might be taken prisoner and used as a political weapon against him. He gave me very specific orders to carry out, should that happen. I have never shared these orders with anyone even though Devin has asked me to several times. My first allegiance is to Chancellor Roché, my second to his son.

"When we followed the directions Armand gave us to the Archive, we feared Forneaux's men might have arrived before us. So we hid several hundred feet on the cliff above it and waited to see if there was any activity below before we went down. Emile and his men approached us from behind. I never heard them coming. There were three of them and they took us down to the site of the Archive at gunpoint.

"Emile had already stationed two more men in the small hut that housed the trap door to the Archive. There were five of them against two of us and to be honest, I wasn't certain Devin could kill a man if he had to."

Devin didn't correct him; he wasn't certain himself but he had a sick feeling where Marcus' conversation was headed.

"Emile asked me to join them," Marcus continued. "He claimed he was authorized to offer me the same position in Forneaux's administration that I held in Roché's. He said I only had to pass one test. The test was to kill Devin Roché, the Chancellor's youngest son, or we would both be shot and killed on the spot."

"I couldn't take out all three men myself so I raised my pistol and I shot Devin in the head," Marcus said. "Because I promised his father I would kill him before I allowed him to be captured."

Gaspard's fork clattered onto his plate as he rose from the table. "You honestly intended to kill him?" he snarled. "Did you miss your target, Marcus? Did your new post with my father fall through? Why in God's name are you sitting at this table with us?"

Devin took a deep breath. "I was standing no more than ten feet away from him, Gaspard. Marcus doesn't miss unless he misses intentionally."

"You're defending him?" Gaspard demanded.

"He intentionally grazed my temple, Gaspard, and then he came back for me," Devin replied. "After he'd killed Emile and two of his soldiers and dumped their bodies in the bay at Calais."

"I'll bet you have only his word for that," Gaspard parried.

"He came back for me, Gaspard," Devin repeated quietly. "I wouldn't be here if he hadn't carried me to safety. If he meant to kill me, he made a very poor job of it."

Gaspard threw his napkin down on the table and sat

down, his expression mutinous. "If you are fool enough to give him a second chance then don't ask me to protect you!"

Marcus leveled a grim look at Gaspard. "I will protect Devin or die trying."

Thankfully, Jules intervened. "How did the reports of Devin's death spread through the countryside then?"

"Two of the soldiers were dispatched immediately to Coreé. Their ship will have to go clear around the southern coast of Llisé and up the Dantzig. News shouldn't reach Coreé for several more days," Marcus said. "However, Emile and his two other comrades bragged of the destruction of the Provincial Archives and Devin's death in a tavern near the docks before I killed them. Up until now the Archive had always remained a secret kept by the Master Bards. News like that would travel fast."

"Your poor father," Madame Aucoin murmured, shaking her head. "He has been through more than one man can stand in the last few weeks. It has been a very sad time for us all."

Devin closed his eyes for an instant. "If you are referring to my mother's death, Madame, I already know. Marcus gave me a letter my father had written before all of this business with Emile happened. Apparently, Emile was to deliver it if he could find me. My father had no idea Emile had changed sides. Marcus said Emile intended to taunt me with the letter but apparently he forgot about it in the excitement of having Marcus assassinate me."

Madame Aucoin wiped a tear from her cheek and patted his hand. "I wish there was some way to spare him this news reporting your death."

"That's been taken care of," Marcus answered. "Devin gave his rosary to Chastel when we left him with Armand because it had a small cross wired to it that served as a token to access the tunnels. I gave my rosary to Devin the night before he was shot because I saw him reach for his out of habit. Emile lifted that rosary from his pocket as proof to deliver to the Chancellor that his son was really dead."

"Thankfully my father will know that the rosary isn't mine," Devin added.

Chastel fumbled in his pocket, extracting Devin's rosary and passing it to him. "I've kept that in my pocket ever since we arrived, praying that you would return safely."

Devin smiled, pocketing the smooth stones. "Thank you for keeping them for me, Chastel. I value them very much!"

Madame Aucoin's gentle face was lined with worry. "I'm so sorry you have had to deal with all this."

Devin turned to Marcus. "I think the thing I have the greatest trouble dealing with is that my father ordered you to kill me, Marcus. Did he assume there would never be a chance of rescue or ransom?"

Marcus shook his head. "Not in these times, Devin. I'm sorry. René Forneaux would think nothing of sending your head back to Coreé on a platter as a means of tormenting your father."

"Well, I think I'll pass on dessert," Armand said jokingly. "I had no idea the discussion would be so serious this evening. I was simply looking forward to welcoming you back, Devin."

"As was I," Angelique said. "Unfortunately the empire hasn't grown any less brutal just because Marcus saved Devin's life."

"And he did save my life," Devin said, making eye contact with each and every person at the table. "There will be no questioning that from this point on. My father's trust in him is well placed and so is mine. I need every one of you to believe that as firmly as I do."

Marcus sat ramrod straight, his head unbowed. "I intend to be worthy of your trust, Devin."

"Just don't shoot me again," Devin quipped, trying to lighten the conversation. "I'm still recovering from the first time."

Gaspard and Angelique laughed but the rest of the group remained silent.

"Have you had any headaches or dizziness?" Madame Aucoin asked.

"I did at first but it passed after the first several days." Devin sighed. "My eyes are still a bit blurry. I can't read very well, which is a grave inconvenience to me. I'm hoping it will pass."

Jules frowned. "That should have improved with rest, along with the other symptoms."

"We had no time for rest, nor will we have in the next few months," Devin replied. "The leaves are already turning in the mountains. Come September, we may be up to our knees in snow. We are going to have to act quickly if we plan to cross the mountains."

Chastel took a sip of wine. "When we thought you'd been killed and Marcus had defected, we decided it might be better to travel together instead of taking two groups. Armand isn't really up to a long trek through rough country."

"I'll do whatever you need me to do," Armand objected. "What's important to me is recovering my daughter and I'll travel half the empire if that's what it takes to find her."

Devin smiled. "I'll go with you to search for Jeanette after the rest of this is settled. I dreamed of her, Armand,

159

when I was lying in the rain by the smoking Archive, wondering whether Marcus had truly intended to kill me. She knelt beside me and spoke to me; I touched her hair and her lips. She looked as real to me as any of you do sitting at this table. I can't believe she isn't alive somewhere in the provinces. I am determined to find her."

Madame Aucoin called for coffee and dessert, although conversation was much more engaging than food at the moment to Devin.

He turned his attention to Chastel. "I thought that Armand was too easily recognized to travel by ship to Coreé?"

"Perhaps from Pirée, he is," Chastel answered. "That's why we've all come to Amiens. We decided to leave here by boat and travel down through Batavie before the river freezes. We'll hire a coach in northern Vienne and go directly to Madame Aucoin's home in Coreé."

"Do you feel that plan needs to be changed because Marcus and I returned?" Devin asked.

"That is entirely up to you," Chastel replied, making a silly salute. "I'd taken over as our supreme commander but I'll gladly turn that job over to you."

"I doubt that Marcus and I can travel by ship from any of the Northern Provinces," Devin replied. "Perhaps we could talk about it tomorrow after I've had a good night's sleep."

Armand leaned forward, his arms on the table. "When this conversation started, you asked me about Lavender's story. You said you had met an old woman in the woods?"

"We did," Devin said. "Whether she was a spirit or some poor old woman who'd lost her mind and her family, I guess we'll never know. Sometimes she referred to herself in the plural, as though there were a host of others with her, as well. She insisted her name was Lavender and she said that she belonged in the story about the little girl who lost her white pony."

Angelique clapped her hands like a child. "What did she look like, Devin? Tell us, please!"

He laughed. "She looked like a withered brown leaf that the wind might blow away with the slightest effort, Angelique. Her dress had faded to a nondescript gray and her face and skin were the color of walnuts from years of living outside in the sun. Wrinkles wreathed her eyes and cupped her mouth. She was filthy dirty and yet she smelled only of earth and growing things. I have never met anyone like her and I doubt I will again.

"After Marcus found me, he stashed me in the mouth of a cave where we had camped on our way to search for the Archive. Apparently we had invaded Lavender's cave and we didn't know it. She had it filled with dozens of carved wooden heads. She claimed they represented everyone in her family and the staff at her father's chateau. She made one for Marcus. He can show it to you later if you'd like."

Marcus reached into the pocket of his dinner jacket. "I have it with me," he said and passed it around the table.

Devin continued while everyone marveled at the detail and the skill of her artwork. "She showed us the heads of her four brothers: Sébastian, Abelard, Michel, and Charles."

Armand interrupted him. "Sébastian Chastain became a priest. He was drowned when the dam was sabotaged at Albion. Would you like to hear the story?"

CHAPTER 21

Albion Revisited

"Of course," said Madame Aucoin pleasantly, oblivious to the looks of surprise on Devin's and Marcus' faces.

Armand settled into his Master Bard persona. His face became more animated, his voice stronger. Devin was relieved to see him display more of his former self.

"*It was an early spring day and the villagers of Albion were enjoying the warm weather and fresh breeze. They had put aside, for the moment, their rash refusal to pay the exorbitant taxes the government had levied on their small community.*

"*The day was sunny and bright for April. Women gathered along the river to wash their clothes and dry them on the stones in the sun. A baby sat and cooed by her mother's side, wiggling her toes in the cool earth. The children were playing, swinging on vines over the water and running and laughing. Most of the men had gathered at the blacksmith's shop to talk.*

"*There had been heavy rains for two weeks before and the dam was stressed by the excess water it contained. There*

162

was no warning, no alarm. A sharp crack rang out and the stones flew explosively into the little valley as the water breeched the dam. Above Albion on the hill, the priest tolled the church bell, hoping to warn the villagers in time to escape the rushing water. Rock and debris swept down through the valley and over the town. People tried to scale the banks but the waters rose too high, dragging them down into their rushing torrent. Mothers were washed away with their babies still clasped in their arms. Fathers held their children on their shoulders but the onslaught swept them both into the flood.

"Halfway up the hill, the priest was dragged away as the raging water tore the nave from the foundation of the church, the bell rope still in his hands. In a matter of minutes, nothing remained of Albion but the foundations of the buildings and a valley swept clean of any sign of human habitation. Above the dam, the militaire *celebrated the annihilation of a group of citizens who dared to defy Coreé."*

"What's the matter?" Angelique asked anxiously.

Devin looked up to focus on her concerned face.

"You're white as a sheet," Madame Aucoin said, standing up to move to his side. "Don't you feel well?"

Devin shook his head. "I'm fine, really," he said, patting her hand. "Please sit down. It's just that Marcus and I spent one night in that valley among the ruins of Albion. I had a dream … or a vision … I'm not sure what to call it. I relived what Armand just described, only some of the details from the Chronicle are not quite accurate."

"According to your dream?" Armand asked skeptically. "This story is part of Tirolien's Chronicle, Devin. Its details aren't open to negotiation."

"If everyone died at Albion then most of your story had to be conjecture," Devin pointed out. "Or did it ever occur to you, Armand, that maybe the men who first told the story were the saboteurs who actually witnessed the flood first-hand? How else could they possibly have known any of those details? If everyone died at Albion, then how was the story passed down to us?"

"Perhaps part of it was conjecture, Devin," Armand conceded. "But you can't deny that the village was destroyed by flood and the people were drowned."

Devin held up a finger. "No, I can't but there are several points that are definitely wrong. For one, the priest survived."

"You can't base facts on a dream, Devin, no matter how vivid and detailed it was," Armand protested.

"I'm not," Devin said. "Lavender led us to the ruins of the church at Albion. The nave was torn away but below it we found steps leading down to a locked room that originally had been part of the basement. Father Sébastian died alone in that room, mourning the deaths of all those villagers who defied the government and drowned because of their dissent. His remains are still there, should you need proof, Armand, but I believe Marcus intends to destroy the key to his tomb. Father Sébastian blamed himself for not warning his parishioners in time when he saw the dam sabotaged."

Devin withdrew the journal. "This is Father Sébastian's journal. It states that the dam was blown up on Avril 12, 1406 by Gascon Forneaux."

Gaspard choked on a mouthful of wine. "Damn it, Dev! Wouldn't you know my ancestors would be involved in something nasty, even back then?"

"Maybe you were adopted," Devin answered jokingly.

"Or perhaps you are the offspring of one of your mother's torrid affairs."

Gaspard grinned. "An affair is entirely possible. My mother always had half a dozen handsome young men who were devoted to her. Maybe that's why my father has always hated me."

"And maybe it's why I have always liked you so much better than your brother," Devin added. He gestured with the journal. "We haven't read very much of this journal. We traveled until dark almost every night and a good bit of that time we were underground." He threw a hand in the air, interrupting himself. "We had an astounding revelation in the caves, too …"

Madame Aucoin placed a gentle hand on his arm. "Finish one thought before you jump to another, Devin. I'd like to hear more about this journal."

Reluctantly, Devin passed the journal over to her. He wanted so badly to be the one to share the information that they had gleaned from it. Now his eyesight had deprived him of that pleasure and someone else would read Father Sébastian's last thoughts to the group. "Would you like to read it aloud?" he asked, as though the question was only a casual one.

She took it from his hand but held the book between them on the table as though he was able to see it just as well as she could. She placed a finger on the first line and began:

"*I, Father Sébastian Chastain, priest to the people of Albion and Rodez, must record the events that led to the destruction of Albion and all its citizens. On 12 Avril 1406, Gascon Forneaux and some of his men destroyed the dam holding back the waters of Gave d'Oloron, subsequently*

165

flooding the town of Albion and drowning all of its inhabitants. I had walked down to investigate when I saw Forneaux's men near the dam. The explosion was triggered while I was still approaching. I saw the flood waters coming over a great distance from the hill above the church and ran to ring the bell to alert my parishioners but my efforts came too late. Every man, woman, and child was swept away by the onslaught and I will forever bear the guilt of their deaths. Had I only reached the church bell sooner, I might have saved some of their lives. I am leaving this journal in the hope that my sister Lavender or one of my brothers may find it and give it to my father. They are the only ones that I have shown this safe room to. Surely, news of my death will bring them here to search for answers.

"This latest outrage has sprung from the continuing feud between the Forneaux brothers over the Chancellorship of Llisé. When Gascon lost hope of any chance of becoming the Empire's ultimate ruler, he formed his own Alternative Government, designed to undermine his brother's rule. His constant attacks on the provincial residents in his brother's name are calculated to turn them against the government. He delivered the news of an exorbitant tax levied on the people of Albion by their Chancellor. When the people refused, no, rather could not pay it, he sent his men to sabotage the dam and wipe the village from the face of the earth. Unfortunately, very few people know of his duplicity. On the other hand, he continues to manufacture false rumors of the savagery of the provincial people to turn the residents of Vienne (the province which houses the Empire's capital) against those of us who dwell in the provinces. It is a plan concocted by a madman and yet no one has the power to stop him. My father has been particularly outspoken and

some days I fear for his life. Only those of us who live here are privy to the actual events that are destroying our Empire from within, like a worm hollowing out an apple until nothing remains but a worthless façade."

"Well, there you have the inception of the Shadow Government," Gaspard said. "Which Forneaux became Chancellor? I don't even know."

"Auberon," Devin said.

"But I can't see why this animosity was allowed to continue up until the present day," Gaspard replied.

Chastel placed his elbows on the table as his plate was withdrawn. "Perhaps the two factions had become so firmly established by that time that they continued to work against each other. Sometimes movements don't die with their leaders but continue to operate in the background. They transform into something completely different from their original inception. If the structure for a Shadow Government was already in place, its purpose may have altered several times in the past four hundred years. It's easy to understand how this might have created a lot of the problems we are dealing with now."

"Whatever happened to Gascon Forneaux?" Madame Aucoin asked.

Devin searched his memory. "He died a natural death. I believe he had a son by the same name who was marginally involved in the government as a minor Council Member."

"And what about Auberon?" Angelique asked.

"Auberon was assassinated in office," Devin answered. "He was poisoned at a formal dinner and died in his wife's arms. They never had any children."

"That's so sad," Angelique murmured. Gaspard covered her hand with his on the tablecloth.

Jules poured another glass of wine as servants cleared the table. "And Gascon never became Chancellor?"

"No," Devin replied. "He was always suspected of causing his brother's death though nothing was ever proven. He made a failed attempt to be elected as Chancellor the year after his brother's death but he had little support."

Gaspard shook his head and grinned. "You are like a walking Archive, Dev. Is there anything you don't know?"

Devin grunted. "There is a great deal I don't know, Gaspard." And a great deal I'll never have a chance to learn if my eyesight doesn't improve, he thought to himself. "Are there more entries in the journal, Madame?"

She nodded and continued.

"I want the Empire to know what really happened here. The dam was blown up by explosives because the residents refused to pay an exorbitant tax that Gascon levied in his brother Auberon's name. No one in this impoverished part of the province would have access to such things except for one of the Comtes from the great chateaus and they never keep explosives in any great amount. No one would have profited from the destruction of Albion except Gascon. It's the kind of spectacular event that feeds his insatiable ego. This was all so unnecessary. The residents of these Northern Provinces already fear him like they fear the rattlesnakes that lie in wait under our rocks and the wolves that roam our mountains. He does terrible things in the name of his brother, the Chancellor, and my people feared him as well."

"And there you have the beginning of the mistrust between Coreé and the provinces," Devin said, with a certain satisfaction.

"Once started, that kind of terror feeds itself and no

doubt led to the church providing a safe haven for the provincial people in danger," Chastel added.

Gaspard toyed with his butter knife, his eyes on the tablecloth. "It's difficult to imagine one man could have set this entire political situation in motion."

"I'm sure he had followers, Gaspard," Devin said. "There were probably other young men who thirsted for power and were more than happy to find a daring young leader." He nodded apologetically at Madame Aucoin. "I'm sorry, Madame. We interrupted you."

"It's quite all right," Madame Aucoin answered graciously. "I am sure this has come as a shock to all of us. Let me continue:

"It is vital that Gascon never know that I survived or that I can identify the men who brought about this tragedy. I will live in this room until my food and water are gone and then I will go to my God knowing that I have done this one small thing to expose the murderer of innocents. I only hope that my father or my brothers will investigate my death and find this journal. My sister, Lavender, knows of this safe room and will tell them how to find my remains. Barring my family's intervention, I hope this journal falls into the hands of someone who will use its contents to bring about justice for those who died here."

The room fell silent. For once the peace of Madame Aucoin's home seemed vulnerable, as though they all existed in an artificial moment in time – something as insubstantial as a bubble or as fragile as an eggshell. Around them the world rioted in chaos, murders were committed for the sake of expedience, poor people served as pawns in a diabolical chess game, and all that remained good and true about Llisé was in jeopardy.

Devin cleared his throat. "Lavender told us that her father's chateau had been burned and she feared everyone had been killed."

"It was," Armand confirmed. "His sons' families and the entire staff of the chateau were slaughtered and the buildings burned."

The muscles in Marcus' jaw twitched as their fears were substantiated with fact. "Father Sébastian was seen ringing the bell on the hillside as the flood waters descended the valley. Gascon must have feared that he survived. By killing all of Sébastian's family, he hoped to eliminate everyone who might investigate the disaster. Lavender told us the truth, then. Gascon obviously hoped to prevent any chance that the information contained in Father Sébastian's journal would be found," he said furiously.

Angelique twisted a napkin in her hands, her cheeks flushed and angry.

"He almost succeeded," Chastel commented. "It also explains why so many of the noblemen with properties in the north have avoided serving on Council. If they believed that Auberon was behind the torching of the Chastain chateau, they would fear defying the government in any way. Had you not found the journal, Devin, we would never have known the real story."

Devin released a deep breath. "The one thing that bothers me about the account from the Chronicle is that it corresponds almost exactly with what I remember from my dream. I told Marcus at the time that it was as though I was actually seeing Albion for the few moments before its destruction and then for the few minutes when the tragedy occurred. Whoever prepared that story for the Chronicle told it like an eyewitness. Is it possible that one of Gascon's men repeated that story to people in other towns and it eventually became part of the Chronicle, Armand?"

Armand nodded. "That could have happened. It doesn't explain your visit with Lavender and your affinity for the people of Albion." He shifted uneasily. "I have to ask – is it possible that these things were a result of your head injury?"

Devin grunted. "Marcus thought the same thing at the time but he and I both spoke with Lavender. We spent two nights and a full day with her. We touched her, she ate with us."

"And yet you said that you touched Jeanette, too," Armand said gently.

"The difference is that Marcus saw Lavender, also. She gave him that carved head. I'll admit that when I saw Jeanette it was a dream," Devin said. "I can't explain what I felt in the valley of Albion. That place is haunted by the terror and screams of those dying people. There is a pathos about it that will probably linger for centuries." He shrugged his shoulders uneasily. "Perhaps I'm just more sensitive to it than some others might be."

"I understand what you are talking about, Devin. I felt the same thing in our chateau," Angelique said quietly. "The rooms and hallways will always hold the terror of my family's slaughter. Some places retain strong emotions and some people are able to feel those sensations much more deeply than others. I know I do."

Devin wished his comments hadn't resurrected Angelique's tragedy for her. She had few enough moments where she was insulated from the horror of her family's murder. "I'm sorry that our ghosts have linked us when so many far nicer things might have formed a connection between us instead," he replied.

Angelique smiled. "*Grandmère* has been teaching me that people aren't just positive or negative things but a mixture of both. I simply have had some experience with ghosts and now, unfortunately, so have you."

Madame Aucoin turned a page or two ahead in the journal. "Father Sébastian has included a list of the men, women, and children who died at Albion."

"Perhaps if you have time later, could you read them to me?" Devin asked. "I would like to match names with the faces I saw in my dream, if I can."

"I will make time," Madame Aucoin said with a gentle smile.

Armand closed his eyes. A sound of despair rose in his throat as he shook his head. "The name Albion has become associated with utter destruction. Until now, it was assumed that it was retribution for their refusal to pay their taxes after a summer of poor harvests. It was a needless tragedy one way or the other. It makes me furious that men of wealth and privilege could value life so little."

"Father Sébastian was also born a man of wealth and privilege," Devin reminded him. "But he chose to devote his life to God and the people of his parishes." He spread his hands, hoping to support his argument. "I have been extremely impressed and reassured that the one constant support of the provincial people has been the church. They have maintained the tunnels to facilitate their escape and have continued that mission for hundreds of years until our present time. Not only that, towns all over the Northern Provinces have assimilated these refugees into their midst. This secret has been kept by countless dozens of priests and who knows how many provincials. It has never been revealed to anyone but those in danger. We, at this table, must be as zealous in guarding that secret as closely as they have."

"Do you honestly believe that no one ever revealed the secret?" Gaspard asked.

"I've seen proof of it," Devin answered.

"As have I," Marcus added.

Devin regarded Armand. The skin across his jaws and cheekbones was stretched taut; he looked old and tired and fragile. Only his eyes burned with an inner light born of hope. "Do you actually believe, then, that my Jeanette is still alive, Monsieur Roché?" he asked formally.

Devin met his gaze unwaveringly. "I do, Armand, I truly do."

Armand stood up and held his hand across the table to Devin. "Then I believe you, Monsieur Roché, and I will follow you anywhere you guide me. Together we will find my little girl and when we do, you have my blessing to marry her. I will put no more impediments in your way!"

CHAPTER 22

Old Alliances

Madame Aucoin forbade further conversation after dinner. Devin was entirely happy to accept her ultimatum. The thought of at least one night amid such luxury made him anxious for bed. He walked up the stairs with Gaspard while Jules and Marcus made hastily arranged security plans in the hall below.

Gaspard followed Devin to his bedroom door. "I was afraid I wouldn't see you again," he said awkwardly. "When word came down that Marcus had shot and killed you, I thought the world was going to end. If even Marcus could be bought off, there would be no hope for the empire, at all."

"Well, he wasn't," Devin assured him. "He was just doing his job. You can relieve your mind about that."

Gaspard hesitated. "Can I talk to you for a moment?"

Devin laughed. "I believe that's what we are doing."

"Privately," Gaspard said, gesturing toward Devin's bedroom. "I don't want to be overheard."

Devin opened his door and ushered Gaspard in. "What is it?" he asked.

Gaspard perched on the window seat. "While you were gone, Angelique and I have grown closer."

Devin smiled. "I noticed that at dinner. I'm happy for both of you."

"It's just that she seems to have formed this connection with you," Gaspard said without meeting Devin's eyes. "I have tried to be a better person. I haven't gotten drunk in days."

"Good for you," Devin commented, sitting down on the bed. It was so soft; he could barely restrain himself from lying back right then and drowning himself in its luxury.

"Angelique has been seeking me out, spending more time with me while you were gone. When she thought you were dead, I was the one she came to for comfort. She cried in my arms."

Devin took a deep breath. "And you think this will stop because I'm alive?"

Gaspard hesitated. "I just think that she has always been attracted to you over me."

"I hope you know, I have never encouraged that, Gaspard," Devin assured him.

"I didn't mean that you had," Gaspard hurried to agree. "It just seems natural on her part. I was hoping ..."

"That I would make it clear that I'm not interested in her in that way?" Devin asked.

"Don't make it sound so calculated!" Gaspard protested. "I wouldn't hurt her for the world."

"I didn't mean to," Devin answered. "I have always tried to discourage her attention. I have no romantic interest in her, Gaspard. You have my word on that."

"Thank you," he said. "I hope that someday I can ask her to marry me but I don't think that Madame Aucoin views me as a suitable companion."

"I've never seen anything to substantiate that," Devin said. "I'm glad you have curtailed your drinking though. We are all going to have to keep our wits about us if we are going to arrive in Coreé safely."

"I was hoping that I might be able to travel with Angelique and Madame Aucoin," Gaspard blurted out. "I want to protect her and I can't do that trekking through God knows what in these mountains."

Devin shook his head. "I don't think that's possible. You might put her in further danger if you go with them. If you are recognized then any attempt they have made to demonstrate that they are simply making a casual trip to the capital for the holiday season becomes a deliberate lie. You don't want to be responsible for landing the woman you love in prison, do you?"

"Of course not," Gaspard answered defensively. "I'm trying to help her – not hurt her."

"Then you'll have to fall in with the plan that we decide on," Devin answered. "If you truly love her, you won't put her in jeopardy just because you want to be with her."

Gaspard sat quietly for a moment, plucking at the quilted pattern on the cushioned window seat. He avoided looking at Devin. "I also don't want to slough through snow drifts and go to bed hungry every night," he admitted.

"Oh God!" said Devin, standing up. "Is that what this is really about? I can't believe you would make a decision like this based on your own inconvenience. People are dying every day because of this so-called Shadow Government and you're worried about getting cold feet? Go to bed, will you? I don't have time for this tonight. I'm bone tired and my head aches. Talk to me in the morning when you are more reasonable."

"God, you're touchy!" Gaspard commented, getting to his feet. "It hasn't been all sweetness and light here, either! We actually thought you were dead and that Marcus would expose us all. We came to Amiens to make plans to escape before La Paix could be found and raided. Can you imagine how we felt? The one place in this empire where I have felt truly safe since we left Coreé, and even it might have fallen because one man decided to sell out to the other side!"

"But Marcus didn't," Devin responded.

"We have only his word for that," Gaspard continued. "Can you swear to everything he did while you lay bleeding on that mountain slope?"

"No, I can't," Devin said. "But I don't need to. If Marcus had wanted me dead, he would have shot me through the heart instead of nicking my head. He wouldn't have come back to take me to safety and he would never have returned here. He had dozens of opportunities to kill me if that's what he wanted to do, but he didn't. Consider the fact that he even disobeyed my father's orders and didn't kill me. I have no intention of doubting his loyalty to me!"

Gaspard's tone was placating. "I'm not trying to make you angry."

"Well, you have succeeded very well for someone who isn't trying," Devin snapped. "Stay here if you like when we go to Coreé. I don't care. You'll be safe, provided for, and warm, but you cannot travel with Madame Aucoin. I will not allow you to put that dear lady's life in jeopardy!"

"You act as though I am thinking only of myself," Gaspard objected.

"Aren't you?" Devin asked. He dropped his face in his hands. "I'm sorry, Gaspard, I really am. I can't discuss this anymore right now. I'm exhausted and I have to get some sleep. I apologize if I've hurt your feelings. Please, just give me tonight to recover my wits and we'll talk in the morning."

Gaspard inclined his head. "Good night, then."

"Good night," Devin said as he closed the door.

CHAPTER 23

Old Habits Die Hard

The draperies in the dining room were thrown back. The view of the harbor below them was spectacular. Another sunny day provided ample light to set the lake water sparkling below them and the blue expanse was dotted with fishing boats. Devin was the last one down. Gaspard didn't appear at breakfast, at all, although the smell of his favorite cinnamon buns wafted through the house.

Devin pushed his chair back and stood up, leaving the others sipping coffee at the table. "Would you mind if I check on Gaspard?" he asked. "He and I had a rather heated discussion last night."

Madame Aucoin frowned. "I'm sorry to hear that. Is there anything I can do?"

He gave her a reassuring smile. "No, I'll smooth things over. It was just a disagreement over the way to proceed."

Taking the stairs two at a time, Devin reached Gaspard's room and knocked softly. When there was no answer he opened the door and blinked at the darkened room. The draperies were drawn and Gaspard was still in bed, a curled-up form in the midst of a pile of rumpled covers. An empty wine bottle lay on the floor by the bed and the room reeked of alcohol.

"Gaspard?" Devin said.

The mumbled response was unintelligible and belligerent. Devin turned around and left, closing the door more loudly than necessary on the way out. If a disagreement was enough to send Gaspard on another binge, he had no doubt what part of Gaspard's problem was with their trek over the mountains. Food would be scarce and they would be carrying no alcohol.

Devin stood a moment at the top of the stairs trying to regain his composure. Gaspard had certainly received more than he had signed up for on this trip and that was Devin's fault. He admitted that. The revelations about Gaspard's family had been shocking and deciding on the necessity of his father's assassination was heartbreaking, but his drinking had reached monumental proportions. Devin couldn't reason with him when he was drunk. No one could. He would simply have to wait until later and hope that at the same time he had a few moments of patience, Gaspard would have a moment of clarity.

"Is everything all right?" Marcus asked from the bottom of the stairs.

Devin shrugged. "Gaspard is sleeping off a hangover. There's no sense in talking to him now."

Marcus walked halfway up the stairs to meet him as Devin continued. "I guess Gaspard hasn't been drinking as much in the last few weeks while we were away. Apparently, I set him off last night. He wanted to travel with Madame Aucoin and Angelique. He said he could protect them. I explained that instead of providing protection he might be placing their lives in greater danger. It turned out that his real concern is that he doesn't want to cross the mountains on foot."

"No one is looking forward to that," Marcus said, descending beside him. "But it has to be done."

"I told him that," Devin said. "He was annoyed. I was angry because I was tired. It didn't go well."

"Let him alone then. This morning we will make our plans. He'll have to fall in with them, no matter how much it inconveniences him, or he'll have to stay here and take his chances. There are times I wish I hadn't hauled him on board when we left Coreé."

Devin didn't answer but he felt the same way.

Angelique rose from her chair when they entered the dining room, her peach gown reflecting the color of her cheeks. "Is Gaspard all right?" she asked.

"He's sleeping in this morning," Devin answered diplomatically. "I guess we talked too late last night." For the first time, Devin realized there were restrictions to living in town. He wished he could escape to the woodland gardens that surrounded La Paix under the statuesque evergreens or stand by the waterfall that plunged down the valley and crashed on the rocks below. Here there was a chance of being recognized if he even took a walk by the harbor dressed like a gentleman. Oddly enough, he had been freer to go where he wished when he was plastered head to toe in filth and his clothes were ragged and torn.

"I think you should leave tonight," Jules said, once Devin and Marcus were seated. "There have been several soldiers patrolling the streets outside the house. It may be nothing or someone may have seen you two enter the house last night."

"There is a boat tied up at the dock almost directly below the house. The captain has been in my employ for years," said Madame Aucoin. "There is a narrow access road that we use to board. We'll travel across the lake and then continue downriver to Vienne. That way we'll avoid leaving from a main port like Pirée. I've invited Annette Dubois and her daughter Sophie to accompany us. They had planned on spending the winter in Coreé, also. By traveling with friends, the trip should appear completely ordinary. We'll leave tomorrow morning."

Devin's heart sank when Jules announced their departure was set for tonight. What he wouldn't give for another night in that sumptuous bed! Apparently, that was not to be. "And what is the best way for us to cross the mountains from here?" he asked.

"Jules and I were talking," Chastel said. "If it's all right with you, I think we should leave Amiens and go back around the eastern side of the lake. Initially, following the path of the river would give us an easier route to follow but the banks are lined with little towns. We'd be better off retracing your steps to the west side of the lake and heading directly south from there. There is no direct road or trail over the mountains. Jules has suggested a guide he trusts, but I wanted to consult with you first."

Devin glanced at Marcus. "How comfortable are you in navigating the Alps?"

"I'm not," Marcus answered. "I traveled them once as a young man but I couldn't guide you safely. We'll need someone else."

"Can you vouch for this guide, Jules?" Devin asked. "The more people we include in this plot, the greater chance there is of betrayal."

"I'm well aware of that, monsieur," Jules said. "But Georges' loyalty to Madame Aucoin is absolute."

"Georges?" Devin asked in surprise. "Georges Mazzei?"

"The same," Jules answered. "He is a former soldier. He offered to make the trip, monsieur."

Devin grinned. "I have absolutely no objection. I'm just surprised."

"Georges has served this house in a number of unconventional ways," Madame Aucoin added. "He has my complete trust."

Devin inclined his head. "Then he has mine, as well. If Armand is traveling with you, how do you plan to disguise him?"

"As a servant," Jules answered. "He has already been fitted with a uniform."

Devin accepted a steaming cup of *café au lait*, cherishing the warmth in his hands as he listened. "You will arrive several weeks before we do, Madame. How will you spend your time?"

"We will open the town house, visit with old friends, and wait until you arrive. The more normal our visit appears, the less chance there will be for speculation. It will be a good time to introduce Angelique to my friends and hopefully we will receive a number of invitations to attend holiday galas."

"Have we decided on a plan and place for the assassination?" Devin asked, hating to have those words leave his lips.

"That is totally up to you," Chastel answered. "But we think Angelique is the only one who can get near enough to René Forneaux to kill him."

Devin glanced at Angelique, dressed this morning in her

183

pale-peach satin. Two braids were drawn back on each side of her head while the rest of her hair tumbled free like a burnished waterfall. "I am very concerned about you, Angelique. Murder is a terrible thing for anyone to undertake. It requires courage and strength. Anyone of us will gladly take this task from you. There is no reason that you have to be involved, at all. I don't want you to feel we are pushing you into this against your will. You have only to say 'no' and we will never broach the subject again."

Angelique held her head high. "I volunteered to kill him, Devin. And Jules has been giving me instructions with a stiletto."

Devin winced. It felt profoundly wrong to ask a sixteen-year-old girl to kill a man.

"One of the holiday parties would provide the best opportunity," Jules said, taking a cinnamon bun from a platter heaped high with pastries.

The enormity of Angelique's task hadn't affected Jules' appetite, Devin thought. Surely, he wasn't the only one who wished to spare her from the violent aspects of their trip back to Coreé.

"But at some point, we still need to present the journal to the Council. It is the only factual information we have gathered against Forneaux and the Shadow Government. Keep in mind, it isn't only René who is at fault. His followers may constitute a larger group than we anticipate," Devin pointed out. "We can't sway the rest of Council if we are all in prison."

"I, for one, would not survive prison," Gaspard commented sulkily from the doorway. His hair stood up, tousled and uncombed, his shirt hung open over his trousers. He was still in his stocking feet.

Devin stood up, not knowing what to expect. "Then we will do everything we can to avoid that," he replied tactfully. He cut Gaspard off before he reached the table and took his arm. "Let's go back upstairs for a moment."

Gaspard wrenched his arm free. "I've just come from there. I don't want to go back upstairs."

Devin took his arm more firmly. "You're half dressed," he hissed. "Come back upstairs with me."

Gaspard teetered backwards unsteadily and slammed his fist into Devin's jaw. Devin went down hard, barely missing the corner of the table.

Devin was aware of both Jules and Marcus grabbing Gaspard's arms but Gaspard struggled in their grasp. Devin righted himself with the aid of Armand's chair. "Gaspard," he sputtered, blood dripping from his lip. "What is the matter with you?"

"What is the matter with me?" Gaspard demanded belligerently, swaying between Marcus and Jules. "Don't blame this on me!"

"Blame what on you?" Devin asked, trying to keep his voice level even though he wanted to scream at him. "What are you talking about?"

"Don't do that!" Gaspard protested sarcastically. "Don't pretend to be all reasonable and nice. Why can't I be the nice one sometimes?"

Devin frowned. "You are the nice one sometimes, Gaspard. What is this about?"

"Everything was fine until you came back," Gaspard muttered. "I didn't want you to be dead but life was easier without having to live up to your perfection every day of my life! I had Angelique all to myself. Madame Aucoin and I played cards together. Even Jules and I got along. And

185

then you arrived and my life is ruined. Everything is 'Devin,' 'Devin,' 'Devin!' It isn't fair."

Devin just stood and gaped. Gaspard still reeked enough of alcohol that he could be drunk again, or still drunk, or just having a horribly maudlin hangover. He wasn't certain how to proceed and then Gaspard dropped to his knees.

"Why does my father have to be the corrupt one?" he sobbed. "Why couldn't it be your father, Devin? I can't do this. I can't plan my own father's murder and I can't stay here and listen to the rest of you plan it!"

Angelique slid off her chair. A soft rustle of satin announced her descent onto the floor. She knelt beside Gaspard and took him into her arms. Rocking him back and forth, she murmured, "I'm so sorry, Gaspard. I'm so sorry."

CHAPTER 24

Honesty

Marcus and Jules hovered, not knowing what to do. Chastel handed Devin a napkin to wipe the blood, which was dripping off his chin. Everything simply stopped for a moment and then Devin knelt beside Gaspard, too.

"You need to go back up with me," he said softly. "We've encountered higher hurdles and we've managed. Come upstairs."

Gaspard nodded, mopping at his face with his handkerchief.

Devin stood up and offered him a hand. "Come on."

Gaspard leaned on a chair and struggled upright. "I'm sorry for ruining everyone's breakfast, Madame," he said quietly. Angelique wisely moved aside and let Devin guide him into the hall and up the beautiful staircase, which neither of them had time or inclination to appreciate this morning.

Marcus followed them out into the hall but he made no attempt to go upstairs with them. Devin opened Gaspard's door and led him inside. Gaspard slumped on the bed and Devin left him alone, busying himself with straightening up the room and collecting two empty wine bottles from under the bed.

"You must hate me," Gaspard said, after a moment.

Devin chuckled. "I was thinking the same thing. You certainly indicated that you've had quite enough of me."

Gaspard looked at him, his eyes red rimmed and his nose running. "And yet it was you who brought me upstairs? Why?"

Devin dumped an armload of dirty clothes in the corner. "Because you have been my friend for as long as I can remember. Because you agreed to come to the provinces and you have been beaten and kidnapped and scared out of your wits, all because you were my friend."

"I was beaten and kidnapped because my father wanted to kill us both," Gaspard answered. "I assume he still would want to do that if he knew we were alive." He looked down and seemed to notice for the first time that his shirt was unbuttoned. Fumbling, he pulled the edges together, matching up buttons and buttonholes. "Can you imagine how that makes me feel?"

Devin sat down on a chair by the bed. "Tell me," he said.

Gaspard held a shaking hand out. "One side of me hates him. He is my father and yet he wrote to tell me that he has named my younger brother as his heir and he has disowned me. In the newspaper report of my disappearance, he referred to me as his heir, again. I don't think he knows how he feels about me! He has tried to have you and me both killed to further his agenda in Coreé and he is conspiring to assassinate the Chancellor or discredit him." He extended the other hand. "But one part of me remembers what he was like before my brother was born. How proud my father was of me and how he showed me off to all his friends. He used to call me his 'little man' as though there was already some sort of pact between us for the future. It all began to fall apart after Louis was born. Louis was smarter and quicker. He excelled at dozens of things I merely dabbled at. My failure at the *Académie* was the final straw." He paused a moment, stuffing his shirt into his trousers. "I wonder what would have happened had I stayed home and worked with a tutor over the summer."

"I never gave you the chance," Devin admitted. "I assumed you still wanted to go with me and when Marcus offered to carry you onboard, I let him. That part, at least, is my fault, Gaspard. And you have never berated me for it. You claimed you wanted to come and you stuck by me even though my whole project fell apart."

"I did want to come with you, more than anything, Dev. I needed time to think. I needed to get away from Coreé, from the *Académie*, and mostly from my father. Had I stayed, I might never have known what kind of man he truly is."

Devin cleared his throat. "There have been a number of unpleasant revelations on this trip."

"Do you think Louis is part of this Shadow Government?"

Devin shrugged. "I don't know. He's still young. He's only fourteen. I'm not sure your father would trust him with that kind of information."

"I hate it when Angelique talks about killing him. I love her, but how could our relationship survive if she kills my father?"

"I wish she weren't the one that seems most suitable for the job," Devin agreed. "Maybe we can find some way around that."

"I know it isn't anything you would ever have planned. She hates him so and with good reason. Devin, how can I reconcile the man who loved me as a child with the man who murdered her family?"

Devin took a deep breath. "I think each of us has the capacity for good or evil. I don't pretend to know why some people turn toward good and others turn away from it."

"You do know that I'm jealous of you," Gaspard admitted. "I have been for a long time. Your parents always doted on you – so did your older brothers. You never take a false step and the rest of us poor idiots just totter from one mishap to the next. How did you get to be the Golden Boy?"

"I never did anything intentionally to earn anyone's friendship or approval," Devin assured him. "I have only lived my life the best way I could. And don't pretend I haven't made mistakes, because I have."

"Like what?" Gaspard asked.

"Like hiding the Head Master's robe at the *université*?" Devin told him. "I never intended on taking it: the opportunity just presented itself. He shouldn't have left it in the dining hall where just anyone could pick it up. I wonder if it's still under the floorboards in our old dormitory room?"

"Don't take all the credit for it," Gaspard said with a smile. "I'm the one who hid it under there!"

Devin laughed. "That's right; you did! But I adjusted the clock in the bell tower to chime two hours ahead of the proper time. I had the entire faculty bouncing out of bed two hours earlier than usual."

"Then you stepped up like a hero and offered to fix it – just as though you'd had nothing to do with it malfunctioning in the first place!"

190

"I thought that was clever," Devin said, nodding. "A little misdirection never hurts."

"But you never got caught," Gaspard remarked. "Because no one ever suspected Devin Roché would cause any trouble."

"So there," Devin said with satisfaction. "You have just proven that I am not the Golden Boy but a sneaky little troublemaker, like everyone else at school."

"You are not Gaspard Forneaux either," Gaspard answered forlornly. "What's my life going to be like when this is over? Will people think I was involved in my father's treachery?"

"Hardly," Devin retorted. "He tried to have you killed. Had you colluded with his plan, you would never have been targeted."

"And what about Angelique and me?" Gaspard whispered. "Is there hope for that?"

"Gaspard, Angelique's family was murdered by your father's order and ultimately he may die by her hand. For her, that may equal the playing field. She seems to accept you for who you are, not who your father is. She was the first one to try to comfort you at the table a few minutes ago. She must care a great deal about you."

Gaspard huffed out a breath. "I'm such an ass. How can I face everyone downstairs after that performance?"

"It might be worthwhile trying to face them now," Devin suggested. "The longer you put it off, the harder it will be." He stood up. "You'd need to comb your hair first. It's standing up like a chicken's."

"Chickens don't have hair. And how would you know anything about chickens anyway?" Gaspard asked, reaching for his comb.

"I had a very close relationship with one on the road to Amiens," Devin retorted. "She was bound for market and escaped. The last time I saw her she was foraging in the marketplace for food."

"Did you have something to do with her escape?" Gaspard asked suspiciously.

"Absolutely not," Devin replied. "Shall we go down?"

Gaspard nodded. "I think I'm as ready as I'll ever be."

"There are cinnamon buns," Devin reminded him.

"There is always that," Gaspard agreed with a grin.

They met Marcus halfway down the stairs as he was coming up. "Devin, you need to come down. The newspaper just arrived from Coreé. Something else has happened!"

CHAPTER 25

Bardic Wisdom

"What now?" Devin asked as he followed Marcus into the dining room. "Don't make me wait to find out; this morning has already been filled with enough tension."

Madame Aucoin handed Marcus the newspaper and he turned to display it to Devin. Even with blurry eyes, the headline was easy to read. "*Chancellor Detained on Charges of Treason*," Devin read aloud. "My God, Marcus, what could he possibly have done that would give them grounds for such a thing?"

"Can you read the rest?" Marcus asked.

"No," Devin answered, shaking his head and handing over the paper.

Marcus laid the paper on the table, amidst the debris from breakfast. "*Chancellor Vincent Roché was detained this morning in Council Chambers on a charge of treason brought by René Forneaux, André Bouton, and François D'Aramitz stemming from an investigation into the apparent deaths of Gaspard Forneaux and Devin Roché.*"

"There wasn't time for news of my 'apparent' death to

reach Coreé!" Devin sputtered. "And René was the one who planned to murder both Gaspard and me – not my father."

Marcus waited for a pause in his tirade and continued. *"Both young men traveled to the provinces in the hope of gathering some of the Provincial Chronicles. Forneaux believes that the Chronicles themselves held information damaging to Roché, in that they differ with reports signed by the Chancellor and housed in the Archives. An investigation has begun and Roché, while detained from leaving the city, remains in office."*

"We have to get home as soon as possible," Devin said, his hands shaking. "The penalty for treason is death! René has blamed his own plan on my father and has no doubt planted evidence to support it. We need to leave, Marcus. We need to leave right now."

"Devin," Chastel said quietly. "The wheels of government move slowly. We have at least a three-week trek ahead of us if the weather holds. I may as well say it now; it won't be your fault if we don't arrive in time to save your father. While your father hoped you might be able to provide him with information about the conditions in the provinces, that was never your intention in coming here. When you realized that Forneaux was behind the Shadow Government, you did everything a son could possibly do to gather the evidence your father needs to fight against it. We will leave tonight, as planned. We still require some time to pack but we'll leave as soon as it is dark."

Devin felt a gnawing emptiness in his stomach that had nothing to do with hunger. What more could possibly happen? Their trip had gone very wrong on this end and yet at home things had gone from bad to worse also.

"Do you remember that I told you before we left, Devin,

that we were on the verge of revolution?" Marcus said, his voice unusually gentle. "I suggested that your father might have allowed you to come on this trip to get you out of the city, away from harm. Ironically, we are rushing back into the midst of that turmoil with information that he didn't even know existed and now may save his position and his life. Things have a way of working out. Trust that events are unfolding the way they are meant to. You can do no more than you have already done."

Madame Aucoin patted the chair next to her. "Sit down, please. Neither of you boys have had any breakfast. And who knows, tomorrow it may be back to raw fish and rabbits! Eat while you can."

Devin slid into his chair wishing he could laugh at her joke but the situation was too serious.

Gaspard's face was white. He stood for a moment and then sat down next to Angelique. "This morning I knelt in this room and I cried for a father I lost years ago," he said. "It's time to put that memory aside and deal with the man who is now threatening Llisé and the people that I love. I apologize for my emotional display earlier. I will do my very best to help you, Devin, in any way I can."

"As will the rest of us," Madame Aucoin assured him.

"I just keep thinking," Devin said. "What if they execute my father on René's trumped-up charges? I can't live with knowing that there was something I could have done and didn't do."

"We will do the best we can," Marcus said. "You cannot do any more than that. And honestly, your father would probably prefer that you remain here where you are safe."

"I am done with staying safe," Devin answered. "If my father's life is at stake then I will stand with him. My brothers may be in jeopardy, too, and I am the only one in a position to help right now."

Madame Aucoin put a cinnamon bun on his plate along with two sausages and half of the remaining eggs. "Then eat, please," she said.

Devin glanced at her eyes, still bright and unfaded. The crinkles at the corners looked like tiny sunbursts. If ever anyone exuded calm, it was she, and he found himself wishing he could travel along with her, just as Gaspard did.

"Devin, did I ever tell you the story of Nicholas Lestrange?" Armand asked.

"No," Devin answered. "And perhaps now isn't the time."

Armand grinned, some of his old bravado surfacing again. "Now is the perfect time," he replied slyly. "Please concentrate, Monsieur Roché, and you can add it to what you know of Arcadia's Chronicle."

Devin put a hand to his forehead in annoyance at the change in subject but he tried to drive everything else from his mind and listen.

"Nicholas Lestrange, who had been a successful farm manager in Ombria, moved to Arcadia and asked for work at the estate of Ambroise Delacroix. Now, Nicholas was an honest man. He was warned about working for Delacroix and knew his reputation but he took the job anyway, saying work was scarce. Delacroix reluctantly extended Nicholas a trial period of two years, at which point he would be reevaluated.

"When Nicholas first took over the position, he found out very quickly that Delacroix had instructed his former farm manager to cheat his customers by adding a small weight to the market scale so that they received less of his products for their money. Delacroix sold only his weakest,

smallest stock at exorbitant rates but claimed it came from finest lineage. He lent money and charged far too much interest. When the borrowers were unable to repay, he appropriated their lands or their homes.

"Nicholas settled into the manager's house with his wife and two children. He managed Delacroix's stables and his fields and also the crops he sent to market. The first thing Nicholas did was to remove the weight from the market scale. He sold the smallest stock for half price and sold prime stock at a good profit. He was always careful to retain the very best to replenish his master's breeding stock. He cut the rate of interest Delacroix charged in half but he lent to more people and allowed them additional time to pay.

"Delacroix was extremely pleased with the income his new farm manager managed to bring in. His customers increased, the number of people he lent money to doubled, and he acquired a reputation for selling the finest stock in Arcadia. One day when he was at the local tavern a man came up to him and thanked him for allowing him additional time to pay off his loan. Delacroix was cordial but inside he was furious. He didn't even finish his drink but rode to Nicholas' house immediately.

"Now, Nicholas was at the dinner table and Delacroix called him outside. First, he told him that he was fired. Second, he told him about the man at the tavern and demanded an explanation. Nicholas knew this day was coming and explained how he had increased Delacroix's income and improved his reputation by the changes he had made to his business. Delacroix sputtered and yelled. After vowing to fire Nicholas twice more, he finally realized that Nicholas had given him something he had never been able to achieve for himself: the reputation of being a shrewd but *honest businessman. He asked Nicholas to become his farm manager permanently and increased his pay."*

Devin leveled a glance at Armand. "And you are telling me this because …"

"Because it shows that one man can make a massive change," Armand responded. "Nicholas could have been fired or sent to prison for adjusting the way his master did business. Instead he was rewarded. You may be one person, Devin, but you can turn this around. You can be the catalyst for change. Don't ever doubt it!"

CHAPTER 26

Remembrance

After breakfast Madame Aucoin invited Devin into the study and closed the door. "Would you like me to read the names from Father Sébastian's journal?" she asked. "I thought it might be something that you would prefer to do in private."

"Thank you," Devin said, touched by her ability to always read people's emotions so clearly.

They sat down at the table, she at the end and Devin next to her at the corner. Again, she followed the script with her finger, pointing out where she was on the page.

"Was there someone in particular that you were interested in?" she asked. "Or shall I read the entire list?"

"I'd like to hear them all but there was a baby. Her mother was washing clothes and she was sitting beside her, wiggling her toes in the damp earth. She was giggling and happy. I can't get the image out of my mind."

"You saw this in your dream?"

"I know it sounds strange, but whatever Armand thinks, for those few moments, I was there among them. I know that I was. I saw their pleasure in that first spring day. I heard their laughter, and no matter how long I live, I will never forget their screams."

Madame Aucoin ran her finger down the list. "*Aimée Granger, age 11 months*? Does that sound about right?"

Devin nodded silently.

"Her mother's name was Corinne Granger and her father was Gustave. He was the blacksmith."

Devin remembered them all, saw them so clearly in his mind that he felt he could reach out and touch them. "There were three young boys swinging on a rope out over the water."

"*Alain Mason, age 10 years, Roland Favager, age 10 years, & Jérôme Favager, age 8 years*," Madame Aucoin read out.

Devin grimaced. "They were having such a wonderful time, laughing and joking and disobeying their parents. I wish I could simply remember that part and forget the rest."

"If you could, Devin, you wouldn't feel so deeply about these people and the terrible wrong that was done to them. That's what we must keep foremost in our minds – especially in Gaspard's. He is overwhelmed by the few kind gestures his father ever made to him and it overshadows the present danger to all of us. You are his friend and you need to reiterate the fact that his father tried to kill you both and that you are still in terrible danger."

"Gaspard is not the most reasonable person, even when he's sober, but I will do my best," Devin agreed. "Could you read the entire list for me, please? I'm sorry to be a bother."

Madame Aucoin squeezed his hand. "You are never a bother, my dear. You remind me of my son. You are so much like him, did you know that? He loved his library and his precious books and he loved the history of Llisé. But most of all he loved its people – the simple provincial people who plowed his fields and tended his crops. I sometimes think it was his idealism that killed him, Devin, and I don't want the same thing to kill you."

Devin tried to reassure her with a smile. "François risked his life to get the Bishop's Book to my father. He undertook the errand himself instead of passing it off to someone else. I can't leave this task to anyone else either." He put his hand on top of hers on the table. "Have you considered that maybe that is the idealist's lot in life? Perhaps we pave the way for change. A good man's death can sway the future. If that is what God put me here on this earth for, I can live with that."

"What of Jeanette?" she asked. "She didn't fall in love with a martyr."

He shrugged. "I try to stay strong for Armand but I have no way of knowing if she survived. The fact that I dreamed of her frightened me."

Madame Aucoin frowned. "Frightened you how?"

"After I was shot, all my dreams were about dead people," Devin said. "I asked Jeanette if I had died and she said 'no.' Perhaps I should have asked if she had died but I never did." "You were out of your head, Devin. I truly believe that when we love someone we form an unbreakable bond that transcends death. There have been times when my dear husband has come to me in dreams with reassurance or advice. I believe he is speaking to me just as surely as you are sitting beside me. His spirit watches over me still and always will until I go to join him."

Devin felt his heart stop. "Then you think Jeanette may be dead?"

"No, no, that's not what I mean. But I think it's possible that just as in death my husband still speaks to me, Jeanette may speak to you from wherever she is. If you two truly love each other, then she must feel your pain and respond to it."

"I wish she could guide me to her," Devin said. "I worry for Armand. He has aged so much since she disappeared. I want him to live to see her again. That would mean more to me than holding her in my own arms. I hope that they will see each other again."

"Armand tried to tell you that things work out for the best when good men work together. I'll keep him fed and healthy while he is with me." She shifted to face him. "Devin, I hate to bring this up now but we left both of your cloaks and your harps at La Paix. If either of us was caught with them we would be detained and you and Armand would be killed. I promise when this is over, you'll have yours back."

Devin stilled the disappointment he felt. The cloak was a gift from his father and Jeanette had embroidered it. He had two reasons that made it very dear to him. "I realize it is not very important right now," he agreed reluctantly. "Maybe someday I can add more provinces' symbols to the back. Perhaps, I will start with Arcadia since I only learned a small part of its chronicle. That will give me an excuse to come back to visit you."

Madame Aucoin bent her head over the journal, her silver hair shining in the gas lights that flared in the wall sconces. She pronounced each name clearly, pausing after each one in case Devin had a comment or remembrance that he wanted to share. Albion had few residents and yet the list seemed overly long. It was impossible to put names to all the faces and Devin was frustrated at not being able to match up all the names with the people he had seen.

"You've no idea what having trouble with my eyesight means to me," he said when Madame Aucoin finished. "My life has been surrounded by books and manuscripts. I've been trained to spot minute facts and details in the Archives and copy brittle ancient texts by hand. At the time that I left, I was considered the very best in the department." He raked his hair back from his forehead. "I don't know what I will do now. Apparently, my education has been for nothing – all those years of study lost because of a gunshot wound. It gives new credence to my father's objections to my trip."

"You still have your memory," Madame Aucoin reminded him. "You know more than most men learn in a lifetime."

"It's not enough though. There is always more to learn."

"And there are different ways to learn it," she countered. "Look at your success with Armand. Even he has accepted that you don't need to repeat stories from the Chronicles over and over to remember them. You hear them once and that is enough. That is a rare gift, Devin. Don't ever minimize its importance."

"I don't mean to sound ungrateful," he said. "It was just that I thought I had my life planned. Now I feel as though I have to start all over again."

"Unfortunately, that is life, my dear. I planned to grow old with my husband, to share long evenings by the fire. I thought we would look forward to visits from our grandchildren together. I thank the Lord every day that you brought Angelique to me. We aren't meant to grow old alone. You've given me a rare gift and I treasure it every day."

They sat quietly for a few moments. The gentle hiss of

the gas lights punctuated by the ticking of the huge grand-father clock and the muffled movements of the household going about their morning tasks formed a peaceful backdrop for their thoughts.

"Devin," Madame Aucoin said, breaking the silence. "You mentioned at dinner last night that you had found something in the caves. I purposely directed our conversation away from it because I didn't want you to discuss it with everyone at the table. I'm fairly certain I know what you were referring to. I think you need to find a private moment to share the information with Chastel, too, but it should go no further than that."

Devin frowned. "I would think you would be proud to disseminate the information that your two families are the only true natives of Llisé."

"My family has always been proud of that fact but can't you see why we wouldn't want it to become public knowledge?" she asked. "Apparently there is something very different about us, some innate protection that allows us to shift from human to falcon. You have seen it in Chastel and his ability to shape shift into a wolf but understanding the process is difficult even for us. I believe the ability first came unbidden. It was strictly a defense mechanism and then later it became more refined. Something we could do at will. I still fly above these mountains but I do so when I please to. Our change isn't triggered by danger or terror like the Chastel family's seems to be. It is a skill that is taught."

Devin interrupted her. "Madame, is there any chance your son escaped the ambush that killed his bodyguards?"

"As a falcon?" she asked. "No, he wouldn't have left his men alone to die for him. Besides, his body was found. They brought it back to Amiens to me."

"To you? Why not to the chateau? To his home parish?"

"Have you forgotten? They believed there was no one left there to mourn him," she said softly. "I buried him at La Paix at the edge of the forest he loved. There is a very simple engraved gravestone among the ferns, nothing ostentatious. He would have hated that."

"Does Angelique know?"

"I haven't told her yet. She is still too fragile. Too close to madness to have any more emotional baggage piled on her. Someday, I will." She squeezed Devin's hand again. "And if I don't live to do it, could you go to La Paix yourself and show her?"

"Of course," Devin agreed but something told him that Madame Aucoin might outlive them all. "Although, without Jules I have no way to find La Paix."

"Georges can show you the way should Jules not survive," she said softly. "Perhaps I will write down the directions and leave them in the secret drawer in your room here in Amiens. That way no one will ever find them but you."

"I don't intend to die on this trip," Devin said firmly. "And there should be even less chance of anything happening to you, Madame. We will both live to see La Paix again and you can show Angelique her father's grave yourself."

She reached for his hand. "I pray God that you are right. There is one more promise I must exact from you, Devin. Can you see that Angelique is cared for, should something happen to me?"

"Of course," he answered. "But Chastel has already offered her a home and Gaspard ... Gaspard believes himself in love with her. I don't know what to think about that."

"Nor do I," Madame Aucoin answered. "Gaspard is almost as flighty as Angelique. She needs a strong, sensible man for her husband. Those aren't qualities I would attribute to Gaspard."

Devin sighed. "He and Angelique have a great deal in common. They can be perfectly rational one moment and unreasonable the next. But I believe he loves Angelique. In all the years I've known him, he has never told me that about another girl. Usually he enjoys their company for a night or a few days and he moves on. I think he was sincere when he told me he wanted to marry her. Whether that is best for her or for him – is another matter."

Madame Aucoin smiled. "It sounds as though we will need to see how he measures up. Hopefully, both of us will be available to make that judgement." She squeezed his hand once more. "Now I must put the finishing touches to my packing and so must you! I put warm hiking clothes in your armoire. Please take whatever you need. I had them made for you."

"Thank you," he said. "Not just for this but for all the comforts and kindnesses you have showered on us. I find myself wishing you were my grandmother, as well."

Madame Aucoin beamed. "But I am, dear boy. I am your mother's mother. Did no one ever tell you that?" She turned and was gone in a swirl of fragrant satin and lace.

Devin stared after her as she left the room and then jumped up from the table and followed her out into the hall. "Wait!" he protested. "Please, come back. Surely, we need to talk!"

She turned to look at him with an enigmatic smile and crossed the distance between them. Putting a hand under his elbow, she guided him back into the room. "I'm sorry," she said. "I couldn't resist leaving you with that little bit of information."

"It's hardly little!" he protested. "Why didn't I know this? Where have you been all my life?"

She sank down in one of the comfortable chairs by the sunlit window and motioned for him to sit on the chair next to him. "Unfortunately, I have spent your entire lifetime at La Paix and here in Amiens. When François' more radical views came under threat from his political rivals, we decided it was important that I provide a haven for his family, should they need it. I retreated to the mountains and virtually cut my ties with your mother's family. I haven't been to Coreé for twenty years. We kept in touch by letter, of course, but even those letters went through a series of false addresses to maintain La Paix's security."

"But no one ever told me," Devin protested.

"The fewer people who knew – the better," she replied. "You have to realize, Devin, that the enforced civility of the capital doesn't extend to the provinces. Here differences are settled by poison or a knife in the dark. Men keep their friends close and their enemies are always under scrutiny. Your Shadow Government is, no doubt, at fault for part of it but there is also an inherent violence here. Perhaps our critics are right and the provinces are primitive. It is our survival instinct that keeps us alive."

"Did you never wonder about us?" Devin asked, feeling cheated of a relationship that he would have cherished.

Madame Aucoin reached out to trace the line of his cheek. "My darling boy, I have watched over you your entire life."

For the first time Devin visualized her as a falcon, strong and free, soaring above the mountaintops and diving into the mist-filled ravines. "The button!" he exclaimed. "You dropped it for me that day on the slope when we came out of the caves."

She smiled. "No, my darling, that was Angelique. She has become very adept at flying."

Devin felt a shiver of excitement go up his spine. "Will you teach me to fly some day?" he asked.

Madame Aucoin patted his hand. "Of course, I will."

CHAPTER 27

Farewells

As though nature sought to warn them of the advance of the seasons, they stepped out of Madame Aucoin's home in Amiens into frosty darkness. Georges guided them down a set of stone steps cut into the steep hillside above the harbor. Despite Madame Aucoin's generosity they packed a minimum of clothing, dressing in layers against the cold night air. Even at midnight, a few lanterns from fishing boats glimmered among the misty spirals on the water, lending a magical quality to the lake.

They descended the hill and skirted the center of the silent town by following the lake shore around to the docks. Two soldiers stood at their posts near the moorings. They were too busy smoking their pipes and talking to notice the group of darkly clothed men who took the road out of town.

It was Marcus who guided them back to the campsite he and Devin had shared the night before they arrived in Amiens. They unpacked blankets and sat, huddled against the cold, waiting for morning. Dawn brought relief as the sun rose in a clear blue sky. Georges had packed an abundance of food in a very small amount of space. They breakfasted on boiled eggs, pastries, and apples before heading south toward the Alps that blanketed the lower half of Arcadia, forming an effective barrier to northern threats to Vienne and its capital, Coreé.

They traveled silently, each of them lost in his own thoughts. The goodbyes this morning had been difficult. Devin had hugged Madame Aucoin, almost ecstatic that he had found another family member, and yet remembering that she had lost her daughter when Devin's mother died. He had really doubted what she had told him, checking with Marcus for verification. Marcus confirmed the relationship, reminding him that she had been at La Paix for twenty years, so that Devin was too young to ever have met her. How odd, Devin thought, that their lives were so intricately intertwined and yet so much secrecy seemed to separate them.

Gaspard bumped Devin's elbow. "Are we allowed to talk?" he asked in a low voice.

"Of course," Devin said, bending to avoid a low-hanging branch. "What's on your mind?"

"I asked Angelique to marry me last night before we left," he whispered.

Devin tried not to show any emotion. "What did she say?" he asked.

Gaspard grimaced. "She said she'd have to think about it."

"Good for her!" Marcus said from behind them.

Devin ignored Marcus and carefully worded his reply to satisfy Gaspard. "Thinking about it doesn't mean 'no.' She's been through a lot of changes in her life lately. Give her a little time to figure who she is and what she wants her future to be like."

"I want a family," Gaspard said.

"Children?" Devin asked in surprise, almost tripping over a rotting log.

"I want someone who belongs to me," Gaspard explained, his tone wistful. "Neither my father nor my brother want anything to do with me. If I have sons I will make sure they know I love them. If I have daughters, I will protect them with my life if necessary. Families were never meant to be like mine."

"I'm so sorry, Gaspard. You didn't deserve this," Devin replied. "Remember you will always have me. What's another brother when I already have five?"

"That's what I mean," Gaspard replied earnestly. "You have five brothers and a father who loves you. Now, you have a grandmother, as well. It's hardly fair."

"Look at it this way," Devin said. "At least, I will never be in competition with you for Angelique. Apparently, she and I are first cousins."

"That doesn't make me feel any better," Gaspard responded morosely.

"Are you certain you're in love with her? Or is that you want a family and she is the only girl around at the moment?"

Gaspard turned to look at him. "That's harsh!"

"I just want you to think about it," Devin replied. "There are a great many pretty young girls in Coreé who thought you were very special."

"I love Angelique," Gaspard protested. "I want to protect her. I want to give her the kind of life she should have always had."

"How are you going to provide that?" Marcus chimed

in from behind them. "How do you plan to buy a home and take care of her?"

Gaspard spun on his heel. "Would you stay out of this, Marcus! It isn't any of your business."

Marcus dropped back a few paces. "As you wish," he said. "But think before you plan this perfect life you are dreaming of. Married life requires security."

Gaspard switched to Devin's other side and lowered his voice. "I'm fairly certain that even though my father claimed he had named my younger brother as his heir in his letter to me at Armand's, he must never have actually done it. Otherwise he wouldn't have referred to me as his heir in that newspaper article. That means I'm still in line to inherit his estate. Once my father is dead, I should be well off financially."

"All right," Devin said. Gaspard's way of thinking was a little cold, but then perhaps they were all thinking that way lately. His switches in mood were beginning to be as erratic as Angelique's.

Ahead a small stream cut through their path on its way to the lake. Gaspard, apparently propelled by his dreams of marital bliss, took a flying leap and landed with one foot in the water and one on the far bank. He thought it was hilarious but Devin imagined that wet boot would be very uncomfortable tonight when the temperature dropped. Georges and Chastel exchanged a look and hauled two large rocks over to use as stepping stones for the rest of them. Everyone else crossed with dry feet.

"Do you think Angelique will say 'yes'?" Gaspard asked Devin, as they started off again.

"I wouldn't even venture a guess as to what her answer will be. She said she needs to think about it," Devin reminded him. "Why don't you leave it at that?"

"It's hard to wait for an answer," Gaspard replied. "Maybe she has already made up her mind to say yes and I'm not there for her to tell me."

Devin sighed. "Well, considering you won't see her for at least three weeks, now isn't the time to get all worked up about it. Enjoy the scenery!"

Their route followed the lake shore. They passed no towns and very few houses. The main population seemed clustered around Amiens and they had left them far behind them. The foothills of the Alps were beautiful, still dotted with an array of purple fall asters and myriad alpine wildflowers. Here more of the trees were beginning to color. Brilliant red and orange branches jutted out from trees still clad mostly in their summer green.

"Why doesn't anyone live along the lake?" Devin asked Georges.

"In winter it would be too hard to travel to Amiens for supplies, monsieur," Georges answered. "Even the fishermen have their own little settlement just south of the docks in Amiens. No one wants to be isolated for six months out of the year."

"Winter encompasses half the year here?" Devin asked in surprise.

"In the mountains it does, yes," Georges replied. "We often have the first snowfall in September and it takes until May for everything to thaw. Perhaps I'm underestimating the length of winter. Maybe eight or nine months is more accurate."

"Why do people choose to live here?" Gaspard asked.

"Most of the residents are fishermen and people who supply them with food and gear. It is beautiful, no?" Georges gestured at the unspoiled landscape. "It is also quiet and remote. Some men come here who may need to avoid the *shérif* or the *militaire* for past crimes. They make a life here and no one bothers them."

"There were soldiers near the docks last night," Devin pointed out.

Georges shrugged elegantly. "Ah, well, I think those men were looking for Marcus, monsieur. I doubt Forneaux only sent five men north to search for you. He cannot risk having you and Gaspard return to refute his charges against the Chancellor. When Emile and his friends disappeared, Marcus would be the only suspect. Luckily, they have not found him."

Devin felt a little less carefree and more wary. The cool weather and beautiful landscape were enough to make him forget they were being hunted, at least for a few minutes. The shadow of René Forneaux's treachery and the urgency of their trip back to Coreé descended on him like a dark cloud and he avoided further conversation.

The farther they traveled into the mountain ranges to the south, the more uninhabitable the country became. Deep ravines cut through the hillsides, carrying water from frigid mountain streams above. Rocks and exposed roots tangled together on the hillsides as evergreens fought desperately to anchor themselves in a constantly changing terrain where landslides followed every heavy rain. Spring floods eroded the banks of rivers and streams, teasing at the trees' tentative anchors until they gave way and tumbled down into gullies, ultimately diverting the course of the same water that detached them.

Their fourth day out, they wakened to snow falling in huge wet flakes. They huddled around the fire and reheated roasted rabbit on skewers from the night before. Georges produced a bottle of brandy from his endless stores and passed it around for everyone to savor a bit of warmth before they started out for the morning.

The snow clung to every twig and branch, coating their entire world in white. Maple branches, some of their leaves in full color, bowed and broke under the weight of the snowfall. The ground was slippery even with good boots and Devin took a tumble crossing a ravine when the grapevine they used to swing across detached, one section after another, and landed him at the rocky bottom of a gully. He climbed back up, glad for the heavy leather gloves Madame Aucoin had provided.

They made less time that day and stopped early before the last light left the sky. Not for the first time, Devin was relieved that Armand hadn't come with them. The distance they traveled each day, the cold wet snow, and the conditions under which they ate and slept would have worn him out. He did miss the possibilities of stories around the fire but the last few nights they had been too tired for conversation, let alone tales from a Master Bard.

The sun set – a pale smear of washed-out gold – in a cold gray sky. Luckily, their isolation allowed them the comfort of a fire every night. They gathered around it as the darkness deepened: a circle of dirty, freezing men hoping to steal some warmth from the fledgling flames. They had gotten into the habit of skipping lunch every day in order to travel as fast as possible and by dark, they were all hungry, cold, and tired.

Suddenly a voice rang out from the darkness. "I'll trade four grouse for a place at your fire."

It took them by surprise and Marcus, Georges, and Chastel leaped to their feet with their pistols drawn.

"There's no need for violence," said a man, stepping into the firelight. "I only hoped to share your fire for the night."

He was tall and broad shouldered and held himself erect like a soldier but his beard and hair were streaked with gray. He held a walking stick in his right hand and a brace of grouse over his left shoulder.

"Did you lose your way?" Georges asked.

"Did you lose yours?" he countered. "I didn't come to share my life's story. It's a cold night. I just hoped to warm up for a while." He threw the grouse on the ground. "There's my peace offering. You can accept it or reject it. I'll move on if you like."

"How did you come by the grouse?" Marcus asked, retrieving them from the ground.

"Trapped them," the man answered. "I sell the feathers to the millinery shop in Amiens."

"Sit down then and join us," Marcus said affably. "I'll just get some wood for the fire."

The man sat, folding his long legs in front of him and holding out his hands to the fire. Marcus walked behind him and in one swift movement, jerked the man's head back and held a knife to his throat.

"Who sent you?" he snarled.

"No one ..." the man stuttered, his hands reaching protectively toward his throat.

Marcus shifted, the blade drawing blood. "Tell me the truth or I'll slit your throat and throw you in the nearest ravine."

"I was hired by René Forneaux," the man spat out. "And I'm not alone."

Marcus' knife slashed quickly across the man's throat, sending a cascade of blood down his chest. "Chastel, help me here," he hissed.

Chastel grabbed the intruder's feet and Marcus took his shoulders. They carried him out of the camp and into the darkness.

"How did Marcus know not to trust him?" Gaspard asked, his face ghostly white in the flickering firelight.

"He lied about the grouse," Devin answered. "They were shot, not trapped. Any man who owns a gun in the provinces is either a nobleman or in the *militaire*."

"God," Gaspard said, swallowing convulsively. "Marcus just killed him. That was awful."

"Pack up," Georges ordered. "Marcus won't want to stay here."

"Shall I put out the fire?" Devin asked.

Georges shook his head. "No, leave it burning. If he really wasn't alone, it may buy us some time. Anyone who sees the fire will assume we are still here and he was able to fool us into letting him stay."

Georges said there were caves about an hour up ahead and they would head for them as soon Marcus and Chastel came back.

CHAPTER 28

On the Run

Marcus returned, carrying Chastel's clothes. His face was grim. "Chastel is following his trail back to see if our intruder really was part of a group or working alone. He had papers identifying him as an elite part of the *militaire*."

Devin frowned. "What group?"

"Not one your father has created," Marcus said. "They called themselves *Le Garde Brun*."

"My father's colors are brown and tan," Gaspard said.

"There you have it then," Devin said.

Marcus grabbed his arm. "Come on, we need to go."

They shouldered their packs and set off into the darkness; the campfire's light faded into the distance and then disappeared. The clouds had cleared off after the sun set but a new moon and a sky full of stars did little to light their way.

"Will Chastel be all right?" Gaspard asked Devin.

"As a wolf, he can follow the scent that man left behind. I hope that his wolves will go with him. He hasn't mentioned them but surely they have come along on this journey. I

218

pray there won't be a dozen men waiting for him. If there are too many, I assume he will follow us and report," Devin answered.

"And then what?" Gaspard asked.

"Then we spend the next three weeks trying to outrun them or we stop and fight. Neither option appeals to me." Devin kept seeing blood spurting down over the intruder's chest and Marcus' complete detachment as he took a man's life. His heart hammered in his chest, imagining every small sound promised another pursuer. He hoped that he wouldn't be called upon to kill a man tonight.

They made slow progress. A dozen things conspired to trip them in the dark – fallen trees, brambles, rocks, and vines. Trees appeared out of nowhere, making them detour time and again. Georges strode ahead of them confidently while the rest of them stumbled onward in the darkness. Devin swore he must have the eyes of a cat.

The wind picked up. It tugged at their jackets, sending chilly drafts down their spines. Twigs crackled and scraped against each other like a dozen assassins creeping closer to strike from the gloom around them. The upper branches made a strange keening sound like a distraught woman mourning her child in the night. Devin's hands were sweating in spite of the cold.

They crossed two streams, walking in icy water up to their ankles. Rocky outcroppings required more agility than they could muster in the depths of the forest at midnight. Hands joined, they scrambled up and over stones, wishing that strange man had never appeared at their fireside. Or that, at the very least, Chastel and the wolf pack would return to protect them from pursuit.

It seemed very late before they finally climbed a rocky

embankment to the caves that Georges had mentioned earlier. Black branches scattered like latticework across the moon as they crept under a rocky overhang halfway up the side of a ravine. Marcus scuttled backwards, lighting a torch and then shielding it with his jacket as he investigated the depths of the expanse behind them. He was gone for what seemed like a very long time, the torch completely hidden from sight, and Devin began to fret at his absence. He breathed a sigh of relief when he returned unharmed several minutes later.

"You can move back," Marcus instructed in a low voice. "This cave appears to be uninhabited. We should be safe from bears or wolves and Forneaux's men, too, I hope."

They crawled in, protecting their heads from low hanging projections of rock. At last they reached a spot where they could stand or sit in relative comfort. The cave was dry, at least, although there could be no fire tonight. Georges offered them a cold supper but no one was hungry. They were all worried for Chastel. The longer he was gone, the more concern they felt. Marcus sat at the cave mouth, his gun in hand, after telling the rest of them to sleep while they could. Marcus announced that he and Georges would take turns keeping watch. Both Georges and Gaspard dropped off easily, but Devin couldn't sleep. His mind kept going over and over the murder of the intruder at their campsite.

He crawled out to the cave entrance and sat down beside Marcus, tucking his feet up under him. "Nothing?" he asked softly.

"I would have told you had there been news," Marcus replied.

They sat together silently. Devin watched the stars move

in their nightly circuits by observing their positions in rela-
tion to the trees. The wind died and the night became very
still. It reminded him of their night in Albion and the
complete absence of night noises, until another thought
occurred to him. "The wolves are with Chastel, aren't they?"
he asked Marcus.

Devin could just make out Marcus' nod of assent in the
darkness. "He'll be all right then," he said aloud, more to
reassure himself than Marcus.

"One would hope," Marcus answered, his voice low. "But
he's been gone longer than I expected."

"There must have been other men," Devin murmured.

"I agree," Marcus replied, "Or for some reason he felt
compelled to follow the man's trail to its origin in Amiens."

"How long would it take him to come back?" Devin
asked.

"We've been gone five days. He can travel much faster
as a wolf than we can. Your guess is as good as mine. If
he isn't back by morning, we will have to continue."

"What if we're wrong?" Devin said. "What if his wolves
weren't there to aid him? What then?"

"The wolves have trailed us since Amiens," Marcus
replied. "I'm surprised you haven't seen them; they are
always flicking in and out of the shadows at the edge of
my vision."

Devin rolled his eyes, a movement that was lost on Marcus
in the darkness. "Obviously, I'm not as observant as you
are."

"I only mean to emphasize that he isn't alone. Whatever
he faced back there, there were teeth and claws to aid him."

Devin let out a deep breath. There was some comfort in
that, then. He studied the woods and rocks around them,

realizing that as his eyes grew more accustomed to the dark, he could see details he would never have imagined were visible at night. Beside him, a vein of some translucent white stone wove its way through the shadowy rock that surrounded the cave entrance, glowing and sparkling in the scant light of the new moon.

"Is that quartz?" he asked.

Marcus shook his head. "I don't think so. It doesn't look like the quartz we used for the top stone for your mother's cairn."

It didn't. This rock drew light to it, bending it and manipulating it into a thin ribbon of luminescence glowing in the darkness around it. "It's beautiful," he commented.

Marcus shifted, stretching both legs out before him on the rocky shelf. "Can't you sleep?"

"No," Devin answered. "I'm worried about Chastel."

"I'm fairly certain he is all right," Marcus replied. He turned to look at Devin. "You haven't had any visions or anything?"

"About Chastel?"

"About anything," Marcus growled. "That stopped after we left Albion, didn't it?"

"Yes," Devin answered.

"Good," Marcus said. "Why don't you go back with the others and leave me alone?"

"Because I'm worried about Chastel," Devin repeated. "I won't talk if it bothers you."

"It does," Marcus responded curtly. "I need to be able to hear someone coming and I can't if you're jabbering."

Devin grinned and leaned his head back against the stone beside him. The night sky glowed a luminescent blue at the horizon; the stars glittered, bright and unhindered by clouds or the constant haze of smoke that plagued the cities. Here, the air felt and smelled completely different than the air in Coreé. It was lighter and cleaner. He could fill his lungs and any memory of Coreé's air was obliterated by the sharp cool mountain air.

Below them, a stone shifted. It tumbled and struck multiple times as it fell. Marcus cocked his pistol, the barrel aimed below them at a pale shape making its way up the face of the cliff. Devin shoved the barrel down. "It's Chastel," he said. The naked figure felt for handholds on the rocks below. Devin knelt at the edge and held his hand out.

Chastel grasped it and scrambled onto the ledge with them. He was shivering, his hands like ice, and Devin removed his coat and placed it over Chastel's shoulders. "Excuse my appearance," Chastel said. "Taking wolf form has some distinct disadvantages. I trust you still have my clothes, Marcus?"

Marcus left to fetch them from the cave, leaving Devin alone with Chastel for a moment.

"Tell me what happened," Devin asked, feeling the cold air seep through the fabric of his woolen shirt. He crossed his arms over his chest and leaned closer to listen as Chastel spoke in a whisper.

"Our friend with the grouse was not alone," Chastel told him, just as Marcus reappeared. He took his clothes and began to pull them on. "There were three other men following us in addition to the one Marcus killed. My wolves took down two others but we lost one man, Marcus. I'm not sure how. The wolves couldn't seem to find his scent and neither could I."

"So, he's still out there somewhere?" Marcus asked.

"He is," Chastel replied. "I'm sorry. It was the strangest

thing. What kind of man doesn't have a scent? I've never known anything like it before."

Marcus was silent.

"But the others are dead?" Devin asked.

"Yes," Chastel confirmed. "Should anyone find their bodies, they will assume they were simply killed by wolves. And for all intents and purposes, they were. I removed some papers from one man's jacket, Devin. I don't know how much help they will be to you but I didn't think it was wise to leave them on the body. We won't be able to read them until daylight anyway."

"You're not hurt?" Devin asked.

Chastel chuckled, pulling his trousers up and fastening them. "Not a scratch. The wolves took care of the other two men. I'm just concerned about the man who got away. The only thing I saw before he turned and ran was dark hair and a scar down the side of his face. I'm sure he will assume we killed his companion and he may connect the wolves to us, too."

"He may not," Marcus said. "Wolves are a constant danger in these mountains. He may simply assume that not only was his friend detected but they had the bad luck to run into wolves as well."

"It seems a bit too convenient," Chastel responded, buttoning up his shirt. "Don't forget, Forneaux is one of the few men who know my secret. No doubt these men were warned to be on the lookout for wolves."

"Then they found them," Marcus said. "Thank God we had the wolves with us. We might all be dead now. We are indebted to you, Chastel."

Chastel returned Devin's jacket to him and shrugged into his own. "You are no more indebted to me than I am to you. We are all in this together. We will succeed or fail as one. None of us will escape the fate of the others."

Devin grunted. "That's not exactly reassuring."

"It wasn't meant to be," Chastel remarked. "None of us can turn back now. I hope that missing man won't be a problem."

"It concerns me that you couldn't track him," Marcus said.

"As it does me," Chastel responded.

"Armand told me a story about a family of men who were famous as trackers when we were at La Paix," Devin said. "It wasn't part of the Chronicle – just something he had heard. The man was unique because no man or animal could smell him coming. Armand said he had a terrible scar on his face ..." He stopped short, his own words resonating in his head. "You don't think he was the man who killed Angelique's sisters, do you? She stated that her nurse made a point of mentioning that he had a scar; she said that it pulled down the corner of his mouth. I believe that she hoped it might help us to recognize him someday."

"There's no way to be certain," Marcus answered. "But he very well may be the same man. His scar fits Angelique's description and his skills as a tracker may explain how he was able to find those children where they were hidden."

Devin felt doubly repelled by a man who could scent out children hiding in a closet. The world seemed filled with horrors that the average man never dreamed of.

"A man who kills children with no compunction has no moral code. Don't ever make the mistake of thinking he has, Devin," Marcus continued. "He won't hesitate to kill any or all of us. Sometimes I think that those who are fundamentally good have a very hard time imagining what motivates the evil men and women of this world. Don't hesitate to kill him because in that instant that you vacillate, he will murder you where you stand."

"I won't," Devin said, and yet he knew he would. He could never kill a man without indecision warring wildly in his head. He changed the subject. "Did you lose any wolves?"

"No," Chastel answered, "we surprised them. There wasn't much of a fight – just the one man running off."

"He must have been fast, too," Marcus pointed out. "Can you describe his face other than the scar?"

"He had dark hair, a beard," Chastel enumerated. "I have nothing more to report than that. We were fighting for our lives."

Marcus grunted. "Except for the scar we have nothing to identify him from any other man we may run into in these mountains. Pull the wolves in closer tomorrow, Chastel. I'll fill Georges in when he takes over my watch. You two need to get some sleep."

"Is there some reason you were sitting up with Marcus?" Chastel asked Devin.

"I was worried about you. Now I can go dream the dreams of the blissfully unaware," Devin said jokingly.

"You can never be unaware again," Marcus said. "This is a dangerous plot you have uncovered, Devin. Forneaux is counting on his men to kill you so that he can convince Council of the primitive violence that exists in the provinces. If either you or Gaspard are able to return to Coreé, you can refute his claims and expose his part in the massacre of Angelique's family. Pray to God that some of us make it out of this alive."

CHAPTER 29

Eviction

The morning was no warmer. They finished the last of the pastries and boiled eggs. Gaspard whined for coffee. When everyone ignored him, he retreated into a sullen heap in the back of the cave. Chastel repeated his story from the night before for Gaspard's benefit, but either Gaspard didn't care or wasn't interested. Chastel turned his attention to the rest of the group. Snow was falling softly, obliterating any footprints made during the night.

"I've heard of this man before," Georges said. "They say he uses the scent and dresses in the hides of the animal he intends to kill and it enables him to sneak up on his prey."

"Still, my wolves sense any wolf that isn't from their own pack," Chastel said. "Surely it must be something more than that."

Georges shrugged. "Last night he may have used the scent of a deer. Your wolves would have ignored it when they were looking for a man. He is famous in Amiens as both a guide and a hunter. It would be best if we eliminate him before he picks us off one by one."

"As much as I resent losing any time," Marcus announced, "I think we should stay here for the day. If Chastel's missing man is searching for us, we'll be able to see his footprints, but in another hour ours from last night will be completely covered. It will give us the upper hand."

"Does this assassin have a name?" Devin asked.

"Jean-Michel Descremps," Georges supplied. "He is well known and excellent at his job. He sells his services for a high price."

"And then what?" Gaspard asked dourly. "Will you hunt him down and kill him, like the rest of his men?"

"Yes," Chastel answered grimly. "We can't let him lead others to our position."

"Others?" Devin asked. "Do you think there may be another group of men hunting for us?'

Chastel shrugged. "I have no way of knowing that. I doubt that Forneaux would have only sent one group, but it would be better to be safe and assume we are being tracked than to suppose that we have eliminated all threats when we haven't."

"Can't you take the wolves out and hunt for him?" Gaspard asked.

"Not in daylight in this snow," Chastel replied. "The wolves will stand out against the snow and it will make them more vulnerable. At twilight, we will search for him again. The gray of our coats will blend in with the shadows and it will be much safer."

Gaspard's expression was petulant. "So we are just supposed to sit and wait?"

"For the moment – yes," Marcus replied. "You are safe, relatively warm, and out of the snow. I don't see where you have any reason to complain."

"There's nothing to do," Gaspard protested.

Marcus blew out an exasperated breath. "Perhaps you'd like to take the first watch, provided you can keep your mind on the job."

"All right," Gaspard responded quite cheerfully. "Show me what I need to do."

After he and Marcus left, Georges snorted. "I wonder how long that will amuse him. He'll be whining for brandy in less than an hour because his toes are cold."

"I'll go sit with him," Devin said.

"You'll reduce the number of men we have to keep watch in shifts," Chastel pointed out.

"Then I'll do double watches," Devin offered. "Gaspard is only here because of me. I'll take responsibility for him."

"He's a grown man," Georges said. "There is no reason anyone needs to take responsibility for him. He needs to stand on his own two feet."

"He will," Devin assured them. He left before the subject could undergo further discussion and crept softly out to the entrance of the cave.

Marcus was giving out hushed instructions about which directions to watch the most and what Gaspard needed to look for. Devin sat down behind them and simply listened.

"This man can mask his scent," Marcus emphasized to Gaspard. "That's why the wolves couldn't find him last night. He must be skilled as a hunter and he isn't apt to be fooled by any tricks we use to throw him off the trail. This snow is a blessing. Perhaps it will convince him that we have gone on and we can get behind him."

"And then what?" Gaspard asked.

"We will follow his trail instead of him following ours," Marcus said. "This snow won't last forever. It's early in the season and it will melt and we will have some warm days again before winter really sets in. Hopefully, we'll be in Coreé before that happens."

Marcus glanced at Devin. "Why are you here?"

"I thought I'd sit with Gaspard for a while," he answered innocently.

"Cover up with this," Marcus said, throwing them a gray blanket. "It makes for great camouflage. And don't talk. Conversations can be heard over longer distances than you might imagine."

"Then stop talking," Devin whispered with a grin.

Devin draped the blanket over them both so that only their faces were visible. Already, the air was warmer; snow plopped off branches onto the ground and the falling flakes mixed with huge raindrops. It would have been a miserable day to be outside even if some world-renowned killer wasn't stalking them. The ledge above them sheltered them from most of the dampness and they sat in silence waiting for something unusual to cross the sloppy landscape below them. They didn't have long to wait.

Devin noticed it first – a bear lumbering up the ravine where they had walked last night. There was something odd about it. It kept stopping, standing on its hind legs, and sniffing the air. It hadn't raised its eyes to the level where Devin and Gaspard were sitting but Devin felt it had already determined they were close at hand. He touched Gaspard's shoulder and pointed to the rear of the cave, holding the blanket up to mask his departure.

The bear continued up the ravine, stopping and sniffing every few feet. It was almost as though someone had led it to where they were hiding. It rose again on its hind legs and called – something between a roar and a growl – and

Devin wished he were anywhere but sitting on the ledge above it. He pulled his pistol from his pocket but didn't cock it. The noise would be enough to call attention to his position and the bear was massive. It called again and another bear appeared below it, following in the footsteps of the one that had come along first.

Devin knew one shot would never bring either bear down and his pistol only held two. He wasn't sure that two well-placed shots would do the job either. Marcus was taking an inordinate amount of time coming to help. He slid back silently on the ledge, reducing his visibility but also his line of sight. Something suddenly occurred to him. If Chastel could shape shift into a wolf, perhaps Descremps could shape shift into a bear. It would explain the confusion over following his trail.

Just as the bears began to climb the slope, Marcus slid in beside him. "What if it's Descremps?" he mouthed to Marcus.

Marcus frowned and then made the connection. He studied the bears below them and then shook his head and pointed back toward the cave.

Devin understood what he meant. The cave belonged to the bears and they were in it. "What now?" Devin hissed.

"Tell them to pack up and move out," Marcus whispered. "I'm not going to wrestle a bear out of his winter hibernation spot. Let's get out while we can."

Devin whirled around and alerted Chastel, Georges, and Gaspard. They exited the cave over the rock ledge, a position that put them way above where they had traveled last night. The bears climbed up into their cave, roaring their discontent that it now smelled like humans. Thankfully, they didn't follow the occupants they had expelled from their residence.

They took a few minutes to pack more securely before they continued. What had begun as a peaceful day of rest ended abruptly in a rushed escape, but as they put some distance between them and the disgruntled bears, they began to laugh.

"I've never seen a bear before," Devin confessed. "And I had no idea that they could walk on two legs. I was sure Descremps had the ability to shape shift and was after us in bear form."

Chastel laughed. "That might have explained my wolves' trouble in following him but I would have noticed the smell of a bear. I've never heard of any story where a man could shape shift into a bear but I suppose up in these mountains anything is possible."

"I hope not," Devin replied. "Those bears were huge! I wasn't sure Marcus and I could stop them between us."

"It depends on how good your aim is," Marcus answered.

"It's not bad," Devin replied, "but I've never shot at a living target before."

Marcus glanced behind them. "We need to keep our voices down. We have no idea where Descremps is and our lives depend on avoiding him."

"Is there any chance he might just leave on his own?" Gaspard asked. "You've killed the men who were with him. Maybe he has already given up."

"Men like Descremps don't give up," Georges said. "They pride themselves on their success. He would lose status with the group of men who hired him should he let you and Gaspard go free. He will only continue to hold on to his position as long as he can add you two to his list of assassinations."

"Delightful," Devin murmured.

"Let's see how far we can travel today," Marcus said. "When it's later in the afternoon, if you would take the wolves back with you, maybe we can still find this killer."

Devin walked next to Chastel. "Where are the wolves now?" he asked.

Chastel pointed to spots along the tree line to their right. "There and there," he said. He waved with his left arm down below the cave where they had sheltered. "There, there, and there. There are four up ahead of us and four behind also."

"Now that you've pointed them out, I can see them," Devin said, watching the shifting gray shadows in the brush. "I haven't seen them at all in the last few days."

"That's as it should be," Chastel replied. "If they were traveling right with us, they could be easily picked off by our pursuers." He adjusted his pack on his shoulders. "You asked me about the wolves in the valley of Albion. I've made arrangements for them to meet us on the other side of the mountains. I thought their services might be needed in Coreé."

Devin grinned. "You made arrangements?"

Chastel nodded. "Wolves understand disputes over territory. It took very little convincing for them to join our cause."

Devin glanced ahead and slowed his steps so they wouldn't be overheard. "I told Madame Aucoin what I found in the caves we entered at the church in Rodez. She said to tell you when we were alone. This may be the only opportunity. There were cave drawings showing people living in Llisé before the first settlers came."

"And the Chastels were among them," Chastel interrupted.

233

"You knew?"

"I've heard stories. I can't say I have ever had the information confirmed. Tell me what the pictures showed."

"I copied them in the back of Father Sébastian's journal. I hated to do it but I didn't have any other paper to use. It shows people hiding in caves because they were afraid of the first settlers who had come in boats. Gradually they learn to shape shift – the Chastels go out to hunt as wolves and the Aucoins as falcons. It is only much later that they begin to live outside again and mingle with the people who have settled there. I thought you should know," Devin said. "When François Aucoin said your family had its very roots in the earth of Llisé, he was right. Your family and the Aucoins make up the only two native peoples in the empire."

"That we know of," Chastel corrected him. "And it's not the Aucoins, Devin. It's your mother's and your grandmother's family. Your grandmother married Comte Aucoin. Her surname was Bonhomme." Chastel turned to smile at him. "Now you are a part of that legacy, too, Devin."

Devin shoved his hands in his pockets, embarrassed by the implication. "The legacy of falcons?"

"It is an old and ancient one," Chastel remarked, "not something to take lightly."

"I don't," Devin replied. "It just takes some getting used to."

"You need to spend some time at La Paix with your grandmother. Even old falcons love to fly. I have no idea whether the process is the same as that of shape shifting into a wolf but consider the possibilities." Chastel slapped him on the shoulder. "You could fly, my friend!"

Devin smiled. "I have already received a promise of flying lessons from my *Grandmère*. I hope when all of this is over

234

that I can return to La Paix next summer." He swallowed a lump in his throat. "And if I haven't already found Jeanette, I will comb every inch of the villages on the map in the Bishop's Book until I do, and then together we'll unearth what's left of the Provincial Archives."

"That's a monumental task," Chastel said quietly. "Would you accept a fellow traveler?"

"Of course!" Devin answered, turning to look at him. "I would welcome your help and your companionship!"

Chastel held out a hand. "Consider it done, then."

CHAPTER 30

The Cabin

On any map of Llisé, Amiens lay in a unique position, sandwiched between two mountain ranges with the Bernese to the north and the Savoie to the south. The Savoie Alps formed a very effective barrier for Vienne's northern border. The rugged mountain range ahead of them seemed to grow higher the closer they came. The peaks shimmered before them, already snowcapped against the azure sky.

"How high do we need to climb?" Devin asked, moving up next to Georges as he led them. Gaspard tagged along, whacking at bushes with a walking stick, matching his strides to Devin's.

"We will have to cross some ridges," he answered, glancing back at him. "As much as possible we will keep to the valleys and passes. Pray God that none of the passes are full of snow already."

"It seems that there are only two seasons in the high mountains: winter and summer," Devin commented.

"The warmer seasons are merely shortened," Georges

answered. "Both spring and autumn in the mountains are glorious. You have only to look around you to see that."

It was true. The leaves of the hardwoods seemed to have turned brilliantly colored overnight here. They were more spectacular in contrast to the proliferation of evergreens around them, forming the perfect backdrop for their flame-colored foliage.

"In Coreé the streets are carefully planted with trees like crabapples that flower in spring, bear fruit in summer, and have colored leaves in autumn. It is nothing compared to the variety of trees that you have here. I feel as though I have never really experienced autumn until now. I want to learn the name of every tree and plant and catalog them in my mind so that when I return home I will never forget them," Devin said.

Georges smiled. "From what I've been told, you forget nothing, monsieur. Would you like me to identify these things for you as we pass?"

"Yes," Devin answered. "I would appreciate that very much."

Georges pointed at the rugged slopes up ahead. "As we travel toward the peaks, there is a height where deciduous trees no longer grow. We will only see dwarf pines there but I'll be glad to teach you the ones we are passing through now."

Their conversation dwelling on ashes, beeches, maples, and pines quickly bored Gaspard and he dropped back to talk to Chastel. Devin noticed that his friend's time at Madame Aucoin's had left him less physically fit for their journey. He tired first and was always asking for something to eat or to take a break. Devin hated to admit it but it was almost like traveling with a small child. Both of them had dealt with so many painful and horrifying ordeals on this trip and yet Gaspard hadn't matured because of it. He seemed to regress into an adolescent schoolboy when things got tough.

"Do you see the difference in the leaf?" Georges asked.

"I apologize," Devin said. "I missed the first part of that."

"Something on your mind?" Georges asked.

"A good many things, unfortunately," Devin replied, as he bent to escape a dangling bramble. "This was never how or when I planned to return home. There are days I wish I'd heeded my father's advice and spent my third year relaxing near the sea in Sorrento."

"Well, if things had gone according to agenda, you would have made it to Sorrento eventually," Georges said. "Madame Aucoin told me you planned to visit every province."

Devin laughed. "I was naïve enough to think that was possible in fifteen months. And I didn't just plan to visit, I intended to learn each province's chronicle as well. Life has a way of sobering us up and pointing out our mistakes."

Georges leaped a small gulley like a man half his age. "You sound discouraged," he said as Devin joined him.

"Disappointed, perhaps," Devin corrected him, "That the world isn't as simple and straightforward as I once imagined. I never realized how interconnected we all are – how one man's misery makes another man suffer on his behalf. I've lost too many people that I cared about to ever view life the same way again."

Chastel sneaked up behind him and grabbed Devin by the scruff of the neck. He shook him playfully. "You are too young to be a cynic!"

Devin turned to face him. "Where's Gaspard?"

"Taking a trip into the bushes," Chastel answered.

Devin jerked to stop, immediately thinking of Descremps. "You didn't let him go alone?"

Chastel inclined his head and chuckled. "The man needed some privacy, Devin. Don't worry, I have two wolves standing guard."

Still, Devin didn't move on until Gaspard rejoined them. Apparently, Descremps hired himself out to anyone willing to pay his price and he prided himself on successfully killing anyone he was contracted to assassinate. If he owed loyalty to anyone, it was a well-kept secret and Devin felt more uneasy with him trailing them than he had about any of Forneaux's men before.

They traveled until dusk. For the past several hours the temperature had plummeted, turning the earth into oddly frozen columns rising above the underlying mud. Mist rose off the river like sylphlike ballerinas, their elongated limbs turning in graceful swirls. Devin hoped they could chance a fire tonight.

"There's a hunter's cabin up ahead where we can spend the night," Georges said. "It's only used a few months out of the year. If we are lucky, we'll find it empty."

"Could Descremps have arrived before us?" Marcus asked.

"It's possible," Georges replied. "But it would be a rather obvious place for an ambush."

Marcus circled the shack when they came to it. There were no signs of footprints or occupancy. He bent to check beneath it and finally nodded that it was safe to enter. Plain horizontal boards nailed to a lopsided framework formed the bizarre structure. A chimney of river rocks tilted as precariously as the building itself.

The door hung partially off its hinges but it was still

secured by a leather thong. Georges turned to Devin as his hand reached for the makeshift latch. "My father used to bring me here when I was a boy. I thought it was the most exciting place in the world. This rickety old cabin with the river right below and all of this deep forest with its wealth of creatures seemed like paradise to a small child." He glanced at the leaves gathered deeply on the roof and smiled. "It is still paradise! I can't promise this will be warmer than the cave last night but it will be more comfortable."

As Georges opened the door, something small and red tumbled to the ground. Two pistols blazed simultaneously from the shadowy interior of the hut. Marcus and Chastel returned fire, the quiet woods recoiling from one concussion after another. Something seared Devin's ankle and he went down, landing near Georges, who lay on his back, his chest already soaked with blood.

"Georges!" Devin gasped, crawling to him.

"I'm sorry ... monsieur," he whispered.

"It's all right. It's all right," Devin murmured frantically, grabbing his handkerchief to staunch the blood. "You'll be fine."

"Avoid ..." Georges began. "Avoid ... Descremps' village ... his mother still lives ..." He stopped speaking, a bloody froth on his lips, his eyes staring sightlessly at the sky.

Devin knelt, his ear to Georges' chest listening desperately for a heartbeat that never came. A sob escaped his lips. "Damn you, Descremps! Damn you to hell and back!"

"Descremps is dead," Chastel said, gently pulling Devin away from Georges' body. "He fired two pistols at once and had two more cocked on the floor. He must have thought he could take out enough of us to grab the other guns and fire again."

Devin didn't care that Descremps was dead; he only cared

that Georges had come along on this trip to guide them and had been cut down by a cold, calculating assassin. "Something fell out of the door when Georges opened it," he said, shivering with reaction.

Gaspard held up two twigs, the center tied with red twine. "Whoever opened this door first was cursed," he said angrily, snapping the twigs in two and grinding them into the earth. "It could have been me or you or Marcus or Chastel. Descremps didn't care who he killed, as long as he kept bettering the odds of killing us all."

Devin took a quick look around. Everyone seemed to be all right. "No one else was hurt?"

"What happened to your ankle?" Chastel asked, pulling up Devin's bloody trouser leg.

"I don't know, something stung me when Descremps shot Georges."

"There's a hole in your boot, too. Marcus?" Chastel called, pulling off Devin's boot.

Marcus was dragging Descremps' body from the shack. Descremps had been shot twice in the chest. His eyes were closed, but a sardonic grin still twisted the unscarred side of his mouth. Even in death, Descremps seemed to believe he had won. Only the pain in his ankle kept Devin from kicking that face until it was unrecognizable. He didn't remember ever having felt this angry and helpless. He'd have mourned any one of their company but Georges had only become involved as a favor to Madame Aucoin. He was not immersed in this political quest for power that was tearing the empire apart. He did not deserve to die.

They were on an exposed ridge; below them a river rushed past, its waters dark and cold in what remained of the evening light. Marcus searched Descremps' pockets, removed money and a letter and then kicked him over the embankment. The body crashed through the bush until a distant splash announced its plunge into the river.

"Georges is dead," Chastel announced quietly, "and Devin was hit in the ankle by one Descremps' bullets."

Marcus seldom allowed his emotions to show but he stopped for a moment and went down on a knee by Georges. He gently closed his eyes and straightened his normally immaculate jacket. After touching him on the shoulder in farewell, he stood up.

"Don't!" Devin protested.

Marcus frowned and met his eyes. "Don't what?"

"Don't roll his body into the river!" Devin said. "I'll dig the grave myself."

"What do you take me for, Devin?" Marcus snapped. "We'll bury him and build a cairn over the grave to protect it. Surely, you don't believe me to be so hard hearted that I would dispose of the body of a friend in the same manner that I would an enemy?"

"I don't think you're up to grave digging, *mon ami*," Chastel said. "Marcus, can you take a look, please?"

Devin glanced down. There was a gouge, as he supposed there might be, from the glancing track of Descremps' bullet.

Marcus' scowl remained but his hands were gentle as he examined Devin's ankle. "The bullet sheared off part of your ankle bone," he announced. "I can't see how you're going to make this trek on that foot."

"I'll make it," Devin replied. "We are almost a week into this journey, with two weeks still to go. Turning back isn't an option."

"Isn't it?" Marcus asked, meeting his eyes. "Are you making the decisions now?"

"I'm making this decision," Devin answered. "Georges died to get us this far. I refuse to have that be in vain."

"I'll help Devin, if he needs help walking," Gaspard offered, hovering beside Marcus.

"And who's going to guide us?" Marcus asked. "I don't know my way around these mountains and neither does anyone else."

"Georges showed me the route on the map," Devin said, resting his back against a tree. "I can guide us."

Marcus sighed. "Knowing the route on a map isn't the same as knowing specific landmarks, Devin. I appreciate what you are trying to do but I'm not sure it's a viable solution. We could spend the winter wandering around these mountains and never make it any closer to Coreé." He turned and went back into the cabin and returned with a lantern. He handed it to Gaspard.

"So what is your plan?" Devin asked.

"I don't have a plan," Marcus replied. "Let's get you into the cabin and bind up this ankle. Then we will take care of poor Georges."

It occurred to Devin as Chastel and Marcus helped him up that Marcus had seen too much death on this trip, too. Was this what the real world was like outside the sheltered atmosphere he had grown up in, he wondered? One calamity after another, the loss of one good friend and then another – where did it stop? Did it ever stop or was this just the way life continued until you were the one who died and others mourned your passing?

Marcus plopped Devin down on a mess of dirty blankets in the corner and took bandages and brandy out of Georges' pack.

Devin shook his head. "I don't need that."

"What?" Marcus asked. "The brandy? It's not for you to drink; it's for your ankle. The chance of infection out here is high."

Gaspard moved closer. "I could use some of that if you can spare it."

Marcus dumped a liberal amount on Devin's ankle that made him hiss between his teeth from the pain. "I'm sorry, Gaspard. From now on, it's only for medicinal purposes."

Gaspard nodded solemnly. "I understand." He found an old shovel hanging from two nails on the wall and went outside.

"I'm sorry about Georges," Marcus said, when they were alone. "He was a good man. I couldn't help but like him. It was kind of him to volunteer to come with us. It's a shame that he lost his life doing us a favor."

"I liked him a great deal," Devin said. "Today he was teaching me the names of all the trees and wildflowers. He had such a strange collection of skills. Who would have guessed that Madame Aucoin's *sénéschal* was a nemophilist and was also trained as a soldier?"

Marcus glanced up as he bandaged Devin's ankle. "A nemo-what?"

"Nemophilist," Devin repeated. "It means someone who loved the woods and visited them often."

"Why didn't you just say that?" Marcus grumbled, shaking his head. "For someone so enamored of words, there's one you've been forgetting."

"What's that?" Devin asked.

"At some point you are going to have to start calling Madame Aucoin, *Grandmère*, preferably before we reach Coreé."

"It just feels strange," Devin said. "Why did no one ever tell me about her?"

"The Bonhommes have always been withdrawn. There were rumors about them just as there have always been rumors about the Chastels. It wouldn't have been an asset for the Chancellor's wife to be known as a shape shifter. Perhaps what you found in those cave paintings might change things eventually, but I don't believe the noblemen of Llisé are ready to accept that kind of information yet." Marcus returned the supplies to Georges' pack. "Years before François Aucoin's family was murdered, your grandmother moved to La Paix. She already had very little contact with your mother's family but once she started her silent vigil for anyone that survived that massacre, she had none at all. She did visit when your brothers were children, long before you were born."

"I'd have enjoyed having a grandmother," Devin said sadly.

Marcus stood up abruptly. "I need to help with Georges. Are you all right?"

Devin nodded. "Tell me when you are ready to bury him. May I say a few words?"

Marcus gave a slight bow. "You may say as many as you like, Devin."

CHAPTER 31

Then There Were Four

They buried Georges under a beech tree above the river. Its leaves had already turned gold edged with orange. They seemed to glow in the light from their single lantern, as though the tree itself carried its own light. Devin had nothing to do with choosing the spot for the grave but he felt Georges would have heartily approved. They lined it with the blankets from the cabin and Devin took one of Georges' blankets from his pack to wrap him in. Marcus and Chastel lowered his body down with the greatest care and dignity. Devin, leaning on Gaspard's arm, took a few minutes to thank this man that they had only recently come to know and who had given his life for them. While he prayed, a gust of wind brought golden leaves cascading down to cover the body and the raw, open wound in the earth around it.

Gaspard helped Devin back into the cabin while Chastel and Marcus filled the grave. Devin couldn't bring himself to watch dirt tumble down on top of the body even though it was protectively wrapped against the elements and the earth that would contain it. He slumped down against the cabin wall, his heart aching, and closed his eyes.

Devin had lied to Marcus about Georges showing him the map. He'd looked at it himself at Madame Aucoin's when Georges had it spread out on the table in the study. He had memorized the route that Georges had marked. Georges' last words warned him to exclude Descremps' village but he had no idea where Descremps was from and neither did anyone else. Devin realized he could kill them all himself by his determination to continue and his misrepresentation about knowing the way well enough to guide them. Was it better to turn back now than to die unburied, unmourned, and forgotten on some mountainside? Should he admit his lie and allow Marcus to make the decision about what they should do next?

Gaspard went back outside and returned with an armload of small branches. He broke them up slowly and methodically, placing them in the fireplace, striking a spark with Marcus' flint to set the fire burning. Kneeling, he blew on the tiny spark until it grew, engulfing the twigs around it in flames. He sat back on his heels and looked at Devin. "What do we do now?" he asked, his face unaffected and boyish in the shadows.

"I want to go on," Devin said. "We'd planned on two more weeks to reach Coreé and we'd need a full week to walk back to Amiens. To me it makes no sense to go back. All of this will have been for nothing."

"Some of us might still be alive, Dev," Gaspard argued. "That, at least, is something."

"We may be alive," Devin reminded him. "But my father may not be. He's been framed for treason and has no one but us to speak on his behalf. Who knows which of my

247

brothers may have been pulled into this too? I have to go back, Gaspard."

Gaspard toyed with some small twigs on the floor. "I can't help feeling as though this entire thing is my fault."

"How could it be your fault? It is not," Devin assured him, "so get that idea out of your head. You've had no more reason to be involved in your father's politics than I have had in my father's until now. Unfortunately, we seem to have been left in charge of setting things right."

"I don't want you to think I'm not willing to go the rest of the way," Gaspard said, adding more twigs to the newly started flames. "I just don't want to freeze to death halfway there."

"We'll be halfway home in three and a half days," Devin pointed out. "I don't think we're in danger of freezing to death yet."

"It could happen," Marcus said, as he opened the door. He brushed his hands on his trousers and went to stand in front of the fire, his hands reaching out for the little heat the flames had generated. The sound of hammering came from outside. "Chastel's making a cross. Maybe sometime in the future we can erect something more permanent, if you'd like."

Devin shook his head. "I don't think he would have wanted that. For all his elegance as a servant, he was a very simple man at heart. A wooden cross would have pleased him. He loved this place. I think it's fitting that he be laid to rest here." The words caught in his throat. They felt false and forced, something you might offer a child to ease the pain of permanent separation from a cherished family member.

Marcus and Gaspard said nothing. Perhaps they knew

how much those soothing words had cost him. Marcus added two more substantial logs to the fire and watched the flames consume them greedily. The fire spit and crackled, sending sparks up the crooked old chimney. But dark, sinister shadows still crouched in the corners of the cabin, refusing to be banished by the cheerfulness of firelight. The shadows in Devin's heart darkened and spread, obliterating any hope this journey had brought him. Tonight only remorse and grief remained.

Chastel came in, a dusting of snow on the shoulders of his jacket and his hair. He divested himself of his jacket, threw his wet gloves on the meager hearth to dry, and sat down with his back to the fire. "I've just been investigating outside a bit," he announced. "Descremps didn't walk into this cabin; he didn't tunnel in from underneath. How did he get in?"

For some reason Devin's eyes went to the chimney and Chastel's followed. "Could a man slide through there?" Chastel asked Marcus.

"Not an ordinary man," Marcus answered. "But we already know that Descremps was not ordinary. He had a reputation for accomplishing difficult feats in unusual ways."

"Gaspard and I went to see a man once while we were at the *université*," Devin said. "He did card tricks and made a chicken disappear. The most impressive thing he did was to climb into an urn and crawl back out again. He folded himself up like rag doll. It was as though he had no bones."

"That, *mes petits*, is magic," Chastel said, with a twinkle in his eyes. "Or should I say illusion? Someone accomplishes what appears to be impossible by misdirection."

"What if it wasn't misdirection?" Devin asked, running a hand down his shin to still his ankle's constant throbbing.

"You believe that it is really possible for a man to fit into an urn?" Marcus asked. "How large was the urn?"

Devin held up his hands to show them.

"I went up on the stage while he did it," Gaspard said in support. "I was three feet away at the most. He went nowhere except down into the urn and back up. The opening was only about as wide as my head."

Marcus rolled his eyes.

"We had a man in the Archives whose thumbs were double jointed," Devin offered as further evidence. "He could bend them either in or out. What if Descremps had some of the same physical characteristics? He could have climbed a tree some distance away from the cabin and jumped limb to limb until he landed on the cabin roof. All he would have had to do was climb down the chimney and wait for us."

"Like Père Noël?" Marcus said with a laugh.

"It's not funny!" Devin snapped. "He got in here somehow. What is your theory? He killed a good and gracious man and he may have killed Angelique's older sisters and her mother and brothers, too. This man was evil! He obviously had some talent that other men lack, Marcus, or you would have seen some sign that he was waiting inside for us!"

Marcus' expression sobered. "Devin, I meant no disrespect."

Devin lowered his eyes and plucked uneasily at the blanket Gaspard had thrown over his legs earlier. "I'm just ... so ... sick of death." To his horror hot tears filled his eyes and ran down his cheeks. Had he been able to, he would have left the room and run out into the snow where he could kneel and weep at Georges' grave in private. He wiped ineffectually at his eyes, realizing he'd used his handkerchief to staunch Georges' wound. "I'm sorry ... I'm sorry ..." he murmured, turning his head away from them all in embarrassment.

Gaspard left the fire and sat down beside him. "I'm sorry, too, Dev. I'm sorry about Georges and your mother. I'm sorry about Angelique's family and that Jeanette is missing. If I could make it all right, I would. There seems to be no respite from death in these provinces. We can't outlive it; we can't outsmart it; we can't outrun it. You and I have just been lucky enough to escape any real contact with it for the first twenty years of our lives. In the provinces they live with it daily. Now, we can only hope to assuage some of the grief that it brings to the people we care about. I'm sorry that you lost a friend today. Georges was a good man and I won't ever forget him. I will do whatever I can to help you through this."

"Well said, Gaspard," Chastel said.

"Yes, well said," Marcus agreed. "But Devin, we need to put our grief aside tonight for a moment to make some hard decisions. Whatever we resolve to do, the decision must be unanimous. One of us cannot force anyone else's vote or speak for them ourselves. You're fond of chess, Gaspard. Well, this playing board has changed. We have lost our guide so there are no rules to follow. None of us knows these mountains the way he did. Our arriving in Coreé requires our taking the right route. We all need to say what we feel is the best way to proceed. Georges has already lost his life. I don't want to bury anyone else."

They sat in silence for a moment.

Devin shifted uneasily. "Before we vote I have something to say. I told you earlier that Georges had shown me our route on the map. I implied he had discussed it with me. Neither one of those things is true," he admitted.

Marcus' head came up like a startled horse. "You lied to me?"

"I did," Devin confirmed. "I apologize. But I did see the route marked out on the map at Madame Aucoin's and I memorized it."

"This changes things," Marcus said.

Chastel stretched his legs out on the floor, the action smooth and relaxed as though nothing disturbed him for very long. "It doesn't really alter anything, at all. You just said that we had lost our guide, Marcus. If Devin claims to know the route, he knows it only as a pen mark on a map. Landmarks change, terrain shifts, and landslides reconfigure the land. I'm certain Georges would have adjusted our course as we went. Things would be no different if Devin points out the way. I say that we vote now."

Grateful to Chastel for his understanding, Devin spoke up first. "You all know how I feel. I want to continue. Without the information I am bringing, my father could hang for treason and perhaps some of my brothers, as well."

Chastel nodded. "With René Forneaux in control and possibly our next Chancellor, I will be hunted down and killed also. I have no choice but to continue."

"Gaspard?" Marcus asked. "You indicated at Madame Aucoin's that you might rather stay behind."

Gaspard shook his head. "I told Devin I would help him and I meant it. Besides, my ancestors started all of this. I intend to end it. I want to go on, too."

"Well, Marcus?" Chastel asked. "It's down to you. How do you vote?"

Marcus gave a humorless chuckle. "This wasn't the way I expected the vote to go but actually, I have no choice. Until his father rescinds the directive, I am Devin's bodyguard. My place is with him. We'll leave at first light."

CHAPTER 32

Night Terrors

Devin found sleep nearly impossible. His ankle throbbed in time with his heartbeat and he was constantly cold. Marcus sat braced against the door, his pistol in his hand. Gaspard and Chastel lay beside Devin. All three had their feet to the fire. Gaspard's gentle snoring indicated he was sleeping but Devin wasn't certain whether Chastel had succumbed or not. Tonight the wolves had joined them, filling the cabin with their musky odor and the smell of wet fur.

The cabin itself had taken on a sinister quality despite Georges' pleasant childhood memories of it. How ironic that the very place he remembered so fondly had been the site of his murder. Georges' death replayed in Devin's mind – the blood soaking his jacket, his last labored words spoken in concern for them, not himself, his sightless eyes staring up at the sky. Devin wondered if he had family members that should be notified. He wished he could tell them himself that Georges had died supporting a good and honest Chancellor who held the provinces in high esteem and hoped to better life for the people there.

Cold air seeped through the sides of the cabin and the floorboards, setting random feed sacks billowing, that had been nailed to the walls to insulate against the cold. The movement was disconcerting, following no prearranged pattern, and contributed to Devin's growing sense of unease.

His eyes kept going back to the fireplace and the exposed chimney that rose to the roof rafters. He was convinced that was how Descremps had come in even though Marcus seemed to find it unlikely. His bodyguard had yet to offer a more plausible explanation for how he had entered without leaving any tracks. A thin, wiry man could have slipped down between those brick walls. But how had Descremps known they would stop here? Did he research his victims before he killed them?

Oddly enough, the children's tale of the three little pigs kept running through Devin's head. He kept thinking of the wolf climbing down the chimney and landing in the pot of boiling water. He would much rather have taken his chances with a wolf than a cold-blooded killer like Descremps.

Two of Chastel's wolves lay sprawled by the fire. Their proximity provided some security but wolves could be shot, too, and he would regret losing even one of them. He should have felt safer now that Descremps was dead but he didn't. Something didn't feel right about the whole incident but he couldn't figure out what. The small gray wolf roused herself from Chastel's side and quietly made her way over to Devin. She curled up in the crook of his left arm and put her head on his shoulder. For the first time that night, he closed his eyes.

He dreamed of arriving at home. His father and his brothers greeted him and then stepped aside as his mother opened her arms to hug him. He could smell her perfume, feel the wispy curls that always framed her face, her arms held him close. When she stepped back, she put one hand on each side of his face, the way she had often done when he was a child. It was her way of ensuring that he listened when she had something important to impart.

"Devin," she said. "Descremps isn't dead. He wears padded leather, lined in metal under his clothes to shield him from bullets. He didn't fall into the river, he rolled over the hill and dropped a stone into it so that you would hear a splash. He plans to kill you one by one. You have to tell Marcus. You are all in terrible danger!"

He fought the vestiges of sleep and sat up, dislodging the small gray wolf and groaning at the pain in his ankle. Chastel sat at the door and Marcus lay beside Devin.

"What is it?" Chastel whispered.

"Descremps isn't dead," Devin said. "He is still after us!"

Chastel stood up and stepped over Gaspard, squatting beside Devin. "Did you dream this?"

Devin was shaking. "My mother told me. Yes, it was a dream but what she said made sense."

"What is it?" Marcus asked, sitting up groggily.

"A dream," Chastel told him.

"My mother told me Descremps is still alive, Marcus," Devin insisted. "Did Descremps bleed?"

Marcus frowned. "What do you mean?"

"He had two bullet holes in his jacket," Devin continued, "but did you see any blood?"

Both Chastel and Marcus looked at the floor where Descremps must have stood in wait for them. There were no blood stains where he had fallen. There was nothing there on the floorboards to indicate that anyone had died there.

"I don't know," Marcus said. "I don't think I even

256

noticed. I was worried about you and Georges. I dragged him out the door and kicked his body over the hill."

"Mother said he didn't fall into the river. She claims he threw a stone into the water instead to make a splash. She said he wears leather lined in metal under his jacket to deflect bullets."

"This was a dream, Devin," Chastel said soothingly. "Perhaps you imagined some of this before you fell asleep. All of us were thinking about what happened today. It's natural that you might have dreamed about it."

Gaspard sat up and rubbed his eyes, listening to the discussion without commenting.

"Devin's dreams are often prophetic," Marcus said. "Some of this actually makes sense. I noticed when I dragged Descremps' body out that while his arms were wiry and small, I thought his jacket seemed unusually heavy around his chest."

"He was smiling!" Devin said accusingly. "Did you notice that? I thought at the time that, even in death, he appeared to take pleasure in what he had just done."

"I noticed that, too," Gaspard agreed. "And even with four pistols, he couldn't have shot all five of us before he had to cock his guns again. He must have known he would be shot before he could kill us all."

"That's true," Marcus said. "Unless he knew that being shot in the chest would never kill him." He stood up and paced the small floor. "If he is alive, where is he? Waiting outside for us? I have his pistols but he could have more stashed somewhere close by."

"He's like a cat," Gaspard said. "Not only does he have nine lives but he wants to toy with us first. He enjoys killing and he intends to take his time about it."

"Gaspard," Devin cautioned. The image his friend had conjured was frighteningly real and he wouldn't be able to get it out of his head. He'd watched too many cats derive almost gleeful pleasure from the suffering of small field mice. The cabin had lost any of the safety he had felt within it. As though on cue, the wolves leaped up to growl and sniff at the cabin wall by the front door.

Devin sniffed suspiciously, glancing at the fire which had died down to just embers. "I smell smoke."

Gray tendrils drifted lazily up between the floorboards and Gaspard dragged Devin to his feet. "Descremps set fire to the damn cabin!"

Within seconds, they could hear the flames crackling beneath them. "Grab your packs!" Marcus yelled, tossing each of them a pistol. He leaned forward, his voice barely audible. "He'll expect us to come out the front door. I'm going to smash this floor in. We'll escape underneath."

"Into the flames?" Gaspard hissed.

"If necessary." Marcus grabbed an axe and chopped through the floorboards as both smoke and flames began to curl around them. He worked backwards toward the north corner which remained virtually untouched. Smashing a hole big enough to exit, he let the wolves out first. Their baying indicated they'd located their target and were in pursuit. Only the small gray wolf remained behind. Marcus dropped his pack and grabbed Georges' and slid through. Chastel followed, coaxing the gray wolf to come but she wouldn't leave until Gaspard helped lower Devin and Chastel caught him from below.

The flames threw an eerie light on a chaotic scene. Descremps must have climbed the beech tree and the wolves were jumping and snarling at its trunk. Gaspard helped

Devin hobble behind a rocky outcropping as a bullet lodged near the spot where they had just been standing.

The beech leaves trembled as Descremps scaled its limbs, climbing higher and higher, but the man himself lay hidden in shadow. Devin aimed and fired just slightly behind where the smaller branches swayed above the burning cabin. A startled exclamation sounded from above as Descremps' pistol fell into the midst of the snarling wolves. Both Chastel and Marcus aimed and blasted at the same spot and were rewarded by another agonized shout but there was no sign of Descremps.

The leaves no longer trembled. The branches remained still as Chastel and Marcus reloaded. Devin and Gaspard held their pistols ready should Marcus and Chastel miss.

"He's planning to jump," Marcus said. "Wait for the leaves to tremble and then shoot just behind them."

Seconds stretched into minutes as they waited, hearts pounding, pistols cocked. When the first branch moved, both Marcus and Chastel opened fire and Descremps crumpled, hitting branch after branch until he came to rest on the cairn of stones marking Georges' grave. Behind him the cabin flared into an inferno, the flickering flames lending a macabre tone to the bloody death of a master assassin.

Marcus bent to check Descremps' pulse and then he grabbed his feet and Chastel took his arms. They hoisted him up, swinging him back and forth a few times before throwing him on the funeral pyre of his own making. Flames flared up around the body, quickly hiding it from sight or consuming it. Devin preferred not to speculate.

Gaspard sat down hard beside him. "God, Devin!" he whispered. "Don't ever ask me to go on a trip with you again!"

CHAPTER 33

Doubts and Speculation

They spent the last few hours before dawn warmed by the burning cabin, which protested its demise, creaking and snapping as it crumbled into a mass of glowing embers. They had saved all of their supplies and all of the wolves, to say nothing about the fact that the four of them were still alive and relatively intact.

They left at daybreak, Devin leaning on Gaspard's walking stick. Marcus had made him keep his boot on all night in case the swelling prevented him from putting it back on in the morning. It had saved them precious time when they escaped the fire. Marcus used Georges' belt and formed an X over Devin's foot and ankle, pulling it as tightly as he could to give him more support.

Devin vowed he would not hold them back and he trudged doggedly along, though his ankle ached horribly. Last night by the light of the burning cabin, he had done his best to draw a map on one of the last blank pieces of paper from Father Sébastian's journal. He realized that his vision had improved immensely in the week they had been on their journey, perhaps because he hadn't attempted to strain his eyes to read while they were traveling. Marcus had labeled the mountains and rivers with the help of Devin's memory and they decided exactly where they were and how much farther they had to go. Devin conveyed Georges' comment that sometimes they would need to travel the ridges and Marcus nodded, agreeing that seemed probable. He also reiterated Georges' final words but none of them knew Descremps' place of residence, so the warning only served to put them more on edge.

The last night's snowfall had merely dusted the ground but the wind had howled all night, fanning the flames of the old cabin. The air felt bitterly cold this morning. Devin felt his cheeks burn as they hiked above the river, using it as a guide to their left. They were already on a ridge that gradually grew higher and rockier. The view below them presented an astounding palette of brilliantly colored trees, the colors deepening along the folded ravines and snakelike rivers. Georges would have loved it, Devin thought sadly.

By noon, the wind had dropped, the clouds cleared away, and the sun came out to warm their backs and their souls. They took a break at mid-afternoon and Devin tottered to a stop by a flaming maple and sank down on a stony ledge. The pain in his ankle made him nauseated but he forced down an apple and some aged cheese. Marcus would need to begin hunting soon. Their rations, even divided by four instead of five, were beginning to run low.

The wolves had traveled with them like a group of hunting dogs. They sniffed the unfamiliar scents and dug up loose dirt and rolled in it. In spite of Georges' death, calmness pervaded today, a welcome respite from the constant watchfulness that had plagued the beginning of their journey.

The rocky ledge the maple clung to had already warmed in the sun and the heat was very welcome. "What was in Descremps' papers?" Devin asked, easing his foot up onto a rotten log as he folded his arms behind his head.

"A contract," Marcus replied, "to kill the following individuals: Devin Roché, Gaspard Forneaux, Marcus Berringer, and Jean Chastel."

"Not Georges?" Devin asked.

"No, Georges was not part of the original equation when the contract was drawn up. You and Gaspard are worth 100,000 francs apiece. Chastel and I are only worth 25,000."

"We can't all be special," Gaspard said with a grin.

"So Descremps could read and write?" Devin asked.

Marcus took another piece of cheese. "That's debatable. His signature was an X."

"But the fact that he asked for a contract shows he had some skill at reading, at least," Devin insisted.

"Perhaps," agreed Chastel. "I'm just glad he's dead."

"You're sure of that?" Devin asked, half in jest.

"Well, allow me to say that he won't be doing any more smiling ever again," Marcus said. "I don't think you want me to give you the details."

"There is some relief in his death," Chastel said. "But I wish we knew whether Forneaux took out any other contracts on our lives."

"The closer we get to Coreé," Gaspard said, "the greater the possibility that there is a bounty on our heads."

"Especially since Chancellor Roché is in no position to help us at the moment." Marcus stretched out on the sun-warmed rock. "I'm getting too old for this. Maybe when we return to Coreé I'll ask for my retirement. I could marry a plump woman from Sorrento, and spend the rest of my days sitting by the fire eating good food and telling her the stories of my adventures."

"I can't see that happening," Devin replied. "You'll be a bodyguard until you die." He wished he hadn't said the words as soon as they were out of his mouth. The ensuing silence made him realize that his comment had chilled the others as well. "I didn't mean that the way it sounded," he amended. "I just can't see you as a man of leisure."

Marcus sputtered. "A man of leisure? God! I don't see myself as that either, Devin. I've honestly never thought beyond serving your father." He shifted, finding a more comfortable position, more at ease than Devin had seen him in days. "Where does your map put us? Is there anywhere sheltered that we could stop for the night?"

"There are caves as we descend this ridge," Devin said, looking at the page where he had reproduced Georges' map in Father Sébastian's journal. "Georges had them circled on his map, so I am assuming he planned for us to spend the night there. Tomorrow we'll go down into a valley. There's a small town there called Notre-Dame-de-Bellecombe. Do we chance buying supplies or bypass it entirely?"

"Small towns in the mountains are used to having hunters stop for supplies," Chastel said. "If we are careful we might be able to pick up a few things and leave without anyone questioning our identities."

"I can go," Marcus offered. "The rest of you look and talk too much like noblemen. I can impersonate a hunter more easily."

"You still carry yourself like a soldier," Devin pointed out.

"And soldiers end their service and come home to their families in the provinces," Marcus reminded him. "I've no doubt that Descremps served the empire at some time. That is probably where he acquired some of his talents for tracking. I intend to research his background when we are home."

Talk of Descremps effectively shut down any idle chatter. Devin looked out across the autumn foliage spread below them and his heart ached. How he would have loved to share this beauty with Jeanette or his mother. A nagging thought invaded his mind, something he had considered once and pushed aside. Was it possible that Forneaux had murdered his mother as well? The explanation his father had given him – that the doctor thought it might have been her heart that gave out – seemed a reasonable assumption until it was placed beside the cascade of disturbing events that seemed to dog his family.

"Devin?" Marcus asked. "Do you need help getting up?"

Devin realized Marcus must have asked him more than once and he accepted Gaspard's hand to pull him upright. Resting seemed to have stiffened his leg and he limped more than he had earlier, letting Marcus take the lead.

By late afternoon the ground began to slope downward. The footing was treacherous and Devin clung to Gaspard on one side and the walking stick on the other. Narrow slopes still dotted with wildflowers cut between jagged outcroppings of rock. Just before nightfall they found the caves that Georges had marked out for them.

Devin was done in. Once Marcus certified the caves as safe, he hobbled in and staked out a spot against the cave wall. The others gathered wood. Most nights, Devin would have been glad for a fire but tonight it only brought back memories of last night's burning cabin and Descremps' body being thrown into the flames. Chastel sent the wolves out to hunt as dusk deepened the shadowy interior of the cave even further. Marcus left and returned with three grouse which he prepared outside in the fading light. Gaspard went out to help him after he built a fire.

Devin wondered when he would be able to look at grouse without shuddering at the memory of their night-time visitor who had been the herald of their encounter with Descremps. Or when would he be able to eat stew and not ache for Jeanette, who he first met as a pretty, dark-haired girl in bare feet bent over a savory stewpot in her father's kitchen? His mother's spirit was everywhere: in childhood memories, in the letters she had written him, and in her hold on his dreams, which had saved all of their lives. Georges' spirit seemed to sit beside him in this sheltered cave, guiding them still, though his physical body had been left behind. Devin wondered if there was something wrong with him. His heart ached physically. He felt as though there was a stone resting inside his chest that was too heavy for him to carry. Had he not feared worrying everyone else, he would have put his head down on his knees and wept.

Chastel sat down beside him. "How is your ankle?"

Devin shrugged. Better than my heart, he almost said. "It's all right. I hope I'm not slowing us down."

"You're not," Chastel assured him. "You've kept up remarkably well."

Devin took a deep breath and kept his voice low. "Do you think Forneaux might have murdered my mother?"

Chastel blinked. "Do you have reason to believe that he did?"

Devin shook his head. "No, I just wondered. It seems convenient, considering the circumstances. My father was already overburdened with rumors of my disappearance and possible death. Then his wife dies, too. And Forneaux picks

265

this moment to file charges of treason against him? Talk about kicking a man when he is down."

Chastel's eyebrows rose. "When you put it that way, it doesn't seem so out of the realm of possibility."

"I don't want to discuss it where Gaspard can hear. He's having a difficult time as it is."

"I agree," Chastel murmured. "Would you like me to mention it to Marcus if we happen to be alone?"

Devin nodded. "Yes, please. I don't feel as though I've had an opportunity."

"All right," Chastel agreed. He let the silence deepen between them for a few minutes. "You know there was nothing you could have done to save Georges, don't you?"

"I know that," Devin said. "It doesn't make his death any easier to bear. It seems as though I've gone through my entire life and I've never lost anyone that I cared about until this trip. Now Jeanette is missing, my mother has died, and even though I had just come to know Georges, I sincerely mourn his passing."

"We all do, Devin. No one more than Marcus, because he feels he should have never allowed Georges to open the door to the cabin. He says he is the one who is paid to take the risks. He feels guilty that you were shot. That bullet could as easily have taken out your kneecap. Remember that Georges was a soldier, too. He knew the risks when he volunteered to come with us. He could just as easily have said 'no'."

Devin smiled sadly. "Georges was too much of a gentleman to say 'no' to a request from Madame Aucoin or his Chancellor's son."

"And perhaps that is part of why you liked him so much," Chastel pointed out. "As a soldier, he was well aware of the risks that lay behind that door. Have you considered that?"

Devin exhaled sharply. "I have considered a dozen options, played that scene over and over in my head. None us had been forewarned about anything amiss. There were no footprints, no tunnels beneath the cabin. There was nothing to make us think that Descremps had laid a trap for us in a place that Georges so obviously loved." Devin cleared his throat, afraid that he might burst into tears again. "I think that is what was hardest. It's the same reason I reacted so violently to your story of your uncle's death. He expected nothing but love and acceptance from his father and yet ultimately his father killed him."

"The cabin didn't kill Georges," Chastel corrected him. "Descremps used it as a means of catching him off his guard and it worked. Perhaps it's a lesson we all need to learn."

Devin nodded. He had run out of things to say. He had millions of words spinning around in his brain, each designed for a specific purpose and yet none truly expressed how he felt. For the first time in his life, he despised the easy platitudes that people offered in these situations: "I'm sorry for your loss." "Is there anything I can do?" "He's in a better place now." "Her suffering is over."

Marcus and Gaspard brought the grouse inside and skewered them to roast above the coals. The cave had acquired a cozy warmth from the fire and all of them moved closer to take advantage of it.

Devin looked at each of the faces around the fire: Gaspard's, Marcus', and Chastel's. Each of them was a man who had stood by him through a host of nasty experiences. He loved them all and he prayed that when this journey was over they would still be together to celebrate the victory that surely lay ahead of so much tragedy.

CHAPTER 34

The Valley of the Shadow

A night in the cave proved uneventful. When dawn came, their route took them constantly downward, leaving the ridge behind them. By mid-morning they had descended the rocky slopes into the valley. The village was clearly visible as they negotiated their way through the boulders clustered near the foot of the incline. Around it on all four sides rose snow-covered peaks but except for a scattering of colored leaves, Notre-Dame-de-Bellecombe might still have been enjoying the last days of summer. It was as though they had stepped from one season into another. Here, the air was sweet and warm, gone was the threat of snow and cold that had plagued them at the higher altitudes.

Notre-Dame-de-Bellecombe lay nestled next to a river, a bridge spanning its width near the center of the village. A church spire rose above the cluster of houses and shops. After the horror of the last few days, the pastoral scene seemed almost too good to be true. Devin longed to simply walk into town like ordinary men and rent a room at the inn. How good it would be to sit at a table and have a real meal served to them. He had no idea where Marcus intended them to spend the night but it was not in a real bed, if the marks on Georges' map had influenced him at all.

They skirted the few farms dispersed across the valley. Small orchards dotted the land surrounding the diminutive barns and sheds. Everything seemed designed on a smaller scale than normal. Perhaps the severe winters made smaller structures easier to keep warm. Black-faced sheep with cream-colored coats grazed peacefully, scattered like dozens of children's toys left forgotten after play.

By mid-afternoon Marcus ensconced them in a grove of trees by a clear brook near the southern end of the valley. "We'll camp here," he announced. "Devin said Georges marked it as a safe place to stay. I'm going to go into town to buy some bread and cheese and maybe some preserved meat that we can carry with us."

"I'll keep the wolves here," Chastel said. "The last thing we need is to have several sheep killed while we're visiting. I pray that no one noticed them traveling with us when we came into the valley today."

"I tried to keep our route against the eastern side of the valley. Unless someone was specifically watching for us, I doubt we were noticed," Marcus answered, laying his packs on the ground. "If, for any reason, I should not return by morning, Chastel, you are to leave immediately and get Devin and Gaspard to safety. Devin has the map with him."

"Understood," Chastel responded.

Devin watched Marcus walk away. He realized that they could have camped much closer and saved Marcus an additional long trek into town but he was certain that Georges had reasons for his nightly stops. He was also certain that Marcus and Chastel had discussed all of this earlier. Marcus had only reiterated part of the conversation so that Gaspard and Devin wouldn't object to leaving, should the situation go awry. He slid down onto the thick grass and fixed Chastel with a stern look. "What could go wrong?"

"Any number of things," Chastel answered, adding his pack to Marcus'. "It never hurts to be prepared."

"Georges didn't seem to have any reservations about stopping at Bellecombe. It was circled on his map." He stopped abruptly when something broke his train of thought. "What happened to Georges' map?"

"Isn't it in his pack?" Chastel asked.

"I don't know," Devin said, struggling to his feet. "But if it had been, why would Marcus have had me draw a new one?"

"That I don't know," Chastel answered.

Gaspard followed Devin and they opened Georges' pack and spread the contents on the grass. Two shirts, extra socks, a scarf and gloves, a few bandages and medicines, and a packet of papers were the sparse contents. Devin opened the papers. The first one made him groan. He sat down abruptly on the grass.

"What is it?" Chastel asked.

"His will," Gaspard said, reading over Devin's shoulder. "Apparently, he has a sister with two sons. He left everything he had to them."

Devin carefully refolded the document and slipped it back into the pack. He opened the second item which was in an unsealed envelope. He saw immediately that it was addressed to Georges' sister. It seemed an invasion of privacy to read it so he simply folded it back up and put it in the envelope.

"It was a letter to his sister," he explained to the others, "perhaps clarifying his reasons for this trip."

"But no map?" Gaspard asked.

Devin shook his head. "It's not in Georges' pack. Maybe Marcus took it out but I actually haven't seen it since we left Madame Aucoin's."

"Maybe he didn't bring it with him," Chastel suggested. "Perhaps his memory was as sharp as yours."

"I can't believe he didn't bring it," Devin replied, carefully repacking everything in the order he had taken it out. "If we had needed to change our route he would have required that map to plan a different course."

Gaspard lifted Marcus' pack. "We could check his pack while he's not here."

"I won't do that," Devin said. "I will ask him about it but I won't go through his things without his permission. That's just wrong."

Chastel looked relieved. "I agree. Is it possible that Marcus has it with him and he had you draw another one just to make sure you were able to take us home if the job fell to you?"

"That's altogether possible," Devin replied. "And now it makes me wonder what possible dangers could lurk in a village as idyllic as Bellecombe."

Their conversation left all of them ill-at-ease as late afternoon turned into dusk and Marcus had still not returned. There was no way to light a lantern or kindle a fire to guide him without calling attention to the rest of them. Chastel's wolves grew restive with the coming night. The craving to hunt proved hard to resist and with no meat on hand to pacify them, Chastel grew tense trying to constrain their natural instincts.

271

"Could you run with them?" Devin suggested. "I don't know how much influence you have over them, but with your direction maybe they would restrain themselves to hunting the mountain slopes rather than the pastures."

"It's not that easy, Devin," Chastel responded despairingly. "They've had the smell of the sheep in their noses all afternoon. It's difficult to resist something so defenseless and close at hand in favor of a wild animal who may give chase. I wonder if Georges didn't think this through completely when he planned for us to spend the night here. He'd had no experience with the wolves and I'm not sure how well he understood the situation."

"If Marcus would come back, we could leave tonight," Gaspard said.

Chastel shrugged. "Traveling at night is dangerous, even across cleared fields such as these, and men who travel at night always fall under suspicion."

"We're not thieves or murderers," Gaspard replied defensively.

Chastel called sharply to a wolf that was moving out of sight and turned back to them. "The people in this valley don't know that. Remember how suspicious we were of the man with the grouse who appeared suddenly by our fire. The provinces are fraught with dangers. People are always wary and prepared to think the worst."

Silence fell between them. The wolves panted and strained toward the pastures filled with sheep. The grass smelled fresh, the earth damp, and the little brook sang merrily as it trickled over stones in its course. The clear night sky glittered with stars and the moon, grown plumper, rose above the horizon, lending its light to the fields below it. It was Devin who spied a figure walking toward them with a lantern. Nothing in his stature or walk indicated for certain that it was Marcus and he grew more uneasy, the closer the man came.

"He's headed straight for us," Devin whispered. "What should we do?"

"Stand up and pull your pistols," Chastel directed. "There's nowhere to hide here. Not with a pack of wolves with us."

"Take them further into the trees," Devin said. "If this is some innocent villager, we'll cause less concern if there are just two of us here."

"All right," Chastel agreed, silently shepherding the wolves off into the wooded area behind them.

Devin consolidated their belongings so that it seemed to be a more probable amount for two men traveling through the mountains. The man had come much closer now and Devin saw by his walk and size that this was not Marcus but some stranger.

"Hello!" the man called out when he was still a number of paces away.

"Hello," Devin answered, with much less enthusiasm.

"I thought I saw some men come through my land to camp," the man said, a slit between his dark beard and his mustache splitting to reveal very white teeth. "Do you have dogs with you, then?"

"No," Devin replied honestly. "Is this your land that we camped on? I apologize for not asking your permission. We'll be gone by morning."

The man grunted. "I'd have sworn there were more of you, at least four men and some dogs. My wife is afraid for our sheep. She wants you to know they are off limits to hunters."

"We have no intention of harming your sheep," Devin replied. "My uncle brought us up from Amiens to do a little hunting. This looked like a fine spot to camp for the night. We can move on, if it suits you better. We ran into snow in the mountains to the north. It's very pleasant here. We hoped to spend a night out of the bad weather."

"You don't have a fire," the man said suspiciously.

"We don't need one," Devin replied. "We've nothing to cook and the air is still mild."

"Seems a bit peculiar to me," said the man, leaning to one side, eyeing up their supplies. "Where is your uncle?"

"He's taken a trip into the bushes," Gaspard said with a knowing wink.

"Would you like us to move on?" Devin asked, an edge creeping into his voice.

The man stepped back. "No, no. Enjoy the mild weather. It won't last. Just know that my sheep are my livelihood. I won't lose one without recompense. We have a *shérif* in Bellecombe. I won't hesitate to call him."

"You haven't made a reputation of friendliness in your village, have you?" Gaspard asked snidely.

"We just don't get many strangers," the man answered. "The *shérif* has someone right now locked up in his jail. He fits the description of a man the Chancellor put a bounty on."

"Chancellor Roché?" Devin asked, his heart thumping.

"No, not him," the man replied. "That new Chancellor, what's his name? Forneaux?

Devin choked. "I don't know. I hadn't heard there was a new Chancellor."

"How long have you been in the mountains?" the man asked. "We heard the news clear out here. A hunter came out to tell us, name of Descremps. Have you ever heard of him?"

"No," Gaspard answered, putting his hand on Devin's shoulder.

The man shifted his position. "Well, I need to be going. My wife will worry. You mind you stay away from the sheep and we'll get along just fine. Maybe I'll be by in the morning and bring you a fresh loaf of bread. You have a good night, now."

Devin waited until the man faded out into the moonlit pasture and slumped back onto the grass. "If your father's Chancellor, Gaspard, do you think my father's already dead?"

"It may not be true," Gaspard said. "Descremps may have made it up to explain the bounty on us. But I think the *shérif* must have Marcus. What shall we do?"

They waited until Chastel and the wolves reappeared out of the trees. "I heard most of that," Chastel said. "God, I wish Marcus had skipped trying to get supplies. Now we're in a bad predicament."

"What is the best way to get him out?" Devin asked. "We don't even know where the jail is."

"Marcus would want us to keep going," Chastel said firmly. "He expressly asked me to take both of you and leave in the morning."

"That's not going to happen," Devin replied. "Do you think, if any of the rest of us were in that jail, that Marcus would go off and leave us?"

"Keep your voice down," Chastel cautioned.

"Well, I don't intend to leave him," Devin said.

Chastel stood a moment, debating. "All right, I'll send the wolves off to hunt and you and I will go into town,

Devin. The *shérif*'s office is apt to be the only building with candles still burning by the time we arrive. We'll say you are looking for a doctor for your ankle; hopefully we can overpower the *shérif* and leave with Marcus. Gaspard, you are our backup plan. If we get in trouble, you need to provide reinforcements."

"Ah, a reinforcement of one," Gaspard said skeptically. "I'm not sure how much good I will do."

"First of all, you can switch jackets with Devin so that you have the journal," Chastel instructed. "If it comes to the worst, you may have to get it to Coreé yourself."

"Absolutely not," Gaspard replied. "I'll switch jackets but I am not going on alone. I refuse to be eaten by wolves or bears or fall down a ravine where someone won't find my bones until spring."

"Then we'll all die here together," Chastel snapped. "Does that make you feel better?"

Gaspard bowed. "Yes, much better! I refuse to die alone."

"I probably shouldn't suggest this," Devin said. "But maybe we should give the wolves free run at the sheep. I don't want any of them to be shot or hurt but if the wolves cause a diversion, we might be able to slip Marcus away without being caught."

"That can be easily arranged," Chastel said. "Now let's go before our visiting sheep farmer decides that maybe we are more suspicious than we first seemed."

276

CHAPTER 35

Wolves in Sheep's Clothing

It was finally decided that Devin and Gaspard should go into the village, leaving Chastel to mind the wolves. Soon after they left, he was to send the pack out after the sheep. Devin spared a moment's consideration for the sturdy little sheep but Marcus' life was more important. With any luck, the farmers would send someone to the *shérif* for help and he and Gaspard could find and release Marcus while the jail was unattended.

As they neared the village, howling broke out in the fields behind them. They hastened their steps, passing tall narrow houses of stucco and half timbers, their steep pitched roofs discouraging the buildup of snow during the winter months. Each had a second-story door and balcony. Devin assumed this unusual adaption enabled the residents to still escape their homes when winter snows rose above the first floor and blocked the front door. Had they come here for a visit, Devin would have loved to explore the quaint mountain village but tonight he and Gaspard were on a mission to save Marcus' life and admiring the architecture was not on the agenda.

Shots rang out from the fields behind them and Devin prayed the wolves would survive. He hated endangering them just for the sake of a diversion but they were all they had at the moment. He knew Chastel would mourn the loss of even one. The more desperate they became, the more willing they were to put themselves and others at risk.

Gaspard grabbed Devin's arm and pulled him behind a building. They had almost run right into the *shérif*'s office. Centrally located, the windows on one side faced the village square; the other side viewed the road into town and the fields beyond. An oil lamp illuminated a cluttered desk and the face of a bearded man, staring out the window. More shots broke the silence and the oil lamp was snuffed. The front door opened and a bear of a man locked up and headed out of town at a run, a rifle over his shoulder.

"You're a genius!" Gaspard whispered gleefully. They checked for any other concerned citizens who might be racing to protect their livestock and rounded the building.

"May I?" Gaspard produced a lock pick from his jacket pocket.

"By all means," Devin replied. "Just be quick about it."

Gaspard had always been the better one at picking locks and he had the door open in under a minute. They went inside and closed it silently behind them.

"Marcus?" Devin whispered.

"Here," he responded from the back of the building.

They felt their way across the room. There was only one jail cell, a simple room with wooden walls and a small barred window on the door. Gaspard picked the padlock and swung the door open.

"Damn," Marcus grumbled. "You two shouldn't have come. Where is Chastel?"

"With the wolves," Devin whispered. "Let's get out of here."

Several more of the villagers were hurrying out of town and they had to move carefully, ducking between buildings to avoid being seen. Devin inadvertently crushed one house's flower bed when they leaped back out of sight. The open fields provided little or no protection so they circled to the west until they reached the foot of the mountains. They followed them until they reached the extreme southern end of the valley where they had agreed to meet with Chastel.

By then the gray light of dawn illuminated the sky. The gunshots had ceased hours before but the tranquil valley with its winding river and quaint tall houses seemed much less welcoming and picturesque this morning. Chastel sat waiting for them, perched on a rock, the wolves gathered around them.

"Are the wolves all right?" Devin asked.

Chastel nodded. "None are missing and we have only one injury." He pointed to the little gray wolf, which was curled by his foot licking her paw.

Devin knelt down on one knee beside her, his ankle protesting. "What happened?"

"She let me look at it. It's not a gunshot wound," Chastel said. "Maybe she just cut it on a rock. I put some salve on it. She should be fine." He stood up and looked at Marcus. "And how are you?"

"Feeling foolish," Marcus replied, "that the man I am supposed to be protecting had to rescue me. Let's move up into the mountains. I've had quite enough of Notre-Dame-de-Bellecombe."

They climbed steadily all day with no sign of pursuit. They walked a little slower because of Devin's ankle and the gray wolf's sore paw. Marcus' story came out as they traveled. He'd bought cheese and meat and then had gone into the bakery for bread. There he had run into the *shérif*, who still had Descremps' description of him fresh in his mind. He arrested him on the spot and vowed to hold him until the magistrate made his yearly visit.

"God, when was that going to be?" Gaspard asked.

"June," Marcus replied. "He waits until the snows have melted and travel is safe."

Devin smiled. "I'm afraid to ask what happened to the cheese and meat."

"He ate most of it," Marcus said indignantly. "Did you see the size of that man? He could have eaten the better part of a whole sheep for dinner and finished it off the next morning for breakfast."

Devin laughed. The sound felt strange to him. He realized how long it had been since he had laughed, since something funny had overcome the deep sadness that threatened to undo him, no matter what. A bit of the heaviness left his chest.

"What did Madame Aucoin say when we left?" Gaspard reminded them. "Eat your breakfast because tomorrow it will be back to raw fish and rabbits! God, she was so right."

They laughed again and Devin recalled the evening of joking and laughter they had shared in the wine cellar of Angelique's chateau amid the ghastly memories of her family's murders. He'd realized then that it was humor that allowed people to carry on, even when things seemed most bleak and good friends had been lost.

"For a while I thought that Georges had a pantry in his pack," Devin said, using the walking stick to propel himself along. "It seemed as though he had an endless supply of food – until it ran out. We checked last night and there is nothing left in there that is edible." He avoided a column of stone poking out of the ground. "Marcus, do you know what happened to Georges' map?"

Marcus stopped until Devin caught up to him. "It's not in his pack. I looked for it after he was killed. That's why I asked you to draw another one."

"It's strange that it's missing," Chastel said. "Has anyone seen it since we left Amiens?"

"He and I went over it the first night," Marcus told him. "He simply gave me a quick overview of where we were and where we needed to go. He put it back into his pack when we were done."

Devin bent to pick up a piece of rock that glittered in the sunlight. "He probably didn't need it to find the cabin. He'd been there multiple times as a child."

"So where did it go?" Gaspard asked.

Chastel frowned. "Was there any time before Descremps was killed that Georges' pack was unattended? Is it possible that Descremps could have taken it? It would have been the perfect guide for an assassin. He would have known which route we were taking and where we planned to stay overnight."

Devin stopped. "Is it possible that Descremps wasn't working alone? What if the men the wolves killed were only part of the group he had with him?"

CHAPTER 36

Evidence and Speculation

"Leave it to you, Devin, to ruin a perfectly good morning!" Gaspard muttered.

"Well, he's right you know," Marcus said. "The moment we let our guard down, we're in trouble. We have no way of knowing whether Descremps had an accomplice that was or is still living. It would be better to assume that he did. We will stay safer if we expect the unexpected. I personally don't remember a time that Georges' pack was where Descremps could have gotten to it, but there was a lot of confusion when Georges died."

"I agree," Chastel said. "Would it be wise to change our route just to throw off anyone who might be pursuing us?"

"That might work if we knew these mountains well enough," Devin said. "I wish I knew which village was Descremps' village. Georges hoped to spare us further problems and we don't know enough to follow his advice."

"The fact that he said that indicated that he thought you would be following his map," Chastel pointed out.

"I guess it does," Devin agreed.

"Then we'll avoid any village from this point on," Marcus said. "We'll eat off the land until we reach Coreé."

They walked on in silence. The missing map seemed to be a mystery without a solution. Devin stopped at the top of a ridge and scanned the slopes below them. His eyes were nearly back to normal and for just a moment, he thought he saw a figure far below them. It disappeared into a clump of dwarf pines and didn't reemerge.

"What did you see?" Chastel asked, pausing beside him.

Devin shrugged. "I'm not sure. It seemed to me that there was a figure below us." He pointed with his finger. "It disappeared into those pines. It may be nothing."

"I'll send several wolves down," Chastel offered. "It will take no time to check and it will relieve your mind that we aren't being followed." He bent and spoke to his pack.

Devin would never cease to marvel at the relationship Chastel had formed with his wolves. They did his bidding without question, even suppressing their natural instincts to follow his lead. When he spoke, their ears pricked to attention, their eyes were fixed on him. Never did they question what he asked of them, even if he sent them into danger. It was something beautiful to behold – this perfect empathy between man and beast.

Three wolves dashed off, sending small stones and dirt scattering as they went. They reached the pines within minutes, circled them and flushed out a mountain goat which bounded down the mountainside as though the devil himself were after it.

Chastel chuckled. "Feel better?"

Devin gave a slight shake of his head. It was not a mountain goat he had seen below them but the figure of man. Perhaps his head wound had left him more damaged than was visible to the eye. He'd had visions, dreams, and now apparently, he was seeing men who simply weren't there. It made him feel vulnerable and, above all, unreliable as a witness or a watchman.

"Not what you expected?" Chastel asked kindly.

"A mountain goat wasn't what I saw," Devin admitted. "I saw the figure of a man. He ducked into the pines when he saw me watching him. Maybe I'm going mad, Chastel. This trip has been enough to drive a sane man crazy."

"Or maybe," Chastel said, "you experienced a phenomenon peculiar to these mountains."

"What do you mean?" Devin asked.

"Just think for a moment. You are traveling with a man who not only can transform into a wolf but controls his own pack. Your grandmother can become a falcon, though I doubt she does it very often anymore. Why is it out of the realm of possibility that a man could hide by changing into the form of a mountain goat? Just because we have never heard of this before, doesn't mean it can't happen." He glanced back down the mountain. Neither the wolves nor the terrified goat were in sight. "By the way," Chastel added, "I hope my wolves kill that goat simply because it's adding to your worries and you have enough on your shoulders at the moment."

The terrain proved as changeable as the weather. Lush valleys still held the remnants of summer close but on the ridges snow flurries swirled and cold winds howled. Oddly enough, Devin found he preferred the ridges. Despite the cold, they provided an unobstructed view of everything below them. Here no one could trail them without being seen. The landscape was barren and rocky except for a few clumps of dwarf pines. He admired the tenacity of the diminutive trees which grew twisted and gnarled, sculpted by the constant force of the northern winds. Their exposed roots clung stubbornly to the mountainsides. Their environment had left them tough and wiry, able to cope with whatever conditions the mountain range dished out.

Devin felt himself changing, too. Gone was the softness of a life spent among his books and manuscripts. His body felt hard and foreign to him, used to strenuous climbs and rapid adjustments to any situation. He lived solely on meat and water and slept on inflexible stone, wrapped in one blanket against the cold.

The transformation was even more amazing in Gaspard. Gone was the drunken, whining *Académie* boy. Gaspard pulled his own weight now. He anticipated needs before they were mentioned, gathering firewood, seeking shelter, and even hunting alongside Marcus. Devin marveled every day that his childhood friend had taken to responsibility with a passion. Devin no longer saw him as an unsuitable partner for Angelique and was anticipating their reunion with pleasure. Gaspard had grown up.

And yet in spite of the fact that they had all become more accustomed to the steep climbs and rough descents, Devin never felt the feeling of pursuit diminish. He didn't discuss it with Marcus or Chastel. Perhaps it was simply his own ghosts that harried and haunted his days and left him wakeful and on edge at night. Twice more, he'd seen a figure out of the corner of his eye, a lone specter that vanished on closer examination. The wolves seemed unaffected by the phantom pursuer, though they roamed on both sides of their group and hunted in front and behind. Surely, if something were following them, they would have sensed it.

Devin lost track of time. Each day was the same: a

meager breakfast of some leftover game from the night before, an endless trek with two breaks to rest and drink the clear water that the mountains afforded in abundance, and an evening meal of whatever game Marcus and Gaspard brought back. His ankle was nearly healed and only ached in the evening after a long day of walking. In the morning, the stiffness lasted only a few moments as they started out.

The gray wolf had healed as well. She had attached herself to Devin and walked at his side in the first few days after they left Notre-Dame-de-Bellecombe, when they were both limping. Since then their relationship hadn't changed. While the other wolves raced and hunted among the rocks, she remained steadfast, padding beside him every morning and curling against him at night.

The mountains before them melted away as those behind them grew more abundant. One day soon, they would descend the last slope and see the foothills north of Coreé. They had left on this mission as five and they would finish as four. Hopefully, they could still right the wrongs that René Forneaux and his Shadow Government had visited upon the people of Llisé and Devin would arrive in time to save his father's life, if God saw fit.

The map's course required a difficult climb up the tallest mountain in the range. The rocky face seemed determined to discourage anyone from traversing its height. Marcus hauled ropes from his pack and linked them all together at one point in case one of them might make a misstep navigating the rocky crags. The wind and snow showers were relentless and Devin wondered if he would ever be warm again. Maintaining a good grip with gloves was impossible and he felt as though his hands were shredded by noon.

They couldn't even stop for a break because the mountain afforded no flat or sheltered places for them to rest.

Chastel showed amazing skill in scaling the mountainside. His wolves leaped from rock to rock in an almost joyful display of fearless climbing. It was as though Chastel tapped into his wolf persona to tackle the stony slopes with his own form of bold alacrity. Marcus allowed him to take the lead and it was all the others could do to keep up with him. Under his direction their frightening ascent transformed into a graceful ballet of holds and pivots that led them surely upward. Fear vanished and they reached the peak before nightfall.

That night they camped on a high ridge, kindling a fire to drive away the chill of blowing snow and a bitter wind. They had been pelted with flurries all day but the last of the gray clouds dissolved by evening, pausing long enough to compose a spectacular sunset of orange and gold. The full moon rose behind them in all its glory, so close it seemed they might touch it if they reached out their hands. The night sky glittered with stars; some seemed incredibly near and others faint and distant; many shimmered blue as ice but others glowed warm as fire. It seemed to Devin that he had never felt so close to God. The fallen snow reflected the moonlight and the world possessed a radiance he had never experienced before. His heart felt so full of the beauty of the night that he thought it might burst. Never had he felt so thankful that his sight seemed to be completely restored!

Chastel and Gaspard played with a worn pack of cards while Marcus scanned the darkness for signs of an intruder. Devin retrieved his rosary from his pocket as he sat by the fire. Sliding the familiar stones between his fingers, he repeated the words silently. The gray wolf crossed their circle and laid her muzzle in his lap and he paused to stroke her head. The fire crackled and popped, the charring wood checkered with glowing coals.

It was the first night since the one in the valley at Notre-Dame-de-Bellecombe that they had spent in the open. Georges' instructions had always provided shelter until now. However, maybe Georges had camped on this open ridge once and felt the hand of God touch his heart, too.

Suddenly, a sound like a boot sliding on pebbles broke the silence. The gray wolf jumped to her feet, the hackles on her back raised up. She growled and the other wolves joined her. They stood as a pack, their tails to the fire with their heads pointed outward. Devin felt a shudder run up his back as the sound of footsteps broke the peacefulness of their formerly silent world. Marcus' gun leveled in the direction of the sound as did Chastel's and Gaspard's. Devin dropped his rosary at his feet and fumbled for his pistol.

CHAPTER 37

The Company of Strangers

A man stepped out of the shadows. For a split second, Devin thought Descremps stood before them, but though the hair and face were the same, there was no scar. He bore no weapon that they could see, his boots were worn, the leather cracked. He stood with his hands stretched outward, his palms up. "I mean you no harm," he said.

Marcus approached, patted the man's coat and removed only a hunting knife. "Were you following us?" he asked, stepping back.

"Yes," he answered. "I've followed you since you left Notre-Dame-de-Bellecombe."

Devin felt a certain relief that his mysterious sightings of someone following them had not been his imagination. But if this man had been shadowing them for days, surely he could have picked them off one by one any time he chose. Why had he waited until tonight to make his presence known?

"What do you want?" Devin asked.

"My name is Ancil Descremps," he answered. "Jean-

Michel was my brother, my twin. He had a commission to kill you – all four of you. He left Notre-Dame-de-Bellecombe convinced that he would. He has never failed before and yet I felt him die several nights before you arrived in the valley. I would like to bury his body. Can you tell me where it is?"

Devin looked at Marcus.

"Your brother killed a very dear friend of ours," Marcus began. "We shot your brother twice in the chest and thought we had killed him. I rolled him over the bank into a river but he came back later. He set fire to the cabin where we were staying in the middle of the night. We barely escaped with our lives but the wolves treed your brother and Chastel and I shot him in the head. We threw his body into the flames of the burning cabin. There is nothing left to bury."

The man winced visibly. "Thank you for being honest with me. I needed to know what happened."

"Did you know what he intended?" Marcus asked. "Did it ever occur to you to question the legitimacy of his killing the Chancellor's son or that René Forneaux would pay to have his own son assassinated?"

"He never shared the name of his employers with me," Ancil replied. "He wanted to protect me and our mother who is very old. All she has ever known was that Jean-Michel was a hunter. She never questioned the large amounts of money he brought her. He was a good son. She never lacked for anything."

"A son who killed people for a living," Devin said pointedly.

"The same thing might be said of any soldier," Ancil replied. "I'm only telling you what I knew of him. He didn't shield me from what he did for a living but he kept my mother comfortable. I cannot fault him for that."

"Your brother killed a good, kind man who only came with us to guide us over the mountains," Devin shouted in exasperation. "He stabbed an innocent woman and her children at Comte Aucoin's chateau. How can you condone that?"

Ancil threw his hands in the air. "I don't condone it. I had no control over any of his dealings, but please know that Jean-Michel meant you no malice. He was simply doing his job. He was a paid assassin and he was very good at what he did."

"He was unusually good at it," Marcus commented wryly. "He was able to sneak up on those he meant to kill without them hearing him. Even our wolves could not track him. Apparently, you have some of those same talents if you have trailed us for days. Can you explain how you did that?"

"When we were boys, Jean-Michel discovered that he could mask his scent by using the scent of another animal. He used the scent of rabbit to hunt fox, the smell of fresh fish to attract bears. If he evaded your wolves he probably doused himself with deer scent to put them off the trail."

"And did you do the same, as you've trailed us these last ten days?" Chastel asked.

Ancil nodded. "It was the only way I could stay safe from your wolves."

Marcus shook his head. "What do you intend to do now?"

"Return to my mother," Ancil replied. "I told her nothing except that I was going hunting. She is used to her sons being gone for long periods of time. We have good neighbors. She will be all right until I return."

"Was there another contract for our lives?" Gaspard asked.

"I don't know," Ancil replied. "This is the first time Jean-Michel has ever failed. Perhaps his employer thought another contract wasn't necessary."

"That would be lucky," Gaspard commented, "but I'm not going to count on it."

"Nor will I," Marcus agreed. He bent and extracted a rope from his pack. "I'm sorry but I can hardly take your word for it that you mean us no harm, Ancil. Perhaps you intend to kill us tonight in our sleep or tomorrow on the trail."

For the first time, Devin felt an objection rising in his throat. "Don't kill him, Marcus," he cautioned.

"I don't intend to," Marcus replied. "But I'm going to tie him up for the night. Tomorrow I will loosen the knots so he can escape in a few hours." He reached out a hand. "Your pack, please, Ancil. There will be no more animal scents to throw off our wolves. If you need the scent to hunt, you can prepare more." Marcus rummaged through the pack, extracting five small vials. He stiffened, pulling out a familiar folded paper.

"That's Georges' map!" Devin exclaimed.

"It is indeed," Marcus said, his eyes narrowing. "We have a consummate liar in our midst. Apparently, the Descremps brothers work together."

"When did you take the map?" Devin demanded.

Descremps cocked his head. "The night our accomplice appeared at your fire. You and your friend were so stunned from watching Marcus slit his throat that you paid little attention to the packs."

"But Georges was there, too!" Devin objected.

"Georges was too busy shepherding you two, to be worried about his own pack," Descremps answered smugly.

"What did you hope to accomplish tonight, Ancil?" Marcus asked. "Did you plan to kill us in our sleep or poison our food?"

Ancil's smile was feral. "Either has a certain attraction, although fire has its merits, too. My brother died by fire – perhaps his killers deserve the same fate."

"Your brother had his head blown off," Chastel retorted. "None of us is cruel enough to burn a man to death – something you apparently cannot say."

"I do what is called upon me to do," Ancil muttered, "nothing more, nothing less."

He moved so fast that Devin saw only the blur of something flung overhead which fell into the campfire. A deafening explosion knocked him off his feet and shook the very mountain beneath them.

Shattered rock, snow, and dust drifted down on five men lying prostrate, the cold light of the moon the only illumination. Devin rolled over, felt fur beneath his hands, as the gray wolf rose and shook herself. He ran a hand over her back and bent to fumble for his gun in the debris at his feet. Not five feet away, Descremps rose up like the Devil himself, his cheeks smeared with ashes and blistered from the explosion.

He dove at Devin, catching him by the shoulders and smacking him back down onto the ledge. A knife gleamed in his hand. Devin's fingers closed over a rock and he slammed it into the side of Descremps' head. The impact stopped the man only momentarily. He paused, hanging over Devin, blood and saliva dripping from his face. Devin hit him again and again until Descremps' hand closed over

Devin's wrist, bending it backwards until the rock dropped from his immobile fingers. A bundle of fur leaped into their silent tussle with a snarl. The little gray wolf latched onto Ancil's throat.

"Stop!" Chastel shouted. What followed was a string of syllables intelligible only to the wolves but the gray wolf ceased her attack and backed off.

Marcus tossed a rope to Chastel, his gun trained on Ancil. "Tie him up."

Chastel dragged Ancil's hands behind his back and tied them securely. He yanked the rope tightly and dragged him to his feet.

Devin rose, grateful that Gaspard was standing to his left, apparently undamaged. He thought of Georges and how they might all have lost their lives tonight. He stepped forward and slapped Ancil across the face. "You can try to justify your profession however you like!" he snapped. "But you deal in death! You and your brother were both cold-hearted killers! Nothing you say or do will make that right."

Ancil turned to face him, his eyes cold, his face impassive except for the bloody imprint where Devin's rock had connected with his cheek. "The world is filled with men like me, Monsieur Roché. It is men like you who are in the minority. If I don't kill you, someone else will. Bleeding hearts don't last long in this empire."

Marcus grabbed Devin's shoulder and pulled him back. "Get away from him! Chastel, find something to gag him with. I've heard enough of his talk tonight!"

"And tomorrow," Ancil said. "What happens when none of you are brave enough to kill an unarmed man?"

"Make no mistake," Marcus growled. "I will have no

qualms about killing you, unarmed or not. I will be ridding the empire of a ruthless killer!"

Chastel forced a bandage into Ancil's mouth and tied it behind his head. He and Marcus walked him to a rock, well away from the campfire, and sat him down. They bound him to it, wedging the ropes beneath the rock so they were impossible to slide up and over it.

Marcus sank down by the fire, his pistol aimed at Ancil's head. "It would be better to shoot him now," he said in a low voice. "He's like a mad dog. There's nothing left to save. He's convinced himself that assassination is a legitimate way of life."

"What will you do?" Gaspard asked, dusting dirt and ash from his trousers.

"I cannot leave him tied to a rock. He'll free himself despite our best efforts to secure him," Marcus answered.

"We have to kill him," Chastel said. "If you leave him alive, he'll follow us. We could all be dead tomorrow, Marcus."

"I know that," Marcus replied.

The evening had been ruined. Above them the moon and stars still shone but before them, in the person of Ancil Descremps, lay a moral and ethical quandary that could easily haunt them for the rest of their days.

"It's a miracle no one was killed," Chastel said, making a tally of wolves and people. "Is anyone hurt?"

Unbelievably, aside from a few cuts and scratches, everyone had survived and none of the wolves had been injured either. Unconsciously, they had all moved away from the fire and toward Ancil as they had talked to him, or they might all have been killed. But Ancil seemed to gloat as his brother had, as though even in defeat he could claim victory, simply because he had made the attempt to kill them even if he hadn't been successful. Devin wondered what other malicious plan he might hold in reserve if this one had failed.

"Devin, you and Gaspard get some sleep while Chastel and I keep watch. I'll wake you later," Marcus announced suddenly.

"But Chastel and I normally keep watch together," Devin protested.

"Do as I say," Marcus snapped.

Chastel rekindled the fire from the few embers that remained. Devin and Gaspard got out their blankets and lay down as close to the new flames as possible. The gray wolf came to lie next to Devin, resting her head on his hip as he lay on his side, watching Ancil. He didn't expect to sleep, not after the evening's events. He didn't even remember closing his eyes, but when he opened them, it was morning and Ancil was gone.

Neither Chastel nor Marcus was there either and the wolves were missing, too. Only the little gray one still crouched by his side. "Marcus!" he yelled.

CHAPTER 38

The Hills of Home

Gaspard sat up, rubbing sleep from his eyes. "What happened?" he asked groggily.

Devin jumped to his feet. "I don't know. Marcus and Chastel are gone and so is Descremps!"

Gaspard rose languidly to his feet. "At least there are no bodies."

"They never wakened us," Devin reminded him. "What if Ancil overpowered them? Or he managed to escape and they went after him."

"Or perhaps," Marcus announced cheerfully from behind them, "both of us are alive and well. It's a fine morning. Let's make an early start."

Devin turned around. Aside from Marcus and Chastel looking a bit smudgy around the eyes from lack of sleep, both of them seemed in good spirits. "Where's Ancil?" he asked.

"Does it matter?" Marcus replied. "He won't be bothering us anymore. Would you unwrap the leftover rabbit from last night? I'm starving."

Devin removed the rabbit from Georges' pack, carefully examining Marcus and Chastel for any sign of bloodstains. Whatever happened last night had left no mark on either man. Both Gaspard's and Devin's questions received carefully veiled answers. Obviously the truth was not going to be forthcoming.

They left after a hurried breakfast, Devin and Gaspard falling behind Chastel and Marcus. Devin almost wished that they could spend another night on that high ridge, a night unblemished by a visit from one of the Descremps brothers.

"Do you think they shot him?" Gaspard asked quietly.

"We'd have heard that," Devin replied.

Gaspard exhaled, his breath misting the air in front of him. "Maybe they slit his throat."

"There was no blood anywhere."

"The wolves could have eaten him," Gaspard suggested. "All of them were gone when we wakened." He waggled his fingers in front of the little gray wolf. "All except for your little pet. Have you thought of naming her?"

"Chastel claims they all have names already," Devin said. "Not ones that translate into human terms but something they use to identify each other."

"Have you asked him what her name is?"

"No," Devin answered. "I probably couldn't pronounce it anyway. Have you heard him talk to them?" That was not the real reason. He had never forgotten Chastel's story that this wolf had been accepted by his pack the night that the villagers of Lac Dupré disappeared. Devin had been fool enough once to voice his theory to Chastel that maybe this little wolf was Jeanette. He'd been witness to her affinity to Armand and now to him. She slept beside him, she had protected him, and she seemed more devoted to him than to anyone else in their group. His hope, that somehow she was Jeanette, trapped within a soft gray wolf skin, was not something he wanted to present for Gaspard to scrutinize. He would allow his affection for this little gray wolf simply to simmer in the back of his brain until he reached Coreé. Then he would not give up until Chastel told him the truth about what he knew.

Whatever Marcus and Chastel had done to Ancil Descremps, Devin saw no more figures following them. The last few days of their journey were more relaxed and though Gaspard continued to press them as to the fate of their last assassin, Devin was content to let the matter go. Had Marcus felt they should know, he would have told them. There had been enough tragedy and death on this trip; if Marcus had conspired to spare them the details of this final execution, and he suspected that's what it had been, so be it.

They camped on what was to become their last night, halfway down a mountain. Vienne's rolling hills stretched out soft and verdant in the evening light. They saw no more peaks taunting them in the distance and for today at least, the weather had been pleasantly crisp, not cold, and the leaves beautifully tinted with a first hint of fall colors. The air still held the memories of summer. How strange that they had experienced all four seasons in the space of a month, depending on the elevation. Devin noticed different scents here and he could already feel the ties of home pulling him closer.

"How do we smuggle the wolves into Coreé?" he asked. "You included me in so little of the planning. I don't even know what you have proposed."

"Doesn't the sewer system run under the Archives?" Gaspard asked. "I believe the plan is to have you bring them in that way, should we need them. Can you find a forgotten spot where they can stay?"

Devin broke off a small piece of rabbit meat and fed it to the gray wolf sitting expectantly at his feet. "I can do better than that. There's a portion of the Archives that is actually blocked off. There's been a problem with dampness and it can no longer be used for manuscripts. It's locked on the Archives' side but there is a back door that connects directly to the tunnels that lead down to the sewers below."

"Perfect," Chastel said cheerfully. "We won't mind the mildew and dampness. Could you smuggle us in some food, please?"

"I'd be delighted," Devin responded. He paused, choosing his next words carefully. "I know that Angelique said she hoped to murder Gaspard's father at one of the first galas of the season. I'd like to suggest another option."

"Go ahead," said Chastel.

"We have to present the information we have to Council – your testimony, Gaspard's, and Angelique's, plus Father Sébastian's journal."

"Don't forget the contract to have us all assassinated," Marcus added. "That was a real piece of luck that we ended up in possession of that!"

"And the contract," Devin continued. "If we ask to present the information, Forneaux will be on his guard and have us all arrested. If Forneaux is murdered at a party, then Angelique may be killed on the spot or thrown into jail. The rest of us could also be arrested as accomplices."

"So what are you proposing?" Marcus asked.

"I've spent a lot of time wondering what makes this

assassination we've arranged any different than the ones Forneaux had planned for us," Devin said quietly. "We cannot convince people that we are trying to maintain a different kind of government if we resort to the same barbaric tactics that Forneaux's men have been using in the past."

Marcus frowned. "Devin, the members of Council are not going to sit quietly by while you present your evidence. Your father has been accused of treason. They will most likely try to stop you or kill you before you can offer the information you have compiled."

"That's where the wolves come in," Devin said. "There is a direct passage that connects the Archives with Council Chambers. It's to facilitate the recovery of records needed during Council meetings."

"I'm well aware of its purpose," Marcus growled.

"If Chastel and Armand could bring the wolves in through there and we enter with them, we could hold the guards at bay while I present my case," Devin finished.

"And what happens to my father?" Gaspard asked.

"He will be charged and tried for treason, Gaspard," Devin answered. "I don't think there is any way we can avoid that."

Gaspard nodded. "Thank you for that, Dev. I do understand. While I still see the necessity of removing him from power, I can't tell you how much I would love not to be party to his murder."

"I agree completely," Devin answered. "Armand has spent the last few months teaching me the power of the spoken word. In order to free my father and clear him of any treasonable offenses, I have to be able to show evidence and present testimony. If I can reach Council Chambers and be allowed to speak, I could bring Forneaux down. If we grant him life in prison instead of a traitor's death, he might be willing to incriminate everyone who has worked with him."

"It puts you in considerable danger," Marcus objected. "I haven't protected you for months only to lose you on the floor of Council Chambers trying to persuade a bunch of hard-headed politicians that the course they are following is wrong!"

"They aren't all hard headed," Devin said. "A great many of them are my father's friends. Surely they would allow me to speak on his behalf."

"Perhaps," Marcus agreed. "But those who support Forneaux aren't going to just sit back and listen. They are either going to run for the door or they are going to fight for their lives and take you and Forneaux down before either of you can incriminate any of them."

"You and Chastel will be there," Devin continued persuasively, "and so will the wolves."

"The wolves aren't bullet proof," Chastel reminded him.

"No, but there will be enough of them to provide a deterrent to keep people in their seats. Marcus, can you take out the guards yourself?"

Marcus exhaled hard. "Probably not, but I do have some trustworthy friends in the guard. Men I can count on. We're going to have to think this through, Devin. It may take a few days to see what the situation is when we arrive. If Forneaux has instituted a curfew, we may even have trouble getting to Madame Aucoin's townhouse."

"Will you consider this?" Devin asked. "We might be able to pull it off without anyone being killed."

"I wouldn't count on that," Chastel said.

"Otherwise we will almost certainly forfeit Angelique's life," Devin said.

"Then you have my vote," Gaspard chimed in.

"There is one tactical advantage we could use, should you care to," Chastel announced, maneuvering his feet so they were closer to the fire. "Devin, do you remember how you asked me why there were no wolves around Albion?"

Devin nodded. "Yes, we thought it was very odd."

"I told you I had contacted two packs from that area. They agreed to meet us at the foot of the mountains. They had already left the region around Albion when you arrived. If more wolves would provide a stronger showing in Council Chambers, I have only to ask these two packs and they will go with us."

"You are amazing!" Devin murmured. "I can't imagine how you control your own wolves, let alone wolves from another pack."

Chastel bit into one of the wild apples they had gathered that afternoon. "It's not so much control, as establishing myself as their leader. Be aware, though, that my 'control', as you call it, will never be as strong with these wolves as it is with my own pack. That might create problems in Council Chambers."

"Still, I'd like to have them with us." Devin looked at Marcus. "Don't you agree, Marcus?"

"I haven't agreed to any part of this plan yet," Marcus grumbled. "And you'll have a great deal of difficulty selling it to Angelique. She has her heart set on revenge against René Forneaux."

"René will be tried for his crimes. That should provide her some closure. Eventually, I hope she will see that revenge through legal means will leave her with a clear conscience later on in life. It might be difficult to explain to her children how she had killed their grandfather," Devin said with a wink at Gaspard.

Gaspard threw an apple core at Devin. "I'll let you explain that to her. Angelique has some very strong convictions. I'm staying out of it."

Devin exhaled. "It's just that if we claim to support the legitimate government, then we have to work within its boundaries."

"It sounds good in theory, Devin," Chastel agreed. "But your government has been seized by men whose only goal is wealth and power. The finer points of a government which serves the people have been completely lost upon them. Remember, this Shadow Government has existed for centuries. It hasn't risen now only to be defeated. Forneaux must have felt he had sufficient support in Council, or he would never have attempted to take over as temporary Chancellor."

Devin leaned forward. "As gentlemen, are we prepared to sit back and allow Angelique to forfeit her life? What of Madame Aucoin? She has only one granddaughter. Do you think this is how she wants her relationship with Angelique to end?"

No one spoke for a few moments. Marcus cleared his throat. "Devin, there are far too many complications with either plan. This is not going to be easy. Some of us probably won't survive. All of us might die; I have no way of knowing. I do know that both plans are flawed tactically. Neither is one that I can throw my support behind unequivocally."

"I understand," Devin replied. "But surely this trip hasn't gone according to plan either. We've been the targets of assassins for almost five months and yet, we are still here."

"By sheer luck, Devin," Marcus said, shaking his head, "by sheer luck."

"What do you think my father would advise us to do?" Devin asked.

Marcus raised his eyebrows. "Your father would tell you to change your name and spend the rest of your life gathering Chronicles in the provinces. His first priority would be to keep you safe."

"Then what of Gaspard and Chastel? With René in power, they are still in danger. And what would you do with your life, Marcus?"

"Follow you, Monsieur Roché, just as I was directed to do," Marcus answered. "But you have one more person to convince that this plan of yours will work. If Angelique agrees to go along with it, then I will too."

CHAPTER 39

High Hopes

In the hastening dark of that early autumn evening, two additional wolf packs crept down the slope and circled them warily. They'd come at Chastel's request and they stood as one entity facing Chastel's pack, hackles raised, lips drawn back to reveal their fangs. Devin feared the merger would not go well. Chastel walked among them speaking in that strange language that only he and the wolves seemed to understand. After almost an hour of Chastel's quiet diplomatic intervention, the new packs lay down together. His own pack relaxed soon afterwards with a few uneasy grumbles and growls. Everyone breathed a little easier once the wolves had begun to tolerate each other, at least.

They slept that night in soft, fragrant grass on the southernmost slope of the last mountain in the range. The crickets' chirping filled the air and the waning moon cast its soft light over their campsite. Though Marcus still insisted on the need for setting a watch all night, Devin felt intuitively that there was no danger here. The feeling of being followed was gone.

Apparently, Forneaux had never put all his trust in either the men from the Chancellor's service or the infamous Descremps brothers. He must have felt that this was a battle he could not afford to lose and only by having multiple assassins tracking down Devin and Gaspard could he ensure that neither of them would return to Coreé. Forneaux was wrong. He'd lost to a group of noblemen with only one soldier among them to defend them. And those same noblemen would see that he was tried for treason before the same body of men he had attempted to rule!

Devin had carefully sowed the seeds of his plan to rescue his father and while Marcus was still a skeptic, he felt he would come around to Devin's way of thinking. Surely, grown men could thrash out their differences without resorting to violence. Forneaux would be on display before a Council he hoped to win to his side. His actions when faced with Devin's evidence could determine whether Forneaux lived or died. Assassinations perpetrated in the forests of Arcadia were not something that most Council members would order or condone. The contract Marcus held, signed by both Jean-Michael Descremps and René Forneaux, was damning enough evidence without all the other information they had amassed. If they could slip into Coreé and reach Council Chambers unscathed he felt they were assured of victory.

Devin took his turn at guard duty at midnight with Chastel. The gray wolf lay between them, her muzzle nestled on Devin's lap as he stroked her head and back. He glanced at Marcus and Gaspard to assure himself that they were still asleep. "When we were at Madame Aucoin's you told me that this little wolf joined your pack the night that the people of Lac Dupré disappeared," he whispered.

"I did," Chastel agreed softly.

"I asked you then if there were a possibility that she could be Jeanette," Devin continued, finding it hard to find the right words to convey what was on his heart. "You never gave me a definite answer."

"Because I don't know," Chastel replied, not meeting Devin's eyes. "If you knew for certain that this wolf was Jeanette, what would you do differently than you are doing now?"

"I'm not sure," Devin answered, running a gentle finger down the soft fur between the wolf's dark eyes. "But I feel a different sense from her than I feel from the other wolves. She has no wildness in her. I have no fear of her, at all; instead I feel a kind of affection. Do you feel that, too? Or is it just me?"

Chastel retrieved his pipe before answering. He seldom smoked and Devin felt that this was a delaying tactic. He waited impatiently while Chastel tamped the tobacco and lit it with a random glowing twig from the fire. Drawing in the smoke, he breathed it out into the cool evening air and Devin recalled the perfect smoke rings Armand often formed to avoid discussing something controversial.

Chastel finally turned to look at Devin. "I can't tell you that this wolf is Jeanette, Devin, because truly I don't know. Do I sense something different about her? The answer is yes, I do. I think my other wolves sense it, too. When I run with them, they tend to protect me. I think they know that I am not quite the same as they are and though they respect and accept my leadership, they also shield me. They shield this little wolf, too."

Devin felt giddy with the possibilities. "What can I do ..." he began.

Chastel sighed. "Devin, you have traveled with her for months. You pet her; she sleeps by your side. She protects you. Don't you think that if she were truly Jeanette and she could have shifted back into a human, she would have?"

The wolf raised her head and looked at each of them in turn as though she were following their conversation. "See!" Devin pointed out. "She's listening."

"Have you not seen my other wolves attend my every word when I speak to them?" Chastel pointed out.

"I have," Devin answered. "I marvel at the relationship you have with them."

"And I marvel at the relationship you have established with her," Chastel countered. "None of my wolves have ever become a pet. If you remember from reading my grandfather's journal, my uncle had a wolf cub that he trained to follow him like a dog. It's possible that this little gray wolf was young when she came to us. She had no pack so maybe she never developed the sensibilities that would have bonded her to the identity of a pack. Perhaps, for some reason, she has bonded to you instead. But, Devin, please don't become obsessed with this. If Jeanette had been going to reveal herself, she would have done so by now."

"Are you sure of that?" Devin asked desperately.

"Let me put it to you this way, since you are forcing the issue. If this little wolf is truly Jeanette Vielle, then she apparently has no idea how to become human again. She's stuck in a wolf's body and you, *mon ami*, need to move on."

Devin looked up at the stars and then closed his eyes. They finished their shift at watch without speaking again.

Despite his conversation with Chastel the evening before, Devin woke with a sense of excitement. Today, he was going home. They had agreed to travel as close to Coreé as possible and spend the evening in hiding. After midnight they would stash the wolves at the Archives and make their way to Madame Aucoin's. Today it seemed that nothing could go wrong and he longed to see his *Grandmère* and Armand again.

As they crossed the open fields north of Coreé, Devin broke into a run. He and the gray wolf bounded through the chest-high wildflowers and grass, blissfully unaware of any security concerns they might be violating. Gaspard joined them, though Devin was certain his heart was not quite so light this morning. Oddly enough, Marcus and he must have felt some of the same enthusiasm because he never once berated them.

They stopped on a hillside with the city spread out below them. For the first time, the Dantzig's dark waters were visible to the west as the great river plowed its way southward. The waters stretched as far as the eye could see, seeming as wide as an ocean. A light breeze stirred the leaves of the trees above them and the sun shone warmly on their shoulders.

"I think we'd better stop here," Marcus cautioned. "I'm not comfortable trying to get any closer to town until later tonight. If we weren't all 'wanted men' I'd walk into the first bakery I came to and order a dozen chocolate croissants and four cups of *café au lait*!"

Devin laughed. Marcus had never seemed to concern himself with food. He was always content with whatever was available – whether it was raw venison or one of Madame Aucoin's feasts. For him to admit that he longed for something sweet and delicious made him seem more human.

"It's nice of you to share," Gaspard said. "I was thinking much the same thing. I swear a moment ago I had a whiff of coffee from that little shop on the Rue de St. James."

"Who said I intended to share?" Marcus said with a completely straight face.

They all laughed. Devin felt the coils of tension unwind from around his heart. They had made it! They had crossed four provinces and a venerable mountain range, braved wolf packs, and assassins, and today they stood on the threshold of Coreé! He'd left his heart in Ombria, if that was where Jeanette truly was. He'd had to abandon both his harp and his cloak but he had returned relatively unscathed. Physically, that was: he had changed in so many small ways he could never enumerate them all.

The fields where they stood were government land set aside for the pleasure of the people of Vienne. Anyone could walk or ride here but the majority of Coreé's residents chose to spend their leisure time at the many city parks. Their regimented rows of trees, flower beds, and sparkling fountains had held little attraction for Devin as a child. Running was frowned on, reserved for games of sports on the school fields. In Coreé he had always had to be aware of his station and behave in a manner befitting the Chancellor's son.

But, Devin had returned a very different man. He'd come back like a knight to rescue his father, put René Forneaux behind bars instead, and speak for the thousands of provincial people who lived in poverty without adequate medical care and education. It was a heady concoction that he had arrived to serve to the staid members of Llisé's Council. One he had never been trained to express but had been called on to do so by default. The question remained, could he accomplish what he'd come to do?

311

Gaspard jabbed him with an elbow. "Why so sober?"

Devin gave a shiver. "I guess the immensity of what we are trying to do finally hit me. If I can't pull this off, we're all done for and it will be my fault."

"Hardly," Gaspard muttered. "We all know who's to blame for the current crisis and, believe me, none of it can be laid at your feet."

"What if my father is already dead?" Devin asked, his voice barely a whisper.

"Then we'll bring his murderer to justice," Chastel said quietly behind them. "Devin, René Forneaux has spun a massive web of deception and deceit. It's possible that dismantling it may have to be done in stages. We have arrived to take the first step, to lay the groundwork for what will follow. Maybe this can't be accomplished with one presentation in Council Chambers but we can certainly stop it from going any further."

"Having second thoughts?" Marcus asked.

"Not exactly," Devin admitted. "I'm concerned we won't be able to smuggle the wolves in and orchestrate entering Council Chambers at the right time. We've had no news at all for weeks, Marcus. What if my father has already been executed?"

Marcus took a deep breath before answering. "We'll know more by tonight. Once we reach Madame Aucoin's we'll be better able to judge what steps to take next."

Devin glanced up at the sun still high in the sky. "That's a long time to wait."

"Well, I won't endanger this mission further by allowing anyone to try to gather more information now," Marcus said. "We wait, Devin."

CHAPTER 40

Unexpected Complications

Dusk finally came and the street lights of Coreé blossomed one by one as lamplighters went about their jobs. Devin had never watched the city come to life at night from this perspective. There was something magical about the process and again he was filled with rising excitement for the task that awaited them. Finally, after hours more of waiting, Marcus ushered them forward.

Against Marcus' better judgement, they had decided to let Devin direct Chastel and the wolves through the sewers and the tunnels to the Archives. Marcus and Gaspard would return to Madame Aucoin's, lessening the chance that all of them might be captured together. They also divided the evidence up so that no one carried all of it.

Devin never had actually considered the logistics of compelling three packs of wolves to go in a particular direction. He could never have done it alone but Chastel's constant whispering seemed to calm them. Late that night, Devin directed them through a seedier portion of Coreé where the *militaire* rarely patrolled and there were no streetlamps to light their way. This area was apart from the docks, where in the morning the very wealthy would wait for ships in their finest clothes. Here the dregs of humanity lived, surrounded by the tanneries and the smell of the sewers emptying into the river.

Devin knew it was going to be a messy business for him and Chastel to slog through ankle-deep sewage but who would have guessed that wolves would be so fastidious? It was only after several minutes of intense urging that Chastel compelled them to enter the fetid tunnel where the city's refuse spewed forth to dirty the deep waters of the Dantzig. Devin lit a torch, though what it illuminated was something out of a nightmare.

"How are we going to keep these wolves fed?" Chastel hissed. "You can't risk coming in this way every day!"

"I'm sure Jules will think of something," Devin said, trying to breathe through his mouth. "I wish I knew what day of the week it is. If we have arrived on a Friday, there will be no Council meetings until Monday. That is a long time to leave you cooped up with all these wolves."

"I don't dare leave them alone together," Chastel replied. "They might kill each other and then where will we be?"

Devin glanced at the small gray wolf at his side. "I don't want her to be a part of this," he said softly.

"And your plan is what?" Chastel said, dodging what looked like a body floating past them. "My God, what was that?"

Devin swallowed as the bloated corpse continued to drift down the tunnel. "Probably some poor man whose family couldn't afford a proper burial. Either that or a cutpurse robbed him and dumped him down one of the city drains."

Chastel gagged. "I can't believe you talked me into this, Mon Sewer Roché."

314

Devin laughed in spite of himself. "I don't believe this was my idea," he said in his own defense. "Gaspard and you had it all thought out before I even had a chance to formulate a plan."

Chastel tied a scarf over his face. "Just so you know, there will be no more sewers where I'm concerned."

"Agreed," Devin replied.

The tunnels that led to the sewers were reached by stone steps. They were rarely used except in the case of flooding which sometimes caused a blockage at the end of one of the branches of the sewer. Some unlucky workers were sent down with poles to break the blockage apart so that Coreé could again present its perfect appearance to the world. The steps were broken and slimy, coated with an evil-smelling black moss, but they rapidly led them above the level of the worst of the sewage. Surprisingly the wolves negotiated the steps easily and arrived dirty and smelly in the hallway that led to the Archives.

"I can't live in this filth for days," Chastel protested. "I really can't, Devin."

"That is easier to fix than you might imagine," Devin said, glad to be able to relieve some of his misery. "There is a bathroom at the end of this hall. No one uses it anymore because this wing is shut down but the last time I was in here there were still soap and towels."

"Thank God!" Chastel murmured.

"I'm sorry," Devin said. "You ended up with the worst job of all."

"I'm not so certain," Chastel said. "You have to walk back through that muck and explain to your *Grandmère* why you smell like dung, rotten vegetables, and dead things."

"Maybe Jules can pour a bucket of water over me in the

315

yard," Devin replied, surprised he still had the ability to joke.

Chastel herded the wolves toward the end of the hallway. "So there will be plenty of water for the wolves, too, until you figure out how to bring more food down here?"

"Yes, of course," Devin answered. "I would never have left you without water. And you have the venison we brought for tonight." The packets of meat had weighed down both his pack and Chastel's, but it was the best way to ensure the wolves were fed for tonight at least.

Devin wove between the wolves, walking ahead to assure himself that all was as he remembered it to be. He found the bathroom dusty and the sinks grimy from years of disuse but there was still a stack of towels, two bars of soap, and the water gushed from the faucet when he turned it. "The wing that is locked from the Archive side is right here." He turned the knob and revealed a spacious area with water-stained walls. "I think the gas lights are even still connected. Do you have a flint?"

"I do. Excellent," Chastel said with some satisfaction. "You'd better be going before Marcus comes after you himself."

"I will," Devin told him. "You might want to stuff your jacket under the door if you have the lights on. I don't want anyone to see a light under the door and come in to investigate."

"A very good idea," Chastel agreed.

"I'll see you get some fresh clothes and boots, too, when I send more food down," Devin said, handing his pack to Chastel. "Goodnight, then." When he turned, the gray wolf moved with him, walking directly under his hand, as he continued down the hall.

"Devin?" Chastel called after him. "You may jeopardize your own safety and hers by taking her with you."

"She won't stay," Devin protested, hoping that it was true.

"She'll stay for me," Chastel answered and followed him to the top of the stairs. He knelt before the little wolf and put a hand on each side of her head. Devin would never know what he said to her but she turned away and joined the others, her tail between her legs.

The trip back through the sewer seemed worse than the trip in. Perhaps it was the lack of company but Devin felt he would never rid himself of the stench that swirled around him. He doused his torch and pitched it when he reached the river. Moving up the bank, he removed his boots and dipped them over and over again in the cold water. He dunked his legs in up to his knees and scrubbed at them. He sat for a moment, squeezing the water out of his trousers before he jammed his wet boots back on his feet. He wasn't certain how much of an improvement he had made. He could still smell nothing but sewer and wished he had one of the bars of the soap he'd left for Chastel.

The waves slapping the river banks sounded peaceful and Devin lingered for a few moments before he made his way back up the bank into the dismal warren that made up the quarter along its shores. He made good time, skirting areas where bars lined the streets, and keeping to the rows of ramshackle houses. Here, poverty was every bit as blatant as it was in the provinces. The tanneries provided work to transform the hides that came from the north into fine leather boots, purses, and clothing. Unfortunately, the chemicals involved in the process were toxic and workers died young, the victims of lung and skin diseases, and blindness.

Many of these people strove no further than to find a

very basic menial job, tending the sewers or scooping up horse dung from the streets of Coreé. If they were lucky, a son or a daughter found work in one of the wealthier homes in the city as a maid or a footman, but those jobs weren't easy to acquire for people like these. Often families worked for the same great houses for generations and there was little chance of advancement for someone who didn't have a relative already employed there.

He passed a house where a baby wailed, its tiny voice thin and piercing. Was it ill or hungry, he wondered? A woman's voice sang soothingly as her steps paced the floor. How could he help them all? What legislation could right all the wrongs in this empire? And how could he persuade those who had everything to even care about the thousands who had nothing?

"What have we here?" a drunken voice called out. "Lost your way, *garçon*?"

Devin backed against a building, knowing he might be trapped but there was no place left to go. Five men had circled him and all he had was the knife in the waistband of his trousers. "I have nothing for you," he said as calmly as he could. "I'm carrying no money."

The first man stepped forward, a toothless mouth marring his grin. "Fallen on hard times, have you?" he said, sarcasm dripping from his voice.

Devin inclined his head. "For the moment."

"God, you stink!" one of them said, laughing. "Did we scare you then?"

They all roared at his joke and Devin took the opportunity to edge away. They smelled very little better, as though they had also worn the same clothes for weeks without washing them or bathing.

"Where are you headed, *garçon*?" the first one asked. "Don't you like our company?"

"I'm expected elsewhere," he answered, backing away.

"Ah, elsewhere!" they taunted and laughed.

They wouldn't have laughed had the gray wolf been at his side! This was exactly what Marcus had been afraid of and he had been foolish enough to walk right into trouble because he was bemoaning the plight of these people. Surely, having just come from a month in the mountains, he didn't present the picture of a wealthy aristocrat ripe for a robbery?

"What do you want?" Devin asked. "I have nothing more than you at the moment."

One man darted forward, his hand clutching Devin's jacket pocket and the bulge of his rosary. The man cackled merrily. "Liar! Liar! He's got something in his pocket! Let's have a look, son!"

"It's a rosary," Devin answered, withdrawing it and holding it out to them. "My father gave it to me. It's the only thing I have."

The laughing stopped. One of them took the rosary and moved to examine it in the dim light from a window. "It's nothing but river stones," he said disparagingly. "Let the *garçon* go. He's got nothing we can pawn for coin."

Devin took the rosary in his hand. "Thank you," he said and left them before they changed their minds.

He made it through the remaining narrow streets lined with makeshift hovels, counting himself lucky to be alive and still in possession of the only thing he'd brought with him. Perhaps even these men had a code of honor not to steal from someone as poor as themselves. Today, he was poor. He hadn't a coin in his pocket. With his father in prison, no doubt all of his bank accounts had been frozen.

Devin's stipend from the *Académie* had probably been suspended, as well. No one paid a dead scholar. If it weren't that his *Grandmère* would take care of him financially, he could well be in the same straits as those poor men who were only looking for enough coin to buy another bottle.

CHAPTER 41

A Time of Reckoning

The moon was setting by the time he made his way to Saint Chapelle. He barely discerned the details of the tall, elegant house before him, just verified the number and walked around to knock at the kitchen door. Marcus opened it, releasing the exquisite scent of bread baking.

"Where have you been?" Marcus demanded. He took a step backward. "God, Devin, don't come any closer in those clothes! Take everything off!"

"Here?" Devin asked incredulously, as the cooks turned to see what ghastly reeking thing had entered.

Marcus shook his head. "I'll get you a robe or something. Don't move!"

Devin stood on the doorstep, half asleep on his feet, until Jules appeared in front of him. "Come with me," Jules said, gesturing outside.

Jules directed him to a carriage house and Devin stumbled after him, so tired he could have slept right there in the yard, filth and all. "The former residents had dogs," Jules explained. "There's a tub out here with running water. Take everything off and we'll burn it. Marcus has gone to get you formal clothes." He cranked the faucets on the whole way and steaming water filled the small backroom.

"Why do I need formal clothes?" Devin asked.

"It's Monday morning," Jules said. "Council is deliberating on your father's charge of treason today. You need to be ready in an hour."

"An hour?" Devin protested, standing naked and shivering. "I need to take clean clothes to Chastel."

"Someone else will have to take them," Jules answered. "Surely there is someone you can trust in the Archives."

Devin nodded. "Pierre Bellac. He will do what you ask in my name but he will have to lead Chastel and his wolves to Council Chambers, too. That's a great deal to ask of someone who could be accused of treason for helping me."

"Today is a day to choose sides. If they are truly your friends they will stand with you," Jules said, handing Devin a bar of strongly scented soap. "I'll send someone to the Archives immediately."

An hour, Devin thought. There was no time to prepare what he would say, no time to memorize eloquent words that would win these Councilmen's hearts. His father's life depended on what he said this morning and he was half dead with fatigue and smelled like a sewer. It was not a good way to start the morning.

He climbed into the tub of hot water, his knees bent under his chin. Apparently, the former owner's dogs must have been one of the smaller breeds. He scrubbed with the brush and soap Jules had left him until his skin was raw and rinsed off twice before Marcus appeared with his clothes.

Marcus took a tentative sniff. "Much better," he pronounced.

"How are we going to manage this?" Devin asked, burying his face in a towel. "Chastel and all those wolves wallowed through that sewer, too. They have soap and water but I doubt that Chastel will try washing the wolves."

Marcus gave an unconcerned shrug. "Most Council members have no idea what a real wolf looks or smells like. It will make them more intimidating."

"Father Sébastian's journal and my rosary are still in my jacket," Devin reminded Marcus. "Don't let them burn it."

Marcus handed him a white shirt. "I've already retrieved them along with Tirolien's Chronicle, which will have to stay here at the house. As things stand, you could be arrested for having it on your person, or have you forgotten that? I don't want to have to break another Roché out of prison this week."

"I haven't forgotten," Devin replied. "Is Armand here? I need to talk to him."

"Everyone is waiting in the parlor," Marcus said. "We'll leave for the Capitol Building as soon as you are ready."

Devin fumbled with his shirt buttons, his mind racing. The stark white shirt and black jacket and trousers almost felt like a costume to him after months in the provinces. He pulled on shiny black boots and followed Marcus back into the house. The floor in the kitchen had been very recently washed but over the scent of soap, a faint reek of sewer still remained. He held his head high and walked past the staff as though he had no idea who the ruffian had been who had marred their spotless floor.

Gaspard and Angelique met him in the hall with hugs. Angelique's color was high, her cheeks flaming and her eyes feverishly bright. Devin wondered if it was the possibility of murdering René Forneaux that had made her so excited.

He thought he had made it clear to her that diplomacy had a better chance of getting them all through this alive.

"Did Marcus tell you that I want to speak to Council first?" Devin asked her.

"Yes, of course," Angelique answered primly. "We all discussed it last night and *Grandmère* believes it is the best way to proceed also."

"That's why there was such a rush this morning," Gaspard explained. "We expected you back hours ago."

"I was detained," Devin replied. "The sewer is an abhorrent place. I don't care to ever visit it again."

Gaspard smirked. "I have heard that the chef prefers that you don't go there either."

Devin cuffed him good-naturedly and went into the parlor. Madame Aucoin sat enthroned on a soft-green quilted chair. Her dress was a similar serene color in watered taffeta that changed subtly with her every movement; her white hair was piled on top of her head with a pearl comb. She rose when Devin came in and held out her arms. He let himself be wrapped up in her sweet, scented embrace. For just a moment, the ordeal they still must face faded away and he felt nothing but a complete sense of peace in her arms.

"My dear boy," she said, stepping back. "We were worried when it took you so long to return."

"The area by the wharves is rough," Devin explained. "I spent a good deal of time avoiding thieves and drunks." His eyes scanned the room for Armand and found him seated at a harpsichord in the corner near the window. "Armand, I need your help. There has never been a time when my words needed to express the correct sentiment perfectly and I don't know what to say."

Armand stood up and retrieved his cane. Devin thought

he had put on some much-needed weight. His face no longer looked so strained and his expression was expectant. "We can talk in the coach," he said. "I'll do what I can to help."

Devin suddenly remembered who was missing from their group and turned to his *Grandmère*. "I am so sorry that Georges was killed, Madame. We all enjoyed his company and we will miss him so very much."

Madame Aucoin smiled wistfully. "He died in a place that he loved, Devin. Not many are able to say that."

Devin glanced around the room; saw Jules, Gaspard, Marcus, Angelique, Armand, and Madame Aucoin. Would all of them be able to gather here again tonight? Or would some be missing from this group, dead in the cause of truth and justice? He turned away as Jules informed them that the carriage was waiting outside.

"I never expected us all to go together this morning," Devin said as they piled into the carriage. It was tight quarters and Angelique threw her arm around Gaspard's neck and plopped down laughing on his knee. Devin's mother would have been horrified but his *Grandmère* simply smiled indulgently.

It was as though they were attending a wedding or a festival; everyone but Jules and Marcus seemed cheery and hopeful. Devin wished he could generate the same enthusiasm. He sat next to Armand, his heart thumping in his chest.

Armand put a hand on his knee. "Monsieur Roché, did I ever tell you the story of Jean de la Tour?"

"No," Devin answered.

"It's part of Arcadia's Chronicle," Armand said. "Make them listen well, *mon ami*, so you can present it to those Councilmen as though their very lives depend upon it, because they do."

CHAPTER 42

Confrontation

The street in front of the Capitol Building was thronged with people, hired cabs, and carriages. A large group of men stood on the sidewalks and blocked the street, although the *militaire* was preventing them from going any further up the steps. They threw rotten vegetables at the Councilmen who were climbing out of their coaches and held up sign boards that read "Free Chancellor Roché!" and "Chancellor Roché Is Innocent!"

Devin stared in amazement. He could never remember any kind of protest in Coreé before. While he had been feeling that the responsibility for his father's release rested squarely on his shoulders, he realized that here in the very stronghold of wealth and affluence, people had been incited to fight against what they felt was injustice, too. Men shouted, horses shied uneasily, and fruits and vegetables flew through the air, splattering off carriages and Councilmen alike.

"Maybe I shouldn't have bathed," Devin commented wryly.

"Thank heavens, you did!" Gaspard replied. "You and Chastel deserve a medal for wading through that sewer!"

"Now if we can just get inside without being plastered with rotten fruit," Devin said.

"They may not recognize you, Monsieur Roché," Jules commented, "but they will recognize Marcus. The trick will be to get inside without being stopped by the *militaire*. I hope they don't bar certain Councilmen so they can sway the vote in their favor."

"Why don't we use the Archive entrance and enter with Chastel?" Devin suggested. "I still have my key."

Madame Aucoin looked at Marcus and he nodded. "That's an excellent idea! Let's do it," she said. "I'll not have my son-in-law tried for treason without the other side of the story being told. We're no help to him stuck in this carriage."

Jules hung out the window to give instructions to the coachman. The carriage inched forward, jostling angry people on the sidewalk. A whip cracked and the horses snorted and reared, clearing an instant path in front of them. They were on their way again in minutes.

While the streets leading to Council Chambers were congested, in contrast, the area around the Archives was deserted. They left the carriage at the curb and walked past the central fountain. A breeze lifted the spray and lightly sprinkled Devin's face. He felt as though it could be May again and he had never left Coreé. One good look around shattered the illusion. The spring flowers had long since died off and the few ornamental trees had already begun to turn red.

Autumn had always been his favorite season at the *Académie*, with its cool nights spent by candlelight poring over documents. And then autumn preceded winter, which offered entire weeks where he could lose himself in the Archives' manuscripts and the art of transcribing them. All of this was achingly familiar. He had forgotten how much he loved it.

Marcus urged him forward. "We haven't much time, Devin!"

They went in on the main level. Oddly enough, it was Pierre who greeted them at the main desk. "I've taken care of everything," he whispered, leaning over the desk. "They're at the door and it's unlocked. Good luck!"

"Thank you," Devin said.

Pierre grabbed his arm. "And praise God, you're not dead, Devin! We were all distraught here!"

Devin smiled. "No. I'm very much alive! Hopefully, we'll set things right today."

They hurried down the stacks of shelved manuscripts reaching from floor to ceiling. Ladders hung on rails that ran the length of the shelves. Their first year, Devin and some of his friends had great fun racing each other down the stacks on ladders, something that was stopped immediately by the elderly Archivists.

Everything even smelled the same and it was all Devin could do not to dash off to his personal work cubicle to see if it was unchanged, too. Instead he directed his group between the stacks, from one room to another. His keys opened every door they needed to go through. As they reached the last corridor, they smelled the wolves before they saw them.

Madame Aucoin's nose wrinkled but she never said a word. Chastel stood at the door, looking disheveled but clean, the wolves pacing around him. The gray wolf left the confines of the pack to greet Devin but Chastel called her sharply back into line.

Chastel put his ear to the door. "You arrived just in time! They are calling for testimony in favor of the Chancellor's not-guilty plea," he told the others.

Marcus nodded his head. "Let's get this insurrection started!" He and Jules waded through the sea of wolves to reach the door. When they were in place, Marcus nodded to the others and swung the double doors open with a resounding bang.

The usual shuffling of paper and subdued whispering of Council Chambers stopped abruptly. Marcus strode into the chamber as if he owned the empire, with Jules at his side. Chastel followed with the wolves in tow and Devin, Gaspard, Angelique, and Madame Aucoin followed. Marcus gave a signal with his hand and the chamber doors were locked behind them by the men loyal to Devin's father, that Marcus had contacted the night before.

René Forneaux stood at the podium. His face flushed with anger. "What is the meaning of this?" he demanded.

"We've come to present testimony in support of Chancellor Roché," Devin announced, his eyes scanning the room for his father's familiar figure.

A gasp rushed through the chamber as men recognized Devin and Gaspard. They strode together toward the raised platform where René Forneaux stood. Chastel escorted Madame Aucoin and Angelique to one side. The wolves surrounded them like one cohesive security unit. Some leapt onto the stage, heads shifting from side to side, hunting for any hint of danger. Their eyes narrowed, gleaming gold. Devin had to admit they made an impressive display.

Forneaux faltered for a moment. "Guards!" he shouted.

"Clear these men and these wolves from this chamber!" The Chancellor's Personal Guard surrounded him, rifles pointed at Devin and Gaspard.

Devin stopped a few feet from the stage. "I invoke the ancient right of free speech in this chamber," he said, his voice ringing clearly through the room.

"This administration revokes the right of free speech to conspirators with the accused," Forneaux snapped. "Leave this chamber now or I will have you shot!"

"In what way am I a conspirator?" Devin countered, making certain his voice could be heard throughout Council Chambers. "You sent men to kill me and your son Gaspard and we survived, yet you reported our deaths to this body of men as one of my father's treasonable acts."

Forneaux huffed, his voice barely audible amid the whispered speculation from the seated Councilmen. "I believed the reports I received to be true. My sources reported that both you and my son had been murdered. I am, of course, grateful to see those accounts were wrong and that you are both alive and well."

"Have you forgotten that the contract to have us killed was signed by you, René Forneaux?" Devin contradicted him. "I have it here it my hand. I am certain that your signature can be authenticated by handwriting experts but it has already been validated by your son."

A wave of angry dissent swept through the building. Forneaux slammed the ceremonial gavel down on the podium so hard that the head flew off, barely missing an elderly gentleman in the front row. "This testimony is out of order!!" he yelled. "Remove these men from Council Chambers!"

A portion of the Personal Guard moved forward but a

good many hung back, uncertain who to believe and where their allegiance lay. The wolves tightened their circle, snarling and growling, their hackles raised.

A sea of men rose from their seats, pistols drawn and cocked. Devin's heart plummeted. He had no idea that Forneaux's influence had become so firmly entrenched. Not only were they never going to be able to testify, they were going to die right here, shot down by men loyal to René Forneaux. This was something none of them had anticipated. It was unheard of for Councilmen to enter Council Chambers armed.

A middle-aged man rose from the center section of seats, gesturing at Forneaux with his pistol. "I want to hear Devin Roché's testimony," he said, his dark hair touched with silver at the temples. Devin recognized him as Macaire Lachance, a landowner from Sorrento, and a friend of his father's.

"I wish to hear it, too," Damien Bouchard agreed, standing to indicate his position. "I second the motion."

Across Council Chambers more armed men stood to support the motion and Forneaux's fists clenched in anger as he unwillingly bowed to their requests. "Go on then," Forneaux snapped. "But only factual information pertinent to this trial will be heard at this time."

"I respectfully request that any information pertinent to this trial and to the current temporary administration be presented as evidence," said Gitan Babvineaux, another friend of Chancellor Roché's.

"I second that motion," declared a gentleman dressed in black, flourishing his pistol.

A wave of Council members swept to their feet announcing their assent and Devin grinned in spite of himself. Forneaux had to back down or risk open war between the opposing factions. He glanced at Marcus and saw the grim set of his face and realized that his bodyguard still sensed danger. He tried to curtail his enthusiasm, as he stepped to the podium.

Marcus grabbed his arm, leaning close to his ear. "Just remember, this will be decided as much by what you do not say as by what you say: the Bishop's Book and the Provincial Archives must remain a secret."

Devin nodded and turned to the chamber of august men. "Honored Councilmen," he began, purposely ignoring Forneaux's claim to the Chancellorship. "When Gaspard Forneaux, Marcus Berringer, and I left Coreé last May, we never realized the dangers that awaited us in the provinces. Yes, they are primitive but the threat to our lives came from Vienne, our capital and our home.

"In early June, Gaspard was kidnapped from Comte Chastel's chateau and held captive for two weeks on his father's orders. The same night he was taken, all of the residents of the village of Lac Dupré disappeared – over 800 men, women, and children. No one knows to this day what became of them. All we know is that uniformed men were seen in the village before it happened.

"Forneaux's men tortured and killed *Shérif* Picote of Lac Dupré and Adrian Devereux, the apprentice bard of Ombria, in an effort to obtain information about our whereabouts. When Gaspard was finally released, it was only in an attempt to capture me as well and kill us both. Comte Chastel is here with me and can testify to both of these events, as can Gaspard Forneaux.

"As we made our escape we came upon Comte François Aucoin's ruined chateau and the sole remaining member of his family, Angelique Aucoin. I will let her tell you her own story."

Devin stepped back and gave Angelique his hand as she stepped up onto the platform. Devin thought she looked very young and fragile in the blue satin dress she had chosen to wear today, but who knew how her mind had scripted today's performance.

"As a child of four," Angelique began, "I accidentally told Monsieur Forneaux about my father's trip to Coreé. I gave him the exact date and port that he would leave from, and my father and his bodyguards were murdered on their way. That same day, the *militaire* came to our home and slaughtered my mother, my sisters, my little brother, and all my family's servants. They poisoned and burned our land and then planted false evidence to make it seem that the provincial people had killed us."

Talon Sauvageon rose slowly from his seat, his expression hard and calculating. "How is that you survived, Mademoiselle, when all the rest of your family perished?"

"I was playing hide and seek with my sisters and brothers. I hid in an empty barrel in my father's wine cellar," Angelique answered. "Luckily one of the maids was only knocked unconscious. She took care of me until just a few years ago."

"How convenient," Talon replied, spreading the tails of his coat before he sat down.

"René Forneaux had my family murdered," Angelique said, fixing him with a vicious stare, "simply because my father did not believe in his political views! He is an evil and dangerous man!"

Devin caught her by the waist and pulled her back against him. "That's enough for now," he whispered in her ear.

Angelique spun away from him and tossed a red cross down on the stage; it skittered across the polished wood and landed at Forneaux's feet. She started off methodically and followed the path of the cross, like a wolf on a scent, her skirts swirling around her. Devin saw a glint of steel in her hand and both he and Gaspard dived after her. Pistols cocked behind them.

Devin flattened Angelique, both of them sliding across the stage on a wave of blue satin as a flurry of shots rang out. He grabbed her in his arms and rolled away to the relative safety of the heavy curtains that draped the side of the stage. Gaspard rolled toward the edge of the stage, dividing the gunmen's target.

The gunfire ceased almost immediately and Devin cautiously raised his head. Bodies littered the platform. Forneaux's guards had been slaughtered by a rain of bullets from Marcus and the guards loyal to Devin's father. Among the dead and wounded lay René Forneaux.

Gaspard rose from the floor only to sink to his knees beside his father. Devin scrambled to his feet, holding out a hand to Angelique.

"Go!" she said.

Devin ran across the stage and grasped Gaspard's shoulders. "Are you all right?"

Gaspard stared at him mutely, his hands covered with his father's blood. He wheeled, rising on one knee to face the Councilmen. "Call a physician!" he yelled. "My father has been shot!"

Devin had seen enough death in the last few months to know that it was already too late to save René Forneaux. "He's already gone, Gaspard," he said, placing a hand again on his friend's shoulder. "I'm so sorry."

Gaspard turned to look at him incredulously. "Why would they shoot him?" He glanced around the stage in shock. "He must have jumped in front of me. Do you think he was trying to save my life?"

Devin took a deep breath, reluctant to destroy Gaspard's hope. "We may never know exactly what happened." The wolves had two of Forneaux's bodyguards on the floor and several more wolves had backed four others into a corner.

"Drop your guns!" Marcus ordered, herding all those who were unhurt into the same corner where the wolves could hold them in one place. Jules collected the firearms on the floor and bound Forneaux's bodyguards.

Angelique had backed toward the side of the stage, her stiletto still in her hand and tears running down her cheeks. Chastel quietly took charge and gathered her into his arms as she sobbed. He wrested the stiletto from her hand and slid it into his pocket, away from sight of the stunned audience before them.

A harried physician arrived from the wings and pronounced René Forneaux dead. Gaspard removed his jacket and covered the upper part of his father's body with it. He rose and stood next to Devin, his hands shaking.

Jérémy Delacroix, Council Steward, took the stage. His voice boomed across Council Chambers. "Please stay in your seats. Monsieur Forneaux has been killed along with several of his bodyguards. But we still need to review some very serious accusations that have been leveled here this morning. No one may leave."

Madame Aucoin moved to Gaspard's side, putting her arms around him, as his father's body was carried from the stage.

Monsieur Delacroix had chairs brought to the stage and

asked Devin and anyone else who had given testimony or who had further testimony to give to sit down. Gaspard slumped into a chair, his face white and Devin sat down beside him. "Do you think my father really tried to save my life?" Gaspard asked, looking up at Devin with red-rimmed eyes. "Why would he do that?"

"I didn't see what happened, Gaspard," Devin answered. "Maybe he couldn't bear to see someone else hurt you right before his eyes."

Gaspard grunted. "Marcus is right. You should be a diplomat. My father was not a sentimental man but thank you for saying that. I'm just grateful that Angelique wasn't the one who killed him. Had it happened here, she would still have gone to prison and been tried for treason, since he was the 'Acting Chancellor.'"

"A case could have been made against that," Devin replied but he was relieved, too. "But now we'll never know who the other members of the Shadow Government are."

Gaspard sniffed and ran a hand across his face. "He'd have never told you anyway, Devin. He wouldn't have broken even under torture."

Delacroix called for order and after a moment the chaos in the chamber subsided. He beckoned to Devin. "Please continue your testimony."

Devin remounted the platform, so unnerved by the preceding events that he forgot where he had stopped in his narrative. Finally, he cleared his throat and continued.

"When we traveled to Calais in August, Marcus and I were seized by members of the Chancellor's Personal Guard. Emile Damien said he was authorized to offer Marcus a position in Forneaux's new government, if he would kill me, as a test of his loyalty. Marcus was clever enough to fake my death and dispose of Emile and two of Forneaux's henchmen. Only two of them returned to Coreé with the news of my death."

Devin shifted, his eyes traveling over the men before him. Some faces were open and receptive but others had grown increasingly hostile. He glanced to the left and saw Marcus standing stalwartly behind him and breathed a little easier. He remembered the tale of Jean de la Tour that Armand had told him in the carriage but at the moment, he felt that something else was called for.

"In Vienne we pride ourselves on our written records. The Archives are overflowing with them. But there is a story about Vienne that has never made its way into the Archives. It's a story of twin brothers. One rose to become Chancellor of Llisé. The other brother, angry and jealous at his success, devoted his life to creating a wedge between the provincial people and the government his brother ruled. He poisoned his brother at a formal dinner and watched impassively as he died in his wife's arms. When Council named another man to succeed him as Chancellor, the angry brother continued his reign of terror in the northern provinces of Llisé. His legacy lives on in the Shadow Government he created and its conspiracy continues to this day."

Raffaele Tolbert rose from his seat, his face puzzled. "Who are these brothers that you speak of?"

Devin paused a moment before answering. "Gascon and Auberon Forneaux."

The Council's solemnity dissolved. Gasps and angry whispers filled the Chamber. Talon Sauvageon leapt from his seat, his eyes narrowed, his face suffused with anger. "On what are you basing this information? Is it one of those fairytales from the Provincial Chronicles you were so determined to collect?"

The Chamber quieted, all eyes were on Devin. "No," he said clearly. "The information came from what archivists refer to as a primary source. On our way back from Calais, we passed through the Valley of Albion and discovered a journal belonging to Father Sébastian Chastain detailing the destruction of the dam of the Gave d'Oloron that was orchestrated by Gascon Forneaux and blamed on his brother, Auberon, who was Chancellor.

"From that point on, Gascon created his Shadow Government, falsifying documents, terrorizing the provincial residents, and attempting to undermine the legitimate government of Llisé. While we knew of its existence, it wasn't until we found this journal that we had any idea how or why the Shadow Government was formed in the first place." Devin handed both the journal and the contract between the Descremps brothers and Forneaux to Delacroix.

"Perhaps among René Forneaux's personal papers, we may find a roster listing the current members of this body," Delacroix commented with a meaningful look at the men before him. "Please continue, Monsieur Roché."

Devin cleared his throat again, wishing for a glass of water. "We were attacked multiple times on our way back home through the mountains to Coreé. Our guide, Georges Mazzei, was killed and I was shot. The cabin we were staying in was burned to the ground, and a bomb was thrown in our campfire. We are lucky to be standing before you today. All this was done by the order of René Forneaux."

Again, the Council Chambers flared with angry voices and Delacroix rapped on the podium with the handle of the broken gavel to regain order.

He directed Devin to sit down. "Thank you, Monsieur Roché. Let me assure you that we will keep your father perfectly safe and that some members of this Shadow Government are already under surveillance and will be arrested before they leave this room today."

Devin stood a moment wondering what would happen next. His father wasn't present and hadn't been for the whole so-called "trial." Was he still in prison? He walked back and sat down while Gaspard presented the information about his abduction and the letters he had received from his father threatening to disown him.

It was late afternoon by the time they had all finished giving testimony. Delacroix removed several dozen men from Council Chambers under suspicion of participation in the Shadow Government. He dismissed the body, announcing they would reconvene tomorrow morning at nine.

At last, Marcus' men were told to unlock the doors. The wolves pricked up their ears at the smell of fresh air and the sunlight streaming through the two massive double doors. Chastel walked over to Devin. "Do you mind if I take the wolves out?" he asked.

"No," Devin said. "They've been remarkably well behaved. Where will you take them?"

"To the meadows outside of town. I doubt we will have further use for them; things seem to be under control."

"But this isn't their territory," Devin protested. "Will they be in any danger?"

Chastel chuckled. "Absolutely not. They will eventually find their way home, as I will, too."

"You aren't staying?" Devin asked.

"Of course he is," said Madame Aucoin, putting her arm around Chastel and leaning her head against his shoulder.

"I've invited him to spend the holiday season with us, Devin. He can go back to Ombria in the spring and become reacquainted with his wolves."

"I'll be back to the house later, *Grandmère*," Devin told her. "I need to find out where they are holding my father." He motioned for the little gray wolf to come to his side and she did. She rubbed her head against his leg and he dropped to one knee to fondle her ears.

"She needs to run with the others," Chastel said gently.

"But I don't want her to go back to Ombria," Devin protested. "I need her here."

"She needs to run with her pack, Devin," Chastel pointed out. "But I'll bring her back to the house with me tonight. We don't have to decide this now. We can talk later."

CHAPTER 43

Realignments

Devin went in search of Jérémy Delacroix. He found him signing off on the imprisonment of a lengthy list of Council Members. Delacroix handed the papers over to another man and turned to smile at Devin. "I imagine you would like to see your father," he said kindly.

"I would," Devin answered, "if it's not too much trouble."

"It's actually no trouble at all," Delacroix replied. "He's been with us all day."

When Devin frowned, Delacroix led him and Marcus down a hallway behind the stage. Delacroix removed a ring of keys and fitted one into a tiny hole in the intricately carved design.

"A secret room?" Devin asked excitedly. "I never knew this was here. It doesn't appear on any of the drawings in the Archives."

"The Council Building was constructed nearly a thousand years ago when Council meetings were often bitter and confrontational," Delacroix explained. "It allowed the Chancellor to see and hear everything that was said during committee meetings without anyone knowing he was there."

When Delacroix unlocked the door, Devin found himself confronted by not only his father but his five older brothers, as well. He had just a moment to assess that his father looked well before he was swept into his strong embrace. Devin had forgotten how tall this man was – how imposing – and how impressive. He felt tears spring to his eyes unbidden.

His father pushed him back gently and held him at arm's length. "You look like you haven't eaten in weeks!" he said. "You promised your mother that they would have food in the provinces!"

"And they do," Devin assured him, attempting to dodge solicitous pats on the back and having his hair rumpled by his brothers. "We've been on the run for months."

His father held out his hand to Marcus. "Marcus, there is nothing I can say or do to thank you enough for bringing my son back home safely."

Marcus inclined his head. "It's what you pay me for, Monsieur Roché."

"And you two brought back evidence that would have convicted Forneaux," his father said. "That was an amazing feat!"

"I never expected him to die here," Devin said. "I imagined he would be tried and sentenced as a traitor. Angelique Aucoin was determined to kill him herself. I thank God she was spared from doing that, at least."

"I think Forneaux placed himself in the line of fire intentionally," Vincent Roché said. "Better to die in an instant than spend a lifetime in prison."

"Don't mention that in front of Gaspard. He has some

idea that his father was killed trying to protect him," Devin said. "Allow him his illusions, please."

"I will," Vincent said, "if not for his sake, then for yours." He paused a moment, considering Devin and then put both hands on his shoulders. "None of us anticipated what you uncovered in that journal! I don't remember sending my youngest son off to the provinces to thwart a coup!"

"We acquired the journal quite by accident," Devin said. "I have a story to tell you about that."

"I imagine you are just full of stories!" his brother André said, laughing.

"I am," Devin agreed. He shook his head. "My God, Father, things are so much worse in the provinces than you ever imagined."

His father patted his shoulder. "You can tell me all of that later. By the way, I wondered if you might be interested in a post as liaison between the provinces and the capital. I imagine there is a great deal of our history that needs to be added to the Archives."

Devin frowned. "How is that possible?"

"If we are going to bring about change, we need to know each other first," his father said. "I can't imagine anyone more qualified for the job than you are. We'll discuss it later when you're rested. For now, I believe we've all been invited out to dinner tonight!"

"How did you receive a dinner invitation when everyone thought you were still in prison?" Devin protested.

"It's from your *Grandmère*. Marcus went to see Delacroix last night while you were wading through the sewers with Chastel," his father said.

"That was an amazing journey, I'm sure!" teased his brother Jean, his grin revealing a stout double chin. "How ever did you manage? You never did like to play in the mud like other little boys!"

His father smiled, ignoring the comment. "It will be good to go to your *Grandmère*'s house tonight, Devin. It's time we were all reacquainted. Besides, it's been a long, hard day; tonight you need to eat some real food and sleep in a real bed." He put an arm around Devin. "Shall we go, boys?"

"Where is Gaspard?" Devin asked Jérémy Delacroix as they passed him on the way out.

"He went back with Madame and Angelique Aucoin," Delacroix answered. "He said he would see you at dinner."

Council Chamber was empty as they crossed the stage and headed out the main doors. There was no sign of Chastel or the wolves. Devin missed the companionship of the little gray wolf at his side. There was an emptiness that only she could fill and he tried to think of every argument he could to convince Chastel to let him keep her.

A carriage awaited them at the curb but Devin would rather have walked. He needed time to adjust to Coreé again, time alone with this city, and with the Archives. He needed to tell his father about Jeanette and how it might affect his proposed position. The carriage full of his five boisterous brothers, his father, and Marcus was not the place to do that.

Madame Aucoin's house was ablaze with candles when they arrived. The warmth that shone through those windows touched Devin's heart. He had lost his mother but he had gained a *Grandmère*. If only he could find Jeanette, his life would be complete.

Jules greeted them at the door, gathering cloaks, and directing them into the parlor. Angelique and Gaspard sat together on a window seat, both of them paler and quieter than usual but they were holding hands, and Angelique's head was resting against Gaspard's shoulder. Chastel and Armand held glasses of wine, chatting in the corner. Madame Aucoin threw her arms around Devin's father and each of his brothers in turn. Devin felt oddly alone and left out. He approached Chastel.

"Where is she?" he asked.

"Who?" Chastel asked blankly.

"My wolf," Devin said.

Chastel laughed. "Oh, I believe she went upstairs to your room. It was a long day for her, too."

Devin walked out into the hall, nearly colliding with Jules who was bringing cheese and tiny quiches to the parlor. He swung around him and took the stairs two at a time, wondering which room had been assigned to him.

He stood a moment, confused, when Chastel's voice boomed out from the hall below. "It's the second door on your right, Devin! Gaspard's is right next to yours."

Devin turned the knob and stood on the threshold. The little gray wolf had been thoroughly washed and lay sound asleep, drying in front of the fireplace. He closed the door and walked downstairs, feeling disappointed and incomplete. He would miss her warmth on his feet at dinner but at least for tonight, she was still his.

Vincent Roché offered a blessing before the meal, thanking God for the safe return of his youngest son, and those who had traveled with him. In the impromptu moment of silence which followed, Devin prayed silently for Georges who had not arrived safely and the Master Bards who had died at their posts.

"I don't know where to begin," Vincent said, as the first course was served. "I heard the abbreviated version of your journey while I listened in Council Chambers, but how did you both become wanted men within a month of arriving in Ombria?"

"Two men who resembled us were killed returning from Chastel's chateau," Gaspard answered, the normal humorous lilt in his voice gone. "I can only assume those assassins were sent by my father when I refused to return to Coreé."

"Later it wasn't just Gaspard and Devin who were in danger. The night that Gaspard was kidnapped right from my chateau, the entire village of Lac Dupré disappeared," Chastel added.

"There is no one left?" Vincent asked, dipping his spoon into a thick creamed soup.

"Not that we know of," Armand answered. "Only those of us who had attended a dinner party at Chastel's or who gone back to the chateau to be certain Gaspard was all right were spared. As it turned out, Gaspard was not all right and two days later we fled Chastel's chateau, fearing for our own lives."

Vincent tilted his head to look at Devin. "You're unusually quiet, son. Is something wrong?"

Devin took a deep breath and blurted out what continued to occupy his thoughts. "Only that I fell in love with Armand's only daughter, Jeanette, while I was studying in Ombria. She is among the missing from Lac Dupré."

Vincent's eyebrows rose but the rest of his face was carefully impassive. "I see. Then I extend my condolences to both you and Armand."

"Had you forgotten that your engagement to Bridgette Delacey has been arranged for nearly ten years, Devin?" Jean blustered. "It's not like you to ignore your obligations!"

Devin laid his napkin down. "My only obligation at the

moment is to find Jeanette if she is still alive somewhere in Llisé."

Devin's brother Mattieu leaned forward. "Do you have reason to believe she may be alive?"

"We do," Devin answered. "I can't go into the particulars now."

"I have already offered my services to help him search for her," Chastel volunteered.

"As have I," Armand replied.

Vincent cleared his throat. "Then it would be courteous to break your engagement, Devin, as quickly as possible."

"I intend to write to Bridgette in the morning," Devin replied.

"News of that sort is more properly given in person," Vincent suggested quietly. "This has been a long-standing arrangement between our two families. I am sure I need not remind you that we require as may allies as possible at the moment."

Devin inclined his head. "I will use the utmost diplomacy, Father."

Madame Aucoin gestured with her spoon. "This is excellent soup, don't you agree, darlings?"

Devin shot her a grateful look. In the provinces he'd only had Marcus to deal with. He had forgotten that in Coreé his entire family analyzed his every move. The position his father had offered him seemed more attractive by the moment. He sat back in his chair as his soup bowl was removed. "Tell me what you imagine this liaison position would involve, Father."

"I believe that you are absolutely right that the Chronicles should be preserved as part of our Archives here in Coreé," Vincent said. "Since the Provincial Archive was burned, it is even more important than ever to gather the stories that were lost during the fire. Obviously, you were unsuccessful in gathering all fifteen Chronicles during this trip ..."

"Aha!" Devin's brother Ethan interrupted. "I told you it was impossible, even for you!"

"I was able to allot less than two months to the project!" Devin objected. "The rest of the time we were running for our lives."

Armand's hand hit the table with a bang. "No one has ever memorized Ombria's Chronicle with the speed and accuracy that Devin has shown! I have no doubt that given the full fifteen months, he would have memorized the entire Provincial Chronicles!"

Only Devin saw Armand give him a slow wink once the dinner guests had broken into a debate over Armand's statement. Devin smiled; at least he had someone on his side.

Devin took a sip of wine. "How much flexibility would you allow me as liaison?"

"You and I will need to work that out in conjunction with the Provincial Affairs Committee," Vincent replied.

Devin leaned closer to his father to be heard above the other conversations at the table. "Would my position begin this spring?"

His father extended a hand and laid it on his arm. "I think we can reserve the details for another time."

How soon he had forgotten, Devin thought. Meal time was sacrosanct in Vienne. Tradition dictated that business never be conducted during dinner and conversation remain congenial and light hearted. The change was jolting. Most of their scheming and planning had occurred over meals in the provinces. They'd barely made it through the first course and already Devin felt constrained. He glanced down the table and caught Chastel's eyes twinkling. Obviously, the Wolf Master of Ombria was enjoying the repartee.

When at last dinner was over, both Angelique and Gaspard excused themselves and went up to bed. Devin didn't think he had ever seen Gaspard look so tired. When Chastel stepped out into the frosty air to smoke, both Marcus and Devin followed him out onto a terrace that overlooked the Dantzig.

Marcus slumped down onto a stone bench. "God, being polite is a trial!' he murmured.

Devin chuckled. "I had forgotten all the intricacies of life in Coreé."

Chastel sighed, blowing a puff of smoke from a pipe he had pulled from his jacket. "It makes me long for my chateau in Ombria."

"There isn't time to return now, is there?" Devin asked.

"The Dantzig closed down to any shipping north on the first of October," Chastel said. "Unless I want to return with the wolves I've missed my chance for passage."

Devin stood looking out at the dark expanse of water. "And you promised my *Grandmère* that you would stay for the holidays."

"I did," Chastel agreed wistfully. "I can see I have lived a rather rustic life in Ombria. I will miss my wolves most of all."

Devin turned to face him. "I will miss your wolves also."

Chastel held up a hand. "Don't ask, Devin," he warned. "The wolves are returning tomorrow and your gray wolf is going with them. I have tried everything I know to coax her back into human form if she is actually Jeanette. You have to let this go. Search across Llisé for Jeanette if you feel that she is still alive somewhere, or renew your ties to this woman that you have been engaged to for years, but please drop this obsession that Jeanette resides inside that little gray wolf. You are only asking for more heartbreak. I will return her to the pack tomorrow. Say your goodbyes." He snuffed his pipe and made his way to the door. "I think I'll have a glass of wine and go to bed. I would encourage you to do the same."

Faint laughter reached them from the house as he departed but the atmosphere on the terrace was anything but cheerful. Silence descended with the closing of the door. Devin sat down across from Marcus, scuffing his left boot toe against the flagstones, his heart heavy in his chest.

Marcus shifted. "I don't want to add to your troubles, but I want you to know I've asked your father to be reassigned."

"No!" Devin protested. "You've been with him for years and years. Why would you leave him now?"

Marcus shrugged a shoulder. "I find my loyalties have realigned. I don't believe I would be happy here in Coreé all year long."

"He'll be devastated!" Devin said. "So will I! I thought we had grown rather close in the last four months. Where will you go?"

Marcus rose and bowed. "Wherever you go, Monsieur Roché. I've asked to be permanently assigned as your bodyguard."

Devin's mouth dropped open. "My bodyguard? Isn't the threat to me resolved with the deposing of René Forneaux?"

"Your father bestowed an honor on you by the job he offered but he has also placed you in a dangerous position. No one is more aware of that than he. You will have the Chancellor's ear on Provincial Affairs; you will shape law

350

and redefine the rights of the provincial people. You will need a bodyguard, Devin. I would like the job, if you'll have me."

Devin held out his hand. "I would welcome your service and your wisdom, Marcus. This is a cause for celebration, not concern!"

Marcus shook his hand and grimaced. "This just means that both your father and I think you need looking after. Don't let it go to your head!"

CHAPTER 44

Affairs of the Heart

Conversation and laughter still trickled from the parlor as Devin made his way upstairs. He was unbelievably tired but if this was his last night with his wolf, he wasn't going to waste it. When he opened the door to his bedroom she raised her head from where it had rested on her paws. Her tail rapped the floor like a dog and she rose to greet him.

He caught her head between his hands, stroking her ears back against her neck. "You and I need to have a talk," he said.

He took off his jacket and trousers and hung them in the closet. The boots he arranged carefully below them and unbuttoned his snowy white shirt while she waited, her eyes always on him.

Devin dropped down on the hearth rug. The wolf rubbed against his back and then flopped down beside him, her head in his lap, her eyes on his. "Chastel wants to send you away tomorrow," he whispered. "There will be no more chances for you to turn back into a human. Winter is coming and you'll have to prowl the mountain slopes for food and watch out for rival wolf packs." His voice broke. "Jeanette, come back to me, please. I would search to the ends of the empire for you but I know you are right here beside me. I love you. I will always love you. Please don't desert me now. I can't bear it."

He lay down on the rug, his face to the fire. On this first night when he could sleep in comfort, he chose to sleep next to this wolf, who had followed him across the northern reaches of Llisé. She snuggled against him, her head in the hollow of his shoulder, the warmth of her body against his bare chest. He closed his eyes, stroking her head and back, feeling the soft fur align under his hand.

He remembered his and Jeanette's only kiss in Chastel's study. It had been sweet and secretive, a moment so fleeting and yet burned into his memory. It was then he had made the decision to marry her, although she had protested. She could never see beyond the differences in their status. He was so in love with her that nothing else mattered. Now, he could also see the intelligence and creativity she would bring to their marriage. He needed her by his side, here in Coreé, more than ever.

Gradually the house quieted. He heard whispered 'good-nights' in the hallway, the closing of doors, the rustle of clothing shed for the night, and finally the creak of antique beds receiving their nightly occupants. Sleep fell over him gently like a blanket and he didn't resist. He closed his eyes as he relaxed, his hand on the wolf's neck, his body curled against hers.

Somewhere a clock struck midnight. Devin didn't open his eyes. He reached out for the wolf beside him and his hand tangled in long hair that flowed over soft skin. Devin startled. He sat halfway up, his arm still heavy with Jeanette's head, her hair draped across his chest in a curtain of dark curls. "Jeanette?" he whispered, afraid that this was just one of his dreams, something he had conjured up simply because he wanted it to be so.

She turned her head and smiled. "My love," she whispered. "My dearest Devin."

"Jeanette." He breathed her name, afraid that somehow this vision would fade away in a moment. He leaned forward, took her hands in his and clasped them together against his chest as he bent his head to kiss her. He ran his hands along her shoulders and down her arms, touched her hair, and he kissed her beautiful, soft mouth again and again. "I was afraid I'd never see you again," he whispered against her hair. "How ...?"

She leaned into him. Her thighs and belly touched his and she laid her head against his chest, her body cool against him. "Adrian sent me away when Lac Dupré was attacked. I tried to reach my grandparents' house but there were wolves in the forest and they surrounded me."

His arms tightened around her, wishing he could have spared her the terror of that awful night. He held her head against his chest as though somehow by his presence, he could block out everything terrible that had happened before.

"Then all of a sudden," she continued, her breath tickling his ear, "I was one of them, racing through the forest with the pack. When they returned to Comte Chastel's, I went with them. But I had no idea how to turn back into myself again."

Devin's mouth descended over hers, memorizing the outline of her lips, the taste of her mouth. "It doesn't matter," he whispered. "Nothing matters except that we are together."

He held her close; afraid to let her go again, afraid that somehow she might slip back into the shape of the gray wolf and be lost to him forever.

"Chastel has been trying for weeks to teach me to shape shift," she whispered. "He wanted me to be able to come back to you. I wasn't sure that I could, but tonight when you said that tomorrow we would never be together again, all I could do was think of what my life would be like without you."

"And I was thinking what my life would be without you." Devin shook his head and laughed. "Chastel told me I needed to move on ... that you might have lost the ability to change back."

"He wasn't sure that it was still possible and he didn't want to disappoint you," she said, brushing his hair back from his forehead.

She seemed to realize suddenly that she was naked and she crossed her arms over her chest. "I need some clothes, Devin."

"Don't," he murmured. "You are more beautiful than I ever imagined."

"Please," she protested, her voice hushed. "My papa is probably sleeping next door."

Devin stood up, releasing her reluctantly. He took his shirt from the closet and handed it to her, his eyes memorizing her pale skin. "If you promise me that you will stay right here, I'll find some assistance."

He slipped out of his room and went next door, tiptoeing to Gaspard's bed as quietly as possible.

Gaspard sat up. "What is it? What's the matter?"

"Jeanette is back," Devin said. "Don't even ask me how. I don't understand it myself but she has no clothes."

Gaspard chuckled. "And that's a problem, Dev? You're losing your touch."

"She's embarrassed," Devin explained hastily. "Do you know which room is Angelique's? I hoped she could help."

Gaspard swung his feet out of bed. For once he was wide awake and cold sober. They both went down the hall to Angelique's room and, seeing a light under the door, they tapped lightly and went in.

Angelique was reading, propped up by at least a half dozen pillows, her hair a halo around her head

After Devin's hurried explanation, she said firmly, "I will take care of this! You gentlemen stay here."

"Dev," Gaspard said, after she had left, "you're certain this is real? I'm sorry to ask, but you didn't ... dream this?"

"No," Devin assured him. "I didn't dream it."

CHAPTER 45

Beginnings and Endings

Devin wakened to a soft knock on his door. Jeanette stood before him in a dress of burgundy silk, her pale shoulders bare. Around her neck hung a silver wolf pendant that nestled in the hollow of her throat. Her cheeks were flushed and she threw her arms around Devin before he had a chance to say a word.

Devin pulled her closer, burying his face in the curve of her shoulder as she had once done to him. "I can't believe you are here. What have I done to be given such an angel after all my bungled attempts to set this empire right?"

She put a hand on each side of his face and raised his eyes to meet hers. "Perhaps God loves the bunglers of this world! Get dressed, my love. I want to see my papa."

Devin took her hand and pulled her into the room after him.

He cupped the back of her head in his hand and kissed her, slowly and gently. "Jeanette," he said softly. "If I have you, I have everything I ever need or want in this world." He dropped on one knee and reached for her hand. "I don't have a ring to give you today, but will you marry me?" At

357

her startled expression, he added, "We already have your father's permission."

She grinned, clapping her hands together and then bent, pulling him to his feet, she laced her hands behind his neck. "Yes, Devin," she said. "A million times – yes!"

Devin threw back his head and laughed. "Then you have made me the happiest man in the empire!!" He picked her up and spun her around the room, both of them giggling like children. He put her down on his bed and bent over her, tracing her collarbones with his lips, and then moving up her neck until she laughed and turned toward him, pulling him down beside her.

The clink of silverware and the clatter of dishes issued from the dining room as they went downstairs, hand in hand, a few minutes later. It was Marcus who happened to catch sight of them from the hall below. Devin put a finger to his lips but it was too late.

"It's Jeanette!!" Marcus bellowed, like a town crier. "Jeanette is here!"

Everyone rushed from the dining room: Chastel, Madame Aucoin, Angelique and Gaspard, giggling like co-conspirators, Vincent Roché, and dear Armand, his thin face white but hopeful. His eyes scanned the stairs, caught sight of his daughter and his bad knees forgotten, he rushed up to take her into his arms. No one spoke at all as Armand rocked Jeanette in his arms, tears streaming down his face.

"Don't cry, Papa," Jeanette implored. "I am here and I am all right. Everything will be all right. We are all together now."

Devin glanced at his *Grandmère* whose hands covered her mouth, an expression of wonder in her eyes, although tears spangled her lashes.

Suddenly, Armand took a step backwards and looked sternly at Devin. "Exactly where did my daughter sleep last night, Monsieur Roché?"

"With me," Angelique added with a delighted giggle. "Devin was a perfect gentleman. He came to get me as soon as Jeanette transformed."

"You did?" Armand asked, a note of disbelief in his voice.

"I did, sir," Devin answered, laying a hand on Armand's shoulder. "And this morning, with your blessing, I asked her to marry me."

"And I said 'yes'!" Jeanette said with a grin.

Applause broke out in the hall and when it quieted, Gaspard stepped forward. "Perhaps it's not too early to announce a second engagement?" He put his arm around Angelique. "Angelique has agreed to be my wife, with her *Grandmère*'s blessing."

Madame Aucoin's face glowed as Devin, Jeanette and Armand descended the staircase. "Two of my grandchildren are to marry and my son-in-law has been restored as High Chancellor of Llisé. I cannot think of a more wonderful way to start the day!"

They all packed into the dining room in high spirits. Initially, Devin was surprised to see that his father had spent the night, and then realized that Forneaux's things must still be cluttering up the Chancellor's mansion. He found himself seated next to him again at the table.

"Jeanette is beautiful," Vincent said, passing Devin a basket of pastries and bread.

"She's not only beautiful; she's intelligent," Devin said proudly. "And I love her with all my heart."

His father nodded. "I have no doubt of that." He turned to the group gathered at the table. "I'm sorry to spoil this festive atmosphere but we're due back at Council Chambers at nine o'clock."

"All of us?" Armand asked regretfully.

"Yes, all of us," Devin reiterated. He chuckled. "Do you have an engagement this morning, Armand?"

Armand shook his head. "No, I've just been working on a new story for Ombria's Chronicle. I'd hoped to add the finishing touches this morning."

"When can we hear the part that is done?" Angelique asked eagerly.

Armand hesitated. "I guess there is no harm in telling it but I may still make a few changes later on. I'll be glad to perform it tonight after dinner, if you will reserve me a place by your fire, Madame Aucoin."

Madame Aucoin graced him with her warmest smile. "There will always be a place by my fire for you, Armand Vielle. But don't keep us in suspense. At least tell us the name of your latest creation!"

They waited a moment as he composed himself. The light in his eyes was bright and engaging; he held his head high, one arm flung around his newly returned daughter. Armand cleared his throat, a smile playing over his lips. "It's called 'Devin and the Wolves of Llisé'."